A Novel

Izzy in El Mareo

Danielle Ledezma

RIVER GROVE
BOOKS

Published by River Grove Books
Austin, TX
www.rivergrovebooks.com

Distributed by River Grove Books

Design and composition by Greenleaf Book Group
Cover design by Greenleaf Book Group
Cover image: ©iStockphoto.com/den-belitsky

Publisher's Cataloging-in-Publication data is available.

Print ISBN: 978-1-63299-206-2

eBook ISBN: 978-1-63299-207-9

First Edition

mareo, el

    noun, from Spanish

1. seasickness, dizziness

2. confusion, muddle, mess
    from *el mar* (Spanish for *the sea*)

Part One

Chapter 1

The plane descended over the ocean, a deep, gorgeous blue fading into a turquoise hue as it neared the shoreline. The entire city of Puerto Vallarta seemed to be shrouded in palm trees or other tropical greenery—a perfect backdrop to the bright, inviting flowers draped all over the buildings along the beach. As the plane descended, the cabin warmed slightly with the humid air taking hold.

Despite the sadness with which Isabella had left Texas, she was full of excitement and hope now. The opportunity to take a sales job at a luxury resort in Mexico had opened a door she desperately needed. Houston, a sprawling city of more than six million people, had become stifling. After three years, three boyfriends, and three jobs, Isabella was ready to make a change. She had taken her time evaluating the logical aspects of the possibility of moving out of the country, but her fluency in Spanish and her desire to start something new had already made the emotional decision for her.

Then she thought about Ethan. Her current boyfriend of only a few months would not be joining her, and now she wouldn't have the ability to talk or text with him for a while until she got settled. At the thought, she felt guilty for leaving him, as well as fear for not having him there to encourage her and help her figure this all out.

Butterflies stirred vigorously in her stomach, and her hands started to feel clammy. *Oh no, please don't get that rumble that means only one thing,* she pleaded with her intestines.

As the plane parked at the gate, she took note of how small the airport was, and how old it seemed to be—not at all like some of the large American airports with terminal after terminal. The main cabin door opened, and the humidity came flooding in like a wave washing over everyone as they waited impatiently to deplane.

Isabella tried to calm herself, taking a few deep breaths. She hated to admit that she was scared out of her mind. Trying to steady herself and be brave, she took inventory of her fellow passengers to distract her mind. The flight had been direct from Houston, and the majority of the folks on the plane were American. Vacationers, she imagined, given all the Hawaiian shirts and Panama Jack hats that surrounded her. One man's Havana shirt was made of silk, not cotton, and his khaki trousers fell, neat and unwrinkled, to his Hush Puppies slip-on loafers. His wife had her gray hair perfectly coiffed and was draped in jewels that must have been the largest emeralds Izzy had ever seen in real life. Her classy white capris reminded Izzy of something her grandmother might have worn, and the woman's satin floral blouse flowed across her shoulders with ease. The couple was likely in their seventies and must have been married for quite a while, given the way they moved together toward immigration without having to say a word.

After they exchanged a few looks, the wife finally spoke. "You packed the keys, right? Please tell me we didn't forget again!"

Again? thought Isabella. *Keys? They must not be going to a hotel.*

"Yes, dear," the husband replied warmly. "I put them in the front pocket and checked it twice." He pointed to the smaller of the two Louis Vuitton carry-ons.

"Oh good. I hope Norma has the food prepared. I'm famished," his wife said.

This couple obviously owned a home here, or perhaps a time-share. Izzy imagined they were retired with plenty of money. She concluded that Puerto Vallarta must be an incredibly popular place for expats to retire and make a new life or have a second home. What would it be like to come for extended vacations where someone named Norma would cook for them? It sounded like a fantastic idea to Izzy.

"Next!" the government official waved Izzy toward another line. She changed course and headed his way, ready to hand over the paperwork and her passport proudly. She had made sure she had everything she needed without anyone else's help.

"Why are you here?" he asked abruptly. The question was so unexpected, it stumped Izzy and she stuttered.

"Uhh . . . for . . . uh . . . work?" she managed to get out.

"What work?" he continued to drill her.

Stumbling, feeling sweat form under her arms, her breath quickened as she tried to remember what the hell she was doing there. She had said goodbye, boarded a plane, and now she didn't know what for. "Yes, um, for a hotel." What was the name of this place she was going to work for? Her brain was no help.

"A hotel?" He frowned. "Why don't you have your ef-emme-tres yet?" he asked, referring to the FM3 work visa she was supposed to be getting.

Shit! I should have said vacation so I wouldn't be answering these questions now. Hadn't they suggested she do that anyway? Dammit—she had let herself get so excited about how strong and capable she was. *Way to go, Iz,* she thought. *Just when you think you've done something amazing and you start to feel proud, you find a way to screw it up. Like when you forced Brandon's hand with an ultimatum, but then he left; and how you're leaving Ethan right when you have something good going.*

"Yes, well, I am supposed to get that on my first day of work next week. So I should have it next time?" she stammered as if asking him if it were true.

His face was worn and beginning to sag under his eyes. She saw that he was probably younger than he looked, but the years, and maybe the sun, had stolen his youth early. Maybe she could try to charm him and use her smile as she had so many times before with authority. Cops were scary if you let them be, but she was normally a quick thinker, and her humor and wit often helped her to ease out of intense situations. She was acutely aware of her heart pounding, and that others were passing through their custom stations with ease while she was stuck feeling separated from the rest of her fellow Houston passengers as they made their way to baggage claim without her. *Think fast, think fast . . .*

"Thank you for being so sweet to let me through with the passport for this trip." She smiled and leaned forward on the desk. "I haven't ever done this before," she said with a slightly detectable hint of sensuality in her voice.

"This time okay, but if I see you again without the FM3, you're going to have a process to follow," he finally said.

She didn't dare ask what process, for fear of changing his mind, so she simply smiled and said, "Thank you so much! I most certainly will!"

He didn't smile back or seem particularly moved by her flirtations, but he did stamp her passport and then slid it across the cold, white counter, indicating she could be on her way. Was it wrong to use sex and beauty to get her way? While women everywhere wanted equality and the same opportunity as men, was it a slam to her gender to revert to flirting? Maybe in America, she reasoned; but she was in Mexico now, or at least trying to be, and in her personal experience with this culture, she found it was still very much about women's sexuality and men's acceptable objectification of women. So really, she was just fitting in with the culture here. *Right?*

Which was so typical of Izzy. Always trying to fit in, yet feeling like a fraud. Izzy never quite felt good enough. Her parents expected her to get straight As, because school seemed to come easy to her, and they questioned her about anything less on a report card. Even making the team wasn't enough; she had to be one of the starting players, one of the stars—of both the softball team and the dance team. When she did make the team and did get the starting positions, she felt proud and loved, knowing she had done well for her parents. When she didn't, she was a disappointment. Early in life, Izzy had conditioned herself to tie love and acceptance to her performance, which set her up for quite the ride in her professional life.

Izzy's public relations major wasn't panning out in the job market as she had hoped. With time running out on her lease on her college apartment in Austin, she had started to explore areas she hadn't considered before. A cousin who was in human resources at a hotel had suggested that Izzy's PR world was similar to hotel catering sales (people who sell weddings, galas, big events) and that Izzy might love planning events. She applied for a sales manager job, drove the two-and-a-half hours from Austin to Houston to interview, and got called back right away with an offer! An offer . . . for an hourly assistant position. Though a bit of an ego blow, the hotel executives who interviewed her explained it was a foot in the door to quickly rise to manager and beyond. Izzy accepted the job because she needed money, and because her boyfriend, who was graduating a semester later, would be moving back to Houston as well.

Houston was massive, however, and Izzy had to find her own way. For someone who had constantly looked to her parents, teachers, and peers for validation and love, the adjustment was not easy. For the first time in her life, Izzy truly had to try and define herself on her own. Find her own gym and workout routine, find her own group of friends, find her own grocery store and ways to entertain herself on days off. The first year was fine with her boyfriend moving back as planned, but when that all ended in a mess, she was faced with the reality that she had nobody else to rely on. Then a beautiful thing happened. Her boss suggested she join a co-ed softball team to meet people "her own age" and even gave her an evening off every week so she could join a team. There, in the space of one night a week, Izzy built a community that was hers—one that was genuine, accepting, and made her feel she belonged.

The hotel industry did what it seems to do often and sucked her into the glamour of sales and travel. Moving from her hourly assistant position, she quickly climbed to a sales role and moved to the Convention and Visitor's Bureau for Houston. Once they learned she was fluent in Spanish, they afforded her an opportunity to travel with the Tourism Board to Monterrey, Guadalajara, and Mexico City, where she was in awe at the idea of being in a foreign land yet able to understand it. She was proud that she had been asked to go due to her knowledge of the Spanish language. It was only a one-week trip, but the impression it left and the confidence it instilled were permanent. She had performed well for the bureau, which showed her that she was valuable to them. Once again, performance became acceptance.

Spanish had been an elective class in middle school that allowed Izzy to start Spanish 2 as a freshman in high school. The curriculum came easy to her, and she felt as if she was in the inner circle of some secret, being able to understand a foreign language. It boosted her confidence; and her professors, and more importantly her parents, were always proud of her and complimented her abilities. Since studying abroad had been too expensive for her family, and her passion wasn't strong enough for her to overcome that obstacle, Izzy had resigned herself to simply practicing her Spanish when the opportunity arose. As she set off for college, she figured Spanish as an elective would be an easy A to help keep her GPA high, and the culmination of her studies earned her a minor, or concentration, in Spanish by the time she graduated—with honors.

Years later, she moved from the Convention and Visitor's Bureau to working in a luxury hotel in the city. Quarterly and yearly goals hanging over her head as a sales manager, she was set up to strive, not only for achievement, but far beyond—to gain recognition and praise. It fit perfectly into Izzy's idea of love. Plus, she was sent on trips to incredible places she'd never been. Only a handful of months into her position, she attended a golf tournament event for prospective clients in Ft. Lauderdale, Florida, to represent her luxury hotel and gain new relationships and, consequently, new business for them.

It was there she first met Gretchen. Gretchen, a German with a beautiful smile, spoke fluent Spanish and was at the tournament representing a resort that wasn't yet built. Spreading the news about its coming, her presentation instantly intrigued Izzy.

Gretchen was the new director of sales for a resort opening in Puerto Vallarta, Mexico. As they cruised the Intracoastal Waterway on a private seventy-five-foot yacht dining on bruschetta and filet after a day of golfing, Gretchen commented to Izzy that perhaps she would be an ideal choice to join her team in Mexico. As the breeze lifted Isabella's hair off her shoulder, she sipped her champagne. She couldn't help but imagine the glamour and adventure of living in Mexico, working for a beautiful resort in a beautiful place. And why wouldn't she, she thought while standing on the top deck of the yacht surrounded by some of the country's most affluent homes? It was like a scene from a movie, or maybe an episode of *Lifestyles of the Rich and Famous*. Everyone thought her job was so incredible and always said how lucky she was, and in that moment, she believed every last one of them.

"Are you sure you are fluent enough that you would be comfortable with this position?" Gretchen inquired.

"¡Claro que sí!" Izzy said. Her heartbeat had quickened slightly, her pupils dilating as she desperately tried to believe her own white lie. The hair on the nape of her neck prickled as the words departed her mouth, and she intently focused on Gretchen's eyes as if to say, *I'm not lying, even though you can tell I might be.*

"Maybe in a few years when we are ready to hire a team we can reconnect," Gretchen said.

"Oh wow! Yes, that would be incredible!" Isabella gasped. They clinked champagne flutes and discussed the events of the day. The tournament, the clients, the extravagant gifts of Movado watches and Maui Jim sunglasses. The evening carried on like a *Sex and the City* episode, minus the sex. This was only the beginning of what Isabella would come to know as "normal," setting her standards much higher than most would ever dream. Not only her taste for luxury, but also her expectations of what life should be like.

Nearly two years later, as Gretchen had estimated, the call came to

Izzy. The resort was ready to hire a team, and Gretchen was reaching out to see if Izzy was still truly interested in the idea they had discussed earlier. *Here it is, Iz,* she thought. *Are you actually going to live up to your own dreams, or are you scared?* Life had been a roller coaster for Izzy in the years that had passed in Houston. Breakups, bad relationships, friends growing apart . . . the life she had built for herself hadn't quite crumbled, but it wasn't what she wanted. It wasn't what she had intended. *Are you turning a corner and becoming a confident, brave person again, or are you running away?* She challenged herself. *How could I be running away when this was a seed planted years ago that is finally coming to life? It's not running; it's taking a leap!* Convincing herself it was a brave thing, she went through the formal phone interview with Gretchen. Only a few days afterward, Izzy was officially offered the position with a subsequent letter from Gretchen outlining pay, starting dates, and the contractual agreements of the position.

"Mom!" Izzy was practically out of breath when she phoned her parents that evening. "Guess what I got today!"

Izzy had kept her parents abreast of the call from Gretchen, and they already had heard the story of the yacht from a few years back when she first entertained the idea of living in Mexico. Her dad was supportive of the idea and had shared stories of his times in foreign lands during his career with the air force, which made Izzy even more hopeful that Gretchen would eventually call her. Her mom, on the other hand, was not so enthused.

"Sounds like you heard from Gretchen about the interview?" her mom responded tentatively.

"Yes! I got the offer letter!" Izzy exclaimed, sounding winded as if she had just run up the stairs to her apartment.

"Well, that's great," her mom said with what sounded to Izzy like fake excitement.

Sensing the lack of support and growing defensive, she asked to speak to her dad instead. "Can I just talk to Dad, *please?*"

"Hey, baby! Congratulations!" her dad said genuinely. "I'm so proud of you. This is gonna be so cool for you."

"Thanks, Dad! I'm scared, but I'm excited. I can't believe this is actually going to happen."

"Well, I know you can do this, and you know you can do this; you just gotta remember that. They wouldn't have asked you to come if they didn't think you could do it." Izzy's dad was always a reassurance, a safe place, to be reminded that she was loved. And that she was good enough.

"But I'll let you finish talking with your mom about the details. Let us know what we can do to help you get down there," he said as he passed the phone back to her mom.

"Hi, sweetie," her mom started, sounding reserved or maybe depressed.

"So, Mom, you really don't like this, do you?" Izzy retorted defensively with a sternness in her voice. "You don't want me to go or what?"

"Well, baby, Mexico is far and it's dangerous! I mean, you already proved you could move to Houston and make friends. I just don't really understand why you need to go someplace so far to try and do it again."

"I'm sorry you just don't understand, Mom." Izzy could feel heat rising in her chest, and the sensation of wanting to lash out became stronger. "Maybe Dad can explain it to you better, since you clearly have never done anything like this in your life."

It worked.

"I moved across the country when I was your age," her mother said, "and that's how I met your dad! It's not that I haven't done anything in my life, Izzy." Her voice was shaky with the hurt Izzy had inflicted.

"This is different, and I'm excited, Mom. It would be nice if you could support me instead of always tearing me down. I'm sorry my choices aren't good enough for you."

"Izzy," her mom tried to soften her voice, or maybe she truly did feel remorse. "I do support you. I just want to make sure you're thinking it all through."

"Well, thanks for the concern, Mom," she shot back, "but I can think for myself."

You hate my boyfriends; you hate that Brandon broke up with me, because he was the one guy you liked; you hate that I moved to Houston, far away from you; and you hate that I like to have fun and drink. Even as she thought it, she knew how childish it sounded. But she did feel that her mom was always judging her, when all Izzy really wanted was for her mother to accept her and tell her she was proud of her. Her dad had figured that out; why couldn't her mom?

When she pictured her Mexican adventure, Izzy pictured serenity and space. Separation and time. Maybe she was running away, but it was brave. Leaving behind all she knew, as painful and dirty as it was, for the dream of something greater. She knew some would accuse her of abandoning family and friends. Some would call her crazy. Few would wish her well and support her, and even fewer might visit. It was a risk she had been willing to take for the promise of adventure, the hope of love and romance, and the unknown doors that might open next. Perhaps she would never return to the US. Perhaps she wouldn't last for more than a month. Either way, Izzy knew she needed this leap, this scary and crazy, never-done-before leap, to reestablish the confidence she had found in Houston. Deteriorated by drinking, poor choices in men and relationships, and distance from her original loving and supportive friends, her Houston life had faded into something unrecognizable. She needed to start over. It wasn't running; it was hitting reset. It was brave.

She scurried out of customs to find where the rest of her travel companions had gone to claim their luggage. The airport was small and, although air-conditioned, the humidity was inescapable. The moisture in the air seemed to pull out smells from everything she might normally pass by without notice. The stark white tile reminded her of high school hallways, and the metal benches seemed to exude the scent of aluminum. Through the giant windows she could see the palm trees, and the sight of those luscious green palm leaves blowing in the warm breeze calmed her nerves, which were still jittery from the immigration encounter.

Finally arriving at baggage claim, she caught up with the older couple she had been watching. One small snake-like conveyor belt moving slowly along the wall produced the bags one at a time with large gaps between each one. Theirs must have been the only flight to land in the last half hour; this was a totally different experience than trying to find her bag at the Houston airport among ten or eleven large conveyor belts of luggage with people pushing forward, children running around, and loud alarms going off as new belts fired up. She spotted her two large suitcases filled with all her clothes and toiletries circulating and about to disappear back into the wall. She walked quickly to the other side, not wanting to look like a scared, silly child running after her bag, but she felt a tug in her stomach that made her speed up her steps.

Grabbing one handle, she heaved it off the belt using both arms and her back, and used her legs to set it down gently on the hard tile. She left it there and reached for the other as it was about to enter the darkened tunnel to who-knew-where, grabbing the wheel and side handle, and yanked on it as hard as she could to slide it off the belt. This one was heavier because she had packed most of her shoes in one place. Why that had been a good idea she didn't know now, because the next step was to try and navigate her way to some sort of transportation with these two bags larger than she was. She got her shoulder bag situated as best she could and positioned herself between both large bags. Taking one handle in each hand, she walked toward the exit, tipping each one onto the front wheels. The turns were a bit tough, so she took wide berths.

As she headed toward the main door, she was hit with what seemed like a full-frontal assault. The time-share representatives. The pushy sales pitches and the shouts coming from all directions seemed to echo across the tile and amplify the chaos.

"Beautiful two-bedroom! You come, come now and see! You never hab to leave!" one woman was saying in her accent as she moved toward Isabella from the right side of the hallway.

"Oh, no thank you, I'm just coming for work," she tried to answer politely. At this point the weight of the bags was causing her forearms to ache and her hands to cramp. It wasn't a long walk, but her bulging bags were definitely over the fifty-pound weight limit.

"Oh!" The woman's face lit up, her bright pink lipstick forming an open-mouthed smile as she continued, the words tumbling out. "How wah-nderfuhl! You are perfect candidate then to buy your own home you can stay when you are here and I can help when you are gone!"

Izzy supposed she would have to be a bit firmer with her, but as the woman reached for Izzy's arm to direct her back to the counter, a gentleman shot out from the left and suddenly was reaching for the bag in Izzy's left hand, trying to take it from her and lead her toward his counter instead.

"Young beautiful lady, you come with me and I will get you a better deal than her," he said, looking at the saleswoman. The woman scowled back at him and said something in Spanish that Izzy didn't quite catch, but she was sure it wasn't a friendly suggestion.

"No! No, I'm not interested!" Izzy exclaimed, continuing to move forward despite their physical attempts to restrain her. Were they truly grabbing at her bags and her arms? The scene was eerily like those from prison movies when a guard walked down the hall between cells, and the inmates threw things, cackling and taunting as he walked by, some of them rattling their bars and others staring blankly. She felt a bit like a prison guard now, as more and more sales reps who had counters lining both sides of this hallway lunged for her and shouted at her, as well as at other newly arriving passengers. They acted like the worst high-pressure car salesmen she'd ever experienced, multiplied by about twenty, and with free reign to say whatever they wanted about the competition.

She focused her line of sight on the sunlight pouring in from the sliding glass doors forty yards ahead and kept her head straight forward. Her hands ached and her forearms were tightening, so she started walking a little faster. She braced herself for the continued onslaught of salespeople, and that invisible but tangible guard went up around her. At least she thought it was tangible to most, but these people didn't seem to care if you ignored them or even if you blatantly said no. The solace in all this was that

Izzy was not alone, and every single passenger departing the terminal was experiencing the same pressure. The beauty of that was she could feel less guilty about ignoring them, because maybe the next poor couple would be suckered into it and Izzy wouldn't feel so rude.

Finally, after what felt like the longest walk of her life, she hit the double glass doors to make her getaway. As the doors swished open, she turned her face upward and took in a deep breath . . . of gasoline fumes and the smell of something burning. The humidity and sunlight soaked into her skin, instantly warming her and calming her after the unwanted assault inside.

Several taxis were lined up at the curb, and they all waved at her vigorously to come, come to their car. She made her way to the closest one—driven by an older gentleman who reminded her of a childhood friend's grandfather who had made it to America as a ranch hand to help provide a better life for his kids. The driver spoke broken English and gestured openly, warmly, making Izzy feel comforted and trusting. After a short struggle with each suitcase, he stored her bags in the trunk and opened the door for her to slide into the back seat. It was an old Honda that must have been from the late '80s, and, while the driver's seat had a seat cover, the rest of the car showed its age through cracked black vinyl seats and nonfunctioning seat belts that draped across the seat onto the floor.

"You go to hotel?" he asked as he started the car and headed for the exit.

"Yes, please," she answered, giving him the hotel name. At least she knew she had this part down and couldn't screw this up. She'd taken taxis to hotels many times in the past, and the security of knowing the driver was familiar with the area and could get her there easily without her help was a relief after navigating unfamiliar airports and baggage claim areas.

"Oh, it's close!" he answered. "For vacations?" He spoke enthusiastically, as if she were the first person ever to come here for a vacation.

"Yes, some for vacation, but also to work at the new hotel," she said without too much detail. She wasn't sure if he wanted all the information or not, so she let him ask her further.

"Which hotel? Where it is?" he seemed confused.

"No, it's north of here, but it's not built yet. It's still under construction."

"Oh, okay . . . " He trailed off, evidently unfamiliar with whatever construction project she might have been talking about. They fell into silence for the short drive, which gave Isabella some time to absorb what she was seeing for the first time. The car didn't have air-conditioning, at least not anymore, so the driver kept the windows down for the ride. So much for trying to straighten her hair that morning. The humidity and breeze sent her locks back into their frizzy, curled, and kinked waves. For once, she didn't mind.

After a short jaunt on the main paved road, they turned right onto a cobblestone street that seemed to lead into an area of condos and apartments. White stucco buildings with Spanish tile roofs, dark orange–painted wood buildings with brown shingles, and small homes of white and sand colors lined the streets. Everything was so vibrant and green, from the palm trees to the grass in the yards to the bougainvillea vines that seemed to grow on almost every wall, their bright pink flowers that looked a bit like fortune cookies draped across the neutral-colored buildings. Some of the buildings looked old, standing behind chain-link fences with rusted aluminum lawn furniture on the patios, and some looked as though they had been kept up nicely.

The wheels of the car rumbled over the stones, and with the windows down she could smell something grilling and something sweet, and then the smell of a tobacco pipe like the one her grandfather used to smoke. An older man in a white tank top, clearly meant to be worn underneath another shirt, stood on the lawn, lamely aiming a garden hose at a corner of his yard. A mangy-looking terrier of sorts darted across the street in front of them, causing the driver to hit the brakes a bit too effectively, rocking them forward in their seats. Before Izzy could recover and sit upright, he hit the gas with such force it sent her backward again. Most taxi drivers she'd experienced always seemed anxious to get back for the next run, which meant they were always stopping hard and speeding quickly, as if stop signs, red lights, or other vehicles impeded them from winning some unknown race. This ride was not much different.

As they took a left turn at what appeared to be the end of the street, she could see water between the buildings. Not the ocean she was hoping for, but a marina with boat after boat lining the docks. It was much larger than she expected, and the size of some of the sailboats was impressive. They stopped briefly at a stop sign, long enough for her to detect the sound of the lines clinking against the masts as the boats rocked slightly in the still waters of the marina. She could see restaurants and shops facing the water, hidden behind the homes facing the street they rolled down. People walked everywhere, slowly and casually. American-looking couples and locals alike strolled, making their way to whatever destination they had in mind. One last left turn had them at the bottom of the small hill approaching her hotel. The impressive building rose like a pyramid in front of them, and her butterflies returned once again.

This is it. This was going to be her home, albeit temporary, for the next few weeks. She took a deep breath and thought about how excited she would be to show her friends, to tell her mother, and to bring people back here. The taxi pulled right up to the front, and the friendly doormen opened her door and greeted her.

"Bienvenida, señorita. Welcome," they said politely. Their white guayabera shirts and dark brown pants were a great contrast to the red-stucco mud building. The large wooden porte-cochère soaring above her and the Spanish guitar music playing overhead announced her arrival in style.

"May we help you with your bags?" one gentleman inquired in perfect English with a huge, warm smile.

"Yes, definitely, thank you," Izzy replied. She wasn't about to drag those things up herself.

The taxi driver helped unload the bags and, returning to the car, Izzy handed him her American Express card.

"No, I don't take card," he said. "Cash only. Forty dollars US."

What? Cash only? Crap. Well, at least she had brought a large amount of cash with her. She pulled out the thick envelope of pesos and asked, "How much in pesos? I don't have US." She had taken the advice of her new boss, Gretchen, and already exchanged US cash for pesos for ease of use.

"Five hundred twenty pesos," he said. *Really? Is that the exchange rate?*

She didn't know and wasn't about to take the time to try and check, so she counted it out and handed it over. She thanked him again and headed through the open-air entrance to check in to her hotel.

The lobby was huge, with ceilings that must have gone as high as the building itself. A waterfall and lush tropical vegetation welcomed her from the other side of the lobby, and the large art pieces of driftwood made the place feel exotic and truly Mexican. She checked in and got her room keys to head upstairs while the bellman organized her luggage to bring up shortly. Her flip-flops echoed on the tile in the cavernous lobby as she headed toward the elevators. She smelled grilled meat, salt, and tequila as she neared the open-air lobby bar and, for the first time since the plane's descent, caught a glimpse of the ocean in the background.

Her breath slowed and even her heart seemed to smile. She had done it, and she was here. Izzy couldn't wait to get to her room, change, and head downstairs to explore. She was a strong woman, after all. Despite the hiccups and minor scares back at the airport, she had made it, and right now it all felt worthy of the struggle. *See, Mom? I can do this. You don't need to worry so much; your little girl has got this.*

Chapter 2

It was her first day, and she would take her first ride up with her new boss, Gretchen, to the resort they would build together. Izzy made her way out of the humid, stuffy hotel room into the open-air hallway to let the cool morning air relieve her sweat ever so slightly. Her curly hair wanted to frizz up naturally, and she was used to fighting the curl with a blow dryer and round brush. But in these conditions, with only a window air-conditioning unit in the room, she had to take breaks from the hair dryer; sweat dripped down her back as she struggled with each lock.

Fuck it, she thought. *At least I have some clips and hair ties.*

She waited on the Spanish tile by the elevator, looking out over the half wall of the open-air walkway into the surrounding marina. The moonlight danced across the calm waters in the early morning darkness. She started playing her first ride up to the resort in her mind. They'd have a great time seeing the gorgeous country and coastline, talking about that night they'd met in Florida. She envisioned the conversation being like old friends catching up after years of not seeing each other.

But once she got in Gretchen's car to head up to the resort about an hour away, those visions dissipated like vapors. Gretchen already had coffee, and when she saw Izzy didn't have any, she remarked, "We don't have time to stop, sorry." *Well, okay, next time I'll get some from the lobby a bit earlier. And maybe Gretchen isn't a morning person.*

"Do you love living here?" Izzy began. "I mean, the hotel is gorgeous and this area is really nice. You must love being here."

"It's fine, yes," Gretchen responded shortly.

Hmm, okay, maybe conversation should wait until they'd both had some coffee. They sat in silence as they drove out of the marina in the dark and headed up the main road, back past the airport and into the areas Izzy hadn't seen.

After what seemed a long and uncomfortable silence, lights appeared around the road denoting homes and stores and signs of life as they drew closer to the resort. Orange and yellow light bulbs cast a glow upon the once-darkened buildings around them, and she was able to catch glimpses of the changing landscape and architecture. "Wow, that place looks nice," she ventured tentatively.

"It's Nuevo Vallarta," Gretchen said. "You could live up here if you want, because it's closer. We've just crossed into the state of Nayarit now."

"Oh cool. Yeah? How did you find your place?" Izzy asked, since Gretchen had been there for quite some time and had her own apartment already.

"I just found something close, and I like the marina. It reminds me of home," she said. *Finally! A clue into emotions and her past.*

"Oh yeah? In Germany? Does it make you miss your family?" Izzy assumed Gretchen must miss her family the way Izzy already missed hers. With the hope of finding someone she could relate to about feeling homesick, she sat up a little in her seat.

"No, of Spain. Mallorca—where I was before this. My parents are fine; I talk to them plenty."

"Oh, you don't miss being home?" Izzy tried to dig deeper to find some common ground and form some sort of bond. Two strong, capable women being in a foreign country, missing home, but having each other. Like a Lifetime movie.

"I haven't lived at home for years, and I'm okay with that. I'll move home someday maybe. It's pretty common for us to leave home."

Izzy assumed by "us" she meant Germans, or maybe Europeans as a whole? Something inside tightened in defense, sensing that was a backhanded way of saying Americans staying close to home, or continuing to live at home, was strange. Tension rose in her throat and, without realizing it, her hips drew in and her lower back flexed as if her body was preparing to run or fight.

They spent the rest of the drive listening to Latin pop music, flipping through stations they could tune into through the different areas of the coast. They were joined on the road by 1980s Honda Civics, 1990s Camrys, and other older models that looked half rusted and probably hadn't had any emissions testing in quite a while. A bus sped past them on the left, looking like something out of a 1950s television show, except more rundown and less cared for. Paint was chipping away from the body of the bus and the door didn't quite close all the way, but that didn't stop the driver from taking the curve ahead of them so quickly it seemed as if the left two wheels lifted slightly off the ground and the bus might topple over on the way around.

As the first rays of morning light permeated the darkness, Izzy could see sections of the road that passed through towns were lined with taco stands, buildings worn from the sun and years of neglect, and piles of tires. What was with all the tires? Stacks so high they must have been close to reaching nine feet. Izzy had counted at least five of these tire "stores," and she wondered how they could stay in business. Then she realized all the cars on the road were old and probably needed a new tire here and there fairly often. Especially the way these people drove! And with all the potholes and cobblestone roads.

Their little car filled with the smell of gasoline, which was fine with the windows down, until they reached the mountainous incline on the north side of the bay and Izzy started to feel sick. The open roadway with views of the ocean gave way to twists and turns, and before Izzy realized it, they were headed into the thick jungle-like forest, rapidly climbing above sea level. Curving to the left, then sharply to the right, they made their way up. *Surely this road must straighten out again*, she thought as they curved to the right then back to the left again. Her stomach gurgled slightly, and a rush of heat came over her. The air-conditioning wasn't on, and the smell of gasoline wasn't dissipating, but the uncomfortable thought of asking Gretchen to turn the air on was stronger than her worry about puking. Isabella focused on her breathing, slowly in, slowly out, trying to keep her eyes on something level in front of her like the dashboard. Dryness began in the back of her throat and crept up into her mouth, and she yearned for some water to calm the knot that had formed in the pit of her belly. She burped, and she felt warm liquid slide up to the top of her throat, forcing her to swallow hard to keep it down. Any minute she might have to let it out. Should she roll down the window? Gretchen had rolled them up as the air cooled in the change of climate with the ascent, which made the car feel stuffier and even more constricted. How embarrassing would it be to puke in her boss's car on the first day?

She reclined her seat a bit and scooted her butt forward in an effort to recline a bit farther without drawing attention to her state of discomfort. She stared out the window up into the tops of the tree line, trying to fool herself that the fresh air was quickly calming her stomach.

As they came around a long, large curve, she saw through a clearing in the trees the deep blue ocean off in the distance below reflecting the early signs of sunlight. It seemed they had climbed a cliff along the coastline, into an area that was underdeveloped and masked by trees and a canopy of lush green foliage. Izzy let out a huge breath and hoped this was the end of the morning roller coaster ride. The road snaked back to the right, inland, continuing to increase in elevation until they reached a plateau and the path traced along the shoreline again. At this point, evidence of human life reappeared along the roadside as stucco walls rose out of nowhere, offering an exclusive entrance into what must have been a wealthy, luxurious neighborhood.

"Is that another resort?" she asked Gretchen.

"It's a private condo development. Those are the things we'll have the most competition with, because the wealthy can rent homes with butlers, maids, and even chefs out here," she informed Izzy, with what could have been mistaken as a desire to teach her something.

The rest of the short drive through the small surrounding villages was pleasant as they turned the discussion from personal questions to work strategies and marketing ideas. Gretchen seemed much more comfortable and at ease talking about the market research she had been doing the last few years rather than answering questions about her parents. She talked Izzy through some of the neighboring villages with high-end luxury homes for rent, and how their resort would offer more amenities than those homes might. She talked about the resort next door that had been established for a few years and the market share they would steal from it once they opened. Izzy suddenly felt much better about her decision to come here. The ride was a great start to feeling informed and capable of understanding everything that was happening.

Unfortunately, that feeling didn't last long.

"¿Qué piensas, Isabella?" her new coworker Nacho asked.

Izzy's palms sweated and her armpits suddenly felt sticky. A heat wave began at the nape of her neck and radiated through her shoulders and into her stomach, which was quickly becoming one huge knot. *What do I think?* she asked herself. *About what?*

She was the only American in the room, and for her entire first week here, she had been lost about fifty percent of the time. Now she felt twelve eyes on her as they anticipated a response from the one American who might know best how to do something for this resort that would attract hundreds, if not thousands, of American travelers each year. She was the seventh employee hired for this construction zone, sitting here in the makeshift conference room where she and the other six all sat working on laptops, making phone calls, and arguing with each other in the same small space. No privacy. No consideration. No independence.

Against one wall was a large folding table covered with architectural renderings of what the resort would soon look like. Drawings of little palm trees dotted the bright blue pools, and heavy black lines crisscrossed, showing how the framework of the restaurant buildings would be laid out. It was the inspiration many on the team needed to help keep spirits up when the debates and the obstacles brought the team to a halt. It wasn't so much the inspiration for Izzy, although she was excited for what it would be in the end; but her inspiration was more about the experience versus the finished product of the physical resort.

But the renderings did offer the only colorful thing in the entire space. The walls were all stark white, and the floor was made up of cheap, large white tiles reminiscent of high school hallways. The bleakness seemed to echo the voices, the keystrokes, and "tap, tap, tap" of people typing, and the irritating snorting of one person who seemed to have allergy issues all the time. Brown metal folding tables with fake wood laminate for tops were pushed together end-to-end forming a large square, so everyone sat around the outside of the square facing toward the center and each other—except when the laptop screens hid their faces, which was most of the day.

For meetings or group discussions, they could simply lower the laptop screens halfway so they could see each other's faces. Notebook papers of hand-scribbled notes, long pages of charts, and complicated-looking spreadsheets were strewn across the tables between the laptops set up at each person's designated area. Metal folding chairs with thin padding denoted the various assigned "places" for every person to set up each morning. Power cords ran across the floor from every laptop, and pencils and pens scattered their way around the room.

Each morning they would arrive, usually two or three at a time as they carpooled from the various areas of town, and would mumble good mornings as they returned to the same folding chair from the day before, plugged in their laptops to the cables they had left hanging across the table, and poured coffee into Styrofoam cups. Usually the general manager arrived first and started the coffeepot for everyone. Without any windows, they didn't seem to notice it was still barely twilight when they arrived and dark outside when they left for the day. They seemed to live in eternal darkness, broken only by fluorescent overhead lights and the blue glow of laptop screens. Each morning featured a regrouping session where each person reported on what they'd completed or started, how it was going, and what issues they might need help with. Soon thereafter, they would each sink into their tasks for the day.

Izzy's job was to compile a list of the top travel agencies that booked vacations into Mexican resorts like this one so she could call them and promote the new resort when it was ready to open. If a specific travel agent, say out of Los Angeles, had several clients who always booked their family Christmas vacations to Hawaii, she would add them to her spreadsheet so she could call the agent and explain why—instead of Hawaii next year—that same family should change it up and try Puerto Vallarta. Mining databases, including lists from her previous jobs, and using online data services the resort paid for, she spent her days copying and pasting names, phone numbers, and emails. While some of the research was exciting, like uncovering a geode in a mound of rocks, the hours upon hours of staring at the computer and the "click, click, click" of her mouse—copying and pasting—was dry and boring.

In addition to finding future agencies to call, she also researched special recognition programs the resort could try to win. Oftentimes, as Izzy learned from Gretchen, when resorts were accepted into special programs with credit card companies or globally known rating systems, they attracted higher-paying customers. As the resort neared its opening, Izzy would need to fill out these applications, create the marketing pieces, and compile all the necessary data for each program Gretchen suggested.

"The more recognition we get early on," she had instructed Izzy on the first day, "the better chances we'll be able to book rooms and fill the resort as soon as we open."

Soon Izzy would begin putting together trips to attend trade shows, visit agencies' offices, and meet with the top-producing travel agents to personally show them what the resort could offer that would be new and different. For now, however, each day Izzy was stuck sipping the bitter local coffee with powdered creamer and searching website after website. She rarely drank coffee, but the early mornings and the late evenings, paired with the entire group around her constantly drinking it, had her into the new routine of caffeinated energy to keep herself clicking.

Unplanned huddles with questions on what cell provider to use or what color uniforms should be ordered would break up the silent spells with colorful conversation and debate. These debates made Izzy the most nervous every day. She could research competitors and find travel agencies online in her own little world, but explaining in Spanish that the walkie-talkie component of the Nextel phones would be a bad idea because they would disrupt any peace and quiet the future guests would be seeking was the most stressful part of the day.

As they pieced together the operational details, she was a part of every meeting and every decision—all the while wishing she knew what decisions they were making.

"Uh, estoy de acuerdo con Gretchen," she would quickly answer.

If she agreed with her new boss, she was probably safe. *But what the fuck are they talking about now?* She was pretty sure they had been discussing what technology to use so the butlers serving the hotel guests would be able to communicate immediately with other departments like the restaurant or the bar. But were they still arguing about Nextel walkie-talkies versus BlackBerries? This vocabulary wasn't in the textbook! She had considered herself fluent—until she'd been thrown into this chaotic position. Her head throbbed around her temples.

¿Qué es eso? ¿De qué están hablando? Such intense focus hadn't been part of her days since trigonometry her junior year, which she surmised was worthless for most people and, therefore, stupid. If she wasn't good at it, she didn't like it. Thrown into this group of six other people who'd spoken Spanish fluently for years, and for some of whom it had been their first language, Izzy felt exhausted and like a fraud. She hated pretending to

give a shit about whatever the hell it was they were arguing about when, in reality, she was totally clueless about it all.

It wasn't only the language barrier. At most of her previous places of employment, people generally spoke with civility and patience, and with at least enough respect to let another person finish their thought or statement. Or at least they feared potential ridicule enough to keep their mouth shut. In this group, nobody had any shame nor any fear of another cutting down their idea. Passion was undeniable, as was the inability to compromise and see someone else's point of view. It was a dynamic Izzy hadn't considered when taking the job. She had expected the same type of environment she was familiar with, where information flowed up and down and across the organization, and ideas were welcomed. How would she have known it would be any different? Now she was learning that the people she worked with—Germans, French, Mexicans, and Argentinians—all had different views and approaches, and not many of them were anything close to what she was familiar with.

Most days she worked on subduing feelings of angst and nerves as she tried to start friendly conversations with all of them in an effort to build relationships. Surely things would gel as the operation got off the ground.

Valeria was one of the only other young women on the team among mostly men, outside of Izzy and their boss, Gretchen. Valeria was also going to be selling and promoting the resort, but instead of family vacations through travel agents, she would be attracting corporations to host meetings or award trips for their top performers each year. She, too, was working on compiling lists of companies that she would call, along with other organizations around Mexico and the United States that might send a group of employees to a resort like theirs. For that reason, Izzy thought perhaps they would get along well; however, their relationship wasn't as natural as she'd hoped it might be.

"How is the research going?" Izzy had asked around day three.

Valeria didn't even look up at Izzy. *Maybe she doesn't realize you're talking to her. There are a lot of people in the room.*

"Valeria," Izzy started this time, waiting for her to look up. When she did, Izzy asked again, "How is the research going?" and gave her a slight smile.

Valeria simply nodded and looked back at her screen. *Maybe she's just on a roll and I'm interrupting? Or maybe she doesn't speak English well?*

"¿Todo está bien?" Izzy tried one more time, in Spanish this time, to see if she might answer.

"Oh, sí," Valeria answered with a small smile. *Well, that's something! Maybe it will just take her longer to warm up to me than it has taken her to warm up to Gretchen. She is her boss, after all, so she sort of has to talk to her.*

Earlier that day Izzy had noticed that Gretchen moved her chair next to Valeria's and they appeared to be looking at something together. They laughed and spoke more casually, from what Izzy assessed, and a slight pang of jealousy had struck Izzy. They must have noticed Izzy looking in their direction, because they both stopped talking and looked over at her. She smiled, almost anticipating they might ask her to join the conversation as the third person from sales, and the third female in the room, but they both went back to their conversation without any invitation. Izzy tried not to let it bother her; she didn't know what they were talking about, so she tried not to assume and make something up in her head. Not long after, her mind was distracted by something else in the office.

"¡No, no, no, no, no!" Nacho was saying loudly into his phone. He proceeded to shout for several minutes into his phone. Because of Nacho's escalating voice, the IT guy who sat next him increased his volume as well.

"¡Tampoco! ¡No me chingues, guey!" His accent was different, smoother, with less differentiation between his words. People in Mexico City, (or the DF or federal district, which they pronounced as "De-Efe"), spoke differently from the rest of Mexico. And within De-Efe, the ones with money who were educated spoke differently than taxi drivers or food vendors. Argentinians like Nacho seemed to have a totally different way of stringing their words together, almost like a song or a melody, which made it difficult for Izzy to distinguish the exact words and understand the message. Words that normally should sound like "yama" sounded like "shama," and "plai-yah" sounded like "pla-shah." Isabella likened it to small-town Texas slang versus English spoken in larger cities. The difference in the accents and cadence was something she had only experienced with ranch hands and folks who avoided large city crowds.

The ache began again in Izzy's chest and spread across her collarbone. It crawled up her throat and threatened, burning and causing her to swallow hard. *Be strong, Izzy*, she told herself. *You chose this, didn't you?* She seemed to be telling herself that every few minutes. The mounting pressure in her head seemed to open the door for doubt to come racing in.

Now, in this small, stuffy space, the dust, the constant layer of sticky sweat under her nicest slacks and button-down shirts, and the dull headache that never subsided seemed a far cry from the romantic vision she had pictured when she first agreed to come here. How could she admit to anyone, including herself, that she was faking it?

As she exited the stuffy room for her lunch break, the sun hit her face with intensity and radiated through her closed eyes, infiltrating each pore, every muscle fiber, opening blood vessels and slowing her breath. The resort was several months from being finished, but one area void of people on the edge of the property provided the only solitude from the noise and the gawking workers. Izzy headed toward that far edge of the resort, where sand turned back into short, scrubby bushes, and strings of bougainvillea vines shattered the haze of green and beige with bright fuchsia hues. Heels and slacks were not conducive for the journey, so she slipped off her shoes, rolled up her pant legs, and continued her escape to where the deep blue ocean and light brown sands offered solace amid the turmoil of loud machinery, banging metal, and shouts of Spanish slang.

Deep blue water, in contrast to the turquoise waters of the Caribbean, stretched out for hundreds of miles. Izzy stood, sinking her toes into the sand and wiggling them slightly so the rocky exfoliate made its way between them, on top of them, and around her heels. Rocking her feet slightly, back and forth, the softly packed damp earth gave way to her weight. Deep breath. Holding it in at the top for a moment or two. Sigh of relief.

Staring out into the sea, her hair ruffled softly by the hot breeze moving the humidity around, and standing rooted in the earth, she felt good. The sun warmed her, and the beads of sweat turned into small trickles running down the back of her neck, slipping behind her collar and tickling her shoulder blades until they came to the levee of her bra strap.

Bob Marley telling her not to shed tears popped into her head. His soothing words had been a source of motivation and comfort for her, and she drew on it often these days.

The sun shifted slightly in the sky, encouraging the shadows to extend a bit farther and the heat to subside just a little. Suddenly she thought about her boyfriend, Ethan. He was nice to her and made her laugh, and he was the last tangible thing connecting her to the life she had left behind; for the first time since starting this crazy new routine and new job, she found herself wishing he were here.

After meeting through mutual friends a few months earlier, she and Ethan had begun dating. Really what that meant is they had begun getting drunk together on a regular basis and having sex. There was no lovemaking, no professions of how special she was, or how she had changed his world completely. Nor was there a feeling of connectedness on Isabella's part. Shortly after they met, she had agreed to take the job in Mexico, so during the few months they spent together, they knew the end would come sooner rather than later. They didn't discuss their future, didn't even bring it up; they were simply content with a relationship that was fun and sexual.

And then, standing at the ticket counter in Houston, checking both bags for the flight, she had turned to him. Emotions had welled up, constricting her throat. The burning had intensified as she tried to hold it in. She feared any attempt at words would let this dragon out. She needed to stay strong; she needed to act as if things were fine. She needed to pretend she wasn't scared or uncertain. Because that's how Ethan had acted. Yet she wasn't sure whether the intense warmth in her chest and desire to reach out and hold him was love for him—or simply the sting of saying goodbye.

"Well, looks like you're all set!" he had said, way too cheerfully. "Guess you better get going." Was he just trying to pretend he was fine, or did he truly not care?

"Yup. Thanks for all your help getting here. I love you, and I'm gonna miss you so much," Isabella had said, tears finally spilling over.

"I love you, Izzy, and we're gonna be fine," he said matter-of-factly. "We'll Skype, and it will be good."

With that, she kissed and hugged him one last time and headed up the escalators, straight up into the unknown part of Bush Intercontinental Airport that led to the international security checkpoint.

Thinking about it now, with her toes in the sand, she wasn't exactly sad, but she did feel lonely. She didn't have anyone to share this with, someone who could understand what she was going through.

The wave crashed a bit harder this time and ran across the sand closer to her toes, reminding her that time was passing and she needed to get back to work. The days didn't end at 5:00 p.m. here; they had a lot to accomplish.

Slowly, pulling her left foot from the sand that had almost reached her ankle, she shook it and almost lost her balance as her right foot shifted awkwardly under the new weight imbalance. Catching herself, she gently placed her left foot back down and pulled the right one out, but now her left foot sunk again. This could be never ending.

Before she let herself get frustrated, she decided to walk back to the building without shoes so the sand could fall off as much as possible. She supposed this was beach life and she might as well embrace it.

Walking back into the makeshift office space, her eyes adjusting to the indoor lighting once again, she felt her heart sink. *Where is everyone?* The rumble in her stomach reminded her what time it was, and she instantly knew the answer. *They went to lunch. Without me.* Just then Nacho walked back in with what appeared to be a microwaved meal from home.

Izzy asked him where they had all gone.

"They went to eat," he said back in English. "I have a conference call with a software company for payroll, so I couldn't go. Glad we finally got that microwave outside!" He jerked his thumb toward the door where an extension cord ran from an outlet under the door to a small table the group had set up outside. After an argument or two about the smells of warmed food, the microwave got the boot to the exterior.

"Oh," Izzy answered, feeling abandoned and suddenly starving. She had thrown a granola bar in her bag from the gift shop of the hotel where she was staying and hoped that maybe the group would bring her something back. *They didn't mean to do that, right?* Her own mind was sarcastically answering the question for her. She sighed and tried not to feel hurt. She had left the room, after all, and hadn't said anything to anyone, so maybe they figured she had brought something to eat and had left to go eat.

~

Izzy got a ride home every night from Gretchen, which put her at her boss's mercy for the hour-long trek between the construction office for the resort and the hotel where Izzy was staying.

"¿Lista?" Gretchen asked, looking up at Izzy for the first time in several hours. The sun had set over an hour ago, but the room remained focused on all the tasks at hand, so Izzy hadn't dared ask if anyone else was thinking of leaving. No such thing as work-life balance here.

"¡Sí, estoy lista y tengo hambre!" she replied. Maybe saying she was hungry would prompt Gretchen to invite her to have dinner. It didn't. But the drives had gotten easier for Isabella and Gretchen after their first.

Now, driving down the winding road in total darkness, Izzy felt exhausted, overwhelmed, and stupid. This first week had been a learning curve she hadn't expected. Everything this week, down to that first car ride, had been a learning opportunity that didn't let her mind relax. Her brain weighed a hundred pounds, and her body seemed weak, like she had spent hours in the weight room or on a treadmill. At least it was Friday, and that meant two days off.

"Tomorrow we can go in a little later," Gretchen commented. "So you can get at least a little extra sleep. I'll come by closer to 7:30."

"Oh, okay, yeah, extra sleep . . . " Isabella paused, not sure how to hide her complete shock. *Tomorrow? As in Saturday?* A feeling of complete disappointment seeped into her tired body. It was like she had just been told she was grounded and not allowed to go to prom.

"Maybe we can end a little early too, or you can catch an early Punta Mita bus so you can go look for a place to live," Gretchen offered. She was trying to be helpful, but it sounded like torture to Izzy. *A little early, like at 5:00 p.m.?*

"Oh, um, okay, sure." Now the disappointment was quickly turning into defiance. She wanted to yell that it wasn't fair, and ask how was she supposed to find a place when they didn't have any resources for her. And *now* she didn't even have a full weekend to do any looking around. She wanted to throw a fit like a cranky kid needing a nap. She knew if she tried to ask anything about "why Saturday?" there was no way it would come off as simply a curious question, but rather complaining or whining. Maybe if she asked a different question, she could draw some compassion out of Gretchen to get a bit more time off, or at least could leave early tomorrow afternoon. Maybe Gretchen didn't realize that Isabella hadn't started looking for a place to live, which required so much time. Maybe she could explain it.

"So how do I even get started looking? I mean, do you have someone to call or something?" The frustration was tangible, even if she tried to make it hidden.

Gretchen picked up on it, but she wasn't taking the bait. "I'm happy to give you the name of the agent who helped me. Or you could just go over to the marina and find someone."

Oh, okay yeah, just find someone. Where the hell is the support? The encouragement? The onboarding plan and training? Izzy's irritation was spilling over, infiltrating her body like spilled milk on the table, creeping ever closer to the edge and threatening to drop over onto the floor, creating an even bigger mess to clean up. But as they entered the marina and the lights signaled they were only minutes from the hotel, her irritation gave way to utter exhaustion, and she gave up the fight. She was simply too tired to be mad.

The clock read 8:44 p.m. as she flopped down on the hotel bed, face down. She could hear the vacationers below, talking and enjoying the evening by the pool. After a few minutes, she lifted herself off the bed and opened the sliding glass door to her balcony. The air wasn't as hot as it had been earlier, and now the pleasant warm summer air wrapped her in a feeling of comfort and peace. Glasses clinked in the bar as bartenders crafted the fruity cocktails and poured Mexican beers, plates scraped the tables as they were set down, and flip-flops shuffled along the concrete. Laughter floated up to her floor, and she imagined the giggles were from a young couple being cute and romantic, maybe here on a honeymoon. Palm trees lined the resort pools that curved and spilled into each other, leading out closer to the ocean a few yards ahead. Soft yellow and blue lights shined up the tree trunks while smaller, bright white lights lined the walkways. Candles danced at the small tables and along the bar near the water, and the moon donated its brightness to the ocean. The breeze ruffled the palm leaves and carried the scent of Mexican food and tequila up to Izzy's nose.

There were worse places to be.

It was late and she was tired, but she was also starving. For the seventh time tonight, she opened the room service menu to peruse the same dinner options she'd sampled all week. Exhausted, irritated, hungry, and helpless, she gorged on the mediocre food room service brought up and fell asleep with the glass door open.

Chapter 3

Thankfully, Gretchen let Izzy take the 4:00 p.m. bus (or the one close to it, at least) home on Saturday to save a few hours for house hunting. She made her way out of her now-familiar hotel lobby and crossed the street to the marina side. Her hotel faced the ocean, the Bahía de Banderas, and across the street the buildings faced the other direction toward hundreds of sailboats and yachts docked in the protected marina. The large cobblestone under her feet gave way to paved sidewalks as she made her way between two buildings into the marina, where an alternate universe consumed her.

The masts of the boats clinked as they rocked, creating the sound of wind chimes, and all the white hulls reflected the sunshine into the windows that lined the large square surrounding the water that formed the marina. The buildings of white stucco, or light-sand color, with Spanish-tiled roofs two or three stories above the water offered even more surface area for the sun to reflect and demand a presence. It was hot, and all the light amplified the heat and humidity like a sauna. And then, right when she was ready to retreat to the first sign of air-conditioning, a slight breeze ruffled the atmosphere, sending relief to her hairline and back of her neck that was already glistening with sweat, as if the universe was reading her mind.

Earlier in the week, Izzy had wondered if she might live in one of the villages close to the resort—if nothing else, to avoid the nauseating commute every day. Gretchen had urged her to stay in the marina where there were other tourists and it was safer.

"A *güera* like you wouldn't do too well in Bucerías," she'd advised. "It seems fine during the day, but don't be fooled into thinking there would be any sort of safety or security. At least in the tourist areas you know the doors lock, and these locations that rent to us have liability for our safety."

It seemed like a logical point, but it definitely removed some of the magic she had pictured in these small villages. And even though these villages looked beautiful and easy to navigate on foot, she wasn't sure if it was quite the right fit for an American city girl.

They had only given her two weeks to find a place and, without resources such as websites to check out, offices to go talk to about leasing, or even any sort of publication that might help her find a rental, she was hard-pressed to do anything other than look around on foot here in the marina. She passed a small café, a jewelry store with gorgeous silver and turquoise, and a large restaurant with generous patio space before finding herself in front of a real estate office. *Perfect!*

She made her way inside through the small doorway, large enough only for one person at a time, and found herself face-to-face with a large desk and a woman with long red nails perched upon the chair behind it.

"¡Hola! ¡Hola!" She greeted Izzy with a red, painted-on smile that matched her nails.

"¡Buenas tardes!" Izzy returned the afternoon greeting. "Estoy buscando un apartamento. Acabo de comenzar un nuevo trabajo aquí."

At the news that Izzy was here for work and needed an apartment, the woman's face fell slightly, and she returned from her standing position back to the relaxed, seated state Izzy had found her in.

"Oh, señorita, I'm sorry. We only do vacation rentals or purchases," she sadly informed her. "You need to find an agency to help with that. We only do real estate."

Isabella's heart sank, and the vision she had started to paint of this lovely red-lipped woman grandiosely touring her through one gorgeous apartment after another faded as quickly as it had been born.

"Okay, well, thank you anyway," she replied as she turned back toward the light and the comfort of the boats. They didn't promise anything and, therefore, didn't risk disappointing her. There was solace in that.

Continuing her walk through the marina, now knowing she probably wasn't going to find an agency around here, she reconfigured her expectations. This was a chance to explore. After all, it was her first afternoon off, so she'd better take advantage.

One store caught her attention with what seemed like hundreds of books in the windows piled up in a chaotic way and spread across what might have at one time been intended as a window seat. She went inside, where the shopkeeper had a rotating electric fan going instead of air-conditioning. The stuffy air infiltrated her nostrils along with the smell of old books and water-stained paper. It had a distinct smell of pulp and ink and must.

"Hi, miss, how are you?" the young woman greeted her.

"Hi, I'm fine. Are these all for sale?" she asked.

"Sale or rent. You can buy and take, or exchange with your own book." Her choppy response indicated that she could speak English, but it was not her preferred language.

"Really? That's cool," Izzy said.

Her eyes wandered from the front window to the left wall and quickly to the back where stands that reminded Isabella of old schoolbook fairs displayed children's books. *Ramona*! *Boxcar Children*! *Babysitter's Club*! The classics. John Grisham, Danielle Steele, and other fantastic authors jumped out of the piles and stacks. *But all in English? All American? How strange to find a bookstore like this in Mexico.* Running her fingers over the books, she let the titles take her back to the places where she'd sat and read them, back in her small blue bedroom with a floral bedspread where Nancy Drew had first become her friend. Excitement built inside her, and she wanted to loudly burst out and read every title she recognized as she moved from stack to stack. Her smile radiated, so wide she thought her cheeks might burst, and, even though she was alone, she didn't feel lonely. In a foreign place, all by herself, Izzy felt like she was home. Relating to nobody and everybody at the same time.

Back outside, sometime later, she breathed in the warm, humid air and held her breath for a second, then released it. The warmth her body felt wasn't only from the heat wafting off the walkways, white buildings, and water. It was the sense of peace that had settled over her. She was proud of being right there in that moment, in Mexico, spending time wandering alone.

She passed more shops and a few restaurants she vowed she'd return to before circling back to the main street and her hotel. Tomorrow she'd ask the hotel for an agent referral. She told herself that using the resources given to her wasn't weakness, but rather efficiency. With that settled, she could let her mind move on to the beach and a drink. It was Saturday after all and, although she didn't know anyone there, she was determined to enjoy the hotel for what it had to offer.

Heading back to her room, she changed into her swimsuit and cover-up—a white cotton sheath that clung to the right places and hinted at the colored suit underneath, making her feel sexy and confident. She knew it hugged her in a way that would draw most men's attention. *But why do you care now about drawing attention?* Even in asking herself the question, she wasn't quite sure of the answer. Exploring solo had been fun and exciting, but now the idea of a drink and a romantic beach alone didn't quite conjure up the same images in her mind.

Making her way down in the elevator to the pools, again she felt the pang of being alone.

Izzy had been helping her friend Jessica cook dinner for her boyfriend over at his apartment when she had first met Brandon. Jessica and her group were killing time on a lazy Sunday afternoon, avoiding the impending homework and projects, enjoying a few beers while watching reruns of *South Park*. The open windows allowed the smell of cigarettes and pot into the living room, creating a familiar, comfortable feeling for Izzy. Jessica told Izzy that they'd be done with dinner before the boys returned, but as it turned out, Shake 'n Bake isn't so fast when neither person cooking knows what the hell they're doing. Both girls were in the kitchen attempting to finish the meal when the door opened and Jessica's boyfriend and his brother walked in.

Laid back, tall, and blond, Brandon had the surfer look Izzy had always imagined being with. Except he had been born in London, the son of an Irishman, so the tanned skin and sculpted body didn't come as part of the package. But he was sweet and thoughtful, and most importantly, he let Izzy be herself. He never tried to change her or ask her to stop certain behaviors. Her flirting was typically a problem for any guy she was with, but not for Brandon. He was secure enough in himself, and in Izzy, to know that it was meaningless and harmless.

Izzy's boyfriends before Brandon had been the first guys who'd showed interest. She hadn't dated much and didn't have the confidence to play the field. Her dad was always telling her she was beautiful, and her mom would make comments about boys eyeing her when they were out shopping. It made Izzy feel embarrassed. Who was she to be looked at like that?

But Brandon was different than any boy she'd ever been attracted to. He wasn't the star of the show, the leader of the pack, or the insanely funny man. He was sarcastic, yes, and he had a great sense of humor. But he was comfortable letting others take the lead, which Izzy loved to do. For the first time, she felt okay to be herself and he would accept her and still want to be with her. They worked well together, and although the sex wasn't mind blowing, they were great friends. They both would light up when the other walked in the room, knowing now the day or night would be more fun having their best friend with them.

"So we were standing on the dock, right—" Izzy heard Brandon saying to a friend as she came through his apartment door.

"Oh wait!" she exclaimed, cutting him off. "You mean last week with that crazy wind gust? Yeah! We were standing there, and of course had to let go of the boat for like one second, then this huge wind gust hit! The sails were halfway up, just enough for the wind to catch them, and the boat shot away from the dock, and we were like, 'Holy crap! Now what?' I was like, 'Yeah, I'm not jumping in there to swim out and get it. Have at it, B!'" Izzy finished the story for him.

Brandon smiled, knowing she enjoyed being the storyteller. He always let her do that without getting angry.

Brandon had been raised Catholic and was conservative, so he never wanted to live with Izzy, but she did have a drawer at his place—and later in their relationship, two drawers—no matter where he lived or who he lived with. They played together, picking up new hobbies like Frisbee golf, and Izzy adopted his love of sailing. They sailed competitively together and did well. The sailing team also traveled to places like New Orleans during Mardi Gras or Jazz Fest, and it always was a crazy time and an amazing experience that played right into the adventure Izzy sought for her life.

Izzy was graduating a semester before Brandon, and she knew that with his engineering degree, he'd end up back in his hometown of Houston. The natural thing to do, of course, was find a job in Austin and stay until he finished, but if not, the next option was to go to the city he'd be in next. At last she had landed an interview in Houston that she was excited to tell him all about.

"Oh, that's cool," he had said without any enthusiasm. "Good luck."

"Aren't you excited? I mean, I could be in Houston already when you get there. Isn't that what we talked about?"

"Sure, babe, but you know, don't make life decisions based on me or anything," he said.

She should have known right then that her future plans were not lining up with his. He was in love with her, no doubt, but he was certainly not ready to commit to her. Nor was he ready to have her commit the rest of her future, or the next step in her career, to him. It bothered Izzy, but she loved him and figured the next step was for them to establish their careers, and then of course to get married. Then to start a family and go from there. While she didn't exactly express this, she was sure he felt the same way. After all, he loved her, right? What other outcome could there possibly be?

She had established herself west of downtown near her job, and when Brandon finally graduated, he started looking at places to live in Houston too. Izzy had been good about not asserting her desire for Brandon to move in with her, or to find a place right near her. But it turned out that Brandon's office was on the same side of town she was in, so he found a location only a few minutes from Izzy.

Brandon laid down ground rules: they would only see each other on weekends because they needed to focus and get rest for their new careers. Izzy pretended to be okay with that, but on the inside she sensed that was a pretty good ploy to put some distance between them. He hadn't been like that about school, even when they had finals and were focused on getting good grades for a better career opportunity. So why now?

As she saw it, they'd been together almost two and a half years, and they were always together around campus unless they were studying or in class. What was so wrong with carrying that togetherness into their relationship now? She was ready for more. She wanted that next level of commitment that wasn't just good friends hanging out and having sex when it was convenient for each other. She wanted that long-term promise. But she tried to keep it in, playing a game with herself mentally and emotionally to not scare him away or pressure him. She didn't want to give him any ultimatums. Yet when it wasn't happening at her pace, she couldn't stand it any longer.

When talking with friends about relationships and what her girlfriends should or shouldn't accept, she prided herself in her advice that spoke of confidence and independence. Now was the time Izzy needed to follow her own advice, but she wasn't. Frustration had set in as she fought with herself about what to do and what to say. Tell him how she felt and risk putting more distance and stress between them, or give in and try to believe he was right and she was the one who needed an attitude adjustment?

He didn't seem too interested in meeting the new friends she had made during the time he was finishing school and she was making her way in the new city, biding her time until he arrived. Instead, they hung out with the same sailing crew from college, and they had pool parties and barbecues and competed at the local yacht club together. That was when Brandon was in his element, as was his entire family. Izzy always tried hard to fit in and make it her element too, but something didn't seem right. She enjoyed the tales of the older men, but at the same time would be bored waiting for Brandon to be done.

"You're crazy, Iz, you fit in just fine," he had said once on the long drive back to the city after the latest race. "You always get all upset, but I told you, I know these guys from growing up. You should be talking with the ladies, like my mom."

Before, they had always done things with people she enjoyed and groups of friends she felt comfortable with. She yearned to go back to the college parties, the 6th Street scene, or the local hangouts where she understood her role and her surroundings.

For Brandon, she thought, sailing was not about spending time with Izzy. It was about doing what he wanted and enjoyed, whether she was there or not. To Izzy, sailing was about spending time together. Her free time was always for him, and she would do whatever he wanted to do whenever he wanted to do it. She had forgotten about her fun Sundays when he was still in Austin—Sundays when she was with the girls, or shopping and taking all the time she wanted, or cleaning while watching football on mute as great music pumped through her apartment. She had given that up for him. So why didn't he understand that their time together should be more important?

One week while grocery shopping, Izzy realized she didn't have mustard at her place and had only mayonnaise. Brandon liked mustard, she knew, so she bought some, thinking of him.

She remembered this later, when she was at Brandon's apartment and he was making them sandwiches for lunch. She asked for mayonnaise on hers.

"I don't have any, just mustard. You know I don't like mayonnaise." He said it somewhat playfully. "Do you want mustard, then?"

"Uh, no . . . you know I don't like mustard?" It came out almost as a question versus a statement. Was this the first time he had ever said something that made her wonder if he really knew her? It was as if the last few years of good times and all the wonderful things he had done for her, and with her, no longer mattered. She stood there thinking this man had no clue about who she was or what she wanted.

They ate sitting on the floor of his living room with no furniture. Reclined on his back after he finished eating, he beckoned her to come lie with him. She obliged and moved to lie next to him with her head resting on his bicep as he wrapped that same arm around her shoulder.

"Brandon, why didn't you buy mayonnaise?" she tentatively ventured. She waited, holding her breath in anticipation of the anger—or worse, his dismissal.

"Why would I? We just talked about this." He seemed to sense this conversation was not about condiments.

"But I have mustard at my place for you even though I hate it," she said. "I got it because I was thinking of you, honey." She tried to temper her emotions so that he would listen and not react. "I always think about things you like. Why don't you do that for me? I mean, I don't know that you never did, but right now, I don't think you do at all."

When he replied, his tone was almost condescending, as if her concern was childish and her feelings were stupid. "It's not that I don't think about you. I mean, Jesus, I just didn't buy you mayonnaise, but that doesn't mean anything."

She decided to dive headfirst into the real question. "Brandon, where do you want to take this relationship? Because I would think we're at the point by now where we do things for each other all the time, just because."

He seemed to sense what she was after. "You know I love you," he started. "And I have thought about the next level."

Her breath caught in her chest, even as she braced for the *but*.

"And I think maybe we can do that in another five years or so," he concluded. "But, you know, not right now. We're just getting started on our careers, and we need to really see where those are going to take us. I mean, I may not even stay in Houston very long, you know?"

Her throat constricted and made her eyes burn. *No, I don't know!* she thought furiously. She tried to steady her heartbeat and her emotions, and she sat up, facing away from Brandon, and reached for her water.

"You okay?" he asked.

"Yeah, just need some water," she said in a steady, unassuming voice. "Hey, I think I'm gonna run."

"Okay, babe, call me later." He didn't even question her abrupt departure. Maybe he didn't realize, or maybe he knew he could play dumb to avoid the impending argument. Either way, she was grateful for the fast exit.

She went straight home and cried for the next hour or so, wondering what the hell that had all been about and what to do about it.

The next day she went in to work and found herself in her manager's office for a work-related matter, but since they had become good friends, it was hard to hide her sadness, and it turned into a heart-to-heart with a woman Izzy had great respect for.

"I mean, to me, it seems you're growing and ready to move forward in life, in your career, and in your relationship," Susan said. "But he's ready to stay right where he is. Maybe you're outgrowing him." It was a statement, not a question.

The strangest sensation washed over Izzy. Was that relief that someone had finally said what she was afraid to admit? It was as if a pressure valve had been opened, and permission to feel that way had been granted.

"Wow...I...uh," she began. "I think you're exactly right. But why do I need to move on? Why do I need to grow?"

"Because, Isabella," saying her name like a parent who was about to explain why something was a bad idea, "you are an achiever, and you are always looking to improve and do more, do better. You've got that built into you. That's why we hired you immediately. Everyone knows you're not going to be an assistant for long. You are too good, and you pick up things so quickly that you'll get bored here before a year's gone by. Think about it. Yes, you moved here with intentions of being ready when Brandon got here, but that is such a huge risk to take—moving here before him and not knowing anyone, then taking a job you knew nothing about, since you didn't even study hospitality in school. You're a brave girl and you're a confident woman, and you need someone who wants to grow and who can keep up with you. I just don't know that Brandon is that someone right now."

Sitting at her desk after the conversation, Izzy stared into space, feeling nothing. Her mind was racing but going nowhere. At twenty-three years old, she felt that she was ready to start thinking about marriage and a family. Yet automatically, instead of owning those feelings as acceptable, she had begun to evaluate why they were wrong, why she needed to try and curb them or change them. But Susan said that maybe her feelings were normal after all. Maybe she wasn't crazy.

Still, although her feelings were validated now, it didn't change the painful idea that Brandon wasn't going to be her husband. She left work that day, skipping happy hour with friends, and went straight home to cry.

Later that week, Isabella found herself back at a house party with all the same old sailing people, the ones Brandon claimed were his best friends, yet who treated Brandon like a toy. Nobody truly respected him, because they could spend hours drinking and recalling the ridiculous things they'd done to him without any mindfulness that he was sitting right there in the room with him.

"Dude," Stevie always started stories that way, "remember when we put B in the dumpster?" Fits of laughter rolled through his body.

"Oh my God, YES!" someone answered. "Where were we? Austin?"

"No! No! That was totally when we were at the races in New Orleans when Brandon was a freshman!" another reminded them.

Izzy looked at Brandon, trying to read his face. He sat there with a goofy smile but not saying a word.

Stevie started in again. "Yeah! That's right! We were leaving the bar and decided he needed a good hazing! 'In you go, FRESHMAN!'" Tears almost ran out of his eyes, he was laughing so hard. "And we just picked up his legs and threw him in there! 'No guys! C'mon!'" He laughed, mocking Brandon's resistance to the entire thing. "You were so scared like a little baby FRESHMAN!"

The entire room was laughing about Brandon's freshman hazing, and Brandon just sat there, smiling but looking at the floor.

Izzy had dealt with this for too many years and was over it. She was over his weakness and his lack of self-respect. She was over the fact that she seemed to be the only one in this group of so-called friends who actually liked him and didn't constantly want to razz him or make fun of him. And since she didn't have the guts to admit it might be time to move on, she let it fuel her frustration.

"Brandon," Izzy said sharply, "I need to talk to you. Right now."

His face didn't register surprise, or even fear, that something was about to happen. He almost didn't have any expression at all. Izzy stood up abruptly and headed for the front door, not the back door where the other half of the party was going on.

"What the fuck was that?" she demanded the minute they were in the driveway.

"What? What the hell do you mean?" he started defensively. "What did I do now, Izzy?"

"They're totally making fun of you and calling you an idiot, and you're laughing about it! You can't stand here and tell me it doesn't bother you."

"Whoa, dude, chill out!" His hands went up, palms facing her, as if to say he surrendered. "I know they're just kidding around, and you should too. Why do you hate them so much? They're my friends, and they were around long before you, so you need to get over this bullshit and fast. Ever since we moved here you've been different, and all of a sudden you don't like any of my friends. What the fuck is *that* about?"

"Hate them? I don't hate them," she said, the alcohol and emotions spurring her on. "I hate what they do to you and what they say to you. And what's this bullshit about not seeing each other during the week anymore because of your career and focus? You never did that to me even when you were going through midterms or finals. Somehow you were able to make time for me then."

"Okay, Izzy, you're being ridiculous, and you're screaming at me in the middle of the street!" He was finally starting to raise his voice louder than hers. "Don't fucking make me choose between friends and you, Izzy. They have been there for me and will always be there for me; they're like family to me. So don't you fucking try to say they are bad people."

"Brandon!" she said, almost at the point of delirium now. "It's not about your fucking friends, okay? It's about how everything else in your life is more important than me! You don't care that I'm uncomfortable here! You don't think about me when you're at the grocery store and think maybe I'd like mayonnaise someday for a sandwich! You love spending time sailing with old men and listening to ridiculous stories over and over again, and you know I'm not comfortable there either, but if I want to see you, I have to go. Do you even give two shits about me and what I need or want? I mean, I moved here just to be with you. I gave up any other place or potential opportunity to follow you. And you conveniently always forget that!"

He stared at her for a second. She thought maybe he was collecting his thoughts and now was the time he'd say what she needed to hear. Now is when he would say he loved her more than anything and he was so sorry. Now . . .

"Then maybe I don't love you, Izzy," he stated flatly, easily.

She recoiled from him and took a few steps back as if he'd slapped her in the face. Her lungs filled with prickly heat and her legs went numb.

He started shouting again. "And Izzy, if you're so uncomfortable with my life now, if you can't stand all the things I love, then maybe you don't really love me either! This is my life, and if you want to be in it, you need to learn to deal with it! If you don't want to, then I can't help you! And I didn't ask you to come here anyway; you wanted that!"

She wasn't sure what stung more in that moment. The fact that he didn't love her, the fact that he was probably right that she didn't love him, or the fact that the first time she finally saw him standing up for himself, it was against her.

She looked him in the eyes, tears flowing from hers as they had been, but the anger stripped from her face. The devastation and sadness had turned to emptiness. As she stood there looking at him, she suddenly felt she didn't know this man at all.

Hours seemed to pass as they stood there in the silence looking at each other. The sounds of the city around them dissipated: the white noise of passing traffic and the ambulance sirens disappeared; the shouts of laughter and music from the party faded into whispers. Izzy heard her breath draw inward, and she held it like she was about to jump off a cliff.

"I'm sorry, Brandon," she whispered. "I'll miss you."

With that, she turned and headed for her car.

She half listened for Brandon to call to her and say, "Don't go," fighting the urge to look back. Maybe he'd be running toward her; maybe he'd be looking miserable enough she knew he'd call to apologize. She resisted the urge until she'd started her car, drunk, and pulled out of the apartment parking lot onto the main street. When she finally looked in the rearview mirror, he was gone.

Now, sitting in a beach chair watching moonlight dancing on the Pacific Ocean as the last glow from the sun escaped below the horizon, she felt that same intense emotion. It was her decision; she had chosen this, but she couldn't overcome the emptiness that she was now all alone and unable to connect with Ethan, since she couldn't call internationally back to the US to get comforting words of encouragement. She was stuck—with nobody to help empower her, nobody to help soothe her, nobody to dry her lonely tears. She looked down at her feet and sighed, hugging her knees into her chest and resting her chin on top of her left knee. It was okay then, and it would be okay now, too, she told herself. *Don't cry, Isabella, you haven't even given yourself a chance*, her inner voice insisted. She concentrated on the sounds of the waves crashing on the rocks methodically, repeatedly, and let her fear go.

Chapter 4

On Sunday morning, she'd assumed she'd missed her ride—*Oh my God, did Gretchen wait forever? Should I call her?*—before remembering it was Sunday. She had the day off. As quickly as the stress came, it subsided again and she relaxed back on the bed.

She had a meeting today with Carmen, Gretchen's property agent. As Izzy waited in the expansive lobby with soaring ceilings, she poured herself a plastic cupful of the cucumber-infused water meant for the newly arriving guests and found a plush wicker chair to sit in while she watched the faces of those coming and going. Her favorites were the people just arriving from the airport for the start of their stay. Her face had probably worn the same impressed, open-mouthed awe these people all had as they stepped in from the driveway.

These two, look at them, she thought. *They must be here on their honeymoon, not able to keep their hands off each other.* Holding hands and grinning from ear to ear, they both widened their eyes, tilted their heads back, and opened their mouths to say, "Wooooooowwww!" As she watched, an older couple walked in from outside as though they had just spent the morning taking a walk around the marina area. The looks they exchanged were different than the newlywed couple but seemed to communicate a friendship, a connection. She wondered about their lives and how they had gotten here. Maybe they had honeymooned here once upon a time and came back year after year to celebrate. Maybe they took one trip a year and tried a new place each time. Whatever they were doing, they looked happy and in sync.

It reminded Izzy somewhat of her own parents. When her Dad would come home from work, no matter how she and her sister tried to be first, their dad would always sidestep or gently unwrap them so he could first give their mom a hug and kiss and look into her eyes. It was like he was relieved to be back home with his best friend. Over time, she and her sister learned not to try and be first, but to let them kiss (*eew*) and *then* they could jump all over Daddy while Mom finished dinner. Even though their dad often poked fun and publicly (and privately to the girls) criticized her, they knew he genuinely loved her. They'd only known each other for six months when they got married in their early twenties, and they'd been through some tough times, but they'd worked it out and stayed together. Isabella admired that and wished for that in her own life.

Of course, as her mom often reminded her, at Izzy's age, her mom had already been married at least four years. Well, she was working on that! And Ethan seemed like a potential candidate, she told herself.

Turning her attention back to the lobby, Izzy realized she had been sitting there over twenty minutes now. She was irritated. Without any way of communicating with Carmen, she could continue waiting, or she could head back to her room and hope Carmen found a way to contact her. Gretchen had been pretty clear that they could only afford her resort housing for two weeks, and this week would be the end of those two weeks. It had taken her this long just to figure out how to find someone to help, and now this lady had the nerve to forget altogether, or at least not care about her time frame. *How rude and unprofessional*, Izzy thought.

The longer she sat, the more her brain ran to stereotypes, expectations she had about Mexican culture. Of course Carmen was late, because there wasn't much sense of urgency around here. Hadn't she seen it in the hotel staff? Whether it was fresh towels, the time it would take to grab a quick sandwich, or the ease in which she would be able to find a taxi, nothing ever panned out the way they said. That familiar warmth of anger started in her belly and rose to her face, and with every recounted memory of injustice, her sense that all Mexicans were so careless and rude grew stronger. She was getting more and more irritated. Maybe they all just said what they needed to say to appease Izzy in the moment without care of the consequences or frustration it might cause later. And now, just to prove Izzy's stereotype correct, Carmen was almost thirty minutes late.

She probably knew she was the only option Izzy had and, therefore, didn't need to worry about losing the business. She was probably off doing something with a friend or family member and would get around to coming eventually. She would probably swoop in here in white pants, towering wedge sandals, and hair all curled up and sprayed into place framing her perfectly brown skin and bright pink lips that would surely match her bright pink nails. Some sheer, floral top would grace her shoulders and lay perfectly on her tiny rear end. Izzy could just see it. *Oh darling Ee-sabella, I'm SO sorry for de wait. Please, you must excuse me. I was with my mother and, ugh, she was just taking forever and, my dear, you know you cannot leave your mother when she is like dat, no?*

She was getting worked up about this as a shorter, older woman in her early fifties wearing a red business suit and pantyhose came shuffling through the front door.

"Isabella?" she called to her from across the lobby.

"Carmen?" Izzy responded.

"Sí, sí . . . yes, it's me!" she responded.

Izzy figured she should be polite. "¿Cómo está?"

"Oh my gosh! ¡Qué *mareo*! It's so hot out there! I am sorry for the delay. I tried your room, but of course you were here waiting. My last appointment ran so late, and I came as fast as I could." The woman looked and spoke like a total professional, nothing like Izzy's stereotypical expectations.

"Oh, sure, that's okay," Izzy heard herself say. *What? It's okay? No it's not! You waited here for forty minutes without any clue, and now everything is okay?* But then she took a deep breath, and she realized that truly, she was just relieved she had someone to help her when she had no idea what else she would do. *And she's not at all what you thought, is she?* With that thought, she dropped any stereotypical expectations, let the anger subside, and gratefully followed Carmen to her car waiting in the front drive. *What is "mareo" anyway?*

Once at the apartment Carmen wanted to show her, Izzy waited in the breezeway between the buildings near the elevators while Carmen scurried off somewhere, saying something about "las llaves." *Look at this place!* From back where she stood, shaded by the building, Izzy could see several interconnected turquoise-blue pools that seemed to stretch from one side of the area to the other, giving it a resort-feel—like the hotel she was staying in. No palm trees crowded the view, but the lush hibiscus and well-manicured grass areas hugged the pools from all sides. Beyond that, she could hear and smell the sand and salt of the ocean before even seeing it.

"¡Aquí están!" Carmen announced as she returned, keys in hand. They ducked into the stainless-steel elevator and rode up to the fourth floor. Striding out of the elevator to the left, Carmen talked with her hands, motioning back toward the marina. The half-walled, open-aired walkway boasted views overlooking the marina out toward the airport and beyond, where her daily commute led her to the far northern part of the Bahía de Banderas. From that vantage point, the city looked like a jungle, full of palm trees and greenery Izzy didn't recognize, and she could see the sharp incline of smaller cobblestone streets rising up from the main road into the hills that were dotted with white, blue, and pink buildings. The warm breeze ruffled her hair slightly, and she could hear laughter in the distance mixed with the cars shifting gears as they rolled past the building below.

"Isabella, now . . . remember . . . this may be pricey, but you are going to fall in love." Carmen spoke with such passion. *She should be the host on a dating show,* Izzy thought, *the way she puts rose-colored glasses on you before even seeing the place.* "This place is only one bedroom, but it is furnished and just *perfect* for you."

Jiggling the key slightly and giving the door a shove, she opened it and led Izzy into the apartment. It was tiny, maybe 600 square feet, and the kitchen and living area were one long rectangle separated by a round glass dining table and four large iron chairs with hideous yellow-and-red cushions. Two equally hideous couches faced each other flanking the left and right walls, and a matching glass coffee table sat between them. The travertine tile was a sand color (*Great for hiding dirt*, Izzy thought), and the countertops were smooth ceramic that gave Izzy a feeling of luxury. But it wasn't the furnishings Izzy focused on. It was the floor-to-ceiling glass sliding doors leading to a large white stucco balcony that drew her in. Light poured in, and tons of beautiful blue sky created a postcard-like impression.

"Wow," Izzy breathed.

"See!" Carmen said delighted. "I knew you would *love* this place! Look, look, come see," she said making her way to the glass doors, opening them for Izzy, and motioning for her to join her outside. She was going for the close and, even though Izzy knew it, she didn't care one bit.

As she stepped outside, Izzy's mind leapt to a vision of herself here, spending time reading or talking on the phone, or watching the scene below while she sipped on something cold. Four white plastic chairs and a white plastic table took up much of the space, and the instant she stepped outside, the sounds and smells enveloped her and wrapped her into a blanket of security and peace. Four floors below her, the pools glistened, calling to her, while a fountain on the right side created a serene and constant stream in the shallow side of the pool as kids splashed and shouted joyfully. A walkway formed an arched bridge over the center of the pools and led to the beach access only a few yards away. There she could see lounge chairs and permanent straw shade covers on the loose, light brown sand, and from there the beach stretched for almost another forty yards before the deep blue water crashed upon it.

Her eyes swept from the pools below, across the bougainvillea winding their way around the villas at the edge of the sand, and beyond to the waves crashing upon the shore. Her shore. Following the coastline to the left, where buildings grew out of the lush, green background, she could pick out the *malecón*, or boardwalk, and the end of the main walkway where the string of old boutique hotels began. As she moved her eyes farther down the waterline, she lost focus on the details as the mountains rose out of the ocean and towered above, almost as if they were protecting the bay, along with all the life inside. Clouds floated across the late afternoon sky, and the same slight breeze brushed a loose lock off the side of her face.

Captivated by the scene, before she'd even seen the entire place, she began bargaining with herself. This was beyond the budget she had set for herself, but without any other expenses, like a car or insurance, she could probably afford to put more into the rent. She was rationalizing again to support the emotional decision she had already made. Just as she had when she chose to take this position in the first place. Her heart and gut always told her which decision to make, but she didn't quite trust them. She was forever trying to explain why she did things. But to whom?

"Can you show me the kitchen and bedroom?" she heard herself ask Carmen, lying to herself as if she weren't one hundred percent convinced this was the place for her.

"¡Claro!" Carmen replied enthusiastically, no doubt knowing this was a done deal.

The paperwork was pretty simple, and the payments would be easy. She got the information about where to send a check each month, and the rent was in US dollars so there wouldn't be issues of trying to convert dollars to pesos. The mailbox system was easy to navigate, and the gym—well, that was just the icing on the cake. It was only two floors from her on the side overlooking the airport and the northern part of the city. This view, while not waterfront, afforded bright green palm trees and the local lush vegetation that grew up around every building, and the mountain along the coast. She could watch planes arriving and taking off, making up stories about who were in those planes and where they were going. Now all she needed to do was check out of the hotel and into her own space— her own place—and start living.

She fell asleep that night feeling excited and proud and confident—something she hadn't felt since she first arrived.

After signing the paperwork, getting the keys, and moving her things from the hotel, one of the first things Izzy did was to change into her swimsuit and make her way down to the pool. When the elevator closed behind her, she stood in the shade of the building as the breeze chilled her body despite the sweltering summer humidity that engulfed the city. The universe was reminding her this was paradise. This was what she had chosen. This was a beautiful place, and there was something peaceful about the bay and this city. She felt her shoulders drop as she took a deep breath.

Low and steady in the background, waves crashed up onto the beach and onto the rocky jetty built to protect the strip of beach in front of her condo complex. On this Saturday afternoon, the pool was one big party with families relaxing together, friends laughing together, and children squealing together.

Then she saw her: a little blonde-haired girl with bouncing curls. She had on a little pink bathing suit with ruffles around her waist that mimicked a skirt. Her water socks matched her suit and gave her the traction she needed around the slippery pool area. She looked at Izzy and was struck with curiosity. Isabella could see the girl's mother keeping close eye from her chair but trying to let her daughter explore and find new adventures. To ease her mind, Izzy smiled at the mother and gave a slight wave, as if to acknowledge she was safe and she understood the mother's position. The mom relaxed a bit in her chair and smiled back, grateful to know Izzy wasn't a danger.

"Hi!" the little girl said. She must have been three or four years old, but then again, without kids or nieces and nephews of her own, Izzy couldn't be sure about kids' ages. Either way, she seemed young and innocent.

"Well, hello there." Izzy smiled back at her. "Are you here on vacation?"

The girl didn't respond with words but tilted her head slightly and pointed back toward her mom as if to say, "I'm with them."

"Are you having fun?" Izzy inquired, assuming this little girl was too young to truly understand her surroundings or what a vacation might be.

"Mommy's happy now…," she said, trailing off slightly. Isabella couldn't help but notice a sadness, a hesitation, that indicated perhaps things hadn't been so good before. Maybe Mommy hadn't been happy recently.

"Where's your mommy?" the little girl asked.

The innocent question struck Izzy directly in her heart. The sting almost made her feel dizzy from the reality of it. The tears didn't have to be called on; they just showed up and started to overflow before she could even stop them.

"My mommy isn't here," Izzy choked out. "I'm here alone." Her voice caught on the word "alone," and she took a sharp breath.

The little girl cocked her head to the side; she seemed to know something had made Izzy feel sad. Then, hesitating at first, she took a few small steps toward Izzy and wrapped her arms around Izzy's legs, pressing the side of her head and her blonde curls into Izzy's upper thigh. Any control Izzy had over her emotions let go, and the dam burst. Isabella bent slightly at the waist to put her arms around the little girl in response, as tears and truth came rushing out.

"Thank you," Izzy said, trying to smile through the tears. The little girl pulled back and flashed one last smile before she bounced off, returning to her mom, leaving Izzy standing awkwardly in her own sad world that seemed to be spinning out of control. Wanting to hide her shame, and feeling embarrassed, Izzy made a beeline over the arched bridge toward the ocean.

By the time she reached the sand and was able to let go, she had been through every emotion and back again, and the exhaustion she had felt earlier in her apartment was back. More than needing to relax, she needed to sleep. Finding a vacant weathered lounge chair, the kind with the plastic straps that lose buoyancy over time, she threw her towel across it and laid facedown in order to hide herself from the beautiful world around her. What a baby she was being: so lonely and scared that she was crying on a gorgeous beach in this beautiful vacation spot. *It's time to put on your big-girl pants*, she heard her internal voice saying, which sounded strangely like her father. Arguing with herself made it even worse, and as her mind fought to overcome itself, her body gave in to the exhaustion, and she fell into a restless sleep in the shade of her private little *palapa* in the sand.

Bing! an email arrived. Finally, Izzy had been able to coordinate with the cable company to get set up with Internet and TV late one evening after work at her little apartment by the sea. She had watched her inbox fill with new junk mail and ads, and she smiled to herself. *This really isn't so far from home, is it?*

Tonight she was having butterflies of anticipation while she opened her brand-new Skype account so she and Ethan could connect. She missed having him around and missed having him to talk to, to ask how her day was, and to listen as she shared stories about what she was experiencing. Before she was able to get the Internet thing working, she had bought a tiny plastic cell phone that she could add minutes to whenever she needed, plus it also could double as a doorstop or even hammer if necessary. And she had used it for both. The old T-9 texting it offered was sufficient, but it took almost two weeks to figure out how to change languages so she could get messages out faster. It was tough to call long distance, though. Puerto Vallarta didn't have quite the number of cell towers her home state did, so calls dropped more consistently than they worked. Most people didn't seem to mind.

She seemed to have lost the ability to function without the connection to someone else. She lived alone and should be independent. When she developed routines like going to the gym or grocery shopping, she was fine. But if she didn't have plans on a Thursday, Friday, or Saturday night, she was lost about what to do with all that time. When she was in a relationship, there was no question. She was ready and waiting anytime they were able to see her.

Now that she had Internet at home, she would bring her laptop home every night so she could use it to Skype. And the recently launched hotel bus ride for all employees couldn't be quick enough. She'd practically run from the bus stop all the way down the main street of the marina to her condo so she could rush upstairs and get online. She knew Ethan was waiting for her so they could both be home and in front of the computer at the same time. Her goal was always to get there fast so he wouldn't be left waiting, feeling irritated. Never mind that she wasn't making friends with folks from work, going out with them after long days, or even taking time to explore her new life. Her days consisted of working, then getting home to talk to Ethan. Weekends she had time to enjoy some things, run to the store, and do whatever else she needed to do, because he had to do the same. It was enough to calm the cravings for the familiar and the personal connection she lacked in Mexico.

Logging in tonight, she saw he was already online. She practically caught her breath in her chest with excitement as she dialed.

"Hiiiii!" she squealed. She was always so happy to see his face.

"Heyyyy," he answered nonchalantly. "What are you doing?"

"Well, um, I just got home, of course, and just logged in. Like every night." She was perplexed that he'd ask what she was doing instead of *how* she was doing, or how was her day. Didn't he know she counted the minutes until they could talk again?

"Yeah, of course." He almost sounded dejected. Maybe something was upsetting him and it wasn't directed at her.

"You okay?" she ventured.

"Yeah fine, just, you know, sitting here without you, trying to pretend like this is enough." Whoa. Now he sounded mad or even resentful about the situation that he had so lovingly supported not that long ago.

"What is that supposed to mean?" she asked, getting defensive.

"Just miss you is all. Why are you getting upset? This is hard on me too, you know." Now he was getting defensive. But if it was just because he was sad and missing her, then, in a way, that was romantic and sweet.

"Oh, babe, I know. I miss you too, and this Skype thing is better because I can see you. But it's not the same as being there." Her tone changed to sympathetic and sweet.

"I'm really horny and can't even do anything about it!" he burst out. Now they were really getting down to it. He was not only upset about the distance, but sexually frustrated.

"Really?" she asked half amused, half turned on at the idea of him wanting her. "You haven't masturbated or anything?"

"Well, yeah, but it's not the same. Have you?" He sounded like a curious little boy.

"Yes, of course! You know I have a toy to help me with that. The same one I've had since college." She smiled, feeling coy and playful. It lived in the bottom drawer of her bedside table, and she only used it in her bedroom. At least up to this point. And only by herself. It was like her little secret that nobody knew about, except that many of her friends talked about it openly, so she always felt obliged to admit that she, too, enjoyed it. Izzy had always been sexually charged ever since her terrible first time with her high school boyfriend. Once she got over the pain, she found that she loved it and could get wet simply at the thought of touching herself, let alone someone else learning to touch her. Her theory was that if she had a vibrator, she wouldn't feel the need to have as much random sex, so she'd bought her toy during her sophomore year of college in Austin.

It did exactly what she was hoping; it helped keep her from getting so frustrated that she made bad decisions with the wrong guys. It empowered her to be able to take care of herself and not to have to rely on a man to make her feel good. What she didn't expect was how much it would help her learn to know how to make herself come, how she wanted to be touched, and what she liked. So when she did actually find a man worthy of sex, she wasn't as shy about asking for what she needed or wanted.

In her opinion, too many women viewed sex as something men liked, but they didn't take the time to understand they could like it too. Sadly, in Izzy's opinion, it seemed acceptable that men liked to have lots of sex and ask for certain things in the bedroom, but if a woman liked to have sex and knew what to ask for, it made her a slut or whore. To Izzy, that wasn't fair. She had spent so many years of high school and early college enjoying sex but letting someone else direct the show. How did he want it? How did he like it? Now, she could say what she wanted or what she liked, and surprisingly, men seemed to enjoy that. In return, she could get what she needed so she could also offer what they might like. As she grew older and even more confident in her ability, and understood her desires, it made for much better sex, even if it was less frequent when she was a single woman.

She rarely shared the vibrator's existence with any men in her life. This night, however, was unfolding in an interesting way. Ethan was lonely, and she could tell. She was hurting emotionally from being alone but wasn't sexually frustrated. The only thing she knew to do was give him whatever he might want in the only way she could.

"Do you want to watch me masturbate?" she asked him, somewhat shyly, but also with an air of naughtiness.

"Really?" His face lit up. "Yeah, babe, that's hot!"

"Okay, hold on. Let me go get my vibrator." She left the computer and ran to the bedroom to retrieve her secret toy. She wasn't sure if she was really up for this, and she was worried she'd look weird; but if he needed this, then she was willing to help. After all, he'd been there when she needed him at different times for emotional support, so why not return the favor with his physical needs?

"So . . . um . . . how should we do this?" she asked when she returned. She had been sitting on the couch with the computer on the coffee table.

"I don't know; I mean, maybe just start touching yourself," he suggested.

"Okay . . . like this?" she asked as she pulled off her pajama pants and her panties and started rubbing her inner thigh with one hand while she slid her left hand under her shirt, leaning back on the couch to relax.

"Wait, no, I can't see anything. Move the camera," he instructed.

Izzy tried to angle the computer screen down toward her lap and prop her legs up on the coffee table on either side of the computer. Surely he could see now.

"Nope, still can't see," he responded. "It's like the light is really dark. Can you turn more lights on?"

"No, there aren't any more lamps or anything in this room. I can try to move to the dining area. Maybe that overhead light will be better?"

"Okay, yeah, try anything." Ethan was starting to sound desperate.

She moved the computer over to the dining table and shivered slightly as the cool air from the vent settled over her half-naked body. Setting the computer on the glass table, she tried to get comfortable in the wrought-iron chair with the horribly ugly yellow-and-red cushions. The iron was cold on her arms and the glass table so high that she had to scoot back from the table, again trying to angle the computer screen down to show what he needed to see.

"Is that better?" she asked.

"Yeah, I think so. Start again."

She started again, running her hands down her stomach to her inner thighs, then running one hand up her shirt.

"Wait, take your shirt off. I can't see your tits." He was starting to get impatient.

"Well, I can't see anything of yours, either. Did you turn the lights on?"

"Do you really need to see anything, though?" he asked, sounding genuinely confused. "I mean, women aren't visual, right? And you're doing this for me, aren't you?"

She had asked him if he wanted to watch, hadn't she? Maybe he was right; she hadn't spelled out that this should be a two-way street. Not feeling entirely comfortable with the idea of someone watching her pleasure herself was making her a bit overly sensitive, and maybe she should just pretend he wasn't there so she could enjoy herself. Taking a deep breath, she tried to let go and get back to the relaxed, focused state where she could use her own hands and her own imagination without worrying about him.

Her left hand made its way to her left breast and began pinching and rubbing her nipple while she ran her right hand down toward her clit and began to move in circular motions, feeling herself start to heat up. She leaned her head back and closed her eyes, trying to remember how it felt the last time she had Ethan's hands on her body.

As she was slipping into a relaxed state of ecstasy, though, she heard again: "Baby, I really can't see anything. I can hear you but can't really see you."

"Okay," she sighed as her momentum dissipated. "Let me switch sides and turn on the entry light by the door."

She turned the computer to the other side of the table and walked over to the door to flip the light on. Returning to the table, he cried out, "Yes! Right there, I can see your body!"

"Here where I'm standing?" she asked.

"Yeah, can you do it standing up there? Maybe just angle the computer down?"

"How about this?" she asked as she moved the computer angle so the camera was pointing at what she thought might be the ground.

"Yes, that's perfect." He sounded enthusiastic.

"Okay, give me a minute then to get to where I was."

Standing up in front of the computer on the cold tile, with the cold air-conditioning on her, it was difficult to get into the mood again. Maybe it was time to use the vibrator, which could bring the mental focus she usually needed. Reaching for it on the table, she turned it on and started at the top of her clit, working it down between her legs and back up again, letting the vibrations stimulate the entire area while her other hand went back to her breasts.

"Okay, I can see that, but now it's blocking any view of your vagina," Ethan informed her.

"Ethan, I have no idea how to do this then." She was feeling frustrated and annoyed yet embarrassed at the same time. "You want the computer on the floor looking up at me instead?"

"No, no, that will block the light. I don't know, Iz, maybe this isn't worth it. Maybe this whole thing isn't worth it," he said with a burst of frustration.

What whole thing? The attempt at cybersex or this entire relationship?

What is he saying? Before she could get upset and start a fight, her body contracted and reacted to the vibrator that she hadn't bothered to move. It felt too good to lose focus now, and pleasure took over any other emotion or reaction she might have had otherwise. Feeling herself becoming wetter, she slipped the vibrator inside and let the vibration take on a new direction. Without thinking about it, she turned around and bent over.

"Holy shit! Yes!" he cried. "That's amazing!" He was clearly climbing toward ecstasy himself.

Letting her body do the talking, she lifted her left leg onto the table behind her in order to open up and show him more of herself. The table was high enough that it started to throw off her balance, so she had to use one hand to steady herself on the chair and the other hand on the vibrator, moving it in and out slowly, bringing her closer to climaxing.

"Oh, yeah babe, put that ass up there."

Now things were going well! She was feeling good, he was feeling good, and he could see. Never mind she was freezing cold and balancing precariously on one leg trying to give him a great show. *Is this what porn stars feel like on the set?* Although the vibrator was doing its job well, she knew she needed that pressure on her clit to get there. Trying to stay focused on the moment and the feeling, she started to search her mind for a solution, seeking only her ultimate pleasure of an orgasm. Maybe if she moved her right hand from the chair to hold the vibrator and repositioned her right foot a little farther from the table, she could balance well enough to use her left hand on her clit without needing to brace herself on the chair. Trying not to interrupt the flow, she scooted her foot out, contracting her abs to try and gain some balance with that left leg up on the table. Slowly, she let go of the chair and reached for the vibrator, switching it to her right hand and holding the table with her left. Slowly, slowly, she was balanced and still moving the vibrator, now with the left hand. If she could just let go of the table edge and stay on one foot, she could reach her clit and take herself there. Her body urging her on, she let go . . . and immediately lost her footing. Her upper body leaned forward, tipping over toward the tile floor.

"Oh shit!" she yelled as she toppled.

"Wait, don't stop!" he pleaded. "Oh my God, I'm almost there, I'm gonna come."

His breathing quickened as she let go of the vibrator and grabbed the chair with her right hand, letting the vibrator fall out of her onto the floor, still on. It started to roll all over the tile, hitting the iron legs of the table. Lurching forward to catch herself, her left leg slipped to the edge of the glass table, sending a surge of pain from her anklebone. The sudden pain sent a shock through her, causing her to jump forward even more. With nothing else left to catch her, the chair swiveled out from under her right hand and she landed with a thud, right knee first, onto the cold tile. Crumpled naked on the cold tile floor, with her left ankle and right knee throbbing, she heard him speak up.

"Oh my gosh, babe, that was great." He sighed. "Babe?"

Miserable, embarrassed, and in pain, she lay there wondering if she should say anything at all. *It's a good thing he just came.* She had been so close! So close, and now so ridiculously far from anything resembling pleasure.

"You didn't fucking hear that?" she responded angrily.

"What do you mean? That noise? I figured you just knocked into something."

Izzy wasn't sure if she was mad that he hadn't even noticed what she had suffered for him, or relieved that he hadn't seen. Part of her wanted to bring it up and play the martyr, because he needed to know how much she cared and what she was willing to do. But most of her wanted him to know that she hadn't enjoyed that. She felt like a porn star, which was demeaning, and she had fallen down and hurt herself. It wasn't worth starting an argument, though; he probably wouldn't understand anyway. So she put her panties back on, wanting to get warm and to have a conversation with him to help her forget about what she had just done.

After retrieving her pajama pants, she returned to the dining table, picked up the laptop, and walked back over to the couch so they could settle in and talk for a bit.

"Oh, babe," he sighed again heavily. "That was good and I'm exhausted. I'm gonna get to sleep, okay?"

What? He cannot be serious. Here I am freezing, bruised, and didn't even come?

"Uhh . . . " She argued with herself on how to respond. Should she tell him that had been irritating? Should she say she needed to talk for a bit? After giving him what he needed or wanted, now she needed the friendship, the conversation, and the reassurance that their relationship wasn't only about the sex. But then again, this relationship was fragile right now. They were far apart without any true reunion planned yet, and he needed her sexually. Most guys need that more than anything else, so women deliver, right? Izzy had been operating under that assumption for years; that it was her job to do what she needed to keep his interest, whoever "he" was at the time. And Izzy did want to keep Ethan's interest. She did not want to be that burden of neediness just because she was lonely in Mexico without anyone. *But look at what I just did for him! Does he not appreciate the humiliation of it all? The fear and the discomfort and the embarrassment?*

"Okay, I guess," she said in a passive-aggressive way, not sure what reaction she was hoping for.

"Cool; sleep well. Bye." And with that, he signed off, and the screen went black.

Izzy sat staring at the black square that used to show his shadowed face in the dark of his room. He hadn't even waited for her to say goodbye. He hadn't said he loved her, or missed her, or that he would talk to her tomorrow. She couldn't even say she was "ridden hard and put to bed wet" because he hadn't ridden anything, and she hadn't even climaxed. Instead, she felt a sort of emptiness sink into her heart and mind. She felt used and left cold and lonely. She sat so long staring at that screen with tears brimming that the entire screen went to sleep, removing the last bit of light in her apartment. Izzy sat in the blackness, the void, and let the empty loneliness and worthlessness sink in as she racked her brain trying to figure out what she could do better, what she could be that would keep his attention.

Chapter 5

The early mornings were still hard for Izzy, but as the resort approached the grand opening date with new buildings completed every week, the sunrises over the almost-finished pools and casitas helped her feel renewed and excited each morning when the employee bus pulled into the resort grounds. The front parking area was still a hole in the ground, but the pools were poured and the large palapas that would be open-air restaurants were up. The thatched coverings against the orange-and-pink morning sky complemented the deep-blue ocean behind them. Palm trees were going in and, although they were young and needed a few years of growth, they framed the walkways and gardens beautifully. Bright allamanda were planted among the lush green vegetation, creating a Mexican paradise.

This week was especially invigorating for Izzy, because they were finally moving into the new office building behind the recently constructed front desk and check-in area. A far cry from the folding tables with cords running every which way, the new office Izzy was moving into featured her own large, light brown desk, computer, and phone. She even had extra chairs on the opposite side of where she sat so she could hold small meetings if she needed to. It was empowering. The struggle and the pain seemed almost worthwhile. Knowing the time would soon come when the resort would be crowded with vacationers and guests all over the pool decks and on the beaches, Isabella wanted to take full advantage of her daily walks before she was no longer able to relax and enjoy the gorgeous setting.

After pinning up some important contact numbers Izzy knew she would need often, she wandered out of her office to see how Valeria was doing with her setup and to see what the rest of the office might be doing. Valeria was in the middle of the open area with the other sales managers. The sales team was still missing two positions that would soon be filled. The general manager already had his door closed and was on a call, as usual, and the director of IT seemed to be waist deep in cables and boxes of hardware that would need to be installed all over the resort.

"¿Qué onda?" Izzy asked Valeria. *"What's up?"*

"Oh, you know, just trying to decide how to organize myself," Valeria answered smoothly.

During the bus rides home, Valeria usually kept to herself, sleeping or listening to music and seeming unapproachable. A few weeks back, as they waited for the last bus home around 6:00 p.m., Izzy had asked Valeria where she learned English. The conversation continued on the bus and all the way home. Isabella was thrilled that she had finally made a friend at work. They didn't live too far from each other, so they made plans to meet for dinner one evening. Valeria loved the idea of the Chili's inside the mall, which was not Izzy's idea of exploring her new city, but she was so grateful to have someone to spend time with that she was willing to do the Americanized version of Puerto Vallarta for the night.

Meeting around sunset, they had walked the mall, tried on a few swimsuits, and then made their way to the restaurant for dinner. Izzy learned about Valeria's time in Germany, the boyfriend she had met while there, her family, and some of why she was in Puerto Vallarta. Valeria had, in turn, listened to Izzy talk about home and Ethan and missing her family.

Finally, someone she could rely on. Someone she could confide in! Someone who cared and who was here and available, not just via phone.

Sensing that perhaps Valeria could use a break, as Izzy did, and drawing encouragement from the time she had spent with her, she took a deep breath and decided to dive in.

"Want to take a break and walk the resort with me?" Izzy asked Valeria.

"No, no, I need to get this finished first so I don't lose my place," she responded. Izzy's heart fell slightly as she tried to ward off the sting of rejection. "But we are going to lunch soon; do you want to go?" Valeria finished.

"Sure!" Izzy lit up. Why hadn't she been invited before? She remembered the feeling of being left behind not that long ago, and wondered what might have changed. "Are you going to the usual place you all seem to enjoy?" She didn't mean for the question to sound bitter, but in her head she scolded herself about sounding jealous.

"I think so," Valeria said. "You haven't been?"

"Um, no, I never seem to be in the right place at the right time to tag along." She tried to finish the statement with a higher pitched tone to recover from any sounds of bitterness that had snuck into her response.

"Oh, well, maybe it's because you always leave to take walks, so we assume you want to be alone," Valeria said with a shrug, without any trace of anger or hurt feelings.

They think I want to be alone? Do they think I'm rude and unhappy? Why didn't they ever ask me in advance, in that case, so I wouldn't go for a walk? She answered her own question with another, saying to herself, *Maybe you should have asked before you always left for a walk.*

"Well, then I guess I'm glad I asked!" Izzy replied, trying to sound genuine without any tension.

Only a few, like Gretchen, had vehicles, so the growing group had to split up into several cars to make their way to the restaurant. Izzy climbed in with Gretchen, Valeria, and a newer gal named Ximena.

To create the sense of royalty and luxury for all the paying guests, the resort was putting together a team of butlers that would be assigned to each casita and available by cell phone to serve every whim and desire the guests might have. As the resort was nearing the opening, the butler team was helping to shape the operation by creating the ways in which they would share information, deliver requests, and execute all sorts of possible scenarios. Ximena was one of the newer butlers on staff and was a vibrant, young, single lady with gorgeous curly hair. Her energy was attractive to Izzy, but she had only seen Ximena from a distance and hadn't taken an opportunity to approach her yet.

"¡Mucho gusto!" she cried, seemingly pleased to meet Izzy.

"Igualmente," Izzy responded. *"Same to you!"*

They chatted easily on the short drive to the restaurant. A small adobe-style building with a large thatch-roofed palapa extended out from the little building. Crushed gravel spread out under the heavy wooden chairs and tables, and a colorful hammock hung in one corner supporting a large sleeping cowboy whose hat rested on his face to block the midday sunlight. A large dog rested just beneath the hammock, taking his own afternoon siesta. Although the group was presented with one-page laminated menus, the large woman who exited the building and kitchen area let the table know they could order anything and she'd make it for them. The group ordered soups, tacos, and sopes, and, while they waited for the food to be prepared, they snacked on delicious homemade chips and spicy red salsa.

Valeria and Gretchen fell into conversation about things Gretchen would soon need help with, which left Izzy and Ximena the opportunity for small talk. A few of the others, such as the director of IT and the director of finance, spoke rapidly about something Izzy assumed was purchasing needs for software programs based on the words she was able to pick up as she listened.

Her head was spinning between all the various conversations in Spanish around the table. She needed to focus on one at a time, so she thought it best to start her own.

What was that word the apartment lady, Carmen, had used to say it was hot? Mareo?

"¡Qué mareo!" Izzy said to Ximena.

"¿Qué?" Ximena asked with a chuckle. "¿Estás mareada?"

"Oh . . . um . . . " She struggled to find a response. Clearly she had mis-used the word.

"New word for you?" Ximena asked. Izzy looked back at her questioningly.

"It means . . . maybe like dizzy or confused. Ummm . . . ¿cómo se dice? I think *disorientated*?"

"Oh!" Izzy suddenly understood what Carmen had meant—she had used it when she was late and frazzled.

"Pues, sometimes we say it when the ocean is really choppy, too. It sort of has a lot of meanings."

Izzy laughed off her mistake. "Well, then I guess yes. ¡Estoy mareada!"

"You know," Ximena started, dropping her voice and nodding toward the IT director, "I saw that guy walking with one of the new front desk girls yesterday."

"*Really*?" Izzy responded, raising her eyebrows and retuning the low tone of voice.

"Sí," she said confirming the piece of gossip, then adding, "and she is supposedly married."

Was it wrong to encourage the gossip? Izzy didn't know either of those people well, and what they did on their own time was their business. So it wasn't damaging, was it? Plus, Ximena was making an effort to share information and bond with Izzy, wasn't she? Truly Izzy felt grateful that someone trusted her enough to make her an insider about the information. Why Ximena did so wasn't exactly clear, but Izzy was sure it was a positive effort to extend friendship. Wasn't it?

They spent a few more minutes wondering what might be going on, then moved on to talk about how they wound up working at the resort, where Ximena was from, and what they thought about Puerto Vallarta so far.

"You know that club on the boardwalk with the badass DJ?" Ximena asked.

"Umm . . . not really," Izzy said a bit sheepishly.

"We should go sometime because the bartender on the second level is super guapo!" Ximena said, giggling. Her giggle caught the attention of Gretchen and Valeria, who both reengaged with Ximena and Izzy, curious as to what they might be laughing about.

The food was some of the best Izzy had tasted in her time there, and being with the group was a great feeling. She was enjoying the conversation and the fact that all levels from directors to managers to hourly butlers could have lunch together without any strange feelings or tension. She hoped that might be the way it would always be even as the staff grew and the resort opened. As the group returned to the resort for the long afternoon that remained, Ximena and Izzy walked together from the dirt parking area toward the side of the building.

"Do you want to get a drink after work?" Ximena asked Izzy.

"Uh . . . well . . . ," Izzy hesitated. "Maybe this weekend sometime? Weeknights are hard since I have to make sure I'm home to talk with Ethan." She felt a bit awkward explaining it to Ximena.

"Ah, the boyfriend back home," Ximena said knowingly. "Sure, some other time," she said, smiling.

The day ended a bit earlier than Izzy had expected, and she found herself home before her 7:00 p.m. standing call time with Ethan. She decided to see if she might be able to reach her mom. It appeared Mom was online, but then again, she left the computer on all day. *Give it a try anyway; at least then you can say you're trying.*

"Hi, sweetie," she heard her mom's voice say as the video was still attempting to connect fully.

"Hey, Mom!" Izzy said, genuinely happy to have caught her.

"¿Cómo ey-stah?" her mom said with a terrible American accent.

"Good, Mom, things are going well. I actually was invited to go to lunch with the group today, and the food was amazing! This open-aired palapa with an older lady who would cook anything you wanted to order—it was so delicious!"

"What's a palapa?" her mom asked. Trying not to be annoyed, Izzy explained the thatched roof, the large wooden pillars, and the restaurant's feeling in a bit more detail.

"Oh, sounds cool," her mom said, followed by, "So who all went?"

"Well, Gretchen; Valeria, a new girl; Ximena; the director of IT—"

"Oh! Gretchen went too, huh? That's interesting," her mom interrupted, thinking she was hitting on a great point Izzy might want to expand on and perhaps talk negatively about her boss, which Izzy had done in the past.

"Yeah, Mom, but that wasn't, like, a thing," she tried to keep the frustration out of her voice. "There was a new girl there, Ximena, and I really liked her. I'm hoping maybe we will hang out in the future. She's a butler and seems to know all sorts of things about the people I have no clue about."

"That's great. So you like her better than that other manager, what's her name? Valerie?"

"Valeria. And no, not better. Can't I have more than one friend?" Izzy could feel the defensiveness rising.

"Of course you can, but you know, you don't typically have lots of friends. You seem more like the type that has one friend you always would hang out with. Remember Heather from middle school?"

One friend? As in, I'm not popular enough to have more than one? It brought up the painful reminder of when Izzy, the brunt of some awful bullying in middle school, sat at the cafeteria table alone for what seemed like weeks on end as her "friends" had decided it was too risky to be seen with her at school. She was an embarrassment since the popular kids had deemed her a nerd. She had befriended one other "nerd" and wound up hanging out with that girl for quite some time—just the two of them. It wasn't a choice; more like a survival mechanism to protect her ego and ward off her feelings of isolation.

"Gee thanks, Mom. I guess I can't handle people very well, can I? Great that I'm in sales and can only have one friend at a time!"

"It's not a bad thing, Izzy. It shows you're loyal and selective, which is actually a good thing!" her mom said, trying to sound upbeat.

"Can we talk about something else? I have to go soon to talk to Ethan."

"Okay, sure. What are you discovering about Mexico?" she asked, sounding a bit hurt but wanting to keep the conversation going.

"Ummm," Izzy took a deep breath and tried to let the anger recede, "well, the grocery store was interesting."

"Oh?" her mom asked, saying as little as possible.

"Yeah, I spent probably twenty minutes circling the cold sections looking for eggs, and when I finally asked someone, they pointed me toward the front door. They were all stacked on pallets in the middle of the floor. Not refrigerated at all!" Izzy was able to talk without sarcasm about the eggs.

"Not refrigerated?" her mom reacted with surprise. "I guess that is pretty third world, huh?"

Izzy felt the heat rise again.

"Third world? What is that supposed to mean? The eggs are just fine. I've actually eaten them, Mom."

"Oh, I just meant, you know, they aren't at the same sanitation level and don't have the same food standards as here."

"Okay, Mom, sure, yeah, it's terrible here, and I shouldn't eat anything."

"Izzy, you're being a bit dramatic. I am just trying to understand—I've never been there!" Her mom tried to retract any offensive statements by using ignorance.

"Or you're just trying to reiterate your point that this is not a safe place and you don't like that I'm here?" Izzy asked rudely, challenging her.

"No." Now it was her mom's turn to get defensive. "I'm just pointing out it's strange and is different than what you're used to."

"Okay, well, I need to go so I can talk to Ethan. Love you," she said, not convincingly.

"Well, I love you too, and call again when you can," her mom responded with true affection.

It wasn't her mom's ignorance or lack of cultural understanding that had Izzy frustrated. It was that Izzy always felt an underlying sense that her choices, her life wasn't quite good enough for her mom. She always seemed so judgmental, and Izzy always seemed to come up short. She loved her mom, and she knew her mom loved her, but talking with her often put Izzy into a negative mood for the rest of the day.

Izzy, you can't keep allowing this to happen. She can't control your mood and emotions, and neither can anyone else. She got up and headed to her kitchen, poured herself a large glass of red wine, and moved to sit on the balcony. She promised herself that from now on, she would be unapologetic about what she wanted and where she was going. If her mom didn't want her to succeed, then she would try even harder to be successful. If someone didn't agree with her choices, she wouldn't stop to care what they thought. This was her moment, and she was going to seize it.

Taking a deep, reassuring breath, she watched the sun set over the beautiful Pacific Ocean and prepared herself to talk to Ethan.

Chapter 6

Izzy's bedroom door was open, allowing gorgeous sunrise colors—orange, yellow, and red—to flood in through her floor-to-ceiling sliding glass doors. She was sure it was late into the day already and that she had wasted so much of it sleeping, but when she finally turned to look at the clock, she saw it was only 8:34 a.m. She had virtually all day to explore, grocery shop, run to the bank, and do all the "normal" things she would have done back home on a day when Ethan had other things going on. Which, if she let herself think about it, had been fairly often.

After putting her hair up in a clip and deciding she was satisfied with her face, she found some cute shorts, flip-flops, and a cotton tank top for the journey. She didn't have a little purse, so she stuffed everything she could into her pockets. The plan was to walk toward downtown and see how far she could get, then on the way back stop at the grocery store for all her essentials. The city hadn't seemed that big when she was touring it during her interview process, so the plan to walk everywhere seemed reasonable. Stepping out of her front door into the open-air walkway, the humidity settled over her skin, giving her face a slight glow and her body a slight damp feeling, which was comforting. Growing up in San Antonio, Texas, she was used to the humidity and warmth. She would feel the heat, sure, and would feel tired or exhausted from it at times, but she didn't hate it. She headed down the elevator and started toward the street, passing the guard station.

"Buenos días, señorita Isabella," Omar greeted her. A light-skinned, blond-haired local who stood out in a sea of dark hair and eyes, Omar couldn't have been much older than her and was always friendly without seeming creepy or suggestive.

"¡Buenos días, Omar!" she responded cheerfully with a big Izzy smile. "Voy al centro para disfrutar el día y descubrir algo nuevo en Vallarta." *I'm going downtown to enjoy the day and discover more about Vallarta.*

"¡Qué bueno! Es una ciudad especial y sensacional," he said, proud of his hometown. "Que tenga un buen día en mi ciudad."

Heading to the right, she saw the pink stucco bus station ahead of her. Her guard went up in a flash and she tensed her entire body.

The taxistas—taxi drivers who hung around bus stops and the tourist areas— waited for someone to need a ride. Smoking cigarettes, lying around on the concrete, and leaning on their old beaten cars, they livened at the sight of her.

"Buenos días, bonita. ¿A dónde vas?"

"¿Necesitas un taxi?"

"Qué guapa, señorita."

"Eres de mis sueños, güerita, linda."

She hated this part of the Mexican culture. Why was it that Izzy dressed herself up in clubs or bars in hopes of catching men's attention, yet when it was freely given in other settings, it made her feel so uncomfortable? Maybe it was the lewd way they stared at her, or the fact that they hung in groups that could easily overtake her if they wanted. It disgusted her to think these men saw her as a sexual object, and she hated them looking at her. Even in broad daylight, she felt nervous and angry before they even opened their mouths.

Maybe she should cross the street. *No! Why should I have to cross the street because they scare me?*

As she got closer to them, they didn't even try to hide their stares. One had been leaning on his car facing the street but stood up and came around the front of the car toward the sidewalk to get closer to her. *Ugh, they are like wolves.* She kept walking and kept her head down until they were finally behind her.

Fortunately, she soon forgot the taxistas. As she passed the familiar buildings of the marina that she had come to know each morning as she walked to the main road to catch the new private resort bus for work, she had, for the first time, a feeling of belonging to this neighborhood. The certain homes with families, the older men who stood outside watering the lawn practically every day, the restaurants, the shops, and the apartment complexes: they were starting to feel familiar and welcoming as folks started to recognize her and acknowledge her with friendly waves. Hitting the main road, she turned right to head south into the city.

How far did this sidewalk go? She knew it would at least lead to the large ports where cruise ships docked across from the Walmart and Sam's Club. No ships were docked today, and she could see all that gorgeous blue water out to the mountainous side of the bay. To the left was the mall, the only all-indoor shopping area that mimicked American malls. Although homesick for familiar people and familiar places, she appreciated everything that was unique and different here and disliked the familiar stores. They tainted the true beauty of the region. Walking farther, she passed the other local grocery store she would stop at on the way back, the one that was a Mexican chain with little English on any signage or products. She'd find her way back later to get milk, eggs, and cleaning products.

This was the only main road going from north to south, and the traffic was heavy, adding to the heat of the day with every passing car, bus, and delivery truck. She watched older cars from the '70s or '80s with broken or nonexistent mufflers, followed by beat-up taxis and then one or two Hondas or Camrys from the later '90s or early 2000s, which were the "nice" cars on the road. The smell of gasoline, dirt, and sweat seemed to permeate the air from every direction and settled on her skin with the moisture from the air. She passed small apartment complexes, strip centers with auto repair shops, banks, and corner stores. Looking down every small side street that led inland, she could see the scenery change within a few yards off the main road. Roads turned to mostly dirt, and shops went from looking like inviting retail spaces with air-conditioning and modern clothing to adobe or concrete buildings without HVAC systems. It gave Izzy the feeling that the main road was a façade, meant to showcase to tourists that Puerto Vallarta was safe and offered similar experiences Americans might expect at home, while a block away mothers raised their own chickens for eggs and meat, hung clothes out to dry, and watched their kids play barefoot in the dirty streets. Paper or cardboard stuck inside shop windows informed passersby of what the shop might be selling, and people sat on the sidewalk curbs to eat fresh-made tamales. This was the real Vallarta, the truth of what life here was like for most hardworking people. Maybe that's how some of her coworkers had grown up and still lived. Meanwhile, Izzy was living and working here in a gorgeous resort condo, totally furnished with all the amenities, in a safe tourist area. She wasn't living in an upstairs apartment over a restaurant or laundry center without air-conditioning, looking out at the alleyways. Most of the world didn't live the way she did.

Her friends and family thought her brave to move out of the country and work in Mexico, but she wondered whether she was really that brave, living in a furnished condo with a private guard gate, resort-style pools, and beach access, while a short walk away, families shared one-bedroom or even one-room homes. She decided not to dwell too much on this. What could she do to change it?

Moving farther down the road, she continued past the larger bank and smaller hotels along the water with bright colors and bright flowers inviting tourists from all countries to come relax and enjoy. She thought about stopping for a cold drink to ward off the intense heat and the near-suffocating humidity, but decided to keep walking to her final destination and find a place overlooking the ocean. *It's not that much farther, is it?* The landscape began to change, and the busy strip centers and hotels transitioned into smaller, much older buildings that housed city offices, real estate brokers, or some buildings without any signage that appeared almost deserted beside the lone junky car parked out front. A chain-link fence arose from across the water to the left of her path, enclosing what looked like a park and blue buildings with the name of an elementary school. It was surprising to see how new the school looked—the landscaping was pristine, and it all seemed well put-together—and as she was pondering whether they had a tax system that paid for this, much like Texas, she noticed the large plaque on the corner of the property boasting the names of what must have been private donors. Now that made sense—a private school. Being a weekend, of course, no children were at play and no other activity was happening, so it was hard to know if this school was mostly the expat children or not, but she guessed this wasn't a place for many of the locals. She started to consider what it would be like to live here permanently. If she had kids here, would private school be the only choice?

The paved main road had begun to narrow, and up ahead, as it entered the main center of town, it turned into cobblestone streets hand-laid from decades past. These weren't small, flat stones; these were two-inch-high rounded stones that stuck up in every direction without much pattern to them. Even in flip-flops, the stones pushed into the arches of her feet, and she turned her left ankle slightly as it slipped from the two-inch-high stone. *How do women in the clubs handle tiny tight dresses and spiked heels out here?* No wonder the taxis and all the vehicles seemed so trashed, and every car had something rattling around somewhere inside.

To her left, steep hills climbed quickly above the ocean, and she could see small stucco buildings. A woman in an old dress, which might have been white when she first wore it, swept dirt from the floors out into the street. *Was that her son and his friends kicking a soccer ball through the narrow streets with no concern for the taxi drivers and bikes that came flying through the cobblestone corridors?* An older man wearing only a white undershirt and worn khaki shorts sat on some concrete steps taking a long pull off his cigarette. A teenage boy in jeans and a t-shirt carried two large plastic bags up the hill, maybe back home to his waiting mother who was fanning herself and her infant from the heat of the day while she breastfed him.

When visiting a place before, Izzy had never really seen the daily ins and outs of life. She saw the gorgeous water, breathtaking sunsets, and the indigenous architecture or city structure unique to it. But before this, she hadn't typically put herself in others' shoes, taking time to imagine their daily lives. Now, however, she wasn't here just for a vacation to enjoy the beauty. The beauty came from something other than the gorgeous surroundings. Something was different about this place, or maybe she was the one who was different.

Izzy wanted to understand how these people, who seemed to be poor in monetary things and income, lived adjacent to beautiful resorts and visiting tourists with so much money. Did they appreciate it? Or did they hate it and have disdain for the light-colored visitors from the U.S. and Canada? Despite her curiosity, she did not turn left and head up the hill to find out for herself. She didn't want to admit it, but she was a little afraid to see the whole truth and allow her eyes to be opened that much. *I'm sure I will know my answers just by living life here and interacting as time goes by*, she thought, making excuses for herself. *Besides, I need to see this city as the tourists from America would, so I can sell it to them better. They certainly wouldn't be wandering too deeply into the local neighborhoods and chatting with older men on stoops or women sweeping.*

Ahead on the right side, the block of buildings was coming to an end and the malecón, or boardwalk, began. The street Isabella had been walking was now bordered on the left by the restaurants Carlos and Charlie's and Bubba Gump, with the malecón to her right, sweeping low along the horizon so as not to impede the call of the deep blue ocean and expansive bright blue skies soaring above. The last store on the right was a jewelry store, and she decided to stop in.

"Bienvenida. Welcome." the shopkeeper said warmly. Her store wasn't small. Instead of beaded bracelets and braided chains hanging in clusters, there were glass cases boasting handmade turquoise, copper, and stamped silver pieces.

"Wow," Isabella said with an exhale. *Has everything been made by hand here in Vallarta?* "¿Todo hecho a mano aquí en Vallarta?"

"No, mija, algunos vienen del campo o de las montañas, y las joyas vienen desde lejos," the woman explained; some had come from the country, some from the mountains, some from remote areas where the jewels were mined. They were beautiful, and Isabella was drawn to them. More than that, she was drawn to the idea of these tokens representing her journey, her adventure. She debated over a few necklaces or a bracelet, but upon finding out how expensive they were, she opted to move on. She had already learned if the store priced things in US dollars, she probably didn't need it that badly.

A little Cuban bar caught her attention with its white stucco walls with black writing and windows without glass. She crossed the busy street, jumping between taxis and scooters to investigate further. Inside, ceiling fans rotated slowly over small worn, wooden tables, and a few old men in white Cuban shirts sat at the bar. The writing on the walls continued all over the restaurant but had a pattern. It was a story, but one she couldn't quite understand. Some of the words escaped her vocabulary, as did many of the cultural references, but the feeling was genuine and easily transferred to anyone who came inside.

"¿Tienes hambre?" asked the young, good-looking man at the door. She hadn't noticed him when she walked in. She wasn't hungry, but should she stay for a minute and have a drink? She checked her watch and realized how late in the day it had already become, and she still had to get to the grocery store at some point.

"No, gracias, pero me gustaría regresar. Vivo aquí en la marina." She smiled coyly to emphasize what she'd said: she lived here in the marina, and she'd love to come back. She held his gaze a bit longer.

"Pues, la pregunta es: ¿Vas a regresar a bailar y tomar conmigo, eh?" he said with a sly smile, inviting her back to dance and drink with him.

Something stirred inside her. It wasn't just sexual tension that was building as she locked her eyes with his, searching for his true intent and meaning, but something more. Something unfamiliar. Her chest felt full, and the back of her neck radiated a slight tingling. Suddenly, instead of feeling like a visitor here, she felt like this was her town, like she belonged.

"Pues, tal vez." She smiled back slyly. *Maybe sometime.*

"Esta noche. Regresa." He said it firmly—*return, tonight*—leaning toward her slightly, almost commanding.

She melted into the moment, letting herself feel the ocean breeze coming through the doorway, feel the coolness of the tile beneath her radiate up her legs slightly, and take in the smells of the rum and mint and mojitos being made at the bar.

"Sí, nos vemos," she said. It was the most sexual response she could think of. She had never really flirted at this level before. Something about this bar, or this situation, banished any insecurity or doubt she had about her sexuality and unlocked her confidence. She could be an object of desire. It was completely thrilling to think that maybe, just maybe, that man would think about her all afternoon, that he would get hard at the thought of her eyes and her blonde hair, at the potential of what the evening might bring.

Leaving the little Cuban bar, she practically bounced up the street, feeling on top of the world, and found herself in the main village square outside a large Catholic church. The square was created from laid bricks and planted trees, large pots with colorful flowers, and vines that wound their way around the walls. Benches under the shade of the trees invited visitors to sit and contemplate, to soak in the sounds of the choir as they stared over the street and the malecón toward the ocean beyond. From here, the bay curved so deeply that Izzy could look out across the water and see her condo complex along with the other hotels in the marina area. Had she really walked this far?

Inside the square, a man sat in a single wooden chair with a spindled back. He had an easel set up and papers scattered around him, held down by pieces of brick. The man was barefoot, and he wore a loose-fitting shirt, unbuttoned exposing his undershirt, and old cargo shorts. His hands were stained a dark brown, and as Izzy approached him, she could smell it. Coffee. He was somehow using coffee beans to create beautiful works of art. Several of his pieces were already drying, laid out on the brick around him.

The one he was working on appeared to be of the Virgin Mary, but with the ocean behind her.

"Buenos tardes, bonita," he greeted her. "¿Te gusta?"

"¡Sí, mucho!" she answered. She did like them very much. "¿Cuánto cuestan esos?" she asked.

"Para ti, 200 pesos por los dos."

She did the math as quickly as she could in her head. That would be roughtly twenty or so US dollars. She chose two drawings, views of the square from different perspectives, and handed over the money, plus a bit more. The man quickly rolled each drawing up and tied them together, creating a little handle for her to carry them easily.

"Mil gracias," she thanked him. "Tienes mucho talento."

"Ay no, no tengo nada, pero tengo amor en mi corazón para mi barrio, mi vida, y este lugar."

I have nothing but love in my heart for my neighborhood, my life, and this place. In that instant, she felt the same way.

As the sun was escaping and the last rays of light shooting over the mountains to the west, Izzy finally returned home in a taxi from a day of exploring and grocery shopping. She opened a bottle of wine and poured a glass before going to sit on the patio to watch the sun go down until the scheduled time to get online and Skype with Ethan.

Although still feeling hurt from their last conversation, Izzy wanted to share this wonderful day with him. At least Ethan cared about her and had supported her move here. She tried not to feel guilty for not having thought about him all day. If she wanted to keep this relationship, she couldn't allow herself to doubt it.

The heat was fading with the sun, and the breeze made the humid air feel less stifling. Families around the pools below were finally packing up their things and moving back inside for the dinner hour. As the sun crept out of sight, the orange blazing beams receded with the outgoing tide, and the winds calmed with the rising moon. A light pink glow emanated from behind the mountains, as if God had taken a paintbrush and widely painted a stroke of rose hues across the purple and blue night sky. She didn't really know God, but she couldn't help but wonder: *Did He do that for me?* She understood scientifically how the sunset was possible, but she felt a deeper sense of something else present this night.

But with the sun disappearing, it was time for her to log in. As soon as his screen name appeared in the "now online" list, she clicked on it.

"Hi!" she exclaimed as he accepted the connection and his picture appeared on the screen. "Hi, baby!"

"Hey," he said, sounding exhausted. "What's up?"

She smiled. "Oh, you know. Just watching the beautiful sunset from my balcony, having some wine, wishing you were here."

"Cool," he said, and then he was silent. *Was he just tired? Or was he annoyed at something?* It couldn't be her, because they hadn't talked all day, so how could she have annoyed him already?

"Are you okay, hon?" she asked, trying to be a consoling, caring friend and girlfriend.

"Yeah," he sighed, "just tired, you know."

"Sure, I hear ya," she said. "So what did you do all weekend that made you so tired?"

"I did a lot!" he suddenly shouted. "You aren't even here, so how can you already be suggesting I don't do anything?"

Where the hell had that come from? What had she done wrong to make him feel this way? "Oh, sorry, no, that's not what I meant," she said quickly. "I just was curious what you did all weekend. Sounds like you must have had fun and been busy?" The butterflies had been replaced with anxious nerves that were already beginning to have their effect on her digestive tract.

"Yeah, you know, working out, out last night and Friday night with everyone, getting the place cleaned up. But I really am not in the mood to detail out everything. I mean, it feels like an interrogation or something." He was being short and irritated.

She wasn't sure how to react. "Should we just talk later?" she offered. He might hear the hurt in her voice and realize he was being a little rude, she thought, and then he might apologize and ask about her weekend.

"Yeah, maybe we should," he said. "This is really annoying, Iz."

Her heart sank into the pit of her stomach. "What's annoying?"

"This!" he exclaimed. "This whole thing of not talking to you, not seeing you, and then having to schedule a time to sit in front of my computer for hours retelling all the details of my day and night, and—whatever! I just don't know how much longer I can take this."

Now Izzy was getting angry. Hadn't he been the one to say they'd be fine? Hadn't he said they'd make it work using Skype and visiting each other? And now he was saying how annoying it was to have to talk to her.

"Then maybe we should talk about you coming to visit, like you said you would!" she said, a little forcefully.

"Really, Izzy? It's about that again? You know it's expensive and that I'm really busy with work. Aren't you coming back to the US soon? Maybe we can talk then."

"Yeah, in another week, but I'm going to Atlanta, not to Houston. As you know." This was a sore point: he was taking off work and going to a wedding in Georgia this coming weekend with old friends. Unfortunately, it didn't coincide with her trip, and she had asked him about staying after the weekend into the following week so they could rendezvous, but he had said he couldn't make that work. She wondered why he couldn't make it work, why extending his stay to see his girlfriend for the first time in months was not something he could do.

"What's really going on?" she asked as she tried to hold back tears of anger and disappointment.

"Let's just talk later. I can't do this right now."

"When later?" she demanded.

"I don't know, Iz. I'll email you or something. I gotta go. Love you."

"Whatever," she said.

With that, he shut down the connection and logged off.

What the hell had just happened? She had wanted to share all of her day's experiences with him, but he was too annoyed to hear about them. How was that love? The walls seemed to close in around her, making her apartment smaller than it had been hours earlier. The departed sun and the quiet of the resort, now that everyone had retired to their condos to play and enjoy the evening together, made her feel desperately alone. What was there left to do but get drunk alone, cry, and go to bed?

She really had a great time all day, but now she didn't remember it that way. It was as if the idea of enjoying the quiet, the aloneness, the entire adventure of living here was nothing without Ethan.

<h1 style="text-align:center">Chapter 7</h1>

In her previous hotel sales jobs, Izzy's goal had been to get large corporations to hold their annual conferences at her hotel. She stood in boardrooms giving presentations, hosted large conference calls, and entertained CEOs and high-level vice presidents over dinner or at concerts. Now, she was trying to convince Mr. CEO to spend his family vacation here in Puerto Vallarta versus Hawaii or Europe or the Caribbean. Helping to create someone's personal family vacation where they would spend thousands of dollars of personal, hard-earned money hadn't been the least bit like creating a reason for a company to spend hundreds of thousands on a conference. But it was turning out to be equally intimidating.

Her upcoming trip to Atlanta, where she wouldn't meet Ethan, was the first stop on a multi-city trade show. She would start the trip in Atlanta, then hop a flight to Jacksonville, Florida, and finish the trip in Salt Lake City. Not exactly vacation destinations, but they were locations where huge call centers with hundreds of travel agents sat. By doing these trade shows with cheap giveaways, she'd have a chance to tell them all about the amazingly beautiful new Mexican resort in Puerto Vallarta. Then, when folks called the 1-800 number to ask for help with booking their next romantic getaway or family vacation, maybe that agent would advise Mr. CEO that his family needed to try a new resort in Mexico this year.

It was a big deal, and now Gretchen wanted to talk to her about it.

"Hola! How are you?" Izzy greeted Gretchen as she entered her office.

With a somewhat blank stare, Gretchen looked at her, almost through her. "Yes, fine. And you?"

"Oh, good; just working on researching for the Signature application," Isabella mentioned, referring to an awards program they were applying for.

"I have that information somewhere; I'll email you when I find it," Gretchen said shortly. Of course she had that information after Izzy had spent hours trying to find it all herself.

"Great, thanks!" Izzy said a bit too enthusiastically. "So, what about this trip did you want to talk about? I brought the agenda with every agency I have confirmed appointments with." She slid a printed-out calendar across the desk, but Gretchen didn't take it.

"Yes, I know who you are seeing. And these trade shows are very important. We need to show well and connect with certain people to make sure we get into this American Express rewards program. Their reach is global, and we need to be top of mind to be exposed to travelers all over the world."

No pressure, Izzy thought. She also couldn't quite tell if she was bothering or disappointing Gretchen, or maybe this was just the way Gretchen talked. She didn't want to continue assuming stereotypes, but after the weeks of sharing a car with her to and from work each day, and having trouble connecting, Izzy wasn't sure if this was a German thing or maybe a Gretchen thing.

Gretchen proceeded to explain what Izzy should say, who she needed to connect with, and what materials she should bring. Izzy had already shipped quite a bit of her materials to the various hotels where she'd be staying by using her own resources to figure it out. *Does she think I'm an idiot? I may not have done this type of sales before, but I'm not brand new to the idea of a sales presentation and business trips on the road.*

Don't let her minimize you! She tried to remind herself of the promise she had made to be successful and to stand up for herself unapologetically no matter what. But she was still afraid to tell Gretchen what she was thinking. On one hand, revealing to Gretchen that she was on top of things already would show that she did have some presence of mind and understanding of the job. But on the other hand, Gretchen might somehow take it as Izzy brushing off her advice. As frustrating as it was to think her boss thought poorly of her, or that she didn't have a clue, she was too intimidated and afraid to correct Gretchen. Her fear and insecurity about her relationship with her boss outweighed her ego, so she took the embarrassment of being instructed like a child.

"This specific trade show is one of the largest in the world, and the cities you're visiting will be the key to getting into this program," Gretchen reminded her, as if Izzy could forget. "You have already reached out to the director for the office visit after the show in Florida, right?" Gretchen confirmed.

"Oh yeah, definitely." Which was a total lie. Isabella had perfected the white lie with her parents as a teenager, but she wasn't entirely sure why she felt the need to use it with her boss. *Reach out to the director in Florida? Crap. Maybe I am missing something. Damn. She'll fire me for acting like I can handle this if I screw it up!*

Izzy's resort was one of thirteen or fourteen of the same brand, and often representatives from each resort would do these trips and shows together to have a greater impact than doing it alone. During every conference call getting ready for the trip, she realized how much she didn't know.

It was time for the weekly standing conference call with everyone who would be on this trip. Dialing in to the call, Izzy heard the tone and announced herself: "Isabella is here."

"Izzy!" A familiar voice rang out. It was Jenny, who worked for the same hotel brand in Atlanta. "*So* great to have you back on. You make the calls so fun and engaging with your questions. Glad you could make it!"

Fun and engaging? I thought all those questions were silly "rookie" questions that annoyed everyone else. While Jenny had been nice and pleasant on the first few phone calls, she was mostly doing the talking and instructing, since she lived in the first city the group would be stopping at. She seemed like a seasoned professional and a nice person, but it surprised Izzy to be called out like that. Instead of feeling as if she needed to impress Jenny or be on the same level of understanding as her, she suddenly felt permission to be the "rookie" and to ask the "silly questions." The feeling of relief and acceptance was almost overwhelming.

The call continued as others joined, and they organized rides from the airports based on flight times, where they'd meet up in the morning to travel together to the location, and what time they'd need to leave for the Atlanta airport together to catch the next flight. As the group hung up, Izzy felt a slight sinking feeling. She hadn't asked about the office visits. The topic hadn't come up and the call had gone a bit long, so she hadn't wanted to keep everyone even longer with her unrelated question. Picking up her phone again, she dialed Jenny's number.

"Thank you for calling the sales office. This is Jenny Mueller; how may I assist you?"

"Hey Jenny, this is Isabella again . . . sorry . . . ," Izzy started to apologize for calling again right after the long conference call.

"Oh hi, Izzy! That call went a little long, didn't it? Sorry about that. I tried to keep us on track, but too many salespeople wanted to talk," Jenny said, laughing. "What's up? Are you getting excited about your first show?"

"Excited, yes, but also still pretty nervous." She had finally found someone she could admit that to.

"That's totally normal, and to be honest, I still get nervous even though I know what it should be like and what I can expect. It's a rough game out there!" Jenny said.

"Well, I know we just took over an hour so I don't want to keep you, but I had a question I was hoping you could help me with."

"Sure thing! Shoot!"

"I was curious how we might be able to get in touch with the center's director and maybe set up a visit to the office after the show," Izzy asked and then held her breath.

"*Great* question!" Jenny said enthusiastically. "We actually won't have the opportunity to do that in Atlanta, given the schedule of the next show, but we could certainly try for some others. I'll send an email to the group to make some phone calls this week and see what we can set up. We do normally have that arranged when we can so it's on the radar!"

A sense of relief set in as Izzy realized she had asked a good question. She had contributed something, even if it was only because she had been asked by Gretchen and lied about her answer.

That became her pattern: after getting some instruction from Gretchen, she'd run back to her office and call Jenny to ask what the heck Gretchen had asked her to do. Somehow it reminded her of the feeling she'd had at childhood softball games when her dad was coaching. Nervous and trying so hard to be the best, she wanted him to think of her as good and valuable. But to "equals" or friends, she could let that guard down and admit that she was lost or confused or scared. Thank God she had found some equals she could lean on early in this process.

This trip would also be her first time back to the US since she moved, and she'd be able to use her phone to call and text. Her parents were thrilled to have a chance to talk without the delays of video calls through Skype. She and Ethan hadn't talked about the fight the other night, but then again, they hadn't talked much about anything due to the later hours Izzy was working as she prepared for the trip. Izzy was still irritated, but she figured that once she got to the US for this trip and had the chance to talk to Ethan over the phone, maybe they could work through some things. She was also trying to get over the fact that Ethan was still insisting he couldn't find a way to extend his trip to see her by even one night when she would be in the same damn city. They had gone around and around again about why he hadn't asked her to come early and be his date at the wedding, and why he didn't care enough to take one day off work on Monday to see her, yet he could make the schedule work to get to the wedding late Friday night.

"Izzy," he had said forcefully, "taking off a bit early on a Friday is totally different than taking an entire day off work."

"Why don't I just change my flight and fly in Sunday morning instead of Monday so we can see each other for a little bit?" she'd asked. "We could at least spend some time in my hotel room together."

"Honestly, I can't afford to help cover that change fee for your ticket now. What is it, like $350?"

"I don't care, babe. I want to see you!" But it went nowhere.

Now that she was clear she would not be having any romantic rendezvous with Ethan, Izzy decided to fill her night some other way. She had never been to Atlanta, but one of her college friends—Jessica, the girl she'd helped make Shake 'n Bake with on the day she'd met Brandon—was living there now. Via email, she arranged to meet Jessica for dinner Monday night once she got into the city. Somewhere in the back of her mind, she tried to fight the fantasy creeping in that perhaps, maybe, Ethan would surprise her and stick around for the weekend. Maybe he'd meet her at the airport or show up at her hotel with roses and dinner plans and love in his eyes. And they'd make love all night and hold each other until his flight out in the morning. *Don't get attached to the idea, Iz*, she told herself.

Looking at the schedule for the rest of the week, she tried to remember if she knew anyone living in Jacksonville or Salt Lake City. No luck there, but she was only in those locations for one night anyway. Those would be great nights to spend on the phone with Ethan catching up and not worrying about sitting in front of a computer the whole time. At least she could call Ethan on a real phone and not feel so lonely in the hotel room by herself.

The trip was coming together. Even if she was faking it a bit, she was sure after a week with some industry veterans she'd have her feet under her a bit more, and wouldn't have to feel like such a fraud.

As she tried to anticipate everything she would need and map out game plans and goals in each city, the week flew past. After a weekend enjoying the pools and the beach, Monday morning was finally here. Her eyes opened before the alarm went off, and she watched the clock until it sounded at 6:15 a.m. Her sleep had been restless, which she guessed was partly from excitement and partly nerves.

Showering, finishing her makeup, and triple-checking her carry-on bag, she was ready to go . . . thirty minutes early. *Well*, she thought, *maybe I can get to the airport a bit early and wander through the shops and really see what traveling in and out of the airport is like so I can relate to my customers.* It wasn't that long ago that she had been ambushed by all the time-share sales people at the airport on the way in. Now she would be able to speak to what the departure would be like: easy check-in and ticketing, short security lines, and great food in the terminal.

The taxistas who would catcall her were not even a block from her condo, so she started downstairs with her roller bag and shoulder bag in tow. It was only 7:30 a.m., and the cloud cover offered respite from the day's heat that was to come. October was a milder season, a rainy season, and the cooler mornings were a welcome change. *Especially this morning*, she thought, since she was dragging her bags down the sidewalk toward the taxi stand.

"¡Isabella! ¡Isabella!" she heard behind her. It was Omar jogging after her.

"Espera güerita," he said playfully. "¿Adónde vas?" He eyed the suitcase and her laptop bag.

"A los estados unidos, Atlanta—para trabajo," she said, explaining her destination. "Necesito un taxi al aeropuerto."

He gestured toward her heavy suitcase. "Voy a llamar un taxi para ti." He insisted on calling a cab rather than having her lug her bags up the street.

"¡Pues, muchísimas gracias, Omar!" she said, thanking him. "Muy amable."

Omar was a sweet man, a brotherly type, always popping up at various times to take care of her. Something about him felt safe and gave her a sense that someone cared. Even if he was only one somewhat unfamiliar person, he was someone watching out for her. And thankfully, on this morning, it gave her an avenue to avoid the catcalls and the discomfort of the taxistas.

When the taxi came, Omar helped load her bags into the trunk, wished her a good trip, and headed back to the guard stand. With a smile, she turned her attention back toward her journey ahead, which caused the knot in her stomach to return. A combination of butterflies and knotted intestines made her need a bathroom. She was anxious and nervous, but she wasn't totally sure why. It was her first trip, which was a bit nerve-wracking, but something else had a hold of her and she couldn't quite pinpoint it.

You'll do great, Izzy! she told herself. But that wasn't it. *Just ignore it,* she advised herself.

She woke with a jolt as the wheels touched down in Atlanta. Her throat dry and her mouth crusty, she realized she had knocked out and slept the entire way here. She was normally a light sleeper, but this flight had been soothing, and the exhaustion from emotional stress had caught up with her. As the flight attendants opened the main cabin door, the humidity flooded in, warming the already stuffy air. It was supposed to be fall in the Deep South, but the day hung on to remnants of summer. Moving slowly through the crowd, stopping in the nearest ladies' room, she tried to adjust her mind to the faster pace of the huge Hartsfield terminal bustling with people of all shapes, sizes, ages, and motivations. After a multi-hour snooze on the plane, she had to wake her body back up to keep moving. Groggy and nervous, Isabella scanned the passing people's faces as she followed the signs to the baggage claim.

Finally, through the fog in her head, past the never-ending carousel of lost bags, she made her way to a taxi and onto the highways of Atlanta. The city stood tall in the distance, but she was awed by the huge Georgia pines and greenery that lined the highways. She was sure neighborhoods were tucked away behind them. *Everything is so green!* The size and speeds of the highway and the five lanes of rushing traffic reminded her of Houston. She'd watched large pine trees disappear out her window as she'd said goodbye to Houston and Bush Intercontinental Airport only a few months ago, and the tall Georgia pines rising up along the highway now gave her a familiar feeling of home.

The ride to her hotel wasn't terribly long, but long enough to allow anticipation to build. *What if?* she wondered. What if Ethan was standing in the lobby, flowers in hand and a goofy smile that lit up, as if movie cameras were sweeping from her point of view to the check-in desk where he was waiting?

But in the lobby, nothing beyond passing guests, ringing phones, and smiling staff who waited to greet her. Her mind logically explained to her emotions why she shouldn't feel sad or disappointed, but her emotions weren't listening.

In the elevator up to her floor, she remembered she was having dinner with Jessica. *Something to be excited about! Stay focused on that*, she tried to convince herself. Now that she was on East Coast time, and Ethan was back in Houston on Central Time, she had an hour leeway after dinner to spend some quality time chatting with him.

Flipping open her pink Razor phone and turning it on in the US for the first time, her heart raced with excitement to see what texts would be waiting for her. Maybe there would be "I love you and can't wait to talk to you" from Ethan. Most likely she'd see "Did you make it safe? Call us!" from Mom. Perhaps a few messages from weeks past that friends had sent, not realizing she couldn't get them in Mexico. Holding her breath for a few heartbeats, she watched the screen light up and heard the sweeping sound of the system loading. Maybe it would take a few minutes for the texts to come through as her phone connected to the network. Maybe a few more? She clicked the text center, but again, nothing. No texts? Really? Not even from her mom?

She texted her mom, and then, taking a deep breath, she opened a new message, typed Ethan's name into the address line, and sent a quick "Hi!! I made it! Can't wait to talk to you later! 9:00 p.m. your time?" Hours seemed to pass as she changed clothes, freshened up, and sent another text to her girlfriend about dinner. Jessica was picking her up in fifteen minutes and taking her to a truly southern taste of Atlanta restaurant to catch up. It was, after all, a work night for both of them, and Izzy had a huge day at her first big trade show the next day. She definitely needed her rest.

Her mom was calling. "Hi, Mom!" Izzy answered pleasantly, happy to finally hear her voice clearly without delay.

"I'm so glad you're back in the US. You know I worry so much about Mexico and all the things we are hearing on the news . . . Izzy, are you safe there?" *Oh boy.*

"Yes, Mom, we talk about this all the time. Puerto Vallarta is not a border town, and I'm not an idiotic teenager getting drunk and wandering into trouble," she replied, trying to keep the sarcasm to a minimum. Her mom was just worried, and it was their first conversation in a while—probably not worth the emotional upset to take her tone as condescending.

"I know, but it's just scary. But tell me, what's the weather like there? Is it hot? We are still having humid and hot summer weather in Texas."

The conversation was light and quick since her friend was arriving soon, but it was nice to connect with home and start her first trip well by telling her parents she loved them. She still hadn't received a response from Ethan. She told herself not to worry; he might still be working.

Bing! From the bathroom she heard the phone sound on the bed. Steadying herself, she brushed through her hair two more times before heading back to see who it was. *Jessica from UT.* Not Ethan. But it was her friend, and she was downstairs. She had nothing to be sad about, she told herself.

The restaurant was an old house that had been turned into a restaurant, and every room had unique tables, artwork, and antique-looking furniture accents. You could eat in the living room, the old dining room, and even the old kitchen, which had cabinets and counters taken out to make room for seating. The hostess walked them to the back and sat them at a table for two.

"This place is so good!" Jessica said for the third time. "I normally only come here on dates, but I figured you have to try it your one time here."

It did feel like a romantic spot, and something Izzy and Ethan would have liked. *And we will like it just as much for friends catching up*, she told herself, pushing the thoughts of Ethan out of her mind.

After ordering glasses of wine, Jessica announced that they would only be eating true southern food tonight. This apparently meant brussels sprouts and okra for starters, and fried chicken, corn, and mashed potatoes for dinner. Comfort food. It was exactly what Izzy needed. They laughed and reminisced and cried a little about the times they'd had together while dating in college. Neither of their relationships then had worked out, but here they were, having dinner together again in a new city in a new chapter of life. It was refreshing, although a little exhausting, to relive and renew their bond.

"Are you finished with these?" the waitress asked the ladies as she gestured to the empty ramekins that had once held brussels sprouts.

"Yes, please," her friend answered.

"They were delicious," Izzy added.

They ordered another couple glasses of wine, and Jessica excused herself to use the restroom before the food came. *Perfect!* Izzy thought. Opening up her purse, she turned her phone over, heart thundering in her ears as she stiffened every muscle in anticipation of that little red light. And it was there! The red blinking light was like a beacon of hope, a calling out from the other side of the ocean of love. *Yes, 9:00 p.m. is good*, he had said.

No *I love you*? No declaration of excitement to speak to her? Obviously he was planning his night around their call, which was good. But that weird feeling she'd had before she left had come back. She couldn't pinpoint it, but her instinct was sending up alarms.

Jessica returned, and they toasted again to their friendship and how it was "just so great to see you again." They shared stories of what had happened after college, how Jessica had ended up in Atlanta, and the guys she'd dated since then. *Only this girl could have ended up in a relationship with a fifty-year-old at our young age of twenty-six. Oy vey.* It was Izzy's turn to tell her story. The breakup with Brandon, the disastrous relationship with Stephen after him, and her current love with Ethan, up to the minute about what she was expecting upon the conclusion of their dinner. Although she did leave out the recent Skype sex incident.

"It's good to see some things never change!" Jessica laughed, but Izzy didn't quite appreciate the humor.

"What do you mean?" Izzy said, trying not to sound hurt or defensive, but interpreting her words as a backhanded insult.

"Oh Iz, you always pick the boy! But who can blame you? When Mick and I broke up, you were still with Brandon, so I never did get to spend much girl-time with you because you still had an amazing relationship. I understood! Bummer it all went down like it did, but you know, you give it all you've got and don't get distracted with friends. I guess that's a good thing that you're so loyal."

Her statement rang inside Izzy's head as she thought about the times in their later college years when she was still dating Brandon, and Jessica had been the single girl.

"Well, we better get the check so you can get back to the hotel and call him!" Jessica exclaimed. Izzy wasn't sure if she was using that as an easy out so they didn't linger, or if she truly was happy for her. It didn't matter, though, because she wanted to get out of there too and get back to the hotel. No offense to her friend, but her mind was in Houston with Ethan right now as the clock ticked closer to 10:00 p.m.

Izzy grabbed the check, assuring her friend she could expense it, and they made their way to the front. It seemed like a shorter drive back, but the goodbye and final words in the car weren't quick as the girls both lingered, knowing it could be months, if not more, before they might have a chance to do this again. Jessica clearly had needed this connection to home as much as Izzy had. Atlanta was good to her, but she missed all she knew back in Texas. How had they lost touch so quickly after school? They both made promises to stay in touch and to be better about catching up more often.

Lots of hugs, thank yous, and good lucks later, Izzy was in the elevator to her room. It was almost time to call Ethan. Washing her face and changing into pajama pants and a t-shirt, she tried to calm the butterflies and fill the ticking minutes with last-minute checks on all her giveaways, business cards, and fully charged laptop. Setting the alarm for 6 a.m., she checked her phone. It was 9:59 p.m.! *Time to call him.*

Shifting and positioning pillows just right, she tried to settle in for a nice long conversation. She dialed his number, holding her breath while it rang. Once . . . twice . . . He was sitting there waiting, wasn't he?

Finally she heard his voice on the other end. "Hello?"

"Hi!" she exclaimed. "Hi, baby."

"Hey, Iz, how are you?" he asked calmly.

They started with small talk. "Good, how are you . . . how was the flight . . . good to see my friend, and dinner was incredible . . . This place is prettier than I thought . . . how was the wedding?"

"The wedding was fun. Actually, um, it was pretty incredible," he said almost tentatively. Something about the way he said it sent up weird flares in Izzy's mind. Her stomach tightened.

"Oh really? Tell me about it!" She tried to sound lighthearted and excited for the rundown.

"It was great seeing the guys and being ridiculous. Oh my gosh, the second night we knew where the girls were getting ready, and since I'm the adventurous one, of course, they dared me to climb the balcony and try to look inside." He was laughing at the thought. "They tried lifting me up to the bottom of the balcony so I could grab on and try to peek over, but we were so drunk already, and the groom was getting upset at us for being too loud. And then—" He had to pause to laugh. "Her *mom* comes outside and sees us!" He busted out with full-blown laughing, barely able to get his words out. "Holy shit, Izzy, her face was the funniest thing!"

Izzy was sort of seeing the humor in this, *but really? Trying to see into the room where the bride and her bridesmaids were getting ready? Are you fifteen?*

"Wow, dude, really?" Izzy started, almost offended for this bride she'd never met. "I mean, wasn't the bride offended?"

"No, Iz, we've known each other forever, and she thought it was funny!" he said defensively. "I mean, we were just being stupid in good fun."

"Oh, okay . . . " She trailed off, unsure of what to say next and feeling uncomfortable. Was it because he'd had so much fun without her there? Was she feeling jealous that he'd had a great time and it didn't appear as if he'd thought, even once, that it would have been nice to have her there? "So what else happened? Lots of fun people there?"

Her mind raced through the seconds until she realized Ethan was being quiet. He seemed to be gathering his thoughts. Finally he sighed loudly, indicating that he was about to launch into something.

"Yeah, actually, some *great* people," he answered passionately. "Izzy, I don't really know how to say this, so I'm just gonna say it. Let me get this out, okay?"

Fuck. She knew it. Women's intuition sucks because it's always right. She'd wanted to ignore her feelings of discomfort and call them insecurity creeping up due to the distance. But he was about to prove her right.

"Izzy, you're a great girl, and I do love you. You're fun, and we have great sex. But you're in Mexico and it's hard. Really hard. I just hate the idea of having to be home sitting in front of the computer at a certain time if I want to talk to you. I mean, it's like I can't have a life because I have to plan around your Skype time. I just think I need a break. Some time, you know, to just see where this might really go. I mean, maybe just for a few weeks or months to see how it pans out. I just need some space right now."

Her entire body was rigid and her heart was on fire. *How could you need a break from a long-distance relationship when we never see each other? How can you get more space than another country?* Her chest was tingling and the fire was spreading through her entire body. *How could he do this to me?*

"Space? Are you kidding me?" she said fiercely. "Ethan, we are in separate countries. How much more *space* do you need?"

"Iz, I know this is hard—"

"Hard for YOU? Or hard for me?" she asked, cutting him off. "I'm the one in a new place without any friends, without any family, and I'm spending my nights rushing home to talk to you on Skype, and *you're* the one who has to schedule your day around our conversation?" She was getting more and more fired up, and her voice was climbing octaves quickly. This heartache didn't feel the same way it had with Brandon. It didn't feel like a sad death of something great. Then, she'd felt a sense of loss; but now, she seethed with anger and betrayal.

"What's her name, Ethan? What is it?" she almost screamed.

"What are you talking about, Izzy? Get ahold of yourself; I'm not breaking up with you. I'm just saying we need to take a break."

"There's no way you go to a wedding in another city with tons of friends and people you've never met and then say you need a break unless you cheated, Ethan. What was her name?"

Now she was losing it. She was accusing him of something she only had a feeling about, with no substantial reason or evidence. But what other reason could there be other than another woman? The alternative was worse: the alternative was that Izzy wasn't quite good enough.

"I'm just saying it makes more sense for us to have some freedom!" His tone was getting harder, and his own anger was building. "Jesus Christ, how can I commit to you when I never see you? And we don't know when we'll see each other? I just wish we could go back to having fun without having to talk about our feelings all the time, and without feeling guilty for wanting to go drinking with the guys, or that I can't talk to any of the women."

Her tone became measured, cold. "Well, Ethan. When I left, you said we would make plans to visit and that we would both find ways to plan trips. How many trips have you planned? How much of all that was really bullshit? And can't talk to other women? What are you saying? That you want the freedom to flirt, or that you want to cheat?" Her head felt like it might pop off.

"It wasn't bullshit, Iz . . . " He trailed off. He had something else he wasn't saying.

"You're full of shit, Ethan. Just say it."

He finally spoke quietly. "Melissa. Her name is Melissa."

The world stopped turning, and not a single sound reached her eardrum. A sort of sick victory emerged from her mind as the fire in her body turned to ice. Instantly her stomach knotted up and her skin turned cold and clammy.

"Listen, I didn't plan it . . . it just sort of happened. You know, we were drinking at the wedding, and I had my own hotel room—"

"Stop! Stop, Ethan, for fuck's sake, stop!" she screamed. Anger and hurt and pain coursing through her veins, she couldn't straighten her thoughts out for any sort of response.

"Listen, Izzy, I love you, and sometimes you have to let things go when you love them. I mean, I slept with her, yeah, but she might not be the only one. I'm not ready to marry you and commit to you, and right now I think we need space to think about it. Especially with the distance."

She felt violated and disgusted. *Is this a fucking country song? If you love her, you let her go? Bullshit: when you're a coward, you run and hide!*

"You. Fucking. Asshole," she said with icy venom. "How can you do this on the first night of my first trip of this new job? When I'm the one making the sacrifices, the one alone, the one staying loyal to you? There's no such thing as space. There's a relationship, or there isn't. Now, Ethan, there isn't."

The walls might agree that she was being dramatic, which she was very good at, but she didn't care.

"I'm not an asshole, Izzy. I'm telling you because I care about you. I don't want us to hate each other. I'm sorry about Melissa, I really am, but I know it was more about us than it was about her. I'm just not ready for this." His voice was soft. "I know I'm risking losing you, but this is what I need. I don't want to quit talking forever, and I'd really like to see you when you are in town, but this is all just too much."

Finally, the tears and sadness overwhelmed her, and all she could feel was hurt. He was willing to risk losing her, willing to walk away, and it was because she had chosen to move to Mexico. She wasn't worth the effort, the sacrifice, and he didn't even pretend she ever had been.

"Okay," she whispered.

"I'm sorry, Izzy. But hey, you need to get to bed, you have a big day tomorrow." As if he really cared.

"Yeah, I do," she said, feeling empty.

"So maybe I'll talk to you later this week? I want to hear how the week goes."

"Sure, yeah. Later this week. Bye, Ethan." Whatever he wanted to think was fine, but she knew she was done. Just like that, the book closed, and she put it down.

She plugged her phone in to charge, and then she buried her face in the pillow and cried. She cried because she was scared about her presentation tomorrow, she cried for the emptiness she felt, and she cried for the loneliness she knew would be waiting for her when she returned to Mexico. Somewhere deep inside, she knew she wasn't crying for Ethan. She was crying for the last tether to her previous life that was finally being severed. Everything was different now, and she was alone on this journey. Nobody was going to come with her to hear her daily struggles. She was going to do this by herself.

Her tears finally ran out, and her sobs became less violent. Her body stopped shaking, and she lay there, softly crying and sniffling in the hotel pillow, body and mind exhausted. Finally, she closed her eyes and let herself drift off to sleep.

Chapter 8

The next morning, at 5:45 a.m., she let the hot water run for a few minutes before stepping into the shower, steaming the mirror of the tiny hotel bathroom. As the water rained down from behind her, she tilted her head back and let it fall onto her forehead and down her face, her shoulders, her back. She took a deep breath, and another one, and let her mind settle into the moment. He wasn't going to text her "good luck." He wasn't going to be there tonight to ask how it went. He wanted space. The thought angered her all over again. She knew she couldn't start off her day this way, but how could she turn off a heartbreak? How could she ignore loneliness? How could she shut down the emotions running crazy circles in her chest? *If only he could teach me that, because he seems so fucking good at it.* The thought strangely comforted her.

Ethan didn't want to be with her. It was tough to stomach, but at the same time, did she really want to keep this long-distance relationship alive for the next year? Was it Ethan she really wanted? Part of her said yes, of course, she loved him, but another part, a tiny part like an annoying buzzing mosquito, was relieved. She ignored it and focused on feeling the hurt of not being loved.

The sobbing had stopped as she had this discussion with herself, and she allowed her autopilot to kick in as she shampooed her hair and finished her shower. Adrenaline pumped through her system, speeding her through the process of getting ready. Her mind was now focused and staying on track, though it wandered to these folks she had never met, only spoken to, in front of whom she would have to perform. She pressed play on the movie in her head to watch the days ahead unfold in her mind. She had learned it was healthy to visualize herself being successful in the future, nailing the presentation or making that shot or connecting with that pitch. She conceptually understood what this trade show would be like and tried to envision herself there, knocking it out of the park. But she had no clue what to expect.

After dressing and packing for the next day, she took one final glance in the mirror, took a deep breath, and let it out. She told herself: *you've got this.*

Downstairs in the lobby, Izzy saw another woman dressed in a suit, whom she thought she recognized.

"Jenny?" Izzy asked tentatively.

"Hi! Yes, I'm Jenny. And you are . . . Isabella?" she asked, cocking her head to the side.

"Yes." She returned her smile.

"Ah!" Jenny exclaimed, stepping closer to Izzy and opening her arms to hug her. "It's *so* great to meet you in person!"

Her hug was genuine and strong, and Izzy returned it gratefully. This was, after all, the woman who had helped her answer all the questions Gretchen posed.

"It's so great to meet you too!" Izzy said enthusiastically. "Thank you so much for everything. Really, you are my lifesaver in so many ways!" she said, laughing.

"Hey, well, I was there once too! Happy to help. How did it turn out with Gretchen about the application forms?"

"Ugh," Izzy sighed heavily, "not so great. But at least they're done and submitted." She smiled.

"Did you eat?" Jenny asked, pointing to the spread of pastries in a plastic case alongside small cereal packets with paper tops.

"Oh, no I haven't. Guess I should?"

"Yeah, grab something . . . Oh! Hey, Carrie!" She called over to the elevators, greeting a curly-haired, blue-eyed woman. Leaving Izzy, Jenny walked over to Carrie and hugged her like old friends. They must have done this before or maybe knew each other from somewhere else? Suddenly, she felt isolation and insecurity creep in.

Distracted from selecting the least dry-looking pastry, Izzy turned her attention to Carrie and walked over to say hello. Meeting new people wasn't a problem for Izzy. What nagged her was the inferior feeling that she was as green as green could be when it came to travel agent presentations, and Izzy knew from past conversations that Carrie was a seasoned vet. She had helped Izzy understand some of the reward programs Izzy was instructed to "get us into" by Gretchen. And she had explained what she could expect on this trip and why it was important. Izzy had never met her, but she respected and appreciated her deeply for the advice and guidance. Although, now, she was feeling as if Carrie had stolen her moment with Jenny.

"Carrie?" Izzy started toward her. "It's me, Isabella!" she said, holding her hand out to say hi.

"Oh my gosh, Isabella!" She smiled warmly. "So great to meet you finally!" She embraced Izzy as she had Jenny. A sense of belonging and shared understanding enveloped Izzy as Carrie's arms did the same.

As they waited for the fourth to join them, Jenny and Carrie filled each other in on stories about people, both clients and colleagues, and about their personal lives. Izzy stood by, listening and appreciating the stories without having any idea who the people in them were. Maybe she'd meet them, but she definitely didn't want to play the question game the way her mom always did:

Now wait, who's Matt?

Mom, it's Becky's older brother. I've told you about him.

Oh! Right, right . . . the firefighter one?

Ugh, no, Mom! That's Michael. I'm talking about Matt!

Thinking about it, she wondered whether she was still that impatient with her mother today, or if that had just been a teenage thing. Either way, she wanted in no way to be like her now, so she refrained from asking any questions at all and simply listened.

"Lovelies!" A new voice echoed across the lobby. "I am heeeeere!"

"Hey, Michael," Jenny and Carrie both said, laughing.

"New girl, new girl, tell me your name," said Michael as he strode toward her. His neatly pressed slacks and crisp button-down shirt looked like a *GQ* model's, and with his suit jacket draped over his left arm, he raised his right arm and motioned with his right hand as if to say "come here" as he spoke.

"I'm Isabella," she said, smiling. She couldn't help herself; this flamboyantly gay man was endearing and captivating. No doubt that's why he was so successful at being remembered by his clients and travel agents. Standing six foot four didn't hurt his sweeping first impression.

"Fantastic. Let's get this thing moving!" he announced, taking long strides toward the front door.

The car ride over had Izzy almost peeing her pants with laughter. Atlanta traffic reminded her of Houston traffic, and they weren't going anywhere quickly, so it was good they had planned for that. What Izzy hadn't planned for was not having another chance to eat. She had been distracted and nervous in the lobby and had never grabbed something to eat. Her stomach was starting to remind her of that, but there was no way she could inform everyone else in the car, the same way she wasn't about to let anyone know that she might have to pee when they got to the building. She was the new kid on the trip, and she wanted to make a good first impression.

"Jenny, darling, you are fabulous for driving us," Michael said as they neared the end of their journey to the agency. "Now, can you be even more fab and drive us to the nearest Starbucks? There's no way I can do this without my Starbucks, and we have ten minutes to spare." He said it as a statement, not a question.

Laughing, she replied, "Of course, Michael. I can't deal with you without it!"

Thank God! Izzy rejoiced quietly. She could grab something for breakfast along with water, which she was already beginning to realize she'd be desperate for later. In that moment she loved Michael. She also made a note to herself not to skip a chance to get food or coffee again, just in case.

She shoveled down her yogurt and granola parfait on the way from the coffee shop to the travel agency building, and as they pulled in to park, she felt the anxiety and nerves kick into full gear. *Maybe yogurt was a bad idea after all*, she thought as her stomach churned.

"So, should I bring my laptop?" Izzy asked the group.

"Yeah, bring it so you can set it up on the table. Do you have photos you can show them?" Carrie asked.

"I have renderings but not real photos yet," she replied.

"Holy shit, girl, they sent you out here with renderings?" Michael was flabbergasted. "That's a tough sell, but you can do it. It's a new place, so just play off the resort next door and say you're the newer, better one. At least they'll know what area you're talking about in Mexico."

He said it offhand, as if anyone would have come up with that same idea, but it terrified Izzy. She hadn't thought about the fact that they might not be impressed with renderings. Or that they might not know where Punta Mita was. She was so naïve.

"Yeah," Carrie added, "these agents see hundreds of hotels and hoteliers every month, so you have to stand out somehow or they'll forget you. So relate to something they might already know so they can remember you."

Is this supposed to be helping? Dammit, she wasn't ready for this! But she had no choice, as they were unloading their bags, laptops, and giveaways and heading into the building. Michael led the pack with Izzy and Jenny in the middle, and Carrie following close behind. They all seemed so calm, so "with it." She tried to let that confidence seep into her own consciousness, but she was shaking. *Yeah, yogurt was definitely a bad idea.* As they were directed from the front reception area to the room that would be used for this trade show, she made note of where the closest bathroom was.

The main room of the trade show produced a white noise you could hear from the hallway, almost like bees swarming around a beehive do. The room was the size of her hotel's lobby and was lined along all sides with six-foot rectangular tables covered with tablecloths. There had to be at least one hundred, and every single one had a unique setup: flyers, pop-up banners, laptops, and iPads. People were slinging business cards across the fronts of tables and stacking brochures neatly, ready for passersby to grab.

She felt overwhelmed, nervous, and—strangely—insignificant. Some tables had their own tablecloths laden with their respective hotel's logo and colors. Others had huge flower arrangements, and still others had candy strewn all over their tables. Carrie told Izzy to bring some things to give away, and all she really had from the office was her business cards. She printed plenty of fliers and had her laptop to show the renderings, but as a new hotel they hadn't yet spent money investing in all the logo pens, memory sticks, or mouse pads. Izzy was sure that, as a new resort, she would get everyone's attention regardless. Finding her table, which was nowhere near her cohorts, she dropped her things and made a beeline to the ladies' room before time got away from her.

Pull it together, Izzy, she said to herself as she sat with her elbows on her knees on the toilet. *You'll be fine and they will love you. You? Did you mean they will love the hotel?* She ignored that voice and hurried back to her station.

In Izzy's last job, people came to her hotel to meet with her specifically, and when she had traveled to do presentations, she knew the handful of people in the room had a meeting they needed to find a hotel for. They had demand, and she had supply. But these people were travel agents who represented hundreds if not thousands of families. Izzy had learned there was a whole new world outside her own sphere of the planet where families had money and spent Christmas through New Year's on tropical beaches around the world, and she was supposed to get them to leave Maui or St. Lucia and come to Puerto Vallarta. Today, her job was to get these hundreds of agents who sat in cubes answering incoming calls to remember her resort, so that when a caller asked, "Can you tell me about a new place I can try? My family is tired of the same old, same old Hawaii," agents would say, "Why yes, you absolutely need to try this new resort in Puerto Vallarta!" But there were so many gorgeous tropical vacation spots in the world, and the competition was immense. She wasn't simply saying that her ballroom was prettier or larger than the one down the street; she had to convince people her resort was better than Costa Rica, or Spain, or Jamaica. And she hadn't the slightest clue, really, how to do that.

Many of the other hotel representatives had obviously been through this circus before and knew each other from past experiences. There were squeals of "How *are* you?" and "Wow, you look great!" mixed with hearty handshakes and "So great to see you again." Then there were the awkward few, like Izzy, who didn't seem to know anyone and tried to keep busy organizing and reorganizing their business card stacks and fliers while shuffling around behind their six-foot tables. Conveniently, one of these types was right next to Izzy, so it was easy to start a conversation.

"So," Izzy said, talking in the direction of the nice-looking lady next to her, "have you done this show before?"

"Yeah, I did the one out in Jacksonville before, but it's been awhile since I hit the Atlanta center," she smiled. "How about you?"

"First time."

"And, where are you from?" she asked, coming around to the front of Izzy's table for a look at her cards and collateral.

"St. Regis Punta Mita!" Izzy responded proudly, assuming the woman would be impressed.

"Oh! Where's that?" the woman asked, still puzzled.

Either this lady was truly a rookie and uneducated, Izzy thought, or Izzy was in big trouble.

"It's in Mexico, actually, just north of Puerto Vallarta," Izzy said, trying to instill pride in her voice so maybe this woman would catch on that this was sort of a big deal.

"Oh! That's great! So you're right on the water?" she asked, sincerely interested.

"Yes, we have private beaches, three huge pools including the adult-only pool, and three incredible restaurants. Not to mention the outdoor showers and amazing spa," she recited, just as she had practiced in the mirror that morning.

"Sounds gorgeous! Maybe I'll have to add this to my list of places I need to see."

Maybe Izzy knew what she was doing after all.

They continued to chat about her resort, the hotel chain this woman represented, and about how long they'd each been doing what they were doing. This woman wasn't all that different from her. She had up and moved across the country to take a job where she knew nobody and had no clue what the culture shock would be. Although it wasn't a foreign country, Los Angeles was a different world for sure, and this woman from the Midwest had a lot of adjusting to do. They discussed the fears they each had and the lonely feelings at night when it was just them alone in a new place. Izzy liked her and hoped she and her new friend might stay in touch. So this was how other hoteliers made friends: it was like a long-distance social network that understood each other because of the lives they lived, the work they did, the families they missed, and the difficult clients they shared. Izzy was encouraged that it would be easy to meet people, which helped her relax a little into the new setting she found herself in.

As she and her new friend were still conversing, they had missed the announcement that the doors were opening, and suddenly, new people flooded the room. The agents! They had already started wandering through from table to table. Both ladies cut the conversation midsentence and manned their stations; lip gloss on, hair brushed, and cue the smiles. They were ready for action.

Izzy was not too far from the front door, so the first round of people formed a line that backed up as they stopped at every table, looking interested and helping themselves to whatever free things were sitting there. Since Izzy didn't have anything to give away, she tried to hold every person there to listen to the same spiel she had just tried on her new friend. The first few seemed to stop and listen, but soon, as the line of agents coming in the door pushed forward, people started skipping her table altogether! If someone had stopped to listen, the next few people in the line went around to the next table. *Why are they doing that? Will they come back around?* She was starting to get frustrated. *Should I stop talking to this person in order to entice the next one to come over and see me, but risk losing the person in front of me who is at least feigning interest?* She was burning energy, not only with constant talking, but with emotional distress and mental energy wondering how to handle the situation.

After what seemed like a half hour into the show, she started to finally get it. They weren't skipping her because they didn't want to see her; they were skipping her because she didn't have anything to give away. As her speech became rote memory, she could mentally disengage with the person in front of her and watch the crowd. They were heading straight for tables with memory sticks, magnets, or flashlight key chains. Candy and rubber stress balls were more attractive than the flashy banners, enticing photos running across iPads, or the smiling hoteliers waiting to tell their story. *Why didn't I think of that?* When Carrie said "things to give away," Izzy had assumed she meant informational things they'd want to take back to their cubes. At least she could have picked up some cheap candy at a store if she had known!

Standing in heels, repeating herself over the noise of the room, and pretending to care about each new person was draining her. How much longer would she have to go on with what seemed a failed event? No new business contacts that were ready to book a family into her new resort, no immediate gratification of a sale, no story to bring home about how she was driving new business to Puerto Vallarta. How would she ever know if she was doing it right and if she was being successful? In her past sales jobs, she knew she had been successful when the contract was signed. Now, there was no "dotted line" for these travel agents to sign. No instant "yes" or "no" by which she could judge her performance. Her expectations, based on her previous career, had been so much greater than this.

The next few hours flew by in a blur. As the crowd began to thin, she could see the wear and tear on other hoteliers' faces around the room. Checking the clock again to see if they were anywhere close to the finish line, she was relieved to see they only had about twenty minutes to go. *Thank God!* Most of the travel agents had made their final sweep of freebies and were heading back to their cubes, as was evident by the few candies strewn across tables and the cellophane wrappers that once held engraved hotel pens scattered on the floor. It looked like a tornado had swept through the room leaving trash and unwanted papers behind, along with the disheveled hotel representatives who had been so tidy and put together only hours before.

"Whew!" Izzy heard Carrie say as she walked over toward her table. "That was crazy, but a good show!"

"Yeah, definitely!" Izzy lied, having no idea what a "good show" even meant. That she had survived? "Can I ask you something? So what does a good show mean to you?"

"Oh, well, you know, I had a few agents who book this area a lot and hadn't known about us, so that's good," she started, thankfully without sounding condescending or taken back by the amateur question. "I have a handful of them to follow up with for a booking they're working on for the holidays that might be interested in our resort."

"Nice! I don't have anyone to follow up with, so I guess it wasn't so great for me," Izzy concluded.

"I wouldn't say that. I mean, you're brand new, so just letting people know you're there is a huge first step. I've been doing these for a while, so at least some of them should know us." She seemed to sense where Izzy was coming from and wanted her to feel good about the day. "You know, it takes time. This time next year will be totally different for you."

Izzy smiled back at her, grateful for the pep talk. "Oh good. I was really wondering how I would explain to my boss that we didn't book any new reservations yet."

"Yeah, that's sort of the hard part on this side of the business," this woman explained. "You won't see immediate results. You just have to track your reservations for the next year and start to see where most of them are coming from. Then you can either trust that it was worth going to the show, or you can cut it out, if not. You'll see you can track results from these sorts of efforts."

If only her boss could have explained that to her beforehand! It seemed that Gretchen not only trusted Isabella, but also assumed she knew more than she did. Izzy was happy to continue trying to live up to those standards if she could meet people like this on the road.

As she finished packing up what little she had on her table, she scanned the room to look for the rest of the crew she had come here with. There was Michael, gesturing wildly with his arms, talking to a couple of men she didn't recognize. Flirting, she wondered? Jenny had found Carrie, and they were both chatting with some other ladies near the door. After saying goodbye and promising to stay in touch with her new friend at the table next to her, Izzy headed over to her group to reconnect.

She realized she hadn't thought about Ethan or the breakup for hours. She felt sad and, if she let herself, she'd be angry all over again. And maybe it was her newfound friend at the table next to her, maybe it was learning how to see this day as a success, or maybe it was being thrown into something she had no clue how to do. One thing was certain: Izzy somehow felt a little bit stronger.

Jenny and Carrie introduced her to the other ladies they were speaking with, and they all praised and congratulated her on the completion of her first big agency trade show. Although Izzy had been in the hospitality industry for several years, she was now being reminded, in close, personal ways, that the people in this line of work had heart. They had genuine concern and care for those they served, those they worked with, even those they might never see again. Izzy found it hard to remember why people said sales was cutthroat, when all her supposed competitors were so friendly and encouraging.

They talked for a few minutes until Michael found them and announced brashly that they were leaving for "a fucking cocktail, stat!"

They didn't go back to the hotel and change, but rather piled back into Jenny's car and headed down one of the hundreds of streets named Peachtree.

"This place we're going is to die for," Jenny said as she steered the car expertly through her hometown traffic. Atlanta had never struck Izzy as a town known for its food, but then again, she hadn't thought much about Atlanta in the first place. The trees were just starting to turn colors, something Izzy had no clue happened in Atlanta, and the air felt crisp. She let herself be lost for a bit, absent from the conversations happening around her. The green maple leaves had edges of red sneaking in, and the stoic Georgia pines towered above them. She missed the breathtaking views of the Pacific Ocean, but something about American life tugged on her heart. She wondered how long she would stay on the beautiful beaches of Mexico before moving home to the US.

Breaking her train of thought, Carrie asked again, "So, can you keep this up the rest of the week?"

"God, I hope so!" Izzy said. "All that talking and repeating myself, I thought I might collapse," she said with a smile.

Carrie laughed as they pulled into a parking spot at what must have been their destination. "No," she said, giggling. "I mean can you keep *this* up?" she joked, gesturing to the restaurant.

What did she mean? Eating out, or rich food without regular gym workouts? "Oh!" Izzy laughed in return. "I guess we'll find out very soon!"

As they pushed through the front doors, they found themselves in what must have been the newest sushi place in town. At least on this side of town: bling everywhere and not only at the bar, but on all the beautiful, well-dressed people as well. This restaurant was one that Jenny's luxury hotel recommended to their guests, which meant they were in an affluent neighborhood called Buckhead. Isabella had never been someplace so exquisite, so gorgeous, so . . . fancy! She immediately felt as if she didn't belong, and without thinking about it, she smoothed her hair and adjusted her suit jacket.

Since they didn't have reservations, even on a weeknight, they had to wait.

"Probably about an hour," the hostess informed them. "You should have called ahead."

"A lot of good that does now!" Michael replied in a huff.

"Let me see what I can do," Jenny announced. "Maybe with our hotel connection I can speed this up. Just go get some cocktails and stop whining." She smiled and gave Izzy a wink.

The group made their way to the bar to order.

"What are you gonna have?" Michael asked everyone. Since he towered over most patrons, he could easily get any bartender's attention.

"Moscow mule for me," Carrie said.

"And a Southern Comfort for me!" Jenny called as she headed back out.

"An Old Fashioned for me," Michael said, and then he turned to Izzy. "And you?"

Izzy was a beer and wine kind of girl without much exposure to cocktails, especially fifteen-dollar cocktails. Her face must have told the story because Michael interrupted her. "Girlfriend, it's not that hard! Just tell me, do you want whiskey or vodka?"

"Um, vodka?" she said.

"Vodka it is! I got you, girl," Michael replied.

Before long, she had a drink in her hand that was strong but delicious. After asking several times what it was, she still couldn't remember, but it was infused with something fruity, as well as, obviously, vodka. Jenny returned shortly, announcing that she had been able to bump them up the list by about twenty minutes, given her employment status at the incredible luxury hotel around the corner.

"This is when I love working in luxury, and all those wealthy people with their noses in the air actually come in handy!" she joked.

"Well, cheers to an incredible first day!" Carrie said, raising her glass.

"Yes! Cheers!" everyone agreed, clinking glasses and swallowing down their cocktail of choice.

It seemed like only five minutes later, after more laughs, stories, and ridiculous assertions by Michael, that they were being beckoned to sit. She looked at her glass, wondering if that could be the bottom of it already.

After nearly two hours, the most delicious sushi she had ever tried, and two more cocktails, they all sat back rubbing their bellies and sipping the last of their drinks. Izzy hadn't laughed so hard in she couldn't remember when, but then again, she could barely remember thirty minutes ago. The drinks were delicious, the sushi was phenomenal, and the company was even better. She barely knew them, but somehow, through experiences and the shared woes of their industry, they had become some amazing friends.

Then the bill came.

For four of them for sushi, plus cocktails, the total was almost $800. That was $200. Each! How on earth could Izzy explain that one to Gretchen? In past jobs, any expenses submitted for reimbursement that were client related would pass, but without clients, the alcohol wouldn't be covered, and there might be a cap on how much she could spend on food. The strong buzz she had going wasn't quite enough to ward off the insecurity of what she was about to sign for. But what could she do? She couldn't give back food already eaten and cocktails already finished!

The others seemed to have no issue with it, so she didn't dare react outwardly as she panicked inwardly. *Do they have larger budgets? What's my budget anyway? Gretchen didn't really say, so maybe I could play dumb for this one dinner? Just this one time say I didn't realize what the restaurant would cost, but in the future, I'll be better? Surely Gretchen will buy that, right?*

While her mind was racing, she laid down her Gold American Express card to pay her portion. It was her own card, after all, and not a corporate-issued card. Maybe she could get away with it this time, and then they'd have a tough conversation and she'd learn what was acceptable or not. At this point she didn't have a choice, so the next best thing was to go with the flow.

The only way she knew how to do that was, of course, to have another drink.

"Let's do one more!" she exclaimed.

"Not me," Michael answered. "I'm on the early flight out, and my fun limit has most certainly been met. But you youngsters go have fun and live it up."

"I'll get one more; why not?" Jenny answered.

Since the hotel they were staying in didn't have a lobby bar, they couldn't simply go back there for a nightcap, so they found a small dive bar nearby they could walk to. One drink turned into two or three, and before they knew it, the bar was announcing last call. It was almost 2:00 a.m. *Tomorrow is going to suck.*

But tonight had been absolutely incredible. She had survived her first show, gotten through the day without emotional breakdowns about Ethan, and begun to make some great friends. When was the last time she had made new friends?

Stumbling their way back to the hotel, they said their goodbyes and "See you tomorrow in Floridas" and headed to their rooms. She washed her face the best she could, at least getting the majority of her mascara off, and filled a cheap hotel cup with tap water for her bedside.

As she plugged her phone in and set her alarm, she saw its red light blinking.

Before she flipped the phone open to read the text message, she braced herself. Her head was spinning, and the giddy buzz quickly turned into a tired state of depression and sadness. After awhile, she flipped the phone open and clicked on the envelope icon to open the messages, catching her breath as she waited the seconds for it to open, and there it was. A message from Ethan.

Hope it was a good day.

That was it? No *I'm sorry*, or *I messed up*, or *I love you*? What an asshole! Fuck him and fuck his good day! Her blood boiled, and she started typing to tell him exactly what she was thinking, but thankfully, exhaustion took over. Setting her alarm for 7:30 a.m. and taking note that it was already 2:43 a.m., she turned the phone over and collapsed on the pillow.

The rest of the week flew by—each city different, each trade show the same, and each night drinking late and laughing with new friends. After a few drinks one night, she told them about the breakup with Ethan. She hadn't had time to talk much with her mom or anyone else about it, and these people on her trip quickly became the listening ears she needed.

"Clearly you are way too good for this asshole," Carrie said matter-of-factly one night in Jacksonville. Or was it Salt Lake City? Either way, it had been funny, but it struck Izzy as poignant. How could Izzy have been too good when Ethan was the one who'd treated her so well after her disaster with Stephen? She didn't deserve the nice guy.

Plus, what she hadn't told her new friend, or even Ethan for that matter, is what Stephen had given her. After a disastrous relationship and horrific ending with Stephen, she couldn't bring herself to honestly talk about it with the next love interest, Ethan. But she didn't want to think about that right now.

Moving through the security lines, the girls had waved their final "goodbye" to Michael as he made his way to another terminal on another airline. Izzy, Carrie, and Jenny chatted easily as they waited to show IDs and remove their shoes. They reminisced about the nights and swapped stories about some of the agents they had met during the various shows.

"Atlanta was by far the best," Jenny decided.

"Well, of course for you, since your hotel is in their backyard!" Carrie teased.

"This entire week was good, I think," Izzy added. "At least for me. My first exposure seemed well received."

"Yeah! So true!" Jenny agreed. "So you survived. And you did well! Congratulations on a week well done," she said, giving Izzy a side-hug with one arm while the other steadied the handle of her carry-on.

"Very well done," Carrie added. "And you know you can call me anytime if I can help, too. I've been at this a long while." She winked.

After security, each had a different gate to find, so they all shared final hugs and agreed to talk again soon. Izzy couldn't help but notice the warmth with which each of them hugged her. Like old friends.

Chapter 9

Izzy couldn't remember to save her life how she had met Stephen. After she and Brandon had ended things, she'd had a few flings here and there, and some terrible online dating experiences, until a few years later when she met Stephen. On one of their early dates, he took Izzy country dancing. While staring into her eyes, he made dramatic gestures about feeling so intensely that he loved her. That was the attraction: his intensity. And she loved the way he made her feel like the center of his world.

"Izzy," he said intently, staring in her eyes as he moved her across the dance floor.

"Yeah?" she asked him, smiling and soaking up all the attention and focus he was offering.

"FUCK!" he said, dropping her hands and stopping in the middle of the floor. Suddenly Izzy was bumped by another couple twirling by, and the romance of the moment ended abruptly as she realized they were in the middle of a hundred other sweaty bodies two-stepping around them.

"What?" she said, confused and a little embarrassed.

"You just," he started to say, looking to his side and then to the floor, then dramatically back up at her and directly into her eyes. "You just are so fucking incredible." He stepped toward her while grabbing her hands and wrapping them back around him as they were before, all in one fell swoop before Izzy knew what had happened. She stared back at him, unsure of what to think, but liking it. This was nothing like the subdued, gentle Brandon she had known.

"I can't *not* say it," he said strongly, firmly.

"Say what?" she asked coyly, half expecting what might come next and, although it was only their second date, she somehow believed could be true.

"I'm in love with you." He pulled her close and kissed her deeply, stopping in the middle of the floor again. This time she didn't feel embarrassed. It was a bit like a movie scene, and she was the star.

As the kiss ended and they started moving again to George Strait crooning about being carried away, another man backed into Stephen as he was attempting to spin the lady he was dancing with.

"What the fuck, man?" Stephen spat at his back as the man stumbled forward into the woman, disrupting the entire flow of the circle.

"Sorry, man, not a lot of room in here," the guy said flatly and started to move toward the edge of the dance floor.

"Oh, no fucking way!" Stephen said, dropping his hold on Izzy and taking long strides toward the man. "You don't just run into me and then try to run. You got a problem?" Stephen antagonized him further.

Izzy watched in disbelief, once again embarrassed, as Stephen picked a fight with a perfect stranger. The dance floor was crowded and most had been drinking plenty, and some, like Stephen, had made sure they had taken a few shots of tequila between beers to "keep the buzz." Bumping into each other was inevitable and mostly understood by the patrons of this country bar. That's just the way a Saturday night went. But not for Stephen. He was looking for a reason to fight. And as the pushing escalated into a thrown punch, the bouncers swarmed the men and within seconds had both out in the parking lot with the local police close behind to ensure they didn't reenter the dance hall. Izzy and the other man's date exchanged sheepish looks, and then she narrowed her eyes at Izzy as if to say it was her fault.

"What the hell, Stephen? We were having a good time, and it's just crowded in there," Izzy said as she trotted toward Stephen, who had somehow lost his button-down flannel shirt in the scuffle and was standing in only his white undershirt, jeans, and boots. He still looked pretty sexy. But also a bit scary.

"Don't fuck with me, Izzy!" he yelled back at her.

Stopping in her tracks, she felt wounded. Hadn't this guy just professed his love to her? Her face must have shown the confusion and the hurt. Through the alcohol-induced rage, Stephen must have seen his chance slipping away.

"Sorry, baby, sorry," he said sweetly as he walked toward her and tried to hug her.

"Sorry for what? Making me feel like an idiot, or for hurting an innocent man?"

"He's the asshole who started it!" He raised his voice defensively. "You hear me? Fucking asshole," he cried over her shoulder toward the other man as he climbed into his truck. "Dick."

"Stephen, you're unbelievable," Izzy said, ready to be taken home so she could retreat to a safer place.

"No, baby, you are," Stephen said. Izzy stared at his intense brown eyes.

Stephen had stirred something inside Izzy she couldn't explain, but she let him pull her close and kiss her. Then she let him take her home and let him get into her bed. Izzy was repulsed and embarrassed, yet aroused by him at the same time. She was his everything.

The problem was that Stephen was good at making anyone feel "his everything" for a moment, just to get what he wanted. He was charming and intense and romantic, dramatic but irrational, the total opposite of gentle Brandon. At the time, she had wanted that.

And Stephen loved her! At least that's what he said, and she let herself believe his grandiose demonstrations of falling for her were real. So when he was too stoned to wake up and make his own kids' breakfast, she had stepped in to do it and let him sleep. And when he'd go to pick up the kids and take over an hour, she had ignored the knot in her stomach telling her she knew he was sleeping with his ex-wife. And when Stephen took Izzy to meet one of his dealers when he needed to buy more weed, and they spent a night in a dark parking lot waiting for the dealer to arrive, Izzy told herself she was becoming a lowlife and that she had to get out. But deep down, she knew she wouldn't.

They had been dating for only a few weeks when Stephen accidentally left his BlackBerry with her one morning. Izzy had met up with her friend at their apartment complex pool.

"You haven't looked at it yet?" her friend had exclaimed.

"No, I mean, should I?" Izzy had asked, so innocently.

"Oh my gosh, give it to me," said her friend. "Then I can look, and you don't have to."

After only a few minutes, Izzy's friend handed the BlackBerry back to Isabella.

"Iz . . . you . . . uh . . . you need to see this," she said.

Taking the device and lifting her sunglasses up to her forehead so she could see the screen better, Izzy had started reading Stephen's texts. Her heart sank as her palms started to sweat. Her breathing quickened, and she could feel the adrenaline pumping through her veins. They felt fuller, like she was prepping for a fight.

Thanks again for last night. You taste amazing.

The number wasn't saved under a name, but it was obvious what had been going on a few days earlier when he was "with the boys."

After that day, she couldn't ignore the situation anymore. They had broken up, dramatically with a fist through a window. But soon, he was trying to win her back. Roses and wine and country music worked on her broken heart, and after one of the most mind-blowing orgasms from oral sex she could ever remember, drunk with ecstasy, she had let him open her knees, climb on top, and then slide inside, one last time. It was beautiful and wrong. She cried and orgasmed, felt bliss and regret.

The next day she felt tired but assumed it was the emotional battle-field she had been on the day before. The second day she woke up feeling almost sick, like she might have a fever, as well as discomfort and itchiness between her legs. Her thong began to feel tight and was rubbing in ways that made sitting still at work difficult. She had gone home early, taken some Tylenol, changed, and gotten into bed. She had slept through the afternoon and into the early evening before she woke to pee. But when she did, the burning sensation that followed and the radiating aches from her crotch were too much to ignore.

The skin around her vaginal opening felt raw and extremely sore to the touch. She got the small makeup mirror from her bathroom and positioned it under herself while squatting so she could see. Looking down, she finally saw the white sores: blisters forming under the opening of her vagina and the skin around them bright red. Something was very wrong.

She called to schedule an appointment at her ob/gyn, and they were able to get her in within two days. Two days of excruciating pain, regret, and embarrassment.

"I'm going to have to take a swab, and it's going to hurt tremendously," her doctor said. And she wasn't lying: it was as if someone had taken a razor blade to the most sensitive skin on Izzy's body and wouldn't stop. Tears formed as she gritted her teeth and tried not to scream.

The results were worse, however. The labs confirmed everything she had read online and everything her doctor had said. She would now live the rest of her life with herpes.

"You'll want to make sure that now, before having sexual intercourse with anyone new, you explain the risk they are taking," her doctor instructed. "And that does include any oral sex."

Even though the doctor told her the virus was common in the US, it didn't matter. Izzy was dirty. She'd been infected by a dirty, cheating asshole, and now anyone else she ever wanted to sleep with would be directly affected by him. For the rest of her life, she'd never be able to fully forget this relationship, this bad decision. Every day for the rest of her life she would have to take Valtrex, which cost her $50 a month, to suppress the virus and help to reduce the pain and the time it took to heal from future breakouts. And before she could ever have sex again, she'd have to stop and say, "By the way, I'm dirty and could give you an STD, but no worries, grab a condom!" No guy would stop because of that, right? Wrong. Wouldn't she? If, as she was ripping off her panties, blood rushing through her body and pulsing between her legs, someone told her she might wind up with an STD, would she stop? And how would she feel if someone *hadn't* told her and she found out later after contracting it?

She hadn't told anyone what happened. She didn't even confront Stephen with it but dropped him out of her life instantly. What a shame that it took something so destructive for her to finally get it, such an extreme for her to finally do what she should have done months earlier. Didn't she know she deserved better? Friends told her. Family had told her. But something inside didn't let her believe it herself. Why?

But now, part of her didn't believe she deserved better anymore. She was no longer a good girl, a clean girl. The kind of girl you take home to Mom and say you want to marry. Embarrassment and shame had taken root and taken hold of her self-image, which was already unsteady enough to have gotten into the relationship with Stephen in the first place.

Ethan was her first relationship after that trauma. The first nice guy to come along and be halfway decent to her. He was sweet and made her blush and paid attention to her, and he was smart. He had a job that she envied, a career that would do well financially. And he didn't have an obsession with Hooters, at least not that she was aware of.

She thought about telling Ethan about her situation but was so afraid he would reject her. So afraid he would say "no." Several times while sitting on his couch, having conversations about her future move to Mexico and what would happen to them, she had wanted to talk about it. If he truly loved her, wouldn't this just be something to deal with together? If he had said, "I love you" one second and then, "Wow, okay, well I don't love you enough for that," wouldn't that have been pretty clear? Maybe that was why she hadn't wanted to tell him. Because really she was so desperate for the whole thing to keep going, for the nice guy to love her and support her through the move, that she hadn't wanted to ruin it. And now she had let him risk his health without even knowing it.

Too good for Ethan. That's what Carrie had said to her during the sales trip. How could Izzy be too good for anyone? How could she have any right to think anyone was beneath her, after that scum she had spent too many months fucking, taking care of his kids, and telling him she loved him? But in the moment Carrie told Izzy that, she loved her like a sister. She'd seen something Izzy couldn't see.

Out of sheer curiosity, Izzy started looking for the things Carrie must have seen. What about Izzy was good? Her smile? Maybe her bravery? Her resilience? Her ability to adapt and learn and change? Maybe she was worthy and beautiful. Maybe she did deserve to be treated well. Maybe she could find a guy who loved her for her, disease or not.

Even though she had lived in her Mexican condo for only a few months, it felt familiar and welcoming after five nights in different hotel beds. Without a Skype session with Ethan to plan around, she had an entire weekend free to do what she wanted.

So what did she want?

Throwing her clothes in the washing machine and surveying her place, she decided the grocery shopping and cleaning could wait until tomorrow. She finally had a Saturday off, since it was a travel day, and she still had hours of the afternoon left. Outside the gated community of Punta Mita, where her resort was located, was the small village of Punta de Mita. She had been down there once with Gretchen on a tour of the area with some potential clients but hadn't gone back to explore. On the tour, she'd met a man named Dave, an American who'd made great money developing real estate in the United States. He had moved out here after falling in love with the area during a vacation. The condos he'd built were incredibly luxurious and could certainly rival anything her resort was offering, especially since they had full kitchens and were meant to sleep an entire family or group of eight to ten in each unit. He'd told Izzy about the surf shack he ran in Punta de Mita and invited her to come visit it sometime. Maybe she would.

Changing into a swimsuit, shorts, and a tank top, she packed a small bag full of sunscreen, hat, sunglasses, towel, and a change of clothes. Transferring her pesos from her purse into her bag, grabbing her keys on the way out, she felt more confident than she had since she'd first arrived in Mexico.

The public busses ran on a loop, but she was never quite sure when they might come by. The schedules posted at each stop were more like guidelines. The ten-minute walk from her condo complex to the end of the marina area brought her to the bus stop at the main road, where a handful of people stood milling around and waiting. Some sat on the rusted old bench and others stood idly by. Since this entire Puerto Vallarta area was a long stretch of various villages and towns along the beach, each bus had the village destination posted on the front window, and as she waited, her nerves acted up with anticipation of which bus to get on. One sign said *Bucerías*, which wasn't far enough to get her to Punta de Mita. She wondered if she should get on and see if there was another bus from Bucerías to Punta de Mita, or wait to see if one coming later would get her all the way there. A moment of panic set in as she toyed with the decision, watching nearly every other person board the bus. She must have been standing there with a dumbfounded look on her face because the driver called out to her, "¿Vas a Bucerías?" In her panic, it took her a long time to figure out what he was saying.

"No, me voy a Punta de Mita," she finally said.

"Hay otro autobús que viene," he responded, jerking his thumb backward: another bus would come.

"Okay, gracias," she said, and the driver closed the rickety door while simultaneously stepping on the gas swerving back into traffic. Had he even looked for oncoming cars?

Letting out a little of the anxiety that built up, she settled into the bench to wait. She wondered if the few folks left standing around her knew how long their wait would be, or if they were just more patient than she was. Everyone drove everywhere in Texas, so they could come and go as they pleased on their own schedules. Here, Izzy was starting to see what life without the instant gratification of a car was like. What a slower pace and the art of *mañana*—tomorrow—was all about. *Slow down, enjoy life, relax a little bit.* She was used to a hurried life, a stressful life, a life where sitting around watching TV or doing nothing had seemed meaningless. Why she lived that way, she wasn't sure. But now, sitting at this bus stop without any clue when her ride was coming, she was forced to be patient and enjoy the moment around her.

It was actually kind of nice.

When the bus for Punta de Mita arrived, she stepped aboard, handed the pesos to the driver, and turned to look down the aisle. There were several empty seats next to a few other faces, but none of them smiled as if to say, *sit with me.* She found two empty seats about halfway back and took the seat by the window. Looking down, she realized she was seeing the road below her. There was a hole in the floor of the bus she could see right through! Not large enough for a person, but certainly large enough to drop something. She pulled her bag onto her lap and held it tight. There was no air-conditioning, and some windows had been dropped open as she remembered doing on old school busses as a child. They only went halfway down, and not every window was down. It was going to be a bit of a stuffy ride, but then again, she did have a vent at her feet.

Shortly after leaving the La Marina stop where Izzy lived, the bus stopped once again. After driving what seemed like a couple hundred yards, another stop. It seemed as if the bus was stopping at every station: even if another bus had just pulled away, her bus would pull right up behind it and stop again. They waited a handful of minutes at each stop.

At the Bucerías stop, a man boarded the bus with a crate of some kind under his arm. A noise came from it: "Ba-gaaaawk!" The guy's crate had not one, but three chickens in it, and as the bus bumped along the road, the chicken got restless. Squawking and flapping their wings, they had soon become the center of a lot of people's attention.

The bus continued to let people on and off at the various stops with faces coming and going, but none as colorful and distinguished as their fellow chicken companions. The chickens rode almost all the way to Punta de Mita before getting off with their owner at what seemed like a stop in the middle of nowhere. Perhaps this farmer was bringing his new crop of egg producers to his farm out here in the countryside, or maybe he was selling them to a restaurant nearby. She hoped it was the former. Although loud and obnoxious, she had come to appreciate the little feathered friends on their short journey together.

Slowing to enter a roundabout that was literally at the end of the road, the bus pulled past a few others that were stopped along the side. Looking back through the dusty window, Izzy could see one begin to take off back toward town while the second pulled forward to take its place. Then her bus pulled around the circle and up behind the remaining bus, as if to assume its place in line for the return trip to town. As primitive as it felt with these 1950s and 1960s buses, with their holes and cracked windows and desperate for a cleaning, they seemed to have a system: two buses made their way up to Punta de Mita and waited for the third to signal the time for their return. The drivers could be casual and laid back, but the buses would still arrive at their planned destination. Maybe there was something to take away from that.

Exiting the bus into the warm afternoon sun, she smiled and took a deep breath. Nobody was expecting her to get home by a certain time so she could Skype with them. After her incredible week of traveling, Ethan was more like a lingering memory than a prime concern. Not that she was over him or totally ready to move on, but she certainly felt stronger. A bit more convinced that maybe Carrie was right about her.

Making her way down the steep hill from the bus stop to the little buildings rising out of the sand and cobblestone roads along the water, Izzy took in the quaint little village that wasn't really large enough to be called a town. Probably less than three hundred yards' worth of buildings and road were developed into condos and shops. It seemed the small village had sprung up as an answer to the resort developments as "the local place to go" for dinner or drinks. Entering through the breezeway between buildings that led to the water, the shade cooled her slightly, and the breeze lifted the stray strands of hair off her neck. Her flip-flops shuffled along the concrete and echoed slightly; she was the only person around as far as she could see.

As she approached the end of the walkway, the light from the white sand, the sun, and the ocean penetrated her vision and warmed her face. The rich aroma of something frying floated past her, and she listened to the sizzle in the skillet of the little restaurant to her right. The soft, light brown sands to her left were dotted with a few plastic chairs and tables waiting for someone to occupy them, and almost behind her left shoulder was Dave's little surf shop.

Dave himself was there when she walked up. "Isabella? Is that you?" he asked, seeming to remember her.

"Dave! Hey!" she answered, reaching out her hand to shake his.

"I'm so glad you made it out here!" he said, returning her handshake happily.

"My little office is right over there." He motioned to the right of the surf shop toward an all-glass box that overlooked the plastic chairs toward the water.

"Not too shabby," she smirked. "Doesn't seem very crowded today."

"Nah, not really. It's slow season here, though, in October, as I'm sure you'll come to know once you're open. Since most of our guests are American, this is back to school and not yet holidays. Things always slow down between summer and Thanksgiving, but it will pick back up soon. But anyway, listen, the waves aren't much this afternoon, but I want you to meet Mauricio." He turned toward the little surf building next to his office. "Hey! Ricio!" he called.

A short shadow appeared in the doorway. "Heeeyyyyyy! Dah-veed!" The new person, Ricio, smiled a disarming smile as he stepped out of the doorway and walked toward Izzy and Dave. "¿Cómo estás, hombre?"

"Bien, bien, Ricio. Quiero presentarle mi amiga nueva, Isabella," he said, introducing her as *my new friend.*

"Mucho gusto—nice to meet you," Ricio said, extending his hand to shake Izzy's. He wasn't much taller than Izzy, but he clearly spent his days working out or surfing, or both, and he was definitely not eating lots of tortillas that would have covered up that six-pack of abs. He wasn't what Izzy would call hot, but he wasn't totally unattractive. His smile made him seem cute and playful, which was always an attraction to Izzy.

"Mucho gusto en conocerlo," she responded, shaking his hand in return.

"I told her the waves aren't great today, but I wanted her to meet you," Dave continued. "She works at the new resort, so I told her we'd take care of her with some lessons over here if she wanted to experience it and be able to sell it to her guests."

"Oh sí, que chido . . . very cool," Ricio answered in a laid-back surfer kind of way. "Well, yeah, today isn't the best, but what I can do is show you what we have and tell you a little about what we do, then maybe we can try tomorrow or next weekend sometime. There's a storm starting to come down from the north that might kick up some of the waves a bit more tomorrow if you can come back. But let's take a walk around and I'll show you about La Escuelita."

"Sounds great! Thank you both very much," she said, genuinely appreciative of not only their hospitality, but the chance to experience a piece of Mexico and the Puerto Vallarta area she might never have found on her own. She knew this was a special opportunity, the kind of opportunity she would have turned down a few weeks back, and now she was feeling even more excited about the split from Ethan. Less than twenty or so yards from the shaded concrete of the buildings, the sand beckoned, so they made their way toward it.

"I'm gonna duck back into the office," Dave said, "but Izzy, come by and say goodbye before you head out. We can set you up with an overnight stay, too."

"I will! Thanks, Dave!" She smiled broadly, unable to hide how thrilled she was to have that offer.

Ricio showed her the little seafoam green–painted office with concrete floors, aluminum chairs, but no desk—only a folding table and gorgeous floor-to-ceiling views of the water through the glass walls and door. He had surf posters up on the walls like a teenager might have in his room—unframed, curling at the corners with a few small tears on a side or two.

"This is my buddy Jack," Ricio said, pointing to one of the posters. The poster showed a big wave and a guy on a small surfboard crouched beneath the raging foam about to spill onto him. The water was dark blue, and the board was white, and this guy, Jack, was a tanned white guy with blond hair from what the picture reflected. "He's up in California but competes a lot down here, too. This was a competition in Cabo a few years back." He seemed proud of Jack and proud to call him a friend.

"Oh wow, so how did you meet him if he's from the US?" Izzy asked.

Ricio laughed a little. "The surfing community isn't that big when it comes to those who are actually good at it." He smiled a toothy smile back at her. "We've competed together for quite a few years. A few of us from around here and Sayulita have made our way all the way up the coasts, and many come down here to practice from the north."

He went on to explain the connection to various surfing locations that these "surf bums" would migrate to, depending on the season and where the next big money-earning competition might be. She recognized a few like Hawaii and the North Shore, but she hadn't heard of Sayulita or Pascuales or Todos Santos. Sayulita was directly north of Punta de Mita, so maybe it was something she could check out while she was here. Of course, as a beginner, Ricio assured, these places would be too tough for Izzy to get much out of them. Better to practice here where waves were more steady and small for learning. As he spoke, they walked back through the building toward the ocean where he had his surfboards set up.

The sand was hot from the sun and, while beautiful, wasn't the fine powder sand of the Caribbean. Grainier and rougher, more light brown than white, with plenty of rocky coastline still evident, it seemed to be a nod to the beaches as far north as Oregon or Washington. Ricio had several large surfboards stuck in the sand, and still more lay side-by-side reflecting the late afternoon sun. They almost blinded Izzy, and she took note of how large they were. The posters in the office all showed boards about the size of the men riding them; these were at least twice as long as she was tall! How on earth would she be able to carve a wave with something that large? If Ricio had heard her thoughts, he would have laughed. Carving waves was definitely not what she was going to be doing.

"What I do," Ricio said, interrupting her thoughts, "is show you a few moves on the shore, and we practice the get-up and the paddle before we get on the water. If you want, we can do that for a little bit today, and then you can come back tomorrow for the actual lesson. I don't have any lessons this afternoon."

"Sure, why not? I'm already here," she replied, anxious to do something different and new, although she felt a little silly about the idea of paddling on the sand.

"Okay great! Let me grab my glasses; this sun is bright," he said, making a move toward the buildings. "Be right back."

Without anyone around her, on the quiet beaches of this late October afternoon during the slow season, Izzy took the precious few minutes alone to survey the area. Off in the distance she could see Las Marietas Islands, the same ones she could see from her resort. She was standing on the northernmost tip of this peninsula that created the northern border of the Bahía de Banderas. The coast curved inward to her left, scooping out the land and creating the deep "C" that was the bay. Through the surf and dusty sky, she could barely see the outline of the malecón and downtown Puerto Vallarta. To the right was a lighthouse—the final tip of the bay. Beyond that the land curved back north and up the coastline, leaving the bay to itself and creating more gorgeous, rocky cliffs, beaches, and lush tropical coves.

Though there was a slight salty breeze, the air was hot and humid, and the sun beat down, creating beads of sweat along her hairline. What storm had Ricio even been talking about? The water was so calm, lapping gently up along the sand and rocks that dotted the shallow waters before the sloping shelf made its way out to sea. If she followed the coastline to her right, it would lead her all the way back to Seattle where she was born, and if she went left, she'd wrap around the bay and head toward Acapulco and unknown places beyond. Standing on the edge of the continent, without anything familiar around her, she felt suddenly free. A strange feeling started in her belly and rose toward her chest, like a bubble of happiness ready to burst with laughter. She smiled until her cheeks hurt.

Ricio returned, jogging toward her with twisted dreadlocks bouncing behind his darkly tanned, sculpted back and broad swimmer shoulders.

"¿Okay, 'Issy,' lista?" he asked. "*Ready?*"

"¡Sí, claro! Enséñame a surfear." *Teach me to surf.*

Ricio had her lie in the sand on her stomach next to one of the larger boards lying on the ground. He instructed her on how to paddle with only her arms, since her legs would be balancing the board. Taking her wrists and standing directly over her head, he moved her arms for her. From all her experience watching people paddle a board, she assumed it would be like swimming freestyle, but apparently watching and doing were two different things. Rather than reaching in front overhead as if only pulling her body through the water, she had to reach farther out and away from her body and the board to create the pull needed to get everything moving. It felt awkward, but she went along with the lesson, assuming maybe she could alter her stroke once she was out in the water.

Later, Ricio talked about how to watch the water and had her sit on the shore looking out into the ocean, learning how to see the next ripple. It was pretty difficult since there weren't many waves, but she thought she could start to see the next little ripple coming up toward the shore. After that, it was time to learn how to go from lying on her belly to standing on the board. He demonstrated, and then she followed suit. Pushing up with their hands while at the same time tucking their toes and pushing off the board, they popped up into a squat stance with one foot in front of the other and arms to their sides shooting out from their shoulders in a "T." It reminded Izzy of when she was a kid, lying on the floor watching TV after school, and then her mom would tell her dinner was ready, and without knowing how, she was on her feet. She felt good at it, and she knew she was in good shape to be hopping, popping, and squatting. This surfing thing should be pretty easy after all.

After what seemed like a long time in the sun, Ricio announced that was all he had for today. The heat had begun to dissipate as the sun started sinking in the late afternoon hour, and she noticed she was hungry. Not only hungry, but starving. It was amazing what the mind could do when it was focused: she had lost track of time, and it felt great. Her body hadn't even told her she was forgetting about lunch, and now it was time to think about dinner.

Ricio began to take some of the boards back up to the shop to lock up for the day, and Izzy grabbed one and followed him. She felt like a character in a movie trying to carry a canoe or kayak bumping into everything, off balance and seconds away from dropping it and falling over. It seemed light since it was hollow, but the length surprised her, and once she had it over her head, she had to redistribute the position of her hands. Was she really supposed to paddle this thing out to sea? Maybe in the water it would be easier.

They moved all the boards up to the shop while chitchatting about Ricio's life. He had lived in Canada for a while and had a daughter who lived with her mother up there. She was only four and was the love of his life. He showed her photos: with curly dark hair and olive skin, she was absolutely stunning. It took Izzy by surprise that this "surf bum" would have such a strong desire to be a good father. She had pegged him for more of a ladies' man enjoying women from all over the world. But he had wanted to be a family man instead, and it hadn't worked out, so here he was now, sharing his passion for the sport and the ocean with others.

"It's like someone showed me how to read the ocean, how to work with her, and I want others to know the incredible joy and frustration she can bring you," he said thoughtfully. "She can be a real bitch, but you love her anyway."

She stayed for a bit longer chatting with him, despite the hunger creeping up, but as the sun was starting to set, he said he needed to get moving. He had some plans with some buddies. As arrogant as it might have been, she fully expected him to invite her to join them. Of course—invite the American blonde girl out for the night; the boys would love it. But he didn't. He was more professional than she'd expected.

"Thanks again for today," she said, hiding her slightly bruised ego.

"¡Ha sido un placer, mi nueva amiguita!" he said, slapping her on the shoulder. Again: *my new friend*. With that, he locked up the shop and departed.

"Hey, Dave, you still there?" she called in to the office next door.

"Sure am! Come on in," Dave welcomed her. "How was it? Great guy, right?"

"Yeah, definitely! I mean, it was fun, given we did mostly everything on land, but I'm excited to try when the waves are good," she said.

"What are your plans tomorrow?" he asked. "If you're able to come back, I can get you into our penthouse for the night, and you can head to work Monday up the hill without having to commute from the marina. Would you want to do that?"

Sunday night away from home: Sunday was a school night. She should get ready for the workweek, she thought, especially after having returned from her trip. But she didn't have anyone at home waiting on her or needing her. Why not do something fun on a Sunday?

"Yeah," she said slowly, still considering it. "I think that could actually work."

"Great! Come by anytime tomorrow, and I'll get your key. You'll have a full kitchen if you want to bring food, wine, whatever. There's wireless Internet and TV, and you can check out one of the restaurants around here if you want."

"That sounds awesome!" Izzy exclaimed. "Should I try to reach Ricio about lessons?"

"Oh, I'll set you up in the morning when he's back. I'm sure he'll have a few lessons scheduled, but we'll work something out. Just come on whenever!"

"Okay, I will. Thank you so much, Dave! This is great!" She felt compelled to start talking about how this would help her sell his condos, compelled to prove that she wasn't just doing this for her own sake, but for his as well, as his colleague and neighbor from the resort up the hill. But then she stopped herself and let herself enjoy the gift with true gratefulness. That was something she hadn't felt in a long time. She had simply been herself, and this friendly, giving man had wanted to give to her. It felt odd, and she wondered what might be different if she approached her life that way. Did she give without expectations? Or did she always have some dream about what was supposed to happen in her relationships? Is that why she always felt so let down?

This thought followed her all the way home. It didn't hurt that there weren't any fellow chicken passengers to distract her.

Chapter 10

On the bus ride north to Punta de Mita with her suitcase in tow, feeling safe and confident that nobody on the bus would try to steal from her, Izzy allowed herself to close her eyes for a brief moment. She considered the idea of going out in Bucerías tonight. That's where Ricio lived, and although it was several stops away from Punta de Mita, perhaps he'd offer to drive her down there so they could get dinner and drinks. Not as a date: he'd just be her tour guide to see the locals in their day-to-day routines. Maybe, while sitting at a bar on a patio with Ricio, she'd see *him*. Maybe they'd walk into a place, and *he'd* stop and stare at the beautiful "güerita" walking through the door. It would be a Mexican romance, something to whisk her away from the hurt and rejection after Ethan, Stephen, and Brandon. Someone to make her feel special and beautiful, someone who thought she was an angel in blonde curls. There had to be something like that in this adventure of hers, far from anything permanent back home.

The bus made the now-familiar turn at the end of the road and pulled into its place in line, waiting for the return to the city. Izzy jumped off and dragged her suitcase down the barely-there dirt road, down the hill toward the building where Dave's office was. It was hot and she sweated easily, grateful to reach the shade of the building and the breezeway between offices on the ground level. She noted that Ricio's office was open, but he wasn't in there. *Must be out with a client.*

"Iz!" Dave exclaimed when she came into his view in the open doorway of his office. "You made it! I'm so excited. I have a penthouse suite for you tonight. Let's get you up there so you can relax."

He pushed a few papers around, opened a drawer, and produced some keys. "Let me take that bag for you," he said. "We're going across the street, but it's not the easiest way to drag your luggage. Are you staying all week with this thing?"

"A girl's gotta be prepared for anything, right?" she teased back. "But of course everything I need for work tomorrow is in there, too."

They headed back toward the road from where Izzy came, but then took a right. Several brand-new buildings lined the sides of this street.

"It has a ways to go," Dave started, "but the development here will continue once the American economy bounces back."

A ways to go? Where could it possibly go? Izzy wondered. The street seemed to just dead-end into the earth.

About halfway up the small street, they ducked into a doorway where Dave entered a code into a keypad and opened the door. It led into a small hallway with a glass door at the end that overlooked the beach. The elevator bank took them to the fourth floor and opened to reveal a door with a sign that said *Penthouse.* For a split second Izzy was ecstatic, but then, this wasn't Las Vegas. This was a tiny beach town, and this was a favor.

Dave helped her settle in and showed her around this four-bedroom, marble floored, granite countertopped, stainless steel everything "Penthouse." Windows in every room boasted gorgeous views of the turquoise water she was about to embark upon for her surf lessons, and the sunlight illuminated every corner of this airy, elegant space. The funny thing was that, although it was elegant, it wasn't comfortable. The beds were a little hard, and the couches felt stiff and made from cheaper quality fabric. It was similar to her place back in the marina area, especially with the tile floors and wrought-iron furniture. But the art was incredible, and the wraparound balcony across the entire backside of the condo couldn't be beat. She saw herself with wine and sunsets and dreamy romantic nights with some local lover. *One night, Izzy; good luck with all that in one night.* It was exhilarating to think about, though.

Dave left her in peace to unpack and settle, and said he'd stop by to see when Ricio might be around. She thanked him profusely. "It's such an incredible treat to stay in a place like this. How can I repay you?"

Of course he answered, "Nonsense! This is from one friend in the industry to another. I'm glad it worked out."

After hanging up her work clothes to help get rid of wrinkles, scattering toiletries around the sink, and placing her pajamas on the bed for later, she surveyed the rooms again. *Wouldn't it be fun to have a bunch of friends here to party and play and relax? Maybe someday I'll come back and bring my Houston girls out here. Tonight, I guess I'll just have to enjoy all the space for myself.* Grabbing a bottled water from the pre-stocked fridge, she bounded downstairs to go find Ricio and see when he could offer her first lesson on the water.

Ricio wasn't in the office, so she took a walk down toward the beach, thinking she might see him there. As she passed the little restaurant, the smell of fried fish wafted through the air. She could smell beans cooking and heard something else sizzling. Around this little tourist area from Punta de Mita down to Puerto Vallarta, seafood seemed to be the meal of choice. Growing up in Texas, she was used to heavy red chili sauces, beans and rice, and lots of meat dishes like chicken or beef enchiladas. Here, she was eating more battered fish, or fish empanizada, and fish tacos. Whatever they were cooking sure smelled delicious.

No sign of Ricio still, so she decided she could get some sun and found a little spot on the beach. Just as she was getting comfortable, she heard him shout from above the sound of a motor. "¡Issy! ¿Cómo estás?" He sounded genuinely happy to see her. He was driving a small boat, painted blue like all the little fishing boats in the area. This one had a small awning fastened over the top to shade the driver, and a couple of small benches that must have been meant for storing equipment or fish. Another guy was with him in the boat, someone she didn't recognize, a little chubby around the middle and soft looking compared to Ricio's chiseled physique. She watched him maneuver the boat into the shallow areas, around some of the fishing boats tied up to the moors, and run it aground on the sand before cutting the engine. They both hopped out and pushed the boat even farther up the sand before they unloaded several boards from the back of the boat.

"Did you just finish a lesson?" Izzy asked as she approached them.

"No, no we just caught some amazing waves over across the cove," Ricio said, tossing his dreadlocks and lifting the board above his head. The saltwater glistened across his deeply tanned shoulders. Izzy tried again to consider what it might be like to have those arms wrapped around her, but she couldn't. Maybe it was because he wasn't much taller than her, or maybe it was the sharp squareness of his jaw, but something wasn't quite clicking for her. *Too bad*, she thought, *but he could still be a fun friend and teacher.*

"This is Paco," Ricio said, gesturing to the guy that was with him. "He teaches with me sometimes when I can book more than a few lessons a day. He's from Tepic and comes down during busy seasons mostly, but he had some extra time to come down early this year."

"¡Mucho gusto!" Izzy said to Paco. "Does this mean you won't have any extra time to squeeze me in today?"

"Of course not!" Ricio said, almost laughing. "It means we have plenty of time!"

She felt relieved and let out a breath. This whole playing-things-by-ear method was somewhat frustrating and stressful. Normally she would have scheduled this and made sure he was available, but she was trying to live the relaxed small town, beach community lifestyle. Her bus experience had taught her that life doesn't have to be so rushed or scheduled, but it still drove her a bit crazy when it wasn't.

"Let us unload a couple of these and grab the ones best for you," Ricio said. "Relax, just hang out, and we'll go in a little bit."

Izzy relaxed onto the sand and situated herself for a wait. It was the slow season, so activity around the little village was mostly the locals or the shop and restaurant owners moving about. The largest industry for this tiny town, as well as a good portion of this entire region, was fishing. Not just commercial fishing and deep-sea fishing, but small motorboats of one or two men that went out with a few rods and some bait, hoping to get enough great catches to barter with the restaurant owners and make some money. Izzy imagined they lived mostly fish sale to fish sale and probably didn't have a lot of savings, or investments, or anything of the like. These towns were made up of small business owners with businesses like fishing or tires or auto repair or tamales, alongside the larger commercial tourist housing and resorts. It was an interesting dynamic, but the culture and the purity of the town was still authentic and less influenced by American tourism than other parts of Mexico seemed to be.

Izzy was starting to truly love the charm, the special feeling that this place gave off to any visitor lucky enough to spend time here. Without realizing it, she was becoming grateful for her time here and her experiences. She was connecting with the community and feeling like she was part of it. While she had felt part of Houston, it didn't seem to reciprocate the love and the appreciation that this little town did. In every "hola" and every grateful smile from the taco stand vendor to the bus driver to the fisherman, she saw genuine gratitude for her time, her attention, and, of course, her money. As insignificant as she was, she felt she could make a positive impact on these people. In Puerto Vallarta, she was one of few versus one of many, and therefore her presence made a difference. She mattered.

"Okay, Izzy," Ricio said as they returned. "¿Lista?"

"Yes! ¡Estoy lista!" Or at least she believed she was ready, if scared at the same time.

"Okay, jump in and throw some of these lifejackets in the back; we'll load the boards."

She climbed into the small boat, a bit awkwardly from the beach into the backside of the boat since it was closest to the ground, and stuffed a couple floating devices into the main storage bench in the back. Paco got in after her and helped Ricio slide a few long boards across the bow and onto the floor. This little boat didn't have a place to fasten boards and store them safely, or racks to secure them for the ride over. Hopefully they weren't going far or too fast. Then Paco jumped back out of the boat with Ricio, and the two of them pushed the boat off the sand and back into the water.

"I'll come help," Izzy offered, feeling a bit strange sitting around watching them do all the work.

"No, that's okay, just hang tight. We got it," Paco said back to her.

She watched them shove their body weight into the front of the boat on the count of three, digging the balls of their feet into the sand as they leaned forward, thrusting against the boat. It worked, and the force threw her backward, stumbling into the side.

"Probably want to sit down, Izzy," Ricio instructed as she felt the heat of embarrassment rising in her face. *Way to go; you look like an idiot who's never been on a boat.*

Once the boat lifted off the sand into the shallow water, Paco and Ricio walked the boat out until they were close to waist deep before pulling the side of the boat down to lift themselves up onto the edge. Flopping over the edge, they moved quickly to start the engine and direct the boat away from the shallow rocks and beach, and out toward the open ocean.

"We are heading to a little cove over across the bay; we had some good waves earlier today, so I think it will be an easier place to try for your first time," Ricio explained.

They motored on, going as fast as the little boat could go with the old engine that reminded Izzy of her dad's fishing boat growing up. Bouncing over waves, the ocean sprayed in their face while the sun warmed their shoulders and backs. The smell of saltwater and sea life made it easy to relax and forget about the shore left behind. Farther out, the water turned to a deep, dark blue, but in this shallow bay they could see what seemed like several feet below the clear water. Breaking through the serenity of the moment, Ricio shouted something to Paco, who quickly turned around and jumped up unexpectedly.

"Whoa! Check it out!" he cried, pointing to the right of the boat.

Izzy stood up carefully, still trying to get her sea legs back so she didn't fall over, and followed Paco's gaze to where he was still pointing. Three gray porpoises were cruising along the side of the boat about thirty yards out, gliding in and out of the water in synch. *How cool!*

Ricio kept the boat headed the same direction to allow the dolphins to cruise along with them, until they suddenly turned and disappeared. Ricio slowed the boat and looked for them to resurface. Paco did the same, moving to the opposite side of the boat.

"Over there!" he shouted, looking almost 180 degrees the other direction from where they had been.

"That's weird," Ricio responded to Paco. "What do you think it is?"

"I don't know, but it must be big," Paco responded.

Something big? What did they mean, 'What do you think it is?' Her mind whirled trying to keep up and follow their thoughts. *Sharks? Something big? What the heck? I don't want to be surfing in shark-infested waters!*

Ricio steered the boat to the left, following the dolphins to investigate. As they got a bit closer, they saw it wasn't just three: there were almost a dozen! *Maybe the three they saw just shot over here to join the group? But why?* The dolphins seemed to be swimming slower, almost floating, and not in a sprint to get somewhere. They disappeared below the surface, popped up again only a few feet from where they'd gone under, and then disappeared again. They seemed to be swimming almost in a circle for some reason. Ricio shut off the engine to drift a bit closer without fear of cutting their backs with the engine blades or disturbing them.

"Are they running from something?" Izzy asked.

"Hard to say," Ricio responded.

Then the pod reappeared only an arm's length from the side of their little panga. They all saw, simultaneously, that the one in the middle of the pod looked sick or hurt and was almost swimming sideways.

"What's wrong with that one?" Izzy asked.

Before Ricio or Paco could answer, the dolphins dove down, becoming shadows again. The three of them stared intensely at the same spot, waiting. As the dolphins returned to the surface again, the one they had assumed was sick turned almost completely upside down, revealing the small tail emerging from her belly.

"She's giving birth!" Izzy exclaimed.

"Holy shit!" Ricio shouted.

They floated, watching in disbelief, as the pod dove deeper again and resurfaced, now farther off the bow of the boat.

"We need to get outta here; our shadow is going to stress them out and could be dangerous for her," Ricio finally said. "They're trying to swim away from us."

Starting the engine again and pointing the boat 180 degrees in the opposite direction, Ricio started slowly motoring away from the pod to give them space and separation. Izzy kept her eyes on the last place they had seen the pod surface. Her mind was like the waves, rolling and floating, weightless.

"That was fucking in-SANE!" Paco finally said, almost jumping with the excitement. "Have you ever seen that before?"

"No, man," Ricio began. "I've never actually seen it in person, but I know when they do this in captivity it can take a few hours to get the baby out. I guess the rest of them are sticking close to her for protection. That also explains why they're in so close to shore; it's not so deep, and the killer whales can't really get here. Normally they're out farther with the fishing boats. But that was crazy cool, man!"

Izzy was speechless and near tears. She had just witnessed, in the wild, something most folks would never even see in captivity. Birth. New life. Wild and unscheduled and messy and uncertain.

The world was telling her something, and she was listening.

They didn't talk much on the way to the quiet little unoccupied beach about fifteen or so minutes from Punta de Mita. They were all still in a daze, in a mode of reflection, after what they had just seen. As the boat approached the beach, Ricio cut the motor, and he and Paco jumped off into the waist-deep, clear-blue water to escort the boat onto the shore. This time Izzy stayed seated as the boys shoved the boat onto the shore so it would stay put, then moved to the same side of the boat together and pulled, digging the boat into the sand as best they could. They didn't have an anchor, so Izzy assumed they must be trying to create a little tension in case the tide started coming in, reaching higher under the belly of the boat, threatening to sweep it out to sea.

"Grab your board, Iz!" Ricio instructed. "Take the big one on the right."

"What?" she protested. "It's like twice my size!"

"Yeah, which means you won't be able to tip it over and fall very easily. It's like standing on a shelf versus standing on a beam," he said with such ease. *He must have this conversation with his new students fairly often to have already perfected that analogy. At least that means I'm not the only person who needs such a huge platform to do this.* It was still a far cry from the vision in her head built upon the few surfing competitions she may have caught on ESPN. Those boards were not like this monster, but, she figured, she had to start somewhere. Maybe before she left Mexico, she would graduate to the cute smaller boards and be carving up those waves like a semi-pro.

She walked into the ocean alongside the board, the water lapping at her armpits, and headed out toward where Ricio and Paco had already paddled, making it look so easy. She could still see her toes through the crystal-clear water, and she was grateful for no sharp, volcanic-black rocks like there were near the village. As the sand crept farther below the waterline, she lifted herself onto the shelf of a board. Surprisingly, she found it was pretty stable in the water as she pushed down. Lifting one leg onto the board, she rolled herself on. She'd expected the board to rock severely, or at least to tilt before coming to rest, but this beast did no such thing. It was like getting on a twin-size bed that lay flat in the water, supporting her every move. Her instructor knew what he was doing, she thought, smiling.

She stopped paddling just before reaching Ricio and Paco, and her board nearly glided into Ricio's. She sat up and let her legs spread across the board, straddling the white fiberglass and allowing her ankles to dangle in the water.

"This must be what the sharks look for," she said with a nervous laugh.

"Nah, this isn't the North Shore," said Ricio. "We'll be good."

As they sat on the boards, Ricio taught Izzy how to "read" the waves: how to see the differences in the undulations, and how to judge which one would, upon approaching shore, create the best possible wave to catch. At first, it all just looked like rolling water, but as he described what to look for, she started to understand. It was not unlike learning to read wind patterns on the water's surface, as Brandon and the sailing team had taught her years before. Knowing what to look for was most of the teaching: the how came later.

"This one," Izzy said quietly, watching a long, seemingly gentle roll of the ocean move toward them. "I think this is the best one."

"Remember, they come in threes," Ricio said, "so it may not always be the first one. Is this the first or the third?"

"I think it's the thiiiirrrd?" she answered uncertainly, dragging out the words into a question. Almost as she had finished the statement, the third roll appeared. *Damn! When am I gonna get this right?* To catch the best waves, Ricio said she had to sit and watch the same ocean for an extended period so she could learn the patterns of the water. But she seemed mostly to be spending time looking at the sun reflecting off the ocean through squinted eyes. Meanwhile, Paco had already caught three waves.

"Ugh," she sighed, frustrated.

"Hey, no worries, Iz, you're learning, and it takes time. Once you can find the wave, you can ride the wave," he reminded her.

She looked at him, annoyed, and rolled her eyes.

He laughed heartily. "Sorry, babe, this is what you paid for!" he joked back, knowing full well she wasn't paying for anything today. "You're gonna learn this if it's the last thing I do! Plus, if you think you can catch a wave you can't see, then you, my friend, are God."

Now it was her turn to laugh. They continued to wait and watch the ocean, chatting. She learned more about Ricio's daughter up in Canada, and her mother, whom Ricio loved but couldn't bring himself to commit to. Izzy talked about her American life and what she was hoping to get out of her time in Mexico.

And then she saw it. "That one! That's the one!"

"Let's see," he answered.

They watched it roll underneath them, lifting them up and setting them back down as it picked up speed heading for shore. Just feet in front of them, the roll separated from the ocean and began to rise, creating the start of the wave. Building strength as it sucked water back from the shore nearly fifty yards away, it began to foam, cresting with force and power and then crashing down on itself from one end to the other.

"That was the one!" Ricio said excitedly. "I guess white girls can be taught!"

"Ha ha, very funny," she teased back. "Can I try now?"

"Yes, let's see if we can get you up there."

"Yay!" she exclaimed like a little kid.

Ricio paddled a bit closer to her and sat next to her to watch the waves as they started to form. She was excited and suddenly nervous. *What if I can't do it? What if the wave comes and all that happens is I fall over?* She hated thinking she was about to do something that she might not do very well.

You'll be fine, Izzy, she told herself. *You're athletic and you have balance and you can do this.*

"Okay, Izzy," Ricio said, breaking through the voice in her head. "I think this is the one; you see it?"

"This one now?" she asked, alarmed.

"No, this is the first of the series. Do you see number two and then three starting to form there?"

"Oh, yes!" she lied. "So when do I start paddling?"

"Go ahead and lie down, and I'll tell you when to start."

She lowered her stomach to the board, and the nerves washed over her, making her feel chilled despite the heat. The hot sun radiated across her back, and the hot air enveloped her body, yet the feeling of cold raced through her core and created goose bumps all over her skin. Raising her head, she watched the shoreline and the first wave starting to break and then crash in front of her. *How close together are these waves?* Her question was answered as the board picked up her feet, then sank down as the front of her board and head were tossed upward and the second wave rolled right under her.

"Okay, get ready . . . now! Start paddling," he yelled.

She moved her arms, trying to pull the board forward to create movement. She had the sensation she wasn't moving at all, and she started to panic.

"Faster, paddle harder!" he said excitedly, as if she weren't already trying the best she could. The adrenaline helped dull her sharp pangs of frustration, but she knew she wasn't doing it well. She was already failing.

Just then, she felt the board launch forward, and Ricio shouted, "Jump now!"

Without thinking, without hesitating, she pulled her hands from the water, slapped them down on the board, and pushed herself up, launching into a low squat stance with right foot forward. She felt the back of her board start to rise up on the water. The rushing, roaring sound of the wave was beginning to break to her right, and her heart rate shot through the roof. As the board lifted, she lifted too, putting too much weight into her front foot, and, having jumped up too close to the front of the board, she watched in horror as the front tip of her board sank into the water and came to a dead stop. The rest of her board kept coming with the power of the wave, and with the front end stopped underwater, the force it created launched her face first into the warm, salty sea.

She had been holding her breath, and now she was underwater. Her eyes squeezed shut as the wave tossed her body in flips; she couldn't tell which way was up. The thought of drowning flashed through her mind. Her legs and arms were heavy bricks, controlled completely by the force of the water. The ocean commanded respect and insisted she submit to its power and authority. She knew it didn't care what happened to her. Her lungs were about to burst.

Then, without warning, the water let go. The shouts and thunderous roar stopped, and serene quiet filled her ears as her body righted itself and headed toward the surface. She broke through what seemed like seconds before her impending death. She gasped for air, sucking in as much as her lungs could take, as if she might never have this much oxygen to drink in ever again.

"Whoa!" she could hear Ricio say from what seemed like miles away.

Now she understood why they had cords that Velcroed the board to their ankles. It floated next her to her like an island sanctuary. All she wanted was to get out of the water so she could lie down, and there it was for her. What a friend this piece of waxed polyurethane was. With the last of her strength, she lifted herself onto it and slid onto her stomach. Face down, she could smell the salt, the fishy scent of shallow water, and the strange smell of the heated epoxy resin. The sun seemed to press upon her in an unfriendly way, as if all the forces of nature were irritated at her.

"You okay?" Ricio asked as he glided up next to her.

"Uuuuuugggggghhhhhhhhh," came the noise that finally escaped her esophagus. "It hates me."

"Nah, we just need to try again!" Ricio almost sounded cheerful. Was he fucking insane? She was never doing this again. Who needed surfing, anyway? She could be just as happy lying on a beach, soaking in the sun from the safety of an umbrella. The look on her face must have shown what she was thinking, because Ricio laughed at her. "Hey, that was your first try! You can't quit after one fall!"

There was that word. Quit. She wasn't a quitter. Lame people quit. Weak people quit.

"Fine, I need water then," she said defiantly.

"We got you right here," Paco said from out of nowhere. He had a bottle of water in his hand from the boat, one that he must have retrieved after seeing her tumble. She took it from him and chugged almost the entire thing

"Better?" Ricio asked.

"Yes, a little," she said. "That was awful."

"Yeah, the first fall can be a little scary. Te da mareo," he said. "But once you get used to it and you know it won't last long, you can move on quicker. C'mon, let's try it again."

Mareo? There was that word again. What did it mean? Muddled or confused? Yeah, I'm definitely that.

"¡El mar te da mareo!" Ricio said, then laughed.

He started to paddle back out. Izzy hated this: she wasn't good at being humbled and admitting she needed help. Ricio had already instructed her and showed her, so she should be good already! But there was no getting out of this: she'd have to woman up, admit she did something wrong, then try to fix it and go again.

They kept working. Ricio would tell her to paddle, and he would paddle next to her to keep up. Just when the wave was about to roll under the board, he'd give her board one last push and yell "¡Arriba!" so that she would jump up as he had taught her. She had a few more spills of different variations, like jumping up too far to the left or the right, tipping the board over, or moving too far back and letting the wave roll out from under her, which would leave her standing on the board but going nowhere.

"Okay, Izzy," Ricio said. "We've gotten through some of these learning curves, right?"

"I guess," she said, frustrated.

"Why don't you tell me which wave you're gonna catch this time? Something seems to change when you own it."

She sighed heavily, feeling weary from all the falls and the sun and the heat and wishing they could wrap up the day and try again another time. But her no-quit attitude reared its head.

Watching the water, looking for the series of waves she could ride, the conversation in her head turned to an argument: *You think you can do this? No, clearly you can't! You've done nothing but fall all day. Maybe it's time to admit you're not going to be a surfer.*

Her head was full of voices from somewhere in her past. The same voices that reminded her of Ethan, of Stephen, of Brandon, of the life she'd left behind in Texas to flee to somewhere new. Voices that reminded her she could run but couldn't hide from the life she had lived up to now. *How can you be proud of yourself when all you're doing is running from your problems?*

But she wasn't running. She was out here in the middle of the Pacific Ocean with people she didn't know, trying to do something she didn't have any experience doing. How could that be running? She was navigating a new work field and a new country, things that terrified her. But every time her fear about those things subsided, she felt happy. If she was running, wouldn't she run to something familiar?

Fuck these voices, she thought.

"This one!" she shouted as she saw the third wave rise up out of the flat space beyond.

"Okay, lie down and start paddling," Ricio instructed. "Go, Izzy! Go now!"

She started paddling, harder than she had before and with a fury she hadn't felt until now. She was going to ride this wave. She wasn't going to try. She was going to do. She felt the water rise at the back of the board, and the heavy push from Ricio to propel her forward even harder, and then his shouts: "¡Arriba! ¡Arriba!"

She sprang from her belly onto her feet in a low squat, balancing her weight above the middle to push the board forward without pushing it down into the water. It clicked. She could feel the wave through the board, and she could tell where it wanted to go. Ricio was shouting behind her, and Paco was letting out a loud *Whoop!* She was up—she was surfing!

She looked up at the shore: she had almost forty yards to ride before she'd have to jump off. Pushing the board forward while balancing the back, she carved to the left to stay in the wave so it wouldn't roll out from under her. She pressed into her heels to drive the board slightly right, and then she shifted to the balls of her feet to straighten it out and point the board at an angle toward the beach. The wave was no longer the enemy trying to pull her under, but the companion joyfully bringing her along for its ride. Like a friend putting their arm around her to walk side by side, or a lover reaching for her hand to say, "I've got you," this wave was rolling with her. She knew what it wanted, and it knew what she needed as the spray jumped up to kiss her face and congratulate her.

The wave began to slow as it lost depth below the surface, and it gave her one last push before it glided up onto the sand. She stood almost erect, no longer in the bended squat, and she smoothly slid up from the shallow waters onto the sand and stopped. Hopping off as the board came to a stop, she turned to see where Ricio might be. He hadn't caught the wave, so he was out in the water where she had started. But he was standing on his board with his arms in the air in a V, screaming, "Yes! You did it! Nice job!" with a huge smile on his face.

They spent the rest of the morning catching other waves and riding them into shore. Not every one was perfect, and she certainly missed waves, fell, and miscalculated, but she was having success in between the falls. She was learning, and every time she fell, she learned one more thing to watch or change or tweak. They worked for what seemed like minutes but what was actually hours, until finally Ricio announced it was time to get back for his next lesson. They caught the last wave into the shore and loaded up the surfboards in the little panga boat to head back across the bay to the Punta de Mita beaches.

Izzy was more relaxed than she had felt in a long time. Her entire body was worn out. The gym certainly was a workout, but this was a full body experience that had her feeling completely exhausted, and she loved it.

"Iz, you did great," Ricio said as they were unloading the boat.

"Thanks! But really thanks to you." She smiled back, grateful for his patience and his determination when she had given up. He pushed her without irritating her, which was something only her coaches had ever been able to do.

"Let's get you back out soon," he said, clapping his hand on her shoulder. "Can't let you forget what you learned!"

"You got it. I'll let you know!"

As he and Paco loaded smaller boards into the boat for the next lesson, Izzy surveyed the beach and thought about what she would do next. She'd had enough sun for the day, and even the idea of lying out on the sand made her feel sleepy. She opted for a nap in the shade and air-conditioning, and she made her way back to the little condo she'd be staying in.

It was the beginnings of twilight when she awoke. The sun hadn't set completely, and there was still enough light out to reveal the movement below. She got ready in shorts and a t-shirt with her flip-flops—*nobody to dress up for in this little beach town*—and she made her way downstairs. The few tourists who had been out on the sand were gone, but now the evening crew had appeared. Fishermen were coming in from their day at sea with their catch, and several of them were talking loudly and gesturing wildly with the restaurant owner.

"¡Tengo el más grande!" one yelled out, claiming that he had the biggest fish: a gigantic tuna he was carrying.

"¡No! ¡No! ¡No lo escuchés!" another protested: *Don't listen to him!*

The boats smelled like fish and sand, and the disappearing sun left a purple haze in the humid evening air as the heat of the day ran out. By no means was it cold, but the sand cooled quickly and was much more pleasant on bare feet than the sand from the middle of the day. Now that she had slept well and showered, the hunger set in, and she could hear her stomach grumble. It might have been the smell and sizzle of the frying fish or the pungent aroma of jalapeño and garlic floating through the air. Suddenly she was famished.

The small restaurant kitchen was to the right on one side of the walkway, and there were white plastic chairs and tables in the empty sand area to the left. She allowed a nice lady to lead her to a table, and she easily chose the *pescado empanizado*, pan-fried fish with rice and salad of mango and jicama, from the small menu. As Izzy waited for the fish to fry, the same young lady returned. She was carrying a small white plate with something on it Izzy couldn't quite see.

"Perdón," the young lady began, "el chef le invita a compartir el pescado fresco del día." *The chef invites you to share the fresh catch of the day.* Resting on the plate the woman presented was a sashimi cut of fresh tuna—the one she had just seen the owner bartering with the fisherman over! Even in that fancy sushi place in Atlanta she'd gone with Jenny and Carrie, she was pretty certain she'd never had tuna *that* fresh.

She thanked the server and inspected the chunks of fish. They hadn't brought rice or wasabi, but they had provided soy sauce packets and chopsticks, like fast-food restaurants might. She put the first piece in her mouth. Firm and cold, without any fishy smell or taste, this was the most incredible piece of tuna she'd ever eaten. It was meaty yet melted on her tongue. *Wow. Pay attention, Izzy. You're going to want to remember this.*

Gazing out toward the last beams of light fading below the horizon of the Pacific Ocean, casting purple remnants on the outcroppings and rocky coastline, she dug her toes into the cool sand below her plastic white chair and breathed in the warm, salty air. Taking notice of the slight breeze that lifted her frizzy curls off her face and listening to the sounds of the open-air kitchen with food sizzling, metal utensils scraping and tapping, Izzy felt a strange emotion welling up in her, encouraging tears to form. It wasn't sadness and it wasn't nostalgia. It was gratefulness.

She had been through so much in recent years: strained friendships, strained family relationships, and terrible romantic relationships. But in this moment, she was fully engaged in herself. Fully aware of her own body, her own emotions, and her own needs. She had been let go by Ethan, and while it hurt tremendously, it gave her the space and freedom needed to focus on herself. Dining alone in a sparsely populated beach town, she felt as if she belonged.

Today she had seen a dolphin giving birth in the open ocean. And this was her life: she was giving birth to the new version of Isabella. The strong version of Isabella. The confident and capable version of Isabella who deserved more than she had given herself, and who would demand more from her future. Something shifted inside her mind, and her anxiety, the uncomfortable feeling she seemed to carry, lifted. Taking another deep breath, she felt her heart expand into a comfortable place. She was proud of herself.

Part
Two

Chapter 11

Alejandra, one of the new hires at the resort, was Venezuelan and had a confident, bordering on arrogant, air about herself. Izzy found learning about how the various Spanish-speaking countries felt about one another interesting: even folks from certain places inside Mexico had preconceived notions about other Mexicans. It wasn't different from the disdain many people felt toward other groups for various social, economic, and racist reasons in the U.S. Alejandra was a good example of that disdain: she felt she was better, smarter, and most certainly more well-off than any of the local staff. And what irritated Izzy more than anything was that Alejandra felt the same way about her, the American. It was a tough pill to swallow, and not only because it bruised Izzy's ego. Rather, it forced Izzy to take a hard look at why it bothered her. *Is it truly the unjust and misplaced arrogance toward all nationalities combined? Is that why it irritates you so much? Or do you think you're better than Alejandra?* The former certainly sounded more ethically and socially acceptable. But was it the truth?

Either way, dining with Alejandra in the past had proven to be tough because the only continuous topic of conversation was Alejandra—her boyfriend, how successful she had been with her hotel career that led her to this job, her country, her preferences. In fact, Alejandra had been the one Izzy and Valeria had talked about at Chili's that first night that Valeria had opened up, laughing and saying things about how Alejandra must really like herself. Valeria had spent more time talking with Alejandra than Izzy had, and had shared some interesting insight during their gossip session.

Alejandra was from Venezuela, a very poor country, and being able to get a job in the hotel industry, then moving to Mexico, made her different than her family. But she had been living in Mexico for a while already, working at a different hotel closer to downtown. The strange part that Valeria and Izzy had discussed that night was how she didn't seem to have any friends from her old job. Surely she would have been touting her popularity from her past life, but she never mentioned it. Valeria then let Izzy in on her personal theory.

"Her boyfriend. That's the reason," she had said, raising her eyebrows.

"Oh, you mean she's always with him?" Izzy had guessed.

"No! He's so controlling and mean to her, so I don't think he lets her go out with anyone."

"Oh wow, that sucks!" Izzy had responded, but the thought had stayed with her.

After spending nearly two back-to-back weeks in Southern California and then Vancouver, British Columbia, Izzy was finally back in the office. The resort wasn't open yet, but the physical buildings were all up and crews were working on the interiors—paint and wood flooring. The pools had been poured but not yet filled; however, the landscaping was coming along nicely. Only a few months to go and they would be welcoming their first guests. That was, if everything was finished on schedule. This most recent trip's presentations had been much easier with real photos versus drawings of what the resort would be like. And with direct flights from Los Angeles every day, Puerto Vallarta was an easy sell for that market. Izzy hadn't had a chance to get back to surfing for a few weeks, but being out on the

California beaches had given her the itch to be back in the warm Mexican waters. And she was excited to get back and tell Valeria about the sushi she had tried out in LA and the amazing crab legs in Vancouver.

Occasionally, Valeria even took the time to ask Isabella about her recent trips and experiences. Nobody else, even her own boss, seemed to care too much what she was doing and where she was going, or how her trips went. She came and went and had incredible experiences, and came home to tell . . . nobody. It made coming back to Mexico that much lonelier after a trip, especially since the Internet infrastructure made calling her parents back home a bit challenging. So when Valeria would ask, Izzy would be thrilled at the chance to share with someone who might care, even if Val was only being polite. Because she had seen Valeria outside work at dinner before the trip, Izzy felt much more comfortable sharing her stories.

"Hey, Val," she said as she left her office and walked toward the opposite side of the room where the girls sat. "Want to get lunch? I want to tell you about another awesome sushi place I tried in Los Angeles!"

"Oh suuuuuure," she responded with her deep, throaty voice that sounded mature and yet childlike at the same time. "Let me check with Alejandra, though, because she said she's ready to eat also."

Alejandra? Since when? What had changed while Izzy had been gone? Silently, Izzy shuddered and hoped that maybe Alejandra was caught up in a phone call or couldn't go at all.

"Okay, see you there. Bye," Valeria said into the phone as she hung up. "She'll meet us there now."

Damn. "Okay, great!" Izzy said, hoping her fake enthusiasm wouldn't be detected. Outside she tried not to seem shaken, but inside she was jealous that Alejandra had somehow swooped in and won Valeria's heart while Izzy had been on the road. But how silly was that? Couldn't they all be friends? If Valeria had decided she liked Alejandra, then maybe Izzy could like her too.

On the way to the cafeteria, they chitchatted in English, which was a great relief to Izzy. She told Valeria about Sushi Masu in the Westwood part of Los Angeles, and about Vancouver, where Izzy had met with many different travel agencies, but had also taken the opportunity to see some famous sights, like renting a bike to ride around Stanley Park and dining in some of the nice restaurants like Cardero's and The Sandbar under Granville Island Bridge.

"Wow, that's pretty cool!" Valeria said enthusiastically. "You know I love sushi."

"It was really neat! I hope someday you get to do things like that, if that's what you want," Izzy responded.

"Oh gosh, of course I want to live in Europe and go back to visit Germany again!" Valeria had learned English in Germany ironically, but she'd also learned the art of blending cultures and the feeling of being the outsider. Her current boyfriend was German, and they had met when she was out there. He had followed her back to her home in Mexico, and they were both working at this gorgeous seaside resort. What a fairytale life! Valeria was in her early twenties, like Izzy, and her life story made Izzy feel like she hadn't done much. She was in a new country, yes, which for her personal world was a huge jump. But for a lot of the rest of the world, especially Europeans, living in a new country was pretty normal. Being connected so easily by train, it was not uncommon for people to move around, attend school, and find jobs all over their area of the continent. Like Gretchen, who was German and who had lived in Spain, France, and now Mexico. She felt connected to Valeria since they both had left home and had both put themselves in tough social situations. Surely Valeria could understand and appreciate Izzy, too.

As they got in line at the cafeteria, grabbing trays and silverware, Alejandra came sweeping in. Never mind the other people who had gotten in line behind Izzy and Valeria.

"Excuse me, oh sorry," she said, pushing her way through the line to the trays and silverware and then making her way up to the girls without regard for anyone behind her.

"I hope today is good; I'm starving!" she said upon her arrival, referring to the menu. The back of Izzy's neck tightened slightly. *Why? Why am I so afraid or invalidated or irritated by this woman? Do not let her win. Do not get mad.*

Flipping her long, light brown hair and checking her long, healthy nails on her left hand, she sighed impatiently. "Some people are just a pain to deal with." She was fishing, and it worked.

"What do you mean?" Valeria asked. "Everything okay?"

That was all Alejandra wanted: an open door to spend the next ten minutes gushing about how incredibly smart she was and how these people couldn't understand it. She had been on a conference call with other reps from the same hotel brand, much like Izzy had done when she traveled in groups with reps from various hotels of the same brand. Alejandra had worked for a hotel from the same company brand in the marina area of Puerto Vallarta for a few years. She had started her hotel career back in Venezuela, which in Izzy's mind didn't mean much because the Latin American division was much different than the North America division, something Izzy was learning more and more clearly during her time here in Latin America. Expectations for the North American division were different, and much higher, than their laid-back Latin American counterparts. The demands for performance seemed to be set at a different level, which caused a more varied business approach than what Alejandra had likely ever encountered. In Alejandra's story, however, the Americans she was planning a trip with didn't seem to understand how good she was and how much she knew. It was all so unjust. Valeria did what Valeria did best and continued to ask questions and react to Alejandra's outcries, which spurred her on.

Was Izzy irritated by Alejandra's arrogance of seeming to know more than the others? Or was she irritated because she had stolen Valeria's attention from her? Or was it because she really, deep down, believed the Americans were better than Alejandra, and she longed desperately to tell Alejandra that? Izzy thought she'd spent enough time here to feel like she was part of the group, part of the community. She wasn't simply a houseguest who needed to be polite and allow others to dominate or direct the conversations, her experiences, and her relationships. Why couldn't she be herself and tell Alejandra what she was thinking? She certainly didn't want to create an enemy, but she also was tired of being the odd one out, the one who was quiet and stood on the outskirts of the group so as not to ruffle any feathers of the peacocks in the middle of the circle. She had made the effort to befriend Valeria and start creating a sense of community, and here Alejandra was commandeering all her efforts. Remembering the promise she made to herself after that Skype call with her mother, Izzy decided today she'd stretch her comfort zone once again and say something.

"Alejandra," Izzy started tentatively, "don't you think that if you're visiting American companies with the American reps, it might help to listen to their advice, since you've only sold to Mexican companies in the past?"

Both girls turned to look at Izzy. Valeria had a look on her face like Izzy had just dared to cross an unholy line. Alejandra's eyes flashed and narrowed, and the beautiful ice blue pierced through Izzy's head to see what was in there.

"I suppose," Alejandra finally answered with an almost too high-pitched tone indicating that she did not agree but was not going to argue.

Izzy quickly sensed she needed to explain further, to ensure Alejandra wasn't pissed. "When I've been traveling with the American counterparts at these other resorts, they've had some good ideas about how to sell to the agents there, and what they're looking for. It might be a bit different than the Mexican agents you've experienced . . . you know?"

"Well yes, they always try to tell me how to speak and what I should try to sell, but I don't listen to them. You know why?" she asked the girls, pausing briefly before starting again. "Because, they keep suggesting the idea that they should come here and try to get Mexican agents to book their American hotels, which is so silly. Proves they really don't have a clue. Mexicans don't leave Mexico," she said matter-of-factly. "And obviously they don't get that. So why should I listen to what they say? I have more experience."

Valeria shifted in her chair. "That's not true!" she said, smiling. "We go other places!"

"Some do, but most don't," Alejandra responded, flashing a smile at Valeria.

To Izzy's surprise, Valeria responded with her own smile, seemingly satisfied with this answer.

Seriously? She let her off the hook that easily? It wasn't worth the argument, but it shed some light on the moment for Isabella. Alejandra was the "mean girl" whom everyone wanted to be friends with, and people let her say rude, hurtful things without challenging her because they feared she would no longer include them in her world if they did. It was high school all over again. But the worst part was that Izzy still wanted to be popular, to be liked and adored by the people she was around every day.

Maybe Izzy was making too big a deal of this. Maybe Alejandra wasn't all that bad. If she reframed the situation differently, it became more bearable and understandable: Alejandra was also in another country, away from family and looking to find acceptance. If Izzy could see Alejandra as more like herself, she could forgive the arrogance and selfishness. At least to some degree.

"You're basically right," Izzy decided to add.

She snuck a sideways glance at Valeria and couldn't help but notice what seemed like slight deflation in her face. Now both girls agreed Mexicans didn't leave Mexico. *But Valeria was fine with it, right? She had just agreed with Alejandra as well.* Izzy brushed it off and let the lunch continue without bringing it back up to Valeria, and the three of them went back to work.

Shortly after the awkward lunch, Izzy had headed out to sunny San Diego, another great market with direct flights. She hadn't had the chance to experience another lunch with both Valeria and Alejandra, and now that she was going to be back in the office for almost two weeks, she wasn't sure what to expect. Would Valeria want to hear about her bus tour of the San Diego Zoo and the baby pandas? It seemed a bit strange to have so much time in the office, but Izzy was excited to have some time at home to explore and maybe create a few more connections in the area. While she had been gone, more folks had been hired as they got closer and closer to the opening date of the resort. It seemed each time Izzy returned from a trip, she was surrounded by new faces on the bus and in the hallways. Not to mention in the cafeteria.

In the beginning, there had always been lots of seats available and plenty of food to go around. This week, it seemed as though they had reached a tipping point. The last yogurt had been snatched already, and the only seats open were outside. She took some of the last papaya and mango she found in the bottom of the fruit bin and made her way to the small outdoor patio. There was no ocean view from this side of the resort, just the bus drop area for the employees. She hoped Valeria was on the next bus, or maybe had been on the earlier bus. Either way, Valeria was nowhere to be seen, so Izzy ate breakfast on her own before making her way to the office.

As the afternoon approached and Izzy got hungry, she started thinking about lunch. Normally she would call Valeria or go by her desk to see if she was also ready to eat. Then she thought of Alejandra. Maybe she was trying too hard just to be liked. Izzy could relate to that feeling. Maybe she, too, was a bit nervous about the new job and new team and simply wanted to be accepted.

Do it now, Izzy. Be nice and reach out to her.

"Alejandra," Izzy said as she approached her office space, "are you hungry for lunch yet?"

"Valeria and I are going to run out for lunch to the village, so we'll have to try next time!" she said. Her voice sounded breezy, but her eyes said something totally different.

You and Valeria? Running to the village? Without any invitation to me?

"Oh! Okay great, it's a beautiful day, so enjoy!" Izzy chimed back, trying to sound nonchalant.

Trying not to let it get to her, she tried to explain the hurt away. *You travel a lot, Iz, and Valeria can't just eat alone because you're gone. You aren't dating her, for God's sake. It doesn't mean Valeria has chosen a new friend. Right?*

But that old feeling started creeping in. It had been decades ago, but the deep wounds reopened, and she felt shunned by Valeria's and Alejandra's lunch date without her.

It had been seventh grade when Izzy was first called "rat girl" by two boys in her grade level. At first they had been teasing, and most of the class who stood idly by laughed but didn't take it to heart. She couldn't remember if it was weeks later or months later, but when the bullying had escalated to the boys throwing cheese at her and making mouse noises across the lunch table, she wound up losing her group of friends because she was "too embarrassing to be friends with at school." Izzy was socially forced to spend what seemed like a lifetime (but in reality was probably a few weeks) eating alone in the cafeteria at "the rejects table" near the door where all the other lonely kids sat without talking to each other. She felt isolated and unloved, and desperately sad. She contemplated suicide and wondered if anyone would even notice. She never truly told her parents about the bullying for fear they'd feel the same way . . . that she was an embarrassment. Or maybe she feared they wouldn't back her up. She still wasn't really sure why she hadn't told them, but it was probably due to the deep shame she felt.

After the isolated lunch weeks, the incident had lost its power, and her classmates seemed to have moved on from it all. The door opened once again for her to establish some friendships, and one in particular became strong. Jana Leigh was a popular athlete that Izzy befriended while attempting to play basketball in eighth grade. Izzy never became a starter, but Jana Leigh was the starting point guard and took a liking to Izzy. Then Jana Leigh developed a crush on one of the two boys who had bullied Izzy the year before. During their class trip to New York City and Washington, DC, while the class wandered through one of the museums, Jana Leigh had wanted to impress the boy and get his attention. So while they were meandering through an exhibit of birds, reptiles, and rodents, Jana Leigh took an opportunity that Izzy had never forgotten, and perhaps had never truly recovered from.

"Look!" Jana Leigh had said loudly, causing a large number of the class to turn and look her direction. "There's Rat Girl's cousin on display!" The boy seemed somewhat entertained and grinned at Jana Leigh. Izzy had stood motionless, heartbroken.

But this isn't middle school. Alejandra is NOT Jana Leigh.

She thought about stopping to ask Gretchen about getting lunch. Their weird trips together up the mountain early in the resort's life had been awkward, but maybe this was a chance to move past that. She wandered over to Gretchen's office, lingering awkwardly in the doorway until Gretchen looked up.

"Hey," she said to Izzy, "everything okay?"

"Oh yeah!" she said a bit too loudly and nervously. "Just, I was wondering if, you know, you might want to get something to eat." She seemed to be stammering. Why, though? She and Gretchen had shared meals and car rides and experiences through the early days, and she had survived that. Why was it awkward now?

"Um, well," Gretchen started, "I am supposed to go with Nico and Nacho. So . . . sorry but no."

No sugarcoating that one. "Oh okay, well, enjoy," Izzy said, forcing a smile.

Before going to the cafeteria, Izzy had to run by the reservations office to give them some information about a few things, so she headed there first.

"Oh my gosh!" Ximena exclaimed. "She is alive!"

Izzy smiled, almost beaming. The feelings of isolation and hurt were swept away with Ximena's enthusiastic greeting.

Since Ximena, who had now moved from the butler team to the reservation team, took the reservations that Izzy booked, they often were in touch about clients and incoming guests, but they hadn't yet spent much time together outside of the office.

"I wasn't gone *that* long."

"Well, you never write or call anymore!" Ximena said dramatically. Both girls laughed and hugged, and Izzy answered Ximena's questions about "where" and "when" and "how was it?" It felt nice that Ximena noticed when Izzy was out of the office for a few days.

Before long, Izzy realized another girl in the office watched tentatively from the computer next to Ximena.

"Hola," Izzy said to her. "Soy Isabella."

"Oh, sorry!" Ximena exclaimed. "This is Luciana. She started while you were gone, and we're just finishing training. Luci, this is Izzy, who does sales."

"¡Mucho gusto!" Izzy said after the introductions and hand shaking. Then, on instinct, she invited them both to lunch. "Voy a comer. ¿Les gustaría acompañarme?"

Without their manager there to stop them, they decided they should both take lunch together and go with her. The line was short, so they moved along easily, adding various sides, slices of meat, and drinks to their trays. The sun was out, and the outdoor tables offered umbrellas to block the midday sun, so the girls opted for some fresh air at a table outside. Normally Valeria and Alejandra didn't like sitting outside, as it was always "too hot," but settling into the shade, Izzy noticed the temperature was quite pleasant with the slight ocean breeze.

Izzy soon learned that Luciana was from Mexico City, but Ximena was from Monterrey. Izzy had been to Monterrey once before when she worked for the Convention and Visitors Bureau in Houston and had enjoyed her time there. From what she remembered, the city was quite metropolitan and had a large university. Nothing like the size and sheer magnitude of Mexico City, but office parks and large corporate buildings gave it a familiar feeling in Izzy's mind. They talked about some of the familiar sights Izzy had seen that Ximena knew, and conversation flowed a bit easier. Ximena and Luciana both spoke English, which was necessary to take incoming calls from travel agents and travelers from not only Mexico but also the US and Canada; however, it was definitely not in their main comfort zone.

"Okay," Ximena suggested, "how's about I speak English, and you must answer in Spanish?"

"¡Claro que sí!" Izzy supported the idea. "Necesito practicar también."

That worked for a while, but everyone wound up falling into Spanish. Although a bit less comfortable for Izzy, she enjoyed being stretched. What really helped was that the girls didn't mind correcting her or pausing to let her find the words she needed.

She tried to tell a story of one of her previous business trips, when she'd arrived at the airport baggage claim to find it empty of bags and people. "Y luego los . . . cómo se dice . . . después del avion, tienes que ir a encontrar su equipaje . . ." Izzy struggled to remember the words for luggage carousel.

"Reclamo de equipaje," Luciana filled in, smiling and nodding.

"¡Sí! El reclamo de equipaje estuvo vacío, y yo empecé a entrar en pánico."

The girls indulged her with "ohs" and "ahs" and nodded encouragingly as she spoke, even if it was a bit broken in her haste to get the story out. She instantly liked them, and they seemed to like her.

Good thing Alejandra and Valeria went off to do their own thing after all, she thought a little too vindictively.

As the three of them laughed and talked and got to know one another better, a couple more new faces entered the cafeteria.

"Oye," Luciana said slyly, "mira al papi por allá." *Look at that hot guy over there.*

Izzy glanced over: he was pretty cute, with a boyish face and handsome smile.

"¡No lo mires!" Izzy almost squealed. *Don't look at him!* She was suddenly a high schooler again, but this time for the fun reasons. This was what she was looking for. Some friends to share in her adventures, some people to go do things with, and perhaps a little melodrama with a love interest.

Ximena, being the loudest and most outspoken of the group, motioned for the guys to come on over.

"Ehh!" she cried to them through the open doorway. "¿De dónde son, guapos?" *Where are you good-looking guys from?*

"Ay, dios mío," Izzy said, remembering a textbook exclamation: *Oh my God.*

The girls erupted in laughter. "¿Tus dios?" they said together. Apparently textbook phrases didn't always translate to casual slang people actually used. "Oh my God" wasn't really a saying in Spanish, at least not like her textbook claimed.

The boys got their food and made their way over to the girls' table, much to Izzy's embarrassment. More than the embarrassment of being part of the group that was overtly hitting on them was the embarrassment that she still didn't feel that confident with the slang they were using, and she certainly wasn't ready to try carrying on a conversation with some hot guy she'd have to face day after day! Combine that with the fact that although not a director, Izzy was still a manager and not exactly an hourly employee on their same level. She didn't have much time to consider it, though, as Luciana grabbed her left arm and hung on as if she was drowning in her chair. Ximena seemed at ease and almost reveled in the direct eye contact they were making with her. She leaned back in her chair and pushed her chest out even farther, which didn't need much help getting "out there."

"¿Cómo te llamas, güey?" Ximena asked one of the guys.

"Yo soy Gabriel, y él es Felipe," he said, nodding to the baby-faced one. Izzy and Luciana both smiled at Felipe. He smiled back, then cast his eyes down to the ground. A bit shy and quiet, he would be a fun one to pursue.

"¿Gabriel?" Ximena said. "Pues, mucho gusto. Soy Ximena." She reached out her right hand, leaning forward slightly to allow the "V" of her shirt to open a bit more. "Ella se llama Luciana, y la gringa es Isabella." She gestured toward Izzy, the gringa.

"Mucho gusto, señoritas." Gabriel smiled at them all on behalf of the boys.

At that they turned to find their own table, leaving Izzy in Luciana's clutches, which still hadn't released, and Ximena's glow of accomplishment. *These girls are crazy! And fun!* Izzy couldn't wait to spend more time with them. She took out her latest discovery, a pay-as-you-go cell phone that worked only in Mexico, and asked for both girls' numbers.

Back in the sales office, Alejandra stood at Valeria's desk laughing about something. Despite the joy she had just felt, Izzy felt that creeping sensation of tingles and tension rise from the backs of her knees to her chest. She felt jealous and hurt. But she would show them. She had new friends now. She smiled at them both and turned back toward her own office.

Chapter 12

Bing! **Her phone chirped,** letting her know a text had come through. Instantly dropping the mascara, she went to the bedroom where her phone lay on the bed.

¿Qué vas a llevar? It was Luciana, asking her what she was going to wear. Isabella had packed all her summer clothes from home, which were mostly casual shorts and tank tops, but not a lot of flirty dresses and club attire. The bars she frequented called mostly for jeans and flip-flops on a deck or patio, and occasionally jeans with heels. The best she could put together for tonight was jeans with heels and a shirt.

She responded: *Jeans, heels, y una blusa. ¿Tú?*

She went back to the bathroom to finish up her makeup and consider her hair. She had been wearing it curly since the early days, when she fought the frizz and lost every time, but should she try to straighten it tonight? Felipe was sure to be there, right? And what man wasn't attracted to long, straight hair? But would it even stay straight? She was deep in this argument with herself when her phone chimed again with Luciana's reply.

Un vestido—en el caso de que Felipe esté allí ;)

In case Felipe is there? Shit. In an instant, the building excitement of a romance that might ignite was extinguished. Luciana was after Felipe. Suddenly Izzy didn't give a damn what she wore or what her hair looked like. Why should she even go?

Don't, Izzy, she told herself. *You're going to spend time with these girls. New friends. Why do you always make it about a guy?* After thinking about this for a moment, she started to work on straightening her hair. Maybe it was better she didn't pursue a romance with a coworker anyway. She had never done so back home, and even though this was Mexico, it was still her job. She decided that she still cared what her hair looked like, but also knew that it would be fine regardless of how it came out.

Perfecto ;), she texted back. Let Luciana throw herself at Felipe, anyway. Izzy didn't intend to be here for life.

About thirty minutes later, Izzy was dressed in jeans, heels, and a short-sleeved tight sweater. Yes, it was a work sweater, but she didn't have much else. It was an outdoor party, and the evening air was slightly chillier. Even still, she thought she'd better do some shopping for more than just sexy swimsuits.

Ximena had a car and was driving the girls to La Posada. It was closer to work than home, and with heels they didn't want to be on the bus if they could help it. After seeing Ximena's text—*Estamos aquí*—Izzy shoved her small toy phone and apartment key into her pockets, gave herself one last look and her straightened hair one last fluff, and then headed downstairs.

"Buenas noches, señorita," Omar greeted her on the way out.

"¡Buenas noches, Omar!" she responded cheerfully. "¡Nos vemos más tarde!"

"Cuídate mucho," he warned, sounding like a big brother again.

Izzy found Ximena's car and hopped in, and they sped away to the north side of the Bahía. They rolled the windows down and turned up the music. Izzy didn't understand all the words, and sometimes the girls said things that she didn't quite catch, but it didn't matter. She was having fun and living a little on the wild side, running around this Mexican town with native speakers, blasting music and anticipating romance. She hadn't felt more at home since she'd arrived. The air was cool and damp with a slight breeze that made Izzy wonder if maybe she should have grabbed a jacket. Shaking off the chill and forcing her mind to stay in the moment, she let go of the worry and figured she'd take a few more tequila shots to stay warm. This night was going to be memorable no matter what.

The venue was an abandoned stadium that had been used for bull-fights years ago. Now it was a place rented out for parties or weddings, which was perfect for this hotel celebration. Parking in the gravel lot, the ladies applied one more coat of lipstick and stepped out of the car. Luciana had come dressed to impress with a very short dress that bloused at the top, giving her a bell-sleeve look that balanced her long, gorgeous legs atop her high heels. Ximena was in jeans and a white see-through tank top. *No hiding those "girls" from anyone*, Izzy thought. Nothing left to the imagination actually stirred the imagination. Without realizing it, Izzy stared at her breasts, wondering what it might be like to lay on them or what they might feel like. Not in a sexual way, but Izzy didn't have those, and they were huge! She could see why men were so drawn to them. Apparently, Ximena could too, and she looked at Izzy with a devilish smile.

"¿Quieres tocarlas?" she asked.

What the hell? No, I don't want to touch them! Izzy started to panic. *Oh God, was she . . . did Ximena . . . ?* Before Izzy could finish that thought, it was broken by Ximena's laughter.

"¡No te preocupes, güera, me gustan los hombres!" she laughed. "Pero después de tequila, quién sabe?" *Don't worry, I like men—although after tequila, who knows? Ximena had to be joking. Right?*

Izzy had expected the scene of the party to be noisy with music and crowded with people, but their arrival fell totally flat. They walked in the door, arms linked, to find . . . nothing. It was more like the beginnings of a family gathering than a raucous fiesta. The band was playing banda-type music, which, with the prominent sounds of tubas and horns, reminded Izzy of the Tejano music from back in South Texas. Some folks gathered around the white plastic tables and chairs, and a few had beers in hand. No sightings of Felipe or Gabriel yet. The girls glanced at each other and then back out at the scene.

"Vámonos," Ximena commanded. "Necesitamos cerveza." *Beer—that was exactly what they needed.*

Getting some beer from the iced tubs, they found a table within view of the stage and dance area. Izzy took a swig of the cold beer and instantly felt better. It went down smooth and cooled her throat. Despite the chill in the air, the cold beer tasted great. A little too great: it wasn't long before Izzy needed another, and she asked if the other gals did too. Luciana declined, but Ximena was ready. *Big surprise there.* She went to fetch a beer when Matías, one of the new servers from the pool area, grabbed her.

"¿Me prometes un baile?" Matías asked, pressing the back of her hand to his lips. Matías was nice and hilarious, great at making anyone within earshot double over in a fit of laughter, but he wasn't good looking or attractive to Izzy in any way. Clearly her feelings weren't mutual, however. She had been a bit too friendly not all that long ago, and he must have taken that as a sign that Izzy had more than his humor in mind. Now, she attempted to backpedal.

"Matías," she started, aiming for a humorous approach that wasn't too hurtful, "¡sabes que somos amigos solamente!" Perhaps reminding him that they were just friends was a gentle way of delivering the message.

"¡Claaaaaaro que sí" he said dragging out the words and rolling not just his eyes but his entire head dramatically. "Pero amigos pueden bailar," he smiled, suggesting that friends could dance without any harm. *Oy vey.* He was going to be hard to get rid of. But then she asked herself: *What is the harm in dancing? Haven't you decided that this is a new version of Izzy, a new opportunity to experience life and all it has to offer?* If the surfing and the dolphin couldn't give her the forward push she needed, nothing else would.

"Okay, okay," she conceded, to herself as much as to Matías. "Un baile."

"Bueno. ¡Vamos!" he said, sweeping her toward the dance floor with his left hand leading her and his right hand on the small of her back. Before she could protest and attempt to release from his hold, she was in front of the entire arena, and the tubas started playing. She froze. She loved to dance and she loved the spotlight, normally, but would she look like a fool dancing with this guy? Would she look like an idiot because she didn't know how to dance? He must have seen the terrified look on her face. Thankfully, he interpreted it as her not understanding the dance moves.

"Sigue," he said, instructing her to follow as he took bigger-than-normal steps to accentuate left, right, left, right. It was a polka-type dance from what she could tell, alternating feet and moving with the "oompa oompa" of the tuba. Watching the joy light up his face, the smile that stretched from ear to ear, and the ridiculousness of the entire moment, she laughed. *If only my softball peeps could see me now!* She imagined they would laugh right along with her, and some of them would jump up there, acting goofy as all get out, and dance right along with her. With that notion, she finally let go and played along. *Who cares who's watching? Who cares if I suck?* This guy clearly didn't, and he was glad to teach her, so why not learn?

She grasped his hands more firmly and, looking at her feet, bopped along with him from right to left to right to left. Using the hand on the small of her back, he pulled her a bit closer in an effort to guide her to turn and go the other way. She felt herself go rigid against his embrace. *Relax, Izzy. He knows the boundary and is just helping you learn the dance.* She talked herself back into relaxing into the move again, and this time, it seemed easier. She could hear the beats of the "oompas" and feel the rhythm of the steps, and it started to click. The song ended and seemed to begin again, moving right into another tuba stanza, but Izzy needed a break. And another beer. And she had forgotten to get Ximena's beer!

Matías conceded and led her away from the floor, where others had joined and were continuing to dance and sing along. More people had arrived, and now there was an actual crowd to maneuver through to get back to the bar.

"Déjame hablar con Ximena," Izzy said, asking for a second to check on Ximena.

"Sí claro. ¡Estoy aquí cuando estés lista!" Matías said, backing off and giving her space. *I'm here when you're ready.*

She found Ximena, who definitely didn't need Izzy's help to get another beer. Gabriel had found his way to her side already. Beers in hand and boobs everywhere, he was mesmerized, and Ximena was indulging in the power of captivity. Seeing Izzy, she waved and motioned her over.

"¡Isabella!" Ximena cried over the music that had seemed to get louder. "¿Recuerdas a Gabe?"

Of course Izzy remembered him from lunch just the other day. She also remembered that Gabe was married, though, with a wife in another city. She wondered if she should ask Ximena about it, but she decided not to. Ximena must have known what she was doing. The real question was, where was his friend Felipe?

"¡Sí, claro!" Izzy said, smiling and shaking his hand. "¿Cómo estás?"

"Bien, bien," he answered benignly. "Bailas bien." He motioned to the dance floor.

"Oh," Izzy said with a laugh, "Matías me enseño." Matías had just been teaching her.

"Sí, claro que sí," he said with a knowing smile.

Glancing around, Izzy saw that Luciana hadn't moved one inch from where they'd started the evening. She sat, perfectly poised with legs crossed and a half-drunk beer in her hand, as if she was posing for a picture that might be taken soon. Nobody was at her side, which meant her attempts to lure in attention hadn't worked yet.

Izzy took the open seat next to Luciana. "¿Estás bien?" she asked.

"¡Sí!" Luciana said, coming to life again. "No me gusta bailar, pero me gusta mirar." *I don't like to dance, but I like watching.* "¿Te gusta Matías?"

"Oh no, solamente es un amigo," Izzy assured her.

"¡Pues, él baila bien!" Luciana said. "¡Disfruta!" *He dances well: enjoy!*

As the party went on, Isabella sat with Luciana, watching Ximena on occasion but also watching the party evolve and more people join the dance floor as the cerveza continued to flow. Luciana didn't have too much to say, and Izzy was afraid that if she pried, Felipe might come up in conversation. So she let them sit in silence.

Strangely, Felipe wasn't there yet. They'd already been there for a couple of hours, and probably most of those who were coming had already arrived. Matías reappeared, asking for another dance, and after finishing her beer, Izzy decided to join. Why not?

That would be a good theme for my time here, she thought. *Why not?* She was so used to asking herself *why* and coming up with reasonable responses. Spending time asking *why* instead of *why not* had focused her decisions in life toward what those around her might think or want, rather than what she thought or wanted. She thought it made her easy to be with and more desirable to be around. But now, standing here with this goofy guy asking her to dance over and over again, she realized she didn't have anyone there to impress or be concerned with. *People will probably think we have something going on. But do I really care?* For once, she didn't! She felt a weight being lifted off her shoulders as she took his outstretched hand and said: "Okay."

The music, movement, and beer had Izzy spinning and sweating, and Matías was sweating through his shirt. It had been slightly cool outside, but with all the moving bodies and constant stream of alcohol, the coolness gave way to heat. *How long have we been on the dance floor?* Making her way off the floor, despite Matías's attempts to grab her hands and whirl her back around, she found Ximena. She had been dancing with Gabriel as well, and her already see-through tank now clung to her stomach.

"¡Necesito agua!" Izzy yelled over the tubas and trumpets, heading for the water.

"¡Yo también!" Ximena shouted back.

The two of them walked, or rather slightly stumbled, over to the area with bottled water and began chugging. It was cold and tasted amazing after all that beer. They spotted Luciana in the exact same chair where they had left her. Perched beautifully still, no sweat dripping from her hair or down her back, she seemed to still be waiting for someone to rescue her.

Someone stood next to Luciana: it wasn't a man, and it certainly wasn't Felipe. Izzy squinted a bit: Alejandra.

Really? Are you serious? Izzy tried to stay positive. *Maybe Alejandra just wants to make friends, and Luciana didn't start working here all that long ago, so maybe she's taking the chance to meet her for the first time. Or maybe she's trying to steal all my friends.*

Ximena leaned her head to the side, blocking Izzy's view, and gave her a questioning look.

"¿Qué onda?" she asked. *What's up?*

"Nada," Izzy said, trying to sound casual. But Ximena wasn't letting it go. Rolling her eyes, she cocked her left hip out to settle in for the explanation as Izzy tried to find the vocabulary.

"Pues," Izzy began. "Solamente . . ."

"In English, por favor," Ximena finally said.

"It's just that it seems like whoever I make friends with, Alejandra tries to make better friends with them," Izzy said. "And she can do it because I travel all the time, and I'm not around. I know it sounds stupid, but Alejandra and I don't get along that great, like we're competing or something, and last week she and Valeria started leaving for lunch together after I had spent some time getting to know Valeria. And now she's hanging out with Luciana. I just feel weird about it."

Ximena raised her eyebrows and did her best to answer in English. "Isabella, why you jealous of her? You're pretty and funny, and she just wants to be friends with you."

"I don't think that's it," Izzy interjected. "If she did, she would be nicer to me. She'd invite me to be part of her birthday brunch, or to go to lunch in the village, or something."

"Do you really care?" Ximena asked. "You're not here forever. Maybe she is?"

Maybe she is. It rang in Izzy's head.

"¿Estás lista para salir?" Ximena asked: *Ready to go?* "Gabriel y algunos otros van a su casa para tomar tequila. ¿Vámonos, eh?"

Oh boy. No, she definitely didn't need to go with Gabriel and his friends over to his house to drink tequila now. It was into the early morning hours, and Izzy needed a shower. Plus, Gabriel was obviously after one thing, which Izzy was sure Ximena was ready to give up, and Izzy wasn't thrilled with the idea of sitting alone in a living room with Gabriel's random friends while the two of them hooked up.

"Oh no," Izzy sighed, "estoy cansada, y quiero bañarme."

"Pues, pasaré por tu casa para dejarte," Ximena said with a knowing smile about what would be happening after she dropped Izzy back at her place. Izzy rolled her eyes and smacked Ximena on her shoulder, laughing at her affectionately.

They gathered their things, including Luciana, and said their goodbyes. Gabriel decided to jump in the car with the girls so he could direct Ximena to his house after she dropped off Luciana and Izzy. That left Izzy and Luciana in the back seat together while Gabriel sat up front with Ximena and flipped through radio stations.

"¡Baja las ventanas!" he said to Ximena, asking to roll down the windows.

The air felt cool again and was a relief to Izzy's sweaty neck and face. She gathered her hair, now curled and frizzed from sweat, and cocking her elbow to the side, she leaned on the inside of the door. Letting the wind cool her and dry her off, she closed her eyes. Reflecting on the night, she was happy with her decision to dance with Matías, even if he had been a bit aggressive, and even if she would still have to explain that she wasn't interested in him. She wished that she, Luciana, and Ximena had spent a bit more time with one another rather than with the boys. *But that's what a party is all about, isn't it?* Her mind wandered to the woman next to her, wondering if Luciana was upset that nobody had asked her to dance. Luciana's eyes were closed.

"¿Estás bien, Luci?" Izzy asked tentatively.

"Síííííí," Luciana answered without opening her eyes. "Sí, estoy cansada." It was close to three in the morning, so of course she was tired. Izzy couldn't help but feel that there might be more, but she figured now wasn't the time to ask further. Izzy returned her head to her hand and let her eyes close until she was stirred awake by the car stopping at her apartment.

"Estamos aquíííííííí," Ximena announced, a little less enthusiastic now than when they left La Posada.

"Gracias, amiguita," Izzy answered as she opened the door to pour herself out onto the private driveway of the condo complex. Walking around to the driver's-side window, Izzy bent down and kissed Ximena's cheek as Ximena simultaneously kissed hers. "Cuídate mucho, y nos vemos el lunes," she said, giving Ximena a motherly look about what she knew the rest of her night would entail. *Be careful, and we'll see each other Monday.* "Drive safe," Izzy instructed sternly.

"Sip," Ximena said, the local slang for sí. She smiled and winked. "Lunes, mi amiga." As they drove off and Izzy turned to head toward the elevators, she heard Omar again welcoming her home.

Stepping inside the elevator, she punched the button for her floor, put her forearm against the stainless steel wall, and leaned her forehead on her arm. She felt the floor beneath her lurch upward with the loud whir of the elevator cables, forcing her legs to bend at the knees with the sudden movement. Her stomach turned, and she felt the all-too-familiar sensation that happened when she drank too much. That beer wasn't going to stay put until morning.

Taking a deep breath, she moved her forearm and let her forehead rest directly on the cold steel in hopes that it would help quell the nausea rising in her throat. It wasn't enough. She looked to her left, pressing the entire right side of her face onto the steel. The sounds of the moving elevator resounded loudly in her right ear, disorienting her a bit too much and intensifying the urge below her ribs.

Please make it to the bathroom, please.

Breathing deeply and trying to talk herself into staying calm, as she had learned to do while waiting in long lines of college bars for her turn to puke, she steadied herself as the elevator stopped on her floor and the doors opened. The bright hallway lights were blinding, flooding her face with what seemed like daylight. Finally making it to her front door, she struggled slightly with the key, jiggled the handle, and, leaning her body weight into the door, felt it give way. The notion of being inside, safe in her own space, triggered the mental block on her physical body, and she ran through the bathroom door, kneeling and vomiting at the same time over the edge of the seat. She had made it, thank God.

After starting the shower and peeling off her sweaty jeans and clothes, she rolled herself in and tried to wash the sweat off, but her arms were heavy and she didn't have the energy to wash her hair. At least she was cooled off and could sleep better. She sat on the hard tile, water falling over the back of her head and neck, and let her head fall between her knees. *What a fun night, right? Yeah,* she thought. *Lots of fun.*

Chapter 13

Something was keeping her from rolling onto her left side. Was it the sheet? She pulled at it and realized it was a towel. Then she remembered throwing up, and she remembered the shower. She must have wrapped herself in the towel and passed out in bed.

Her head was pounding. Taking the last few sips of the bottle of water at her bedside, she lay back down and wondered what time it was. At least she had today off.

Her hair in the bathroom mirror was all over the place, and her eyes lacked any sort of spark or life. Pulling on the shorts and t-shirt that lay on the bed, she wandered through the small hallway into the main room. The gorgeous sun, blindingly blue ocean, and fantastically free sky shone in the floor-to-ceiling glass doors to her balcony, there to greet her. This is why she had wanted to live in this apartment.

She got herself some more bottled water out of the fridge and made her way to the balcony. The humidity and heat hit her face as she slid the door open and stepped outside. Scents of salt and sand rose from below her, along with the unique smell of heating concrete and plastic from the table and chairs and surrounding stucco building. The white paint was dull from the elements but still reflected the sunlight warmly. Below her, the pool was already alive with a few families and a couple of young boys playing loudly in the middle of the pool. The fountain was going as usual, offering the steady sounds of splashing water, and beyond the pool was the private beach dotted with straw umbrellas and lounge chairs, and then the ocean, the deep sounding bass to this song.

Returning to the air-conditioning, she put a few things together in a small tote bag she had acquired from a vendor who had come by their sales office. She had been given a small notebook before she left Texas, but she hadn't found a use for it. Now she threw it in her bag along with a pen, her toy phone, sunscreen, and a towel. After pulling on one of the new bikinis, shorts, and a top, she headed out the door to the beach.

She slipped her flip-flops off as she hit the sand. There wasn't much breeze and the air was hot, but the sand hadn't yet heated to the point of burning her feet. Finding a spot closer to the water's edge, she laid out her towel, set her tote down, and settled onto the ground. Her sunscreen smelled like coconut and felt good as she glided it onto her arms, shoulders, neck, legs, and stomach.

Through her sunglasses, she squinted at the reflection of the sun dancing on the ocean. The beach wasn't packed, but bodies stretched up and down the shore all the way to where the strip of beach started to curve, heading into the main downtown area. She knew the hotel she'd stayed in upon arriving was in that direction. Maybe she could walk all the way there.

She left her things and started making her way. She passed a large Marriott hotel, then another condo complex, then another she didn't recognize, looking into the distance for the hotel she had lived in. Who were the people all over the beach? Were they Americans here for vacation? Were they Mexicans here for a getaway? Surely none of them were living here, like her. None of them belonged here like she did. Something about that notion made her smile inside, and the seed of confidence that had taken root grew a bit more. She wasn't afraid to be out here alone, walking the beach by herself.

Ahead of her, the beach seemed to end, and a large rock outcropping parted the waters. Built out by man, these jetties were created to break the sea and to help calm the waters as they approached. This morning, what appeared to be a yoga class was happening on top of one. The jetty had been landscaped on top with grass or maybe Astroturf, and three women moved to silence, or maybe the sounds of the waves.

The sun was weakening her hungover body, so she turned and headed back to her spot. After thinking for a moment, she pulled out her notebook.

Things to try, she titled the page. *Number one, yoga. Number two, whale watching. Number three, salsa dancing.* Before she knew it, she had an entire page of things, but to her surprise, her hand kept moving, and ideas kept pouring from her head. Her emotions welled up, but instead of wanting to cry, she felt like she wanted to write: to explain and share what she was feeling.

After some time, she was sweating a bit too uncomfortably and needed a break. She felt relieved to have gotten all that out. Now that she'd spent time sweating out the alcohol and pouring out her emotions on paper, her stomach signaled with a growl that it was time to find something to eat. It felt so great to have sat there with herself for an unknown amount of time, with no restrictions or deadlines, and nobody else's schedule to consider. What surprised her even more was that she'd actually enjoyed it. She was fun to be around.

Stepping back into her apartment, she shivered in the cold air. Without even rinsing off, she changed into another pair of shorts and a loose-fitting cotton shirt with the same flip-flops. Sunglasses would hide her lack of makeup, and it was hot enough out she didn't need to worry about doing her hair. Such small things created a sense of freedom. She counted out some cash and decided she'd hit up the little taco stand up the road.

The sun continued to heat the world around her, and she turned her face toward it, soaking in the sense of freedom reverberating through her. Ahead of her on the sidewalk was the little concrete bus stop where a few taxi drivers, or taxistas, were gathered. As always, they reminded Izzy of a group of high school boys hanging out around their trucks in the parking lot before school. She tucked her chin slightly and walked ahead.

Then she heard, "Eres de mis sueños, bonita." *You're from my dreams, beautiful.*

The catcall angered her, and her entire body went rigid. She should have known that was coming. Her mind flitted back to the sand and sun, and the peaceful confidence she had just experienced on the beach. Recalling the feelings of happiness with herself, she searched her mind for the vocabulary she would need and continued walking toward them. This time, she decided, they needed to know. She had been here for a few months already; didn't they realize she wasn't a tourist? Today she'd set them straight. She had learned enough curse words and slang from the guys at work that she felt she could arm herself.

"¡Oye!" she started loudly. "No soy de tus sueños, y no soy turista estupida. No me mires y no me hables, pendejo!" she said angrily. *Don't look at me, and don't talk to me, asshole!* She directed this last command at the one who'd said something about her being from his dreams. It didn't work like she thought.

"¿Pendejo?" he cried angrily. "¡Eres una pinche gringa!"

Her blood boiled, and she walked faster. *How can they curse at me when they're the ones who're being rude and indecent? God, I hate this!* They backed up, and one spit at the ground. She ignored them and kept walking as fast as she could up the street without looking back. *Next time*, she decided, *I'll just cross the street and avoid them altogether.*

She kept her quickened, angry pace all the way to the taco stand. Finally, irritated that she'd let them get to her, she took a deep breath and tried to slow her steps. She could feel the heat subside in her chest, and her neck and back released the tension she had been holding. Now she needed more than just tacos. She needed a beer.

The cobblestone road gave way to paved cement sidewalks that at one time may have been smooth and even, but that were now cracked and lifted slightly, creating great places to trip. It gave the road character, she thought. She could smell the beef before she heard the sizzle, and her mouth watered. A large green awning covered the metal tables and chairs that were meant to be shared by people eating the tacos or the pizza next door. Since this marina area was a large center for hotels and American tourists, on the right side of the awning was a Pizza Hut window. *Seriously, who comes to another country and eats fast food pizza from back home?* She supposed enough people did, otherwise it wouldn't be in business. On the left side was the window to order tacos, quesadillas, and beer. Every taco came on open corn tortillas instead of flour, and the meat was cut into small, bite-sized pieces. Cilantro and cebolla, or onion, was all that came on them, unless she ordered the quesadilla, which was the same taco, but with cheese and folded in half. It was all delicious.

She ordered her beer and tacos—one al pastor and one de res—and sat down at a table to watch the people come and go. She had no view of the ocean, which was on the other side of the hotels across the street, but it was a shaded area and the beer was cold. In what seemed like seconds, her beer arrived with the server. Taking a big swig, she felt relieved of any lingering hangover. It felt good going down, and it tasted cold and effervescent like beer always should. *What a great afternoon. A morning sleeping in, time at the beach, and now tacos and beer.* She tried to forget the angry interlude with the taxistas that could have ruined her entire day. Maybe she should feel bad for them that they could never have such a beautiful American girl. She regretted thinking that as soon as she'd formed the thought. She was stereotyping them in the worst way, to make herself feel better. That wasn't fair. Plenty of amazing people lived here, generous and friendly and helpful. She only felt this way about the group of taxi drivers who made her uncomfortable every time she walked by! Okay, not every time: early in the mornings on the way to catch the bus for work, few of them were out, and if only one or two, they didn't say anything besides "good morning." They only catcalled when they were in a small crowd like the one today.

She asked herself: *If they were white guys doing it, would I feel the same way?* She would, she thought. Wouldn't she? Before she could answer, the server arrived with her tacos, breaking her train of thought. She didn't want to think about it anymore. She had tacos and beer and life was good. Her life was a Jimmy Buffett song.

Chapter 14

Although the calendar showed December, the heat from the sun didn't let up, and the humidity hadn't yet subsided for "winter." The entire year in Puerto Vallarta is about 85 degrees, and seasons are marked more by changes in rainfall than in temperature. But Izzy had made it through the rainy summer season, and the resort was getting closer and closer to opening. Now she was getting amped up about her holiday trip home.

She had highlighted, circled, and drawn little Christmas trees all over the five days she'd be home; now only four days remained before her departure. At least for Christmas, Gretchen understood that Izzy might want to take time off and fly home. The United States can be great about allowing other cultures to celebrate their respective holidays and religious observations, but that didn't necessarily go the other way. On Thanksgiving, she was in the office as usual, and she decided if she couldn't be home, she'd use the hotel's long distance to call home. After about an hour chatting with her mom, dad, and sister, she got tired of passing the phone around and listening to them describe the food without her being there to taste it.

But now, for Christmas, the rest of the country understood her. They, too, wanted time off to be with family. Gretchen wouldn't go home at all so she could hold down the fort while Alejandra, Valeria, and Izzy took time off. Izzy found it strange that Gretchen wouldn't want to go home, but a flight from Puerto Vallarta to Berlin was probably more expensive and more exhausting for a quick trip home than one from Puerto Vallarta to San Antonio. She felt far enough from home as it was, and she couldn't understand how Gretchen could feel fine spending Christmas alone thousands of miles from her loved ones.

At work, Alejandra and Valeria were civil to her, and Izzy had learned how to have lunch with them without feeling irritated the entire time. But something was still a little off. She didn't quite trust them, and she always had the feeling they were nice to her face but acted otherwise when she was gone. She wanted to be with people she trusted and loved more than anything. Her mom, she knew, she could trust. Her dad, she knew, would adore her. And she couldn't wait to see them.

First, though, she needed to get her passport back from the human resources manager, Maria. Izzy's work visa, called an FM3, would allow her to come and go as a temporary resident of the country rather than simply as a visitor. Thus far, she had been traveling with her passport for business, but she'd handed it over to Maria when she'd had a couple weeks in the office so that Maria could finalize the paperwork for the FM3.

When Izzy arrived at her office, Maria was shuffling papers around and picking up large file folders. Maria's office was more like a storage closet with a computer. Stacks of boxes, papers, and folders lined every inch of space; some of them, half opened, revealed new uniforms or samples of others they hadn't ordered yet. Maria appeared to be looking for something. *I hope it's not my passport*, Izzy thought lightly.

"Hola, Maria," Izzy said.

"Buen día, Isabella," she said politely. "¿Cómo le va?"

"Muy bien, claro. Me siento emocionada con la inauguración, pero más para mi viaje a casa." *The resort opening soon will be exciting, but I'm more excited for my trip home.*

"¡Ah!" Maria said, her face lighting up in recognition. "¿Entonces necesitas tu pasaporte, verdad? Pueeeeees . . . creo que está en la caja fuerte."

She didn't sound confident to Izzy. *In the safe? What safe?*

"Lo busco y te llamaré," Maria instructed. *Let me look for it, and I'll call you.*

Izzy tried not to let her lack of confidence show on her face. "Sí, claro. ¿En diez minutos? ¿Treinta?"

"Hasta mañana," said Maria. "La caja está en el banco."

Izzy was restless that night, and what was normally an easy evening to fill with journaling, walking the beach, or playing around on Facebook was a heavy void of uncertainty. She kept crawling off the couch and wandering the five feet over to the fridge, opening it—there was still nothing in the fridge—closing it, opening it again, forgetting why she was in the kitchen, and finally returning to the couch to browse the four channels she was getting on TV. Finally, relaxing with a long hot shower and telling herself it would all be fine, she climbed into bed.

The next morning, she felt much better about the whole thing, and she was sure Maria had made it to the bank the night before to retrieve her passport. The idea of Maria taking such care to secure her passport had her feeling a bit better. *Probably not a great idea for it to have been lying around her office anyway, so of course she'd take it someplace safe.* The thought comforted her, and she dressed and headed for the bus stop without another worry entering her mind.

Maria wasn't there when Izzy arrived at the resort. *Maybe she had to wait for the bank to open this morning, and then she'd be in.* Izzy made a mental note to check back in a couple hours. After a minimal breakfast of fruit and yogurt, because she still hadn't adjusted to the idea of sandwiches for breakfast, she settled into her day at the office: sending back quotes to travel agents, explaining again to Mr. Silverton that no, she could not make the rates any lower even if he did have a Black American Express card (*because if you have a Black card, you can freakin' afford it!*), and checking the rates on some travel websites filled her morning and into the lunch hour.

At lunch, Ximena appeared in her doorway, right on cue.

"Vámonos, güerita," she insisted as usual. "¡Tengo muchísima hambre, guey!"

Over lunch, Ximena asked about her trip, and her life in America. "Sooooo, wait, you mean you open some presents the night before, and then again in the morning?"

"Yeah!" Izzy grinned from ear to ear.

"And you don't cook that night?"

"No, we go out to this one Italian restaurant my parents love, usually." Visions of past Christmas Eves danced in Izzy's head. In their younger days, she and her sister had let their mom dress them in outfits as if they were twins, even though they were over two years apart. Through middle school and even into high school, their mom would have them open one thing that night before dinner, knowing it was something they might want to wear: sweaters or shoes. It was the smaller boxes the girls got excited for now, of course, and the smaller the better. One year when they'd both received gorgeous small pendants with their birthstones on them—matching yet unique—they'd put them on instantly and were so proud to wear them out.

After lunch, Izzy gave Ximena a quick hug and went to Maria's office. The human resources director was there, her back to Izzy, bending down as if to file something away.

"Hola," Izzy said a bit tentatively. She hoped she hadn't interrupted something.

Maria didn't respond, but merely turned slowly around to face Izzy, eyes cast downward and a tissue in her hand. When she finally looked up at Izzy, her eyes were watery and about to spill over, and were knitted together, causing her forehead to wrinkle, showing her early forties much more than usual.

"¿Estás bien?" Izzy asked, concerned that perhaps she had just interrupted something personal.

"¡Izzy!" Maria said rather loudly as a sob caught in her throat. "¡No puedo encontrarlo! ¡Se me perdió, y no sé cuando y no sé donde, pero no lo tengo! Lo siento. ¡Por favor, discúlpame! ¡Lo siento!" Her shoulders heaved, and she blew into her kleenex.

"What?" Izzy responded in English. *Holy shit. Please tell me I didn't understand her correctly. She didn't just say she lost my passport and can't find it anywhere. Please say I'm misunderstanding.*

Maria was crying almost uncontrollably now, unable to get any rational sentence out.

The floor fell out from under Izzy, and a loud "woosh" roared through her ears. Her blood was boiling, and suddenly she felt hot and confined in this storage closet, this pathetic excuse for an office.

"Tienes que recuperarlo," Izzy said. "No, no, no puedes . . . mi viaje . . ." She was having trouble doing the translating in her head. "You have to FIX THIS!" she finally yelled, sending Maria into a crying fit like a teenage girl who has been caught cheating on her midyear exam. She was sorry, Izzy could see that, but how was this forty-something human resources manager sitting here crying and apologizing? How was she not taking control of the situation and fixing it? Did Izzy have to do this shit herself? Where would she even start? *Dammit, this is fucking insane!* Her rage built, and she wished there was somewhere to direct it. There was Maria: pathetic, wailing Maria.

"No me importa como," Izzy began, "no me importa con quien, pero tienes que arreglar la situación—HOY!"

And with that final vicious command to fix it today, Izzy stood and turned to leave the office.

"¡Espera!" Maria pleaded. "¡Por favor, espera!"

Wait for what? For you to fucking cry all over your desk? Never in a million years could Izzy imagine any of her previous bosses or directors of human resources, or even an HR admin, for that matter, breaking down bawling about a mistake, no matter how large. And this was a huge one: not only could Izzy not leave to get home for Christmas, she couldn't leave the country, period! She was trapped! Feeling claustrophobic, choking on anger, and head spinning with fury, Izzy gave Maria one last opportunity to say something as she glared ice cold bullets straight into her eyes.

Maria drew in a sharp breath, like a child calming down after a tantrum. "Podemos llamar a la embajada para ver si pueda hacerte un nuevo pasaporte."

"¡Llámalos inmediatamente!" Izzy said venomously. *If you can call the embassy to get a new one, you better fucking do it right fucking now.*

"Por favor," Maria started, "dame una hora, más o menos—"

Without answering her about it taking an hour or so, Izzy stormed out of the office, nearly running into Felipe in the hallway. She didn't even care. She was livid and wondering whether she could illegally sneak into the US at the border in time for Christmas.

Back in her office, Izzy couldn't think of anything except how unjust and unfair this whole thing was. Breathing didn't help, and the more she thought about the mess, the closer she came to tears all over again. She was still too amped up to calm down and get any semblance of work done. She wasn't sure if Gretchen had been informed or not, but she had a feeling Gretchen wouldn't have much sympathy. She wanted to close her door and throw a fit like she was nine years old again, crying into her pillow and screaming and letting out all her anger about how it wasn't fair. She ran in circles, unable to escape the red-hot monster that had formed in her mind.

The anger made her feel out of control, like when the wave had taken control of her entire body after she fell off her surfboard for the first time. *Maybe a walk. The ocean*, she decided.

Once outside, she could breathe deeper, and the salty air was a welcome friend. The heat of the day matched the heat of her emotions and seemed to balance her. The whoosh of the waves, constant and predictable, sounded in her ears and penetrated to her heart. *Relax*, they said. *It will be okay.*

It was the Saturday before Christmas, and she had no idea if she'd be seeing her family. She had already missed Thanksgiving, and now this. *But you wanted to be here*, she reminded herself. Plenty of people came to Puerto Vallarta for Christmas as well.

Yeah, but they bring their families with them! She sighed heavily. What could she do now? Was there anyone she could call? Anyone in the US government she could file a complaint with? Maybe, but most likely not.

Okay, Iz, worst-case scenario is you can't go home. Then what?

Her mind went through the options and tried to help clear the anger as she worked toward a positive outcome. She could Skype from home and see everyone, since she was off work. She could spend time surfing again, maybe see if Ricio and his friend wanted to hang out. She could even approach Gretchen to see whether this might be an opportunity to try building a relationship again. There were plenty of restaurants she hadn't tried, and there were plenty of bars and clubs to experience. If nothing else, she was living on a gorgeous beach with a pool and could spend her days on the sand.

It could be worse, she thought. *You could be stuck in some awful place instead of on a beach in a resort town.*

Taking a final deep inhale and letting it out slowly, timing it with the sound of the waves rushing from the shore, she felt better and returned to her office.

The day dragged by as she waited for an update. The clock mocked her, and the seconds slowed down just to spite her. An hour had passed with no updates. An hour and fifteen minutes. Almost two hours. *Okay, her time is up. I'm going back to her office.*

A line of people had formed outside Maria's office. *What the hell?* Izzy thought impatiently. *She doesn't have time for you!* She decided she would look in the office for a moment before taking her place in the line. If she poked her head in and Maria saw her, maybe Maria would wave Izzy in ahead of everyone else. *What the hell could they possibly need that was more urgent, anyway?*

Maria's assistant Carlos was behind her desk. He must have seen her confused look.

"Hola, Isabella," he greeted her. "Maria se fue a la embajada para usted. Ella me dijo que iba a llamar a tu cellular cuando esté terminanda."

Maria was at the embassy and would call Izzy's cell when she was done. *But if she's calling my cell, that means she expects it to take longer than today's workday?* Izzy wanted to ask more questions and maybe even follow Maria to the embassy herself. Instead, she meekly answered, "Oh, okay, gracias," and slunk back to her office. There was really nothing to do but wait.

She stared at her computer screen without really seeing it when Ximena appeared in her doorway again.

"Hey," Ximena said quietly. "You okay?"

"Hola," Izzy said back weakly. "Not really."

"I heard. Everyone heard," Ximena shared.

"Everyone? What do you mean?" Izzy asked, a little panic settled in her throat.

"Well, Izzy," Ximena started to explain, "these offices aren't that large, and Maria's door wasn't closed. Sooooo I think pretty much everyone knows."

"Oh, well, good then, they realize how stupid she is!" Izzy said defensively.

"Just be careful. You know our big boss really likes her and hired her from his old hotel."

By "big boss" she meant the general manager, who wasn't a warm and fuzzy type of guy. Undoubtedly Ximena was trying to offer some helpful advice, but it sounded like a divisive taking of sides in Izzy's clouded state of mind. Was she taking Maria's side? Did everyone think Izzy was a bitch for yelling at her?

"But she lost my *passport*! I can't even leave this country for work, let alone for my Christmas vacation to finally go see my family!" The anger that had been cooled by the ocean was starting to simmer again.

"I'm sure it's hard, but you also were pretty mean to her when she was already sorry to you," Ximena offered, shrugging her shoulders. Izzy stared at her, feeling wounded. What the hell did Ximena know? She hadn't been there! Before she could remind her of that, Ximena started again.

"Listen . . . I understand you, and how upset you are. But not everyone here knows you like that and understands how important this is. They just heard how mean you were and how Maria cried so much. I guess a lot of people saw her afterward."

So that was it. Maria had retreated somewhere, and people had asked her why she was sobbing and so upset. And without knowing Izzy well, it was clear whose side they were on. Izzy felt desperate to justify her behavior to everyone. Suddenly, she wanted to reach out to all the staff she passed in the halls every day and ask for their support and their understanding. Ximena must have seen it on her face.

"Don't worry, it's just something to talk about, but I'm sure it will pass." She gave Izzy a hug before heading back to her own office and added, "It's just that more people here know Maria, and they don't know you."

Izzy left as usual around 3:00 p.m. and headed back to the city. Ximena had asked her about going clubbing tonight, but Izzy decided to take a rain check because she felt more like wallowing in her sadness. At least Ximena had felt some compassion and sympathized with her about how crappy it would be not to see her family. Izzy was grateful for Ximena's attempt, but it only made her feel more bummed about the whole idea of spending the holiday alone.

At her apartment, she sulked over to her fridge. Finding nothing appetizing, she grabbed a bottle of water and heaved herself onto one of her couches. She didn't want to try to have fun. What could be fun when she was being stripped of the only thing she'd been looking forward to? At that moment, all of her experiences here felt empty, pointless—her stupid job, friends she wasn't sure she liked, even the surfing lesson and the dolphin. She wanted to erase all of it. In fact, this entire move seemed like the worst thing she'd ever done.

She'd been sitting on the couch for what felt like a lifetime when her toy phone started buzzing.

"¿Bueno?" she answered, her breath catching in her throat.

"¿Isabella? Habla Maria." Maria sounded hopeful, which could be a good sign there was decent news coming.

"Hola, Maria," Izzy said, sounding like a parent speaking to a child they had just scolded.

"Tengo buenas noticias," she said. "Pero tienes que salir mañana." *Good news—but you have to leave tomorrow.*

"Okaaayyyy," Izzy responded, leaving an awkward silence as a fill-in-the-blank.

Maria explained. She'd been to an office where an embassy representative sat, but it wasn't an official embassy office, and they couldn't process anything there. The closest American embassy that could reissue an American passport was in Guadalajara. They had already booked Izzy's flight there, and she would leave tomorrow. A private escort from the government would meet her at the airport and take her through security. They had arranged an appointment for her first thing Monday morning when they opened as a special favor, and they had arranged for a hotel stay in Guadalajara right next door to the embassy office. Maria gave her the addresses, names, and information she needed. She had also apparently faxed all the documents directly to the gentleman at the embassy, who would be waiting for her in the morning.

"Wow," Izzy said after Maria finished her entire story. "Pues . . . gracias por tu ayuda."

Maybe Maria wasn't so pathetic after all. She had found resources and put this all together—and pretty quickly, Izzy had to admit. She had just enough days left before her trip home to get to Guadalajara and back with a new passport if everything went as planned.

"De nada, Izzy. Lo siento otra vez." *You're welcome, Izzy. I'm sorry again.*

"Está bien, Maria. Gracias por arreglar todo."

It was actually okay, and she was in that moment extremely grateful that Maria had fixed everything.

~

The official who met Izzy at the airport was wearing jeans and a polo shirt, and he certainly didn't appear to be some government official as Izzy had pictured in her mind. She was thinking more like black suit, white shirt, black tie, and an earpiece of some sort. He told Izzy he was happy to help her: surprisingly, this happened more often than Izzy would have thought. Visitors would lose their passports or forget where they put them, and would be panicked about trying to get home. Oftentimes he could help make things happen from Puerto Vallarta, but in this case, since it was the hotel, her employer, and not herself who lost the passport, he had to send her directly to the offices in Guadalajara. Once she had passed through the security stanchions, he waved goodbye and wished her luck.

Normally her flights took her through the main terminal for the larger planes, but for this quick domestic flight she headed downstairs and into a small area of the airport she'd never seen. It was like one big glass holding tank, and they called over the PA system when a little plane drove up from the runway and parked outside. It felt surreal that just a day ago she had been walking the beach, listening to the waves telling her to relax, and trying to dream up a solution, and now she sat waiting for the flight that would hopefully get her what she needed to get home.

Breathing a bit more intentionally, she picked up the book she had brought for the trip. Her book collection had started to grow considerably since she had taken this job and found herself bored in airports and on planes. But she loved all the travel. Every trip was a new adventure, a new possibility, a new friend, or a chance meeting. The romance of the entire thing was, originally, about the time she'd spend in Mexico and who she might run into and meet. She was quickly discovering, however, that the romance was also in every new city she'd never experienced. She was already anticipating her next trip, and then Toronto, then Chicago, then New York City, then back to Los Angeles, and then to Vegas. But first, today: Guadalajara. She wondered what it would be like. Sitting in the airport, she suddenly saw the lost passport as another adventure, and she couldn't help but laugh. She owed it all to Maria.

If she could handle this, she decided as the PA called her flight, she could probably handle just about anything.

Chapter 15

Christmas had been wonderful, relaxing, and a bit annoying, as the time home often could be. She loved her family, but the strange feeling of competition, or whatever it was, could also be draining.

Now back in the office, time went by quickly, and in what felt like the blink of an eye, she was packing for her next trip.

Her last few trips had been to the Los Angeles area to see the myriad travel agencies there that catered to people with lots of money who could afford her resort. This time she was traveling all the way up the Pacific coast to Seattle. She'd go from Seattle to Chicago to New York City and back. Not bad, except it was winter, so flight delays would be constant, and she'd need lots of luggage. Surveying her few winter clothes, she tried to piece together different outfits in her mind. Wearing the same thing in each city, even if nobody was with her to know, somehow seemed wrong. Laying things out day by day, she paired pantyhose and tights, panties and shirts, along with the little bits of jewelry that might make each outfit seem different. It was all a far cry from the shorts and flip-flops she had been wearing for months now, but she was excited to wear something different than the same old summer clothes.

As she made her way downstairs to catch her flight, her mind rechecked where she had put her new passport, her ID, her headphones, and her phones, including the US phone she turned on when back in the States. Preoccupied with her mental checklist, she had been on autopilot to get downstairs and now found herself at the driveway as her mind jerked her back to the current reality. As long as a taxi was ready and waiting as they normally were, she'd be fine. The security guard would get one for her from the waiting taxistas, and she'd make her flight.

But this morning, a car was being checked in at the welcome station, and the guard didn't have time to get her a car. She looked down the sidewalk in the direction of the bus stop, where many of the taxistas usually bided their time waiting for the next ride, the same place she had walked through feeling like a piece of meat and calling them assholes. But she couldn't miss her flight, could she? *Okay, this will be fast, and there are always at least a few drivers over there.*

Taking matters into her own hands, she lugged her oversized suitcase to the sidewalk so she could wave to one of them for a ride. Sweat formed at her hairline from the humidity; she steadied the bag and dropped her laptop case next to it. When she looked up the road to the station, however, it was empty.

"Shit," she said out loud. "Don't tell me there isn't a single one in sight." The butterflies were back, and her mind worked to find another way. She calculated the time it might take her to get to the nearest hotel, where they'd have the number of the taxi dispatcher, when a yellow taxi rounded the corner from her left, coming out of a small residential area she'd never noticed before. She jumped into the street and waved him down as he drove, at a snail's pace, toward her. *Could he be any less concerned about my waving? Use the other pedal, the one that makes the car go,* she thought impatiently.

The car arrived at the curb and the trunk popped. Without greeting the driver, she immediately started lugging her bag to the edge of the sidewalk.

As she struggled to get a handle on the heavy bag, the driver's hands intercepted her and easily lifted the bag from the sidewalk and into the trunk. It was him. The one she'd called a pendejo as he'd called out to her about being someone out of his dreams.

Closing the trunk, he looked at her. Did he recognize her? Of course he did. How many other small, blonde, curly-haired girls roamed around the marina area regularly? How many of them had spoken rudely in Spanish to him? Her palms started to sweat in fear.

"¿Está lista?" he asked. *Was she ready?*

"Sí," she answered meekly. "Estoy atrasada." *She was running late.*

"Vámonos, entonces," he instructed, and he opened her car door.

The trip was silent for the most part, as they bumped along the cobblestones and over the speed bumps. Traffic was building on the main road out of the marina area, so he took a quick left and started down another route she didn't recognize. She wondered if he'd ever thought about retaliating against her; if he was abducting her now that he had the chance.

"Es un chort-cut," he said, looking into the rearview mirror at her. "To miss traffic," he added plainly.

More awkward silence ensued as they bumped along past what looked like private homes and chain-link fences. She hadn't known this neighborhood was over here. It appeared to be homes people lived in full time rather than vacation spots or condos. The views were of the overgrown areas that hadn't been developed, rather than the ocean or the mountains on the other side of the highway, so maybe the pricing was different than the oceanfront places. She would have asked normally, but knowing who this driver was and what she had said to him, she opted out of the small talk. Trying to look around at the scenery and relax a little bit, she couldn't help but notice the cross hanging from his rearview mirror. Like many Catholics, he had a rosary swinging with every bump and turn and a small picture of the Virgin Mary on his dashboard. To the right of that was a picture of a young boy holding a soccer ball. The boy must have been six or seven and was beaming at the camera, his dark hair falling every which way as if he'd been running around without a care in the world.

"¿Su hijo?" she asked him tentatively.

"Sí, mi hijo," he answered flatly. "Tiene cuatro años."

He's four? Okay, she was a little off on judging children's ages. But the photo and rosary showed he was a father, a religious man, and a provider. Suddenly she wondered if she should apologize to him for what she'd said. As soon as that thought formed, she felt defensive. *If he was such a good guy, why did he stare at me and try to get my attention? He must have a wife, too, or at least there was a mother somewhere in the picture. And they were angering me and making me feel uncomfortable. I was right to say what I said.*

As she was making this argument in her head, the taxista turned into the airport and navigated toward the drop-off line. She decided she didn't need to say anything or apologize for anything. She would just hand him the cash and be done.

Stopping at the curb, he exited the vehicle and popped the trunk. Setting her suitcase on the sidewalk, he opened her door as Izzy repacked her wallet after getting the necessary pesos out.

"Gracias," she said as she handed him the cash.

He refused payment. "No, señorita, es gratis."

Izzy stood in the beaming sun, damp from the humidity and hair amiss after the ride with windows down, as a bead of sweat formed below her bra line and slid down to the small of her back. Time seemed to stand still as she looked into his face. At first she felt guilt. Then she felt anger; he was making her look like a jerk. Finally, however, she felt prideful. Of course it would be free; he had offended her deeply and owed her something. But then he turned to leave her outstretched hand, still awkwardly lifted in an offering, and in the end, she felt sad.

"¡Gracias!" she said to his back as he walked around the back side of the car to climb into the driver's seat again.

He glanced at her over the top of the car, face unchanged, and then he ducked into his vehicle and closed the car door firmly. Without looking at her again, he drove away, leaving her standing at the sidewalk's edge.

Her eyes stung and her throat tightened. She desperately wanted to be right, to not have to feel the truth of the moment. The noise around her returned, and the next taxi pulled up to drop off another passenger. Breathing deeply, she grabbed the handle of her suitcase with her left hand and adjusted the laptop case on her right shoulder, and then headed through the sliding glass doors to the ticket counter. She had a plane to catch.

~

Seattle was a gorgeous city, and she was excited to spend time in it. Izzy had been born there, and although she had been back to visit her grandparents on the outskirts of the city, she only vaguely remembered what the city was like. She had been to Pike Place Market as a child, which she had fuzzy memories of, but if she was being honest, her expectations were solidly built on what she had seen in *Sleepless in Seattle* with Tom Hanks.

She had chosen to stay at a competitor's hotel so she could get a better rate and be closer to the market. She had a few appointments in the downtown area that she would be able to walk to, and a couple across the water in Bellevue she'd need to take a taxi to, but she had intentionally built free time into her Seattle visit rather than spending her time running around from one appointment to the next. She had learned to do this after several trips to Los Angeles. Her colleagues from other hotels who were more well traveled than she was had also encouraged her to take the time to experience each place. She might never be back again, they said.

It had been easy to enjoy Los Angeles because she always had other people with her. They knew the restaurants to try and the places to go in between appointments, like little cafes where they might catch a glimpse of a star, or small markets—Joan's on Third was one—to use for catered lunches with big travel agent offices. The idea of all these people who didn't seem to have anywhere to be, who sat at small sidewalk tables sipping espresso and contemplating the world, had been such a delight to Izzy.

For this trip, she was on her own. She'd have some folks to meet up with in New York when she got there, but on this trip she'd planned everything herself and set her own appointments based on the business inquiries she'd received from a few of the agencies here.

After months of heat and sunshine, Seattle's cloudy, cool climate was a welcome change. Beyond invigorating her senses, it signaled to her body that she had arrived in this new place, alone, and she was about to take control of her visit. She felt excitement and a surge of energy. *I can do this.*

At the front desk of her hotel, she asked for a good local seafood restaurant, and the concierge recommended she take a trip to someplace called Salty's. The taxi ride gave her a chance to see the city. The route took them down toward the ports where all the huge tankers unloaded. Cranes and big equipment had ceased work for the evening but boasted their power and strength just the same. As they crossed the bridge to the other side of the Sound, the scene changed from big city to a residential feel. Although the sun hid behind the layers of clouds, everything was bright green and seemed to brighten the world around her.

Within a few minutes, the restaurant came into view: an old gray building with blue scrawled lettering that said *Salty's*. The driver offered to return when she was finished and gave her his card, which she gladly took and thanked him for the offer.

"Good evening, miss. Welcome to Salty's," the host greeted her. "Are you meeting someone here?"

"No," she replied, "table for one."

She asked to sit by the window, and it was everything she had hoped it would be. The view across the water was gorgeous with tall downtown buildings and the lights coming on in the evening twilight, the beautiful Space Needle standing valiantly over them all. Between the shore where the restaurant sat and the city beyond, she watched sea lions play in the sound, jumping out of the water and climbing over crab pot markers. She laughed to herself.

"Good evening, miss," the waiter greeted her as he reached for her water glass to fill it. "Are we waiting on someone this evening?" he asked.

"Nope, just me," she said back to him. She hadn't meant to sound defensive or aggressive, but she must have, because he quickly answered, "Oh, yes, of course," and quickly removed the extra place setting.

He explained the menu, the raw bar, and the specials for the day. She'd never tried oysters, and she knew her dad would be excited if she did so now, but she opted out. Instead she went for the lobster bisque and the catch of the day.

"Would you like a glass of wine with that?" he asked.

She smiled from ear to ear. "Why not?"

As the sun disappeared and the sea lions made their way to wherever they spent their evenings, the city lights began to dance along the calm waters of Puget Sound. The last of the small fishing boats had been docked and tied up for the night. She had never tasted soup that delicious, and the fish was perfect. Savoring the last few sips of the second glass of wine, Izzy sat back in her seat and assessed her situation. Was she lonely? A little bit. It sure would have been fun to have her dad there, or both her parents, to enjoy a bit of their past. But despite not having someone to share this with, she had done it anyway. She might never be back to Seattle, and she might never have the chance to eat at Salty's again. A new feeling began to grow and spread through her body. Not angst or worry or tension. She took another sip and let her shoulders drop. Taking a deep breath, she tried to put words to her feelings. Satisfaction. She felt pride and satisfaction that she had done something on her own without feeling scared, and had truly enjoyed it.

Huh, she thought. *Who knew.*

One evening at her hotel, as she was looking through all her friends' pages on Facebook—softball games she'd missed, hilarious drunken bar scenes, and some strange food pictures she could have done without—a notification popped up. It was a friend request from Jenny. Isabella's heart rate jumped, and her stomach did a nervous and excited flip. It was as if an imaginary line had been crossed from work relationship to friendship, inviting Izzy in to her personal stories and pictures. Essentially into her life. Maybe she felt strangely excited because Jenny was the first face she'd connected with on her first trip, the first person she felt she could rely on, other than Carrie, to help her through this intimidating new career and life she was building. Jenny represented not only a great person and new friend, but the proof that Izzy could make new friends and build new memories without having to rely on the past. She was going to make it no matter where life took her.

Accepting Jenny's friend request, she got back to work. With only a few hours left before heading back to the airport, she needed to ensure that no emergencies had popped up anywhere. Opening her email, she poured herself some water from the tall, slender glass bottle they had sent up as a welcome amenity, and she sorted through her 102 new inbox messages. One caught her eye, and adrenaline surged through her. The contact she had been working with to get in to the rewards program from the trade shows a few months ago had sent her an email.

She remembered Gretchen's words about how important these shows were. It was a bad habit, but her self-esteem was tied to performance; and if she wasn't performing, whether at softball or dance competitions or work, she felt worthless and would spend mental energy and emotions beating herself up. For months, she had been building up so much pressure about this first attempt to get into the resort program, the evidence that would prove whether she could make it in this job.

But then she caught herself. *Izzy, you just spent a nice dinner alone by yourself and enjoyed it. And you surfed and made new friends and ate freshly caught sushi. Even if you don't get into this thing, you're a brave person, and people want to be friends with you. You are successful. Don't get so caught up in this.*

With that, she took a cleansing breath and clicked the email to open it.

Congratulations. We are extremely pleased to welcome your resort into our program for 2009–2010.

Jumping out of her chair, Izzy threw her hands over her head, tilted her head back, and let out a "woohoo!" Stepping over to the window overlooking Seattle, she looked out at the world and said to it, "Do you see that? I can do it! I got us in!" Smiling so hard her cheeks were starting to hurt, her mind ran through the list of names she could call to celebrate with.

Going back to her computer, she searched for Jenny's name in her inbox. Noting her office number in her signature line, Izzy picked up her personal phone and dialed her new friend. As it rang, she thought about how tomorrow she'd go home and share with Gretchen the good news, and maybe, just maybe, Gretchen would show a sign that she was proud of Izzy. But for now, she would enjoy this, she thought, as she heard Jenny pick up the phone.

Chapter 16

"¿Qué vamos hacer esta noche?" she texted Luciana and Ximena from her apartment back home in Puerto Vallarta, asking what they should do tonight.

"¡Cenamos y luego bailamos!" Ximena responded. Of course: eating and dancing. What else would they do?

They made plans to meet at what Luciana called Los Mapaches—"The Raccoons"—a restaurant Izzy hadn't heard of or tried, and then to hit the downtown area for some dancing and fun. Izzy spent the afternoon soaking in some sun and getting some much-needed reflection time in her journal. She took the time to take mental snapshots of the views, the mountains, the ocean waves crashing upon the rocky jetties, and the brilliant blue skies above. Her focus had shifted: instead of looking inward, feeling insecure and worried, she was looking outward at the beauty around her and the experiences she could create. Once her mind shifted, this place shifted. Now she was comfortable alone, and she sort of enjoyed it. Only in spurts, of course: she was still excited to spend the evening out with the girls.

The nights were warm, and even with a breeze, the air felt heavy with the day's heat. Add dancing and tequila, Izzy would soon be sweating and her hair turned to frizz. Instead of opting for jeans, heels, and a satin blouse, she went with shorts, a cotton shirt, and flip-flops. Who was she there to impress anyway?

"Okay, no te preocupes de los mapaches," Luciana explained. "No son peligrosos. Son como mascotas." *Don't worry about the raccoons. They're not dangerous—they're like pets.*

Wait, what? The restaurant where they'd met turned out to have a different name than "Los Mapaches," but she hadn't thought too much about it, since the girls were there when she walked in. Now it was clear that, yes, it was a nickname, but the reason had her a little jumpy!

They were led to a small table outside on the patio. Not long after the waiter brought their chips and salsa, they appeared: raccoons the size of small dogs tentatively made their way out of the surrounding bushes. At first only one or two came, and they sat, eerily watching the girls eat their chips.

"Holy shit!" Izzy exclaimed in English: Luciana hadn't been joking. "¡No estabas bromeando!"

"¡Sip!" Luciana said in return. "¡Cuídate, porque si no tienes cuidado, los mapaches tomarán la carne de tu taco!" *If you're not careful, they'll steal the meat from your taco!*

No freaking way. Izzy couldn't believe it. But she continued to watch the other tables feeding them, dropping chips on the floor, some trying to get raccoons to take the chips from their hands. It was like a show for them. And no wonder the raccoons weren't bothered by people.

Izzy decided to join the fun. *When are you going to have a chance to interact with a raccoon?* Taking a chip in her hand and leaning slightly to her right, she displayed the chip. One of the raccoons looked her dead in the eyes. He hesitated. *Is he deciding if he can trust me? I should decide if I can trust him!* Taking a few steps toward her, then a few more, he approached her hand and reached for the chip with his. Looking at her as he tenderly grasped the fried tortilla, as if to make sure she was offering, she invited him to take it.

"Sí, tómalo," she said. "Es para ti."

He took the chip with his hand, like a small child, and he put it to his mouth, crunching on it and eating it completely. *How cute! They are like little pets!* Amused by the situation, she didn't notice the other raccoon approaching from her left side until Luciana and Ximena both started laughing.

"¿Qué pasa?" she asked. "¿Se están riendo de mi?" She turned in time to see the second raccoon standing up on his legs and reaching over the table to take the rest of Izzy's chips from her plate! *What the fuck? You little assholes!* They had worked as a team, one distracting Izzy so the other could get all the chips, not just one.

The girls thoroughly enjoyed themselves at Izzy's expense. In spite of herself, Izzy laughed too.

A few drinks and tacos later, they were ready to head to the club. They decided to take a taxi instead of having Ximena drive this time so they could drink whatever they wanted without worrying about driving or leaving the car somewhere. Windows down and Latin pop music blasting, per their request, the taxi driver made his way through the busy main road that ran parallel to the ocean. The same road Izzy had walked months before, admiring the local scene, now looked like a new place with vibrant lights and music in the air. As the pavement gave way to cobblestone, the taxi slowed and bumped his way down the main malecón: the strip that overlooked the boardwalk and ocean, where the Cuban club Izzy had once visited was located. But instead of stopping somewhere along this road, the girls directed him to take a left, taking them from the tourist area of bass-pumping night clubs and into the residential areas with small shops and laundromats like the one she had noticed on her first stroll downtown. Nothing seemed familiar.

"Ya llegamos," the driver announced. Pulling paper bills out of their small clutches, the girls combined their pesos to pay the driver and got out at the bottom of a staircase leading to what seemed like a small apartment complex.

"¿Qué es esto?" Izzy asked the girls.

"¡Una sorpresa!" Ximena and Luciana shouted in unison. *A surprise.*

Climbing the rock staircase, hand firmly on the black steel railing leading them upward, Izzy eyed the entrance and looked for clues as to what exactly they were about to do. There wasn't exactly loud club music pouring out, like the open-air clubs on the malecón. *Maybe a smoking lounge or something?* Paying the cover at the door, they entered the dark room. To Izzy's surprise, it was packed with tables full of people laughing and drinks clinking. And there, in the front of the room, was the surprise: a karaoke stage with handheld mics, monitors, and a screen for the audience to see and sing along. It wasn't occupied as they walked in, but as they were shown to their table, a brave man stepped up and started to belt out what must have been an old Mexican ballad from decades ago.

Luciana asked the server for their book of songs. "¡Vamos a cantar!" she said.

"¡*Ustedes* van a cantar!" Izzy said. "¡No lo puedo! I can't!

"¡Síiiiiií!" Ximena chimed in. "Si prefieres, puedes cantar en inglés. Pero vas a cantar esta noche." *You can sing in English if you want, but you're going to sing tonight.*

"Okay. ¡Pues, tienen que cantar primero!" Izzy teased. "Y luego yo lo intentaré. ¡Pero no antes de más tequila!" *You have to sing first, and later I'll try. But not before more tequila!*

They ordered shots and gulped them down with salt and lime. Then another round. Guzzling water in between not just to stay hydrated, but to try and wash out the taste of nasty silver tequila, Izzy was starting to feel looser and more at ease. Perusing the song list, she decided to try one in Spanish, but one she knew. *How about Shakira? Yes! I can do that one!* Without thinking it through, she flagged down the cocktail server and pointed to the song on the list.

"¡Éste!" she exclaimed.

What seemed like seconds later, she was ushered up on stage and handed the mic. Looking out at the crowd, she found Luciana and Ximena back at the table cheering and clapping with their arms over their heads.

Oh shit, Iz, you just did this. No, tequila did this! Either way, she was up here, so no backing down now.

The MC announced that "la güerita" was about to sing Shakira. The music started, and Izzy stared at the screen blankly. *I don't know those words! I know the English ones. What the hell am I doing?* The words on the monitor started changing color rapidly. She was missing them all! The entire first verse was gone! *Damn, this lady sings so fast!*

She looked up at the quick breath between verses to see Ximena nodding pointedly. Taking a deep breath, she started in on the second verse, just reading along and trying to keep up. *Thank God for tequila.*

"Yo puedo escalar los Andes," she sang. It didn't sound half bad; she had the accents right, at least. Soon she began to lose herself in the song, no longer even thinking about all the people in the audience. She was enjoying herself and moving with the beat as she bobbed around, trying to keep up with Shakira's quick transitions between words. Laughing when she missed and playing with the audience, encouraging them to sing along, she finished the song amid claps and cheers. *They liked it! Or they liked that I tried.* Of course she was fun to watch. What other white, curly-haired girls attempted to sing karaoke in Spanish in the middle of Puerto Vallarta? Even if it required shots first. Beaming, she left the stage and returned to the girls.

"¡Tu turno ahora!" she laughed, telling the girls it was their turn now.

"¡No! ¡Nunca!" Luciana protested. *Never!*

"¡Ay, chica, no canto—nunca! Solamente bailo," Ximena added. *I don't sing, girl! I just dance.*

"¿Cómo?" Izzy demanded. "¿Ustedes me forsaron a cantar, pero ustedes no lo van a hacer? ¿Qué onda?" *You made me sing, but you won't do it yourself? What's up with that?*

She felt as if they'd set her up to be a fool, but she knew it was good fun. If they didn't have the confidence to do it too, even with tequila, so be it.

They were sitting at the table watching a couple young guys on stage attempting to serenade the crowd with an oldie but goodie love song from Luis Miguel when Ximena's phone lit up.

"Gabriel," she said, and her face lit up along with her phone as she checked the text message. Luciana and Izzy looked at each other, rolled their eyes, and then clinked their glasses. They knew this would go one of two ways. Either they would meet up with Gabriel and his friends, or Ximena would leave them on their own. Both had happened before, and some nights it gave Luciana and Izzy an easy out, a way to get home at a decent hour. Decent, as in before 4:00 a.m.

"¡Están en el malecón!" Ximena cried to the girls. Gabriel and his friends were on the main strip, only a few blocks away.

"¿Pues, vámonos, eh?" Luciana responded, as if there were any other answer.

Waving down their cocktail server to pay the bill, they headed down the stairs, which seemed quite a bit steeper this time, and out to the streets. Now that she had made the mistake of wearing heels out once or twice, Izzy was grateful her flip-flops helped keep her steadier over the cobblestone streets, even if inside the club she felt a bit dressed down. Just one wrong move and she'd go crashing down, twisting an ankle, and then it wouldn't matter how cute her shoes were. Passing late-night taco stands, late-night laundry facilities, and young kids still out playing in the streets, the girls made their way back down the hillside, spilling out onto the main road parallel to the ocean. *It must not be that late if the kids are still out. Then again, do kids around here really have bedtimes and rooms of their own to play inside? Probably not.* Even in her drunken haze, Isabella noticed the difference in lifestyles. For that moment, as brief as it was, she acknowledged that she was lucky to have grown up the way she did.

The malecón was alive and jumping with the sounds of the passing cars and open-air clubs competing to have music louder than each other. They passed the little Cuban place she had seen before, but it seemed a bit too relaxed for where Gabriel's crew would most likely be. Ximena led the way, darting across traffic to the flat boardwalk, where she could walk along the water and look back across the street at the names of the clubs. It was easier to see them from this side of the street than it was to stand underneath them.

"¡Aquí está!" she pointed, finding the name of the club Gabriel had sent her. Without looking both ways, she darted again, this time across both lanes of traffic, leaving Luciana and Izzy stranded on the malecón on the other side. Luciana shouted at her to wait, but Ximena was on a mission and wasn't turning back.

"Ay, cabrón," Luciana said, sucking her teeth and rolling her eyes.

Traffic was building, so as people pulled over in their taxis to get out, blocking one direction, the girls had an easier time sprinting across the one lane that might be moving. Finally, at the door of the club, they showed their IDs, got their hands stamped, and joined the hot, sweaty mass of people pushing one way then another trying to get to the bar, to the dance floor, to the bathroom.

The club was on multiple levels: one at street level, another three or four steps above, and then a third floor up circular staircases at the back, where the restrooms were. On the second level, they spotted Ximena in a booth with several men at a low table that held four or five almost empty bottles of vodka, tequila, and rum. *Wow; bottle service, huh? Wonder what they're celebrating.* Ximena waved dramatically for them to come over.

Gabriel was the nicest dressed, which meant he was in jeans, sneakers, a white tank top, and a button-down shirt with the bottom three buttons still buttoned. The others wore only undershirt tank tops, shorts, or jeans. A few had tied their other shirts around their heads. *Is that supposed to be cute? They look ghetto as hell—definitely not from the hotel. Ugh. I am not talking to these fools. I need a drink.*

"¡Luci!" Izzy yelled over the noise. "¡Vamos a los baños!"

Luciana nodded and grabbed Izzy's hand, preparing to snake their way through the crowd toward the bathrooms.

"¡Nos preparo las bebidas, chicas!" Gabriel shouted, letting them know he'd be mixing their drinks while they were gone. *Should that worry me? Eh, probably not. I know where he works.*

"¡Okay, muy bien, gracias!" Izzy shouted back.

The throngs of people were dancing and mocking sex on the floor, basically dry humping each other. It didn't seem contained to one area. They were all over the place, including against the walls under the stairs right by the restrooms. *Ugh, that can't be a romantic place to fake sex. But who said anything about being romantic in a club?* The lines were long and the girls were drunk, so the conversation was limited. Izzy and Luciana pointed at people they were watching as they stood in line and laughed at some idiots on the first floor by the open-air archways. The tourists were easy to find; they were the ones dressed in button-down shirts with loafers. And, typically, they weren't great at dancing. Something about the sexual hip movements of Latin America didn't quite translate to non-Latinos. *Well, your hips definitely don't move like Shakira's either,* Izzy told herself. *Maybe you should practice that.*

Breaking their way back out of the steamy ladies' room, the girls emerged and had a decision to make. Should they head to the bar and the dance floor, leaving Ximena where she was in the capable hands of Gabe and his friends, or should they return to the table to ensure she was all right? Something about the idea of this group of men pouring and serving drinks to Ximena alone didn't sit well with Izzy.

"¿Tenemos que regresar a Ximena?" she asked Luciana, who nodded in return. Grabbing hands again, the girls wound their way between groups of friends, through circles of girls, and squeezed through gyrating bodies grinding on one another, finally making it to the table.

"Ah!" the men shouted as if they'd been buddies forever and were reuniting. "¡Regresaron!" Gabriel handed them drinks, which Izzy eyed for a moment before pouring down her throat. The cold liquid felt amazing in the stifling hot club. Then the bite came. *Whoa! What the fuck is in this?*

"What the fuck is in this?" she said out loud, in English.

"¿Qué?" one of the guys asked.

"¿Qué contiene esta bebida?" Izzy asked. "¡Es muy fuerte!"

"¡Oh! Un poquito de vodka y un poquito de tequila, con jugo y hielo," Gabriel explained.

Vodka and tequila? Fuck. This is going to get ridiculous.

As Izzy tried to deaden her taste buds near the back of her tongue to take another sip, Luciana elbowed her hard, nearly sending her sideways into the guy standing to her left.

"¿Qué pasó?" Izzy asked assertively, gesturing to where Luciana hit her.

"¡Mira quien es!" she said as she motioned toward the front door.

It was Felipe. He had disappointed them at La Posada, but now here he was. *He looks good outside his work clothes*, Izzy found herself thinking.

Luciana fluffed her hair and adjusted her clothes. She unbuttoned one of her top buttons to reveal a bit more cleavage and hiked her skirt up a tad more as she flung her hair off her shoulders to reveal as much skin as possible. *Damn, get it, girl*, Izzy thought. *I can't compete with that!* Izzy couldn't do much adjusting with her pullover blouse and shorts, but she made sure they were on straight.

As Felipe made his way around the table to greet the men with firm hand slaps and the girls with tender cheek kisses, the group shifted around to make room for him to stand.

"No, no, estoy bien aquí," he said, waving his left palm at the group to say that they didn't need to move. He went to stand by Luciana. *Oh okay, that's cool*, Izzy found herself thinking. She guessed that Luciana would probably go home with him, or vice versa, after first bumping and grinding on the dance floor as practice before heading home to do the real thing. *Whatever, it's fine*, Izzy thought. *I'm not really looking for a relationship, and for sure not with someone I work with. I'm just here to have fun.*

Drink after drink, the group started to split off as the buddies found interests in other scantily clad women, and Ximena and Gabriel tuned the world out. They shoved their tongues down each other's throats, and he fondled her breasts. It was like a train wreck; Izzy couldn't stop watching them. *It's like soft porn, but reality soft porn. Wait, am I turned on?* Horrified at the notion that she was getting turned on by watching, Izzy slapped Luciana's arm and said, "¡Vamos a bailar!" As Izzy pulled Luciana away toward the dance floor, Luciana grabbed Felipe's hand to pull him along with them. The three of them squeezed through sweaty bodies toward the middle of the second floor and formed a small, tight circle as best they could in the crowd. Moving to the music, the bass and drums, and looking out over the crowd toward the ocean, Izzy smiled. She didn't need to be here all dressed up getting attention from men to enjoy herself. The drinks and dancing were enough!

"Me voy al baño," Luciana shouted into Izzy's ear.

"Okay," she responded. "Voy contigo." *I'll go with you.*

"No, no, quédate aquí con Felipe. No queremos perdernos el uno al otro," Luciana instructed. *Stay here with Felipe so we don't lose each other.*

She made her way toward the bathroom and out of sight, and suddenly Felipe moved closer to Izzy. She wondered if someone had bumped him from behind, but then he looked her straight in the eye and put one hand around her waist, pulling her toward him. *Oh, um, I guess he wasn't bumped. I probably shouldn't.* But his hands felt good on her waistline, and it had been so long since someone had touched her like that. She gave into the music, the alcohol, and his warmth, and let him pull her in to dance.

Now she, too, was grinding on the dance floor, but she was loving it. When they spotted Luciana returning a few minutes later, however, they created a bit more space between them. Izzy wondered why she felt like she was sneaking around with Felipe. *He isn't dating either one of us!*

They moved to the music together, nobody touching anyone, for another hour or so. Sweat pouring out and alcohol taking over her thoughts, Izzy was numb to the world and her surroundings, except for the fact that she was dancing, wasted, looking out over the Pacific Ocean. *My peeps have got to do this with me! My girls from back home in Houston would love this!*

Suddenly, Izzy realized she was thirsty. "Vamos a tomar un trago de agua!" she suggested to Felipe and Luciana. They nodded their heads and followed her back toward the table. Everyone was gone, the bottles were left empty, and the booth was vacant. Had they all found their way home? *I hope Ximena is okay*, she thought.

"Bueno, ¿están listas para salir?" Felipe asked. *Ready to leave?*

Looking at each other, they shrugged. Izzy's head spun with the room, and she dripped with sweat. She could definitely use a shower and bed. "Sí, seguro, vámonos."

Exiting the club, they flagged down a taxi. The girls climbed into the back seat, and Felipe took the one up front. The taxi bumped its way through the downtown area and back onto the main paved road toward home. Luciana's place came up first, and as they pulled up to her apartment door, she kissed Izzy's face and said good night. Before heading to her place, she walked over to the passenger side window to tell Felipe "bye" with a simple cheek peck and one-armed awkward hug through the window.

"La Marina," Izzy slurred to the driver. *Where does Felipe live, anyway?* she wondered. *Who cares? I'm going home first.* The ride from Luciana's to Izzy's was only fifteen minutes, which they spent in silence except for the sounds of the radio and street noise through the open windows. Everything was turning, then starting over, then turning, then starting over, the world around her shifting as if she was still on the dance floor. *How much did I actually drink?* She couldn't remember back to the first margarita at Los Mapaches. *What time is it anyway?*

The car slowed and pulled to a stop.

"Llegamos, güerita," Felipe said quietly.

She sat up straight, opened the car door, and stumbled out. She felt guilty she was coming home late and drunk, like the security guard might ground her.

"¿Está bien, Isabella?" the guard asked, sounding concerned.

"¡Sí, claro!" She tried to sound with it and not so trashed.

"Voy a ayudarla a su cuarto," came Felipe's voice. *He's going to help me to my room.*

Ready to pass out, Izzy didn't wait for him, but made her own way to the elevators and pressed "up." She was ready to lie down.

"¡Espera, Isabella!" Felipe instructed, jogging lightly toward her as she waited, leaning on the wall. She glanced in the direction of his voice in enough time to notice the taxi pulling away. *I guess he's going to call another one?* Through the opening in the buildings, she could see the ocean and the mountains beyond, and she smiled. She might be wasted, but she still knew where she was. She was in paradise.

Look at that. The sun's starting to sneak a tiny bit of light across the land. So pretty. Wait, what? The sun? Holy shit, I need to sleep.

Practically falling out of the elevator, Izzy made her way down the hall toward her door, Felipe behind her. *Nice guy*, she thought. Arriving at her door with her back to Felipe, she searched her clutch for her apartment key. As she was putting the key in the lock, she felt him press against her from behind.

She froze, mind whirring and blood pumping. With his hands on her hips, he pressed her slightly toward him and whispered something sexy and Spanish in her ear.

Adrenaline flowed, shaking her out of her tired drunken haze. Her body tightened, and she felt herself quiver between her legs as blood rushed and pulsed through her. Tilting her head to the right, she exposed her neck to his face, and he took it. Kissing her neck, below her ear and then the top of her shoulder, he ran his hands down to her inner thighs.

What about Luciana? Izzy found herself thinking. *Is she going to be pissed? Will she find out? Fuck it.*

She turned to face him and let him kiss her, soft and sweet but with such urgency it made her arch her back and press herself into him further. *Oh yeah, he's ready.* Turning to get the key back into the lock and opening the door, they fell through it to the entryway. Slamming the door and locking it behind them, they stumbled to the bed, hands everywhere and clothes coming off awkwardly. She hadn't been touched like this, wanted like this, in months.

"¿Tienes un condon?" she asked quickly.

"Sí, bonita, lo tengo," he said as he slipped a condom out of this pocket. *Oh thank God, because I am not about to stop and have some conversation about herpes.* Undoing the condom wrapper with one hand and his teeth, he slid his fingers between her legs, showing both of them how ready she was. Arching her back, she urged him forward.

"Rápido," she whispered, "por favor."

The first glimpse of dawn was beginning to sneak through the window, lighting the room just enough so she could see his face. She didn't know this man, and she didn't care. He was sexy, and other women wanted him, but he wanted her, out of the whole club. *Of course he did*, she thought. *And it's okay that he did.* She felt her newfound confidence and pride solidify her choice. *He isn't with anyone, and nobody can claim him. Just let it happen.* And so she did.

Chapter 17

"So he's a lot of fun, huh?" Jenny had asked excitedly when Izzy recounted her newest relationship as of the past few weeks: with Felipe. "I bet he can get you into clubs and VIP rooms since he's a native!" *Wrong; news flash that everyone here is a "native."*

"He's definitely fun," Izzy answered, "and hot!"

"But?" Jenny sensed slight hesitation in Izzy's response.

"Well, I mean, I'm not going to stay here forever, and I certainly don't love him," she admitted. "He's just a fun distraction when I need it, and someone to do things with when I'm lonely."

Hearing it out loud, she felt guilty. *Poor Felipe. He keeps telling me he loves me. Does he honestly think we have something special? He has to realize this is a fling. Plus, why can't a woman date without getting attached? Men do it all the time!*

Reflecting on the romantic weekend she'd just finished, she had to admit it wasn't just a fun fling where they partied together and made love. This last weekend Izzy was home, Felipe had made reservations at a beautiful restaurant perched on the top of a cliff overlooking the Pacific Ocean.

It was south of the main downtown area, so from their table they watched the sun set over the horizon while sipping on red wine as the lights came on in the town below. They could see her own apartment on the other side of the bay and all the lights between the city and the hills. They laughed about people at the office, and shared stories about what was happening in each of their daily experiences. Like friends. They felt comfortable. Even the language barrier was something Izzy could overcome most of the time. Felipe didn't speak a word of English, and though he professed his desire to learn, Izzy knew better.

"Eres hermosa," Felipe said, reaching across the table to hold Izzy's hand.

The conversation had fallen silent as the wine clouded Izzy's mind, and her English-to-Spanish translations were becoming more and more difficult. Maybe it wasn't her lack of vocabulary, but more about his lack of ability to relate. Izzy enjoyed telling him about her life because she loved the peace and joy she felt when she did, but she somehow felt a bit lonelier afterward because the person on the other side of the table didn't get it. He couldn't. Nor could she truly connect with him regarding the lifestyle and experiences of Mexico City, where he was from.

But as the silence fell, and the lack of connection was apparent, he would do something like that. He would tell her she was beautiful and hold her hand or brush her hair out of her eyes. *Just a fling, Izzy?*

"Quiero regresar a los estados unidos contigo," Felipe said, surprising Izzy with that bold declaration. *I want to come back with you to the US.*

"¿Qué?" Izzy responded, her mind whirring to find words to say no.

"Sí, preciosa, eres la mujer que me hace mejor. Te quiero," he gushed, as if he had been holding that in now for some time. *You are the woman who makes me better. I love you.*

Izzy swallowed a large gulp of wine and tried to think of how to respond. She thought she would have loved to hear a man say those sweet things to her, and to declare she was the one for him. But inside she panicked. Her heart sank to her stomach and she felt clammy. As fun as he was, she didn't connect with him on a soul level.

"Felipe," Izzy started to respond gently, "sabes que no es posible." *You know that's not possible.*

The intensity on his face softened, and he cast his eyes down toward his lap. *Maybe that was a bit harsh, but it's the truth! I don't know where I'm going after this, and we can't start a life together. He doesn't even speak English! How does he think he could live in the US when he doesn't speak the language?* Of course she knew he absolutely could live in the US without speaking English, but the lifestyle that would offer wasn't anything close to the future she envisioned for herself. She couldn't find the words to explain that to him: she didn't want it.

"Pero, Felipe, estamos aquí ahora. Vamos a disfrutarnos por lo momento y vemos lo que el futuro nos trae." *But Felipe, we have right now. Let's enjoy each other for the moment, and we'll see what happens in the future.*

He looked up at her and smiled, warmly but weakly. It wasn't what he wanted to hear. Izzy wondered if he, too, had feelings and words he didn't know how to express.

Luciana wasn't on the bus the Monday after Izzy returned from a business trip to LA. Ximena didn't seem to know where she was, so she and Izzy spent the ride up talking quietly off and on as others on the bus napped for the ride up. Valeria sat with Alejandra, as she always did now. Izzy decided not to worry about it. Alejandra could have Valeria because, honestly, she needed at least one friend. *Good of Valeria to be there for her.* Then Izzy wondered, was she there for Luci? Had she made an effort to be the one she could confide in and trust after all these months? Or was she just a backstabbing bitch who stole Luci's love interest? The thought made her shiver, so she forced her mind back to the present and focused on the passing towns out the window.

Arriving at the resort, Ximena and Izzy made their way to the cafeteria for breakfast before clocking in for the day. Still no sign of Luci. Filling

Ximena in about her latest trip to Los Angeles and the crazy paparazzi incident at the sushi place she tried, Izzy couldn't shake the strange feeling of discomfort that had crept in when Luciana was absent. *What are you worried about? Maybe she just came in early, or maybe she isn't feeling well. It probably has nothing to do with you, Izzy.*

The day dragged on like any other as Isabella recorded all her trips' activities in a report for Gretchen and set reminders for herself to follow up on specific requests. She was just getting through her inbox and feeling caught up when her phone rang. *Luciana! She must be calling about lunch.*

"Hey, Luci!" Izzy answered.

"Hola," she said a little flatly. *Is she okay?* "Tenemos que hablar." *Have to talk? Why does she sound so serious?*

"Okay. ¿Todo bien?" Izzy asked her, trying to force her mind to believe this was about a reservation or perhaps a client issue.

"Um, no, no exactamente. Por favor, venga a mi oficina."

This must be a work thing, then, if she insists on chatting in her office. Izzy was trying to convince herself this wouldn't be about Felipe. Leaving her office and making her way through the hallway to where Luciana and Ximena sat, she tried to think about what guests at the resort might have been an issue that Luciana would need her to fix. No one came to mind.

At the office, Luciana turned in her chair without getting up to hug her as her normal "welcome back" greeting. Something was definitely off.

"Sit, please," she said in English. *English? She doesn't normally speak to me in English.* Izzy sat, her mind going crazy. Ximena was in the corner, typing. Izzy searched her face for some sort of sign, something to indicate whether she knew what might be about to happen, and if she did, whether she was on Luciana's side or Izzy's side. Ximena looked back at Izzy, but her face didn't provide any guidance or help.

"Listen," Luciana started, "I want to say in English to make sure you understand me. I know about Felipe."

Izzy's stomach dropped to the floor and heat rose in her neck and up to her face. *Oh fuck.*

Luciana's face registered no emotion. No anger, but no excitement, either. It was empty, which felt even worse. Izzy didn't say a thing. The tension was so thick that another reservation agent got up and left the shared office space, no doubt as an escape.

"You know I have liked him since he came," Luciana said. "And you know I am here for my life, but you will leave soon. Very soon, I hope." Venom crept into her voice, overpowering her broken English. "How long have you been sleeping with him behind my back?"

"Luci," Izzy started, stammering. "Just a month or so, but Luci—"

She was cut off by Luciana putting her hand up.

"You were my friend, and now you betray me." Her words were cold.

"Luci," Izzy tried to say softly, "I didn't mean for it to happen. We were drunk one night after the club, and when he took me home, it just happened. You weren't seeing him, though, were you?"

Maybe she should have told Luci earlier than now, but what was there to tell? That Felipe had asked Izzy out and they were dating? It wasn't like Izzy (or Felipe for that matter) needed permission from Luciana before they could go out together. Now Izzy was starting to get defensive. *He's the hottest guy working here; any one of us could have said she liked him. You can't have some sort of claim on him!* Her face tingled with a strange mix of embarrassment, shame, anger, and sorrow. She didn't want to hurt her friend. *But he chose me! He wants me, not you! Should I hold myself back just because of your crush?* Maybe the "old Izzy" would have been afraid of that and would have sacrificed her own desires to please someone else. Now she wasn't afraid to go after what she wanted, so why should she feel so awful?

"¡No me importa!" Luciana cried, tears welling up as she started to lose her calm. "You knew, and you fucked him anyway!"

The sting went deep under Izzy's skin as emotions whirled inside her. *Fucked him? As if I'm some cheap whore who just goes around "fucking" people? We've actually been dating and spending time together, not just having sex! Maybe we really like each other!* She was about to say that when Ximena stepped in.

"Luci," she said as she rolled her chair over to her. *Yeah, Ximena, tell her she's overreacting. Tell her Felipe and I really do like each other.*

"No hables con ella ahora. Lo que hizo fue desconsiderado, pero tienes que trabajar, y tienes que olvidarlo." *What the fuck? What I did was inconsiderate? How could she say that when she's the one running around with a married man?*

They both looked back at Izzy. Ximena had chosen to stand by Luciana's side. Izzy's entire body went cold, and her hands and feet felt clammy. They were against her. *It isn't fair! I didn't mean for it to happen, but it did! Why can't Luci be happy for me, and mature enough to see that Felipe could make his own decisions? His decision was to date me, not Luci. Why is that my fault?*

Then her mind flipped and she saw two women who had been friends before she'd arrived, and would most likely be friends after she was gone.

"I'm sorry, Luci," Izzy said, feeling defeated. "I didn't mean to hurt you." Then she stood and slunk back to her office. The next business trip couldn't come fast enough.

As Izzy boarded the bus home, she watched Alejandra and Valeria sit down beside each other. *Do they know?* They looked at Izzy as she moved past them, and she saw the answer. *Yup, they know.* She could see the judgment all over their faces. *Who fucking cares. I'm not staying here forever. I'm living my life the way I want, and if others can't handle it, that's their issue. Fuck all of them.*

But something inside felt empty. Staring hard out the window all the way home, taking in the serene beauty and the scenes from everyday life, she tried to forget about the pain and the hurt. But as she walked through her door and looked around at her empty apartment, the tears came. Alone again, without anyone there to understand, she let herself cry and mourn the loss of the friendship she had ruined. *Will they ever forgive me? Will they ever see my side of it?*

Taking a deep breath and wiping her face, she found her plastic phone. She hadn't seen Felipe much today and hadn't wanted to see him last night when she landed, but tonight she needed to see him. He answered immediately and said he'd be there in under an hour. *Does he know? Does he even care? Guys never seem to get the shit end of this deal.*

She moped around while she waited for Felipe, picking up and tidying the bathroom slightly since she had ignored it last night after she got home. Finally, he knocked on the door. When she opened it, he stood there in a white button-down shirt untucked with the sleeves rolled up over his tanned, brown forearms. Khaki shorts and brown loafers with aviator sunglasses and a slight smirk, he leaned on the doorframe and crossed his arms.

"¿No me visitaste hoy?" he asked playfully, scolding her for not visiting him today during work.

She smiled back playfully, letting the day's drama wash away for the moment. *Of course she's upset; this guy is hot! Can't blame her for being sad she lost this one.* She feigned confidence and let her ego drive her forward. It was safer that way. She didn't have to admit she'd made a mistake, and she honestly wasn't convinced she had.

Reaching for his shirt, she grabbed a handful of it right between his pecs and pulled him into the apartment. For the next few hours, it would all be worth it.

Chapter 18

Sitting alone on the bus to and from the resort wasn't what bothered her the most. On the way up she slept, as did most people, and on the way back she listened to her music and daydreamed about where she'd take her friends from back home when they'd come visit. She didn't mind lunch or breakfast in the cafeteria, because now that people knew, she and Felipe started sitting together. And most weekends, she relished the time on her own beach or at her own pool, where she could just be with herself and not feel judged by the strangers coming and going each week in the condos around her. She surfed and golfed now, sometimes, taking lessons in both from locals that neither wanted her nor judged her. It created space to be free. It created time for Izzy to know herself without the eyes of others, including Felipe.

Felipe still claimed to love her. She found truth in the stereotype of the "Latin lover" and the passion that came with it. The same passion created jealousy, and when Izzy would be in conversation with other male coworkers, Felipe made no secret he was displeased and made sure the coworkers knew it. The sex was great, and when they were salsa dancing or dining together, things were fantastic. At other times she second-guessed her decision, like when she felt he was getting a little too close for comfort and she was his possession of some kind.

But what bothered her the most was that nobody seemed to understand her side. Plenty understood Luciana's side, and the men seemed to high-five Felipe for winning the güerita, but nobody seemed truly to understand Izzy. Nobody in Puerto Vallarta anyway. She was more and more grateful for the friends she had made on the road, who lived her lifestyle of travel and entertainment and thought her life in Mexico was great and exciting. Maybe she didn't belong in Mexico, but she had found a way to belong to something. And that helped her through the weeks she was in the office. Even still, each new trip was a welcome respite.

"Vegas, baby!" She laughed into the phone with Jenny as they talked about their upcoming trips. "But not before New York, which will be a whole other adventure!"

"Can't wait to see you, girl. Travel safe!" Jenny said.

Izzy's sleep was restless that night. Although only two and a half weeks had passed since her last trip, with all the drama that had unfolded, it seemed like months. She was ready to get out of the telenovela that had become her life and get into something close to "normal."

She knew spring was coming back home in Texas, but much of the country was still getting snow and cold. New York was no exception. The flight delays were ridiculous, and when she finally got to New York, she realized a taxi wouldn't get her to the hotel before midnight. *If I don't call them, they'll think I'm not coming and might give my room away. Better let them know I'm on the way.*

"Oh, miss, I'm so sorry for that; sounds like a hectic day," the front desk agent said. Izzy loved her luxury hotel chain and was ecstatic to see this gorgeous New York version, but at the moment she was just grateful for the kind voice on the phone.

"Well, that's what you get traveling in the winter," Izzy responded heavily. "I should have never connected through Chicago. A hot bath and glass of wine and I'll be fine," she said, half joking.

"We will be here ready for you; take your time," she assured Izzy. *At least I know they won't be giving away my room so I'll have a place to sleep!*

After arriving and getting checked in, Izzy turned toward the elevators and took a moment to revel in the luxury surrounding her. Ornate gold carvings and hand-painted ceilings reminded her of a book she once read that referenced the tearoom here. The main character had made a ritual of getting ice cream here with her mother, and it was a memory she had drawn from later in life to ease her through tough times. Standing in that same lobby now, Izzy could see what that woman had felt. The opulence and feeling of royalty seeped inside, and Izzy felt important. Stepping into the elevator with her head held high, despite feeling so tired, she instructed the man inside which floor she was headed to. *I don't even have to push the buttons on the elevator? Man, this is the life.*

Down the hall, she found her room and let herself in. Turning to the left, she saw through the bathroom door that the tub was full of water and a bathmat was lying neatly beside it, with slippers set carefully on top. A glass of red wine had been delicately placed on the end of the tub near the gold faucet. *Wow. That's the most incredible customer service I've ever seen.*

Pulling her luggage all the way into the room, her jaw dropped as she took in the incredible detail of the furniture, the giant king-sized bed, and the glass coffee table adorned with the signature Bloody Mary cocktail. Crown moldings and soft, supple sheets; winged-back chairs and an ornate antique dresser. Turning in circles, she breathed in deeply and caught a glimpse of herself in the mirror. The world of drama was draining, and it was hurtful. But Izzy did get to do some incredible things and experience incredible adventures that most people—not only in Puerto Vallarta but everywhere—never would.

She undressed and slipped into the bathtub to soak. She'd barely remembered the comment on the phone about a warm bath and glass of wine, and here they were, waiting for her. *So that's what it means to really listen to someone and to work hard to surprise them. Is that how I serve my clients?* Then her mind jumped to another track. *Is that how I serve my friends?* Dismissing the thought, she let herself relax and appreciate the service that had been provided just for her. She was worth the effort, and she would accept the thoughtfulness gratefully.

The next day was filled with running around the city from appointment to appointment, hopping in taxis and then trudging the huge New York City blocks on foot. The gang reunited for dinner in a restaurant above the craziness of the streets with windows overlooking the busy intersection below. Two clients were with their group, but they had known Michael and Carrie for so long, they felt like friends. The drinks and food kept coming, and Izzy stopped to soak it all in; looking around the table, she felt at ease. This is where she belonged. This is what she missed so much. How much longer could she stand the drama of Mexico? How long had she committed to being there? *Only a year. It isn't all that far off.*

The thought lingered uncomfortably despite the smile she wore on her face for the table to see. She had been so excited about the adventure of Mexico and couldn't wait to start her new life there. Now, she felt like she was living in a dramatic mess and was ready to jump out of it. *You can't leave like that, Izzy.* She knew it was the truth.

"Oh, my gawd!" Michael gasped at the elegantly presented cotton candy dessert, distracting her from her thoughts. "It's absolutely gorgeous!" Everyone at the table laughed, and Izzy was beside herself. It was presented well for a state fair–type of dessert; very trendy. But it wasn't the dessert that had Izzy almost peeing her pants; it was Michael's face and gestures, his ridiculous, overdramatic delight in the thing. He was unequivocally himself without apology. Dramatic and flamboyant, professional and fun. While he did keep a more professional demeanor with clients for the trade shows and formal events, he was pretty much the exact same person in any setting. *I wish I could feel comfortable like that,* she thought as she watched him with admiration and wonder. *What would I be like if I stopped trying to fit in and be accepted? What am I like when I'm alone? Should I try it?*

Before Izzy could spend too much time in self-reflection, the table was passing around the bill for everyone to pay their portion as the night wound down. Perhaps it was the sugar rush, but several at the table weren't ready to turn in for the night.

"Where to next?" Jenny asked the table.

"Next?" Michael exclaimed as if she had said something terribly taboo. "Well, if it's that kind of a night, then we need to hit up a little spot by the hotel so we can all stumble back. Forget finding a taxi at three a.m."

"There's this really cool spot I found running around today, not far from the hotel on Park Avenue," Carrie said. "Let's check it out!"

As the group made their way down to the street level, a few sane members of the pack opted out and jumped in a taxi to head back to their respective overnight accommodations for some much-needed rest. The others, including Izzy, piled into a taxi and headed for the bar. *Why waste a night in New York City with sleep? This is the city that never sleeps, after all.*

The bar was dark but modern in feel—not brass and dark wood, but sleek black tables, mirrors, and glass. The scene was loud, and the music inspired a feeling that something was about to happen. Sometimes Izzy imagined what the sound track to her movie would be. A girl walks into a bar, and some gorgeous man sees her from across the crowd. She doesn't see him yet, and he watches her laugh with her friends and order a drink. What song would fit this scene? The song playing right then seemed to be perfect. She couldn't help it; she scanned the room as subtly as she could, searching for that gorgeous man. But within seconds, her group pushed up to the bar and she was lost in the shuffle, desperately searching for the name of that amazing drink Michael had ordered for her back in Atlanta. *I've got to get better about ordering. What is "my drink"? Anything vodka? Anything that gets the job done, I guess.*

Carrie, Jenny, and Izzy found a group leaving their small cocktail table and jumped in the chairs right behind them as Michael and some of the others stood firm near the bar, waiting to give them the long list of drinks. Before long, a couple of men, dressed in suits but clearly having been out of the office for some time, approached the three women. They appeared a little scruffy from a long day's work, with slight wrinkles in their sleeves but fine-looking slacks that fell neatly to the tops of their perfectly polished shoes. One of them had light brown eyes and inviting, slightly ruffled brown hair, and he smiled right at Izzy. Her heart instantly fluttered, and her stomach turned to butterflies.

Offering his hand in a friendly but businesslike way, he said, "Hi, I'm Blake." *Damn, what a smile.*

"Izzy, or Isabella," she offered hers in return.

"Where are you in from?" he asked.

"How do you know I'm not from the city?" she asked playfully.

"If you were, I would have found you by now," he said. "Someone as naturally gorgeous as you doesn't walk into my bar on a Wednesday night."

I want to think that was cheesy, but damn, that was well timed and almost sounded sincere. Did he set me up for that line? Does he use that line on every woman? How do I know he isn't traveling too and just acting like he knows the place?

"Oh, that was good," she said, smiling. Flirting in a teasing way was the easiest for Izzy. A light punch-in-the-arm sarcasm was much more natural for her than trying to sit pretty, act aloof, and be mysteriously sexy.

"Here you are, my dear!" Michael exclaimed, coming out of nowhere and pushing between Blake and Izzy to set her requested drink on the table. "And who is this yummy transient you've found?" he asked, turning toward Blake.

Seeming unperturbed about the underlying suggestion that he was "just another one" in the sea of objectified suits, he responded, "I'm Blake. And you are?"

"Michael." He offered his hand. "And I screen anyone that wants Isabella's time. So tell me, what are your intentions this evening, sir?"

She thought she should probably be horrified and embarrassed, but instead Izzy laughed out loud and enjoyed the scene. *Let's see how this guy takes it! Maybe I do need someone to screen them for me.*

"I was just saying to her that a natural beauty like this doesn't walk into my bar on a Wednesday night, so my intention was to find out how long she might be here and if I'd get to see her again." Blake smiled and looked around Michael, locking eyes with Izzy.

"Hmmm," Michael began, "good line. He'll do. Have fun, sweetie!" He gave Izzy a look as if to say: *I won't see you again, so I'm saying goodbye now.* Then he bent over as if to give her a hug and whispered in her ear, maybe not so quietly, "Don't let the polished shoes fool you; this guy isn't very successful if he's in this bar. The real men are in their own penthouses entertaining the important people with thirty-year-old Macallan and strippers. Byeeee!" He practically pranced off, delighted with himself and his humor.

Catching Izzy's eye, Jenny lifted her glass and her eyebrows at Izzy, and winked.

Why is everyone assuming something is happening here? Am I putting off some sort of crazy vibe? Or are they encouraging me to enjoy the attention? Izzy tilted her head and furrowed her own eyebrows back at Jenny, asking, "What does that mean?"

"You know I don't care," Jenny started, "and you know I would never judge, right?" she asked Izzy, as if testing the water before jumping in.

"Of course," Izzy said back. "What is it? Tell me."

"It wasn't that long ago Felipe was gazing into your eyes at a romantic restaurant saying he loved you," Jenny reminded her.

"True . . . ," Izzy said, hesitating to finish the thought.

"Just be mindful, that's all. I know you are a great person and you're having fun with Felipe, and you're definitely not committed to him; but just make sure you make your choices so you can live with them versus letting the choice make you."

With that, Jenny hugged Izzy, kissed her on the cheek, and left to find where Michael had pranced off.

Blake took a step closer to Izzy's chair. "So, how long are you in town for then?" he asked, grinning.

"I'm afraid I leave tomorrow," she responded with an almost devilish smile.

"Well then, we'd better make the most of tonight," he answered suggestively.

Could I? Could I let something happen with this perfect stranger on my last night in New York City? She hated that Felipe was so jealous all the time and that she couldn't even have harmless conversations with other coworkers without him getting upset. *But how would he ever know? I'm in another country! And even if something does happen, I never told him I love him or that we are an exclusive couple with intentions of a future together. In fact, I've said the opposite! So screw it.*

"Well, how about you start with who you are and what you do, Blake?" *Game on.*

What seemed like minutes later, Blake was riding up the elevator with Izzy to her room. He hadn't quite forced himself in, but she hadn't quite resisted his assertive behavior, either. The awkward silence between them was more than simply a lack of something to say. It was the realization that they didn't know each other at all but were about to give each other the most personal, intimate thing one person could give another. *Thank goodness for alcohol. Otherwise, I'd know better.*

As she opened the door, she half expected him to push her into the wall and start going at it, but he didn't. *He must not do this often, or maybe this is all part of the act so he doesn't feel like such an asshole for sleeping with women he'll never have to see again.* He walked through the room admiring the furniture, the bathroom, and the ornate details of the luxury hotel.

"Nice view," he said as he walked toward the window, taking off his jacket as he spoke.

"Yeah, not bad for a girl from Texas, huh?" she joked, alluding to the flirtatious jabs he'd given her earlier in the bar about being a Podunk, Texas, girl.

"I meant the view in here," he said coyly, closing the curtains and turning toward Izzy. *Damn, he's good. Maybe he's a little too practiced and this is a little too rehearsed, but who the hell cares?*

She sank into one hip, cocked her head to the side, and smiled, telling him with her body that she knew it was a line, but she wouldn't throw him out because of it. He took a few more steps toward her and put one hand around her waist, then gave a little tug to pull her close to him. Leaning in, he kissed her lightly on her lips, then her cheek, then below her ear, then her neck. Pulling back, he looked her in the eye to see what her reaction would be.

Izzy could feel herself tighten as she started to feel wet. Her heart pounded and her mind raced. *Holy shit, he's good. But how am I going to get rid of him later? I can't have him staying! I have coffee with a travel agent first thing in the morning, then a plane to catch!*

You've come this far, her other voices reminded her, *you can't stop now.*

He must have seen the hesitation in her face. Instead of backing off, though, he tried again. Picking up her left hand, he kissed the back of it, then the soft crook of her elbow, then her shoulder, then her neck. The anticipation grew, and Izzy could barely contain herself any longer. She let her head fall back, offering him more of her neck, which he gladly took as he put his other arm around her and slid his hands down to her backside, giving it a squeeze. *They always like that part*, she thought, smiling.

As they made their way to the bed, hands and lips everywhere with both of their breathing escalating, Felipe popped into her head.

Shit, her other voices said, *you just lost a friend over him and said he was worth it. And now? He's not worth much, is he?* She was practically yelling at herself.

Well, I can't stop now! I mean, I could, but do I want to? She gasped as Blake pulled her bra down and took her breast into his mouth. *Not really!* And then, as Blake unzipped her skirt and slid his hand down her panties, the voices subsided, and she let him take over.

The alarm went off with a shrill, jolting Izzy out of her restless, alcohol-induced sleep. Blake was gone. *Thank God. I don't even remember him leaving.*

Rushing around to get herself presentable for the coffee meeting, she didn't have time to pack her bag. She'd be running back to the hotel and hoping that she could find a taxi instantly to get herself to the airport on time. The traffic was bad as expected, but her schedule had her at the airport with time to spare. She could finally sit with herself, and her thoughts, as she waited to board the plane.

I don't even have to tell him, do I? I mean, we aren't in a relationship. We just like to drink and have sex. Or, well, that's not true. I do like him, and he's good company. But I definitely do not love him or have any intention of keeping the relationship going when I leave. If I leave. Does he know I might leave? Have we even talked about that?

Suddenly a new thought broke in: *Isn't this supposed to be my time to get back to me? To stop losing myself in relationships and worrying all about what others think of me? Why can't this be fun for me?*

"Now boarding group three," came the announcement over the loudspeaker. *Oh, thank God.* Almost collapsing in her seat, she fell asleep in minutes and didn't wake until the wheels hit the ground.

Chapter 19

The sun was already up when Izzy opened her eyes. She had slept well into the midmorning after the long days of running around the city, the late nights, and the exhausting travel. Although her body felt rested, her mind did not. As much as she had convinced herself her actions back in New York City were acceptable, she felt the weight of the guilt pressing down on her. *Should I tell him? Maybe I should find a way to let him know so I can once again explain that we aren't exclusive?* Maybe not. What he didn't know couldn't hurt him, could it?

She rolled over and planted her feet on the cold tile floor. Washing her face and preparing herself for the day, she debated about how she might bring it up, and what she might expect him to say in return. Jenny had been right. She had made the choice, so she needed to own it. She made the choice knowing what the stakes were, but had decided her own moment and her own adventure to find Izzy was the path to take, versus letting someone else's potential feelings be her guide. Of course, that choice was much easier to make with the help of distance and alcohol. *Man, this is not going to be easy, but I think I have to.*

Settling herself outside on the terrace, then deciding it was too hot for what might be a tough conversation, she moved back into the air-conditioning and relaxed back onto the couch while putting her bare feet up on the wrought-iron-and-tile coffee table. Finding his name quickly in her little toy phone, she dialed his number. Her heart thudded in her ears and sweat formed on her palms. *Should I tell him now over the phone, or just make plans to hang out and tell him then?* Her breathing escalated with every ring, and her chest tightened with anticipation. By the fourth ring, she realized he wasn't going to answer. *Wonder where he is?* His voice mail came on, and she decided not to leave a message.

Breathing a sigh of what could only be described as relief, she headed back to her bedroom to find a swimsuit and her journal and proceeded to the pool. She heard her mom's voice pop into her head: *Relax and enjoy today because tomorrow will come, whether you like it or not.*

Monday morning was back to the grind—the early alarm, the long walk to the front of the marina, and the sleepy bus ride up to work as the sun rose over the Pacific.

Updating Gretchen on the trip, logging activities and follow-up from the trip, and sending "thank you" emails, her morning flew by. Despite how focused she felt on her work, she couldn't help but get a strange feeling. Everything had seemed mostly normal that morning, but she could feel some unsettled energy in the office. Maybe the entire resort. Breakfast had been a little weird without Felipe there, and she was more worried than hopeful that she might see him there. She had eaten in peace outside on her own, but the way people had looked at her made her feel weird. Was it accusation? How could they know about New York? Trying to shake it off and logically explaining to herself that it was absolutely impossible for anyone to have known, she decided it was all probably in her head.

As she made her way to the cafeteria, Ximena greeted her. It wasn't the usual friendly greeting, but Izzy was relieved she didn't flat-out ignore her. And that she wasn't with Luci.

"¿Cómo estás?" Ximena asked how Izzy was doing.

"He estado mejor," Izzy replied a bit sheepishly that she had been better.

"Pues, tienes mucho en que pensar. Y tenemos mucho de que hablar." One thing Izzy loved about Ximena was her boldness and her fearlessness about what needed to be said. She was right. Izzy had a lot to think about, and they did have a lot to talk about.

"¿Conoces Sayulita?" Ximena asked.

Izzy had heard about the incredible surfing at Sayulita from Ricio, but she didn't know it and hadn't been there.

"He oído hablar del pequeño lugar, pero nunca he estado allí."

"Iremos, entonces, para hablar y pasar tiempo sin el grupo y sin los clubs. Esta cosa es tan importante que necesitamos un lugar tranquilo." *Let's go then, to talk and spend time together without the group and without the clubs. This thing is so important that we need a quiet place.*

Izzy wasn't sure what to feel. She was nervous about what Ximena's intentions were, yet at the same time she was immensely grateful that Ximena wanted to talk and spend time with her versus letting the friendship die. Maybe there was hope that Ximena would be willing to hear Izzy's side of it all.

"Okay!" Izzy said enthusiastically, maybe a little too enthusiastically, given the situation, because Ximena looked at her a little funny.

"Okay, pasaré por ti el sabado por la mañana." Ximena instructed that she'd come pick Izzy up Saturday morning.

"Okay. Perfecto." Izzy smiled meekly.

~

Ximena said she'd be picking Izzy up at 9:30 a.m. The clock said 9:17 a.m., and Izzy sat impatiently on the couch, already packed. She knew what the intention was behind the invite, but wasn't quite sure how to emotionally prepare. If Ximena was really pissed and going to say something about ending the friendship, she wouldn't have invited her to go camping. Would she? So their relationship must have been salvageable. Right? Her mind had been racing since the girls finalized their plans, and now it seemed to stand still as her eyes waited for the numbers to change; 9:19 a.m. Izzy debated if she should dive in and be the one to address the elephant in the room, putting out her version of the story first, or wait for Ximena to start the tough conversation.

Estoy aquí, the text message read. Izzy's stomach did a backflip as she headed downstairs to meet her.

They packed to stay for the night and had brought a tent for camping. The first campsite they came across looked a bit too dirty and was pretty open to the sky, and it would be too hot without any shade cover. They walked on down the road, and a small white sign pointed them through what looked like the wild jungle. Once under the protection of the banana tree leaves and thick vegetation, they found a little shack waiting for them to reserve a spot.

"¿Cómo te parece? ¿Está bien?" Ximena asked Izzy if she thought this would be okay as they walked toward the little shack to pay for the campsite.

"Sí, si podemos encontrar un lugar con mucha sombra, seriá perfecto," Izzy answered. *Yes, if we can find one with lots of shade, that will be perfect.*

Paying the cheap rate for one night, they were directed toward an area with a few open spots. They picked out one that was on the sand but under the trees and near the walkway so they could easily find their way out.

Ximena began to work on the tent. "Voy a ver la playa mientras tu haces eso," Izzy said to Ximena playfully.

"¿Cómo? ¡Vente para acá para ayudarme!" she shouted. "A menos que quieras dormir sola en la playa."

What? Get yourself back here and help! Unless you want to sleep on the beach by yourself!

Once they got the tent set up, laughing and messing up a few times, they headed to the beach to check out the scene. Izzy had heard it was beautiful, but she was amazed as they exited the lush jungle that faded into sand. It was as if they had been taken back in time to what it looked like before human beings ever stepped foot here—the pure jungle, sands, and mountains untouched by bulldozers and concrete. Some areas of town were built up to the sand, and homes dotted the tree lines, but for the most part it wasn't a very developed area, and the beauty was incredibly stunning. Children in diapers played in the shallow waters as mothers in worn, dirty dresses stared on with baskets of trinkets resting next to them. A place the locals lived and fewer tourists played, it was an entirely different world. The waves were larger than El Anclote at Punta de Mita where she had surfed, and the beach stretched to the north far beyond where her eye could see. She was in love.

"¿Te gusta?" Ximena asked of Izzy's first impression.

"¡Sí! Mucho," Izzy said passionately.

"Es un lugar de paz donde me gusta pasar el tiempo cuando necesito recuperar de la vida loca." Ximena explained that this peaceful place was one she came to when she needed to recover from the crazy life.

"¡Pacífico! ¡Pacífico fría!" An older man with two white plastic buckets made his way up and down the shore peddling Pacífico beer.

"¡Sí! ¡Por aquí!" Ximena cried, motioning for him to come over.

"Yes!" Izzy agreed. "Hace calor aquí, y eso suena increíble." *It's hot out here, and that sounds incredible.*

"Después de fumar eso, vamos a necesitar algo que tomar," she said, smiling. *After we smoke this, we're gonna need something to drink.* Of course Ximena had brought weed. There was no question about legality here, and it had been awhile since Izzy had partaken.

"Well, of course!" she said, smiling. *What could be better than cold beer, a little high, and this gorgeous beach?*

Cracking open the beers, they said cheers and took their first of many sips for the weekend. Izzy almost forgot about the drama she and Ximena had yet to totally work out. The sounds of kids shouting and playing, the hum of fishing boat motors in and out of the shore, the yells of the men as they returned and ran the boats aground to take in their catch, and the never-ending gentle rustling of palm and banana leaves created a picture Izzy knew would stay etched in her mind forever. More than that, it was the feeling of freedom, of peace that she sought but lately was having trouble finding. This place seemed to ground her, to remind her of the incredible things she was doing and seeing, and all the ridiculous decisions she had made. In the beginning, she had taken time to reflect and journal and be alone on the gorgeous beaches of Puerto Vallarta. Lately, her traveling had picked up so much, and her time spent with Felipe was so distracting that she had forgotten to make time for herself. Even with Ximena sitting next to her, she didn't feel the need to fill the time with small talk. *This is what I imagined. This is what I wanted my Mexico experience to be. Beautiful beaches, beer, and relaxation.*

Then Ximena finally spoke up.

"Listen," Ximena said in English. "I have to speak English because I want to make sure you hear me."

Izzy's serene moment came to an abrupt halt. This is what Ximena wanted to do, and Izzy knew it, but she wasn't quite ready. Would she ever be? She looked back at Ximena's face and saw care and concern, not anger from someone about to attack. It helped Izzy brace herself without allowing defenses going up.

"I like you, Izzy, and I want to make right everything. But I can't understand you. Do you love Felipe?" she asked pointedly.

Izzy paused, preparing herself for the reaction of what she was about to say. "No, really I don't love him. I like him a lot, and we have fun, but I cannot say I love him," Izzy admitted out loud.

"Why, then, do you pick him, not Luci?" Ximena asked. Izzy wasn't sure she understood the question and looked inquisitively at Ximena, who tried then to explain further. "If you no love him, why hurt Luci, your friend, who you do love?"

The question was intended to be surface level, but the significance of what Ximena had assumed, that Izzy loved Luci, had her reeling. She had never thought about her feelings for Luci. Or Ximena, for that matter. Or really anyone else. Could she say she loved Luci, or was Luci just another person to pass the time with? If Izzy had been so hell-bent on starting a new life here, how deep were these connections going? The answer was really in the question.

"Pues," Izzy started, but then changed her mind. How could Ximena sit there and ask Izzy about picking Felipe over Luci when Ximena constantly ditched them for Gabe?

"Oh, like how you always pick Gabe over me and Luci?" Izzy said sternly. "You leave us in clubs and cancel plans whenever he wants you to! You pick him all the time! Does that mean you don't love us?"

Ximena took a deep breath, almost as if she might have expected that response, and said, "Sí, pero nunca te robo de lo que quieres, y nunca te lastimé." *Yes, but I never rob you of what you want, and I never hurt you.*

The truth rang in the air and hit Izzy hard. Before she could find words or a response, Ximena continued.

"And now you use your trips as a way to run, and you never apologize to Luci. You make me mad, Izzy, because I thought better of you."

It stung. It wasn't that Izzy had just done something hurtful to their friend, it was that Ximena had held Izzy to a higher standard than that. That she respected Izzy, and now that was compromised. Izzy's feelings of defensiveness dissipated into a mixture of regret and disappointment. She hadn't thought about what Ximena would think, only what Luci would think. But what damage had Izzy caused as a ripple effect to others? Who else had held Izzy with high esteem but now felt otherwise?

"That's not fucking fair!" Izzy cried, now getting angry at Ximena again. "You know what I went through with Ethan, and everything I've been feeling, and now you throw it in my face and say I've disappointed you and made you mad? Do you think you're being a good friend by trying to hurt me back by saying all this?"

"I'm not trying to hurt you. I'm just a mirror, and you no like it." She let that hang in the air, taking a long drag off the joint as Izzy absorbed what she meant. Then Ximena added, "Tell me you didn't sleep with someone in New York."

Izzy's heart almost stopped, and she suddenly felt cold. Her mind was too clouded with pot and beer to come up with a good response other than the truth.

"What if I did?" she asked defensively as tears formed, despite her willing them away.

"You say you need to find you again, but before Felipe you keep telling me stories of sleeping with that guy in Los Angeles, Vancouver, wherever. Why do you do it? You don't need to," Ximena said. "And now you did it even to Felipe."

Izzy couldn't look Ximena in the face. She was ashamed and angry and exhausted all at once. The tears she fought were winning.

"And you don't even love Felipe," Ximena kept on. She was getting through and she could tell, so she didn't want to stop now. "Have you thought about how the people around you feel, and how what you think is explainable might be really hurtful? That you don't respect them as people and care about their feelings? You think just telling Felipe you don't love him will make him change his feelings for you? Or telling Luci she wasn't dating him anyway so she will then not be upset? C'mon, Izzy, you haven't really thought about anyone but yourself in a long time. Maybe was good for you after the breakup, but how big of a mess do you want to leave? And in how many other lives?"

In the bright sunshine, Izzy felt chilled. Her mind swirled with arguments of defense about how she always thought of others and never herself, and how that always sent her into relationships where she was second and they were first in everything. That it was unhealthy, and she needed that to change.

But then her mind whispered: *You swung too far the other way. That's not who you are. You are a caring person, not an asshole, but you've been one for sure.*

As much as she didn't want to, she was under the influence enough not to care what Ximena would think. She put her beer down in the sand, pulled her knees into her chest, and cried. A small part of her hoped the crying would make her friend feel bad for saying those things, but a large part of her knew Ximena was right. Izzy had taken her own hurt, and her need to discover herself and cleanse herself of being pushed around, and she had asked others to bear the hurt with her. Although it was unintentional, it wasn't right.

"That's not what I meant to do," Izzy said through soft tears.

"I know, Iz, and I don't think you realized it," Ximena said, moving closer to Izzy and wrapping her arms around her. "That's why I took us out here to tell you. Look, I still love you and you are still my friend; I am just sad and mad to watch all this. I'm mad at a lot of people right now."

Ximena continued to hold Izzy, lightly stroking her hair. Neither said anything as Izzy reeled from the hard truth of what she'd said. *I didn't mean to do that, and I thought I was being a good person by saying things up front and being honest. I don't want to do to others what has been done to me.*

She suddenly considered: maybe Ethan had felt the same way. He had gone out of town and slept with another girl. Hadn't she just done that to Felipe? And she wasn't even sure if she was going to tell him! *Just like Ethan*, she realized.

"So what am I supposed to do, huh?" she finally asked Ximena out loud a little too forcefully.

Ximena pulled her head away from Izzy's so she could look Izzy in the face before answering. "You need to figure out what the fuck your deal is so you can change it," Ximena said, trying to lighten the mood a bit with her tone. "I mean, only if you want to." She took a final drag from the joint. "We need more beer."

With that, she got up and walked down the beach to find the beer man, leaving Izzy sitting on a beach towel alone on the beach in Mexico. Alone. Was that how she preferred it now? Certainly not. But the way she'd been conducting herself, she had only been worried about her own experience and her own feelings. She hadn't even stopped once to consider what anyone else might be going through. Like Luciana—or Valeria, for that matter, or Alejandra, or even Gretchen. They, too, were all away from home and their families and parents.

Why is my story so much more significant? Why am I so much more of a victim?

Ximena returned with two more cold beers and, standing over Izzy, handed her one. "¿Tienes hambre?" she asked. *Are you hungry?*

"Actualmente, sí." Taking a deep breath, Izzy let out all the hurt, the shame, and now the guilt that had erupted in her system. *Okay, so you messed up. You swung too far to the other side for self-preservation. But you can come back and right things. It's time to stop playing the victim.*

Taking a few big swigs of beer, they left their towels and snacks on the sand and, barefoot, she and her friend wandered up the beach toward the smells of sizzling beef, charred chicken, and pungent, spicy peppers.

Chapter 20

The bus ride to work was much shorter than normal as Izzy replayed the scene over and over again of approaching Luci, imagining different outcomes and how she might respond. Would she go straight to her office? Should she call her and ask to talk? Invite her to lunch? Either way, after the weekend with Ximena, Izzy was certain of one thing: she *had* to say something; she *had* to make things right.

She didn't see Luci in the morning, so she started her Monday with the usual emails and reservation requests. As the hours ticked past, Izzy got more anxious. She knew the longer she waited, the worse the anticipation would be. *Her reaction isn't going to change. Delaying it won't make her get over it faster and make this any easier.* She finally had a few small ounces of courage and knew she had to take them instantly or they'd be gone. Quickly picking up her cell phone, she decided to text Luci instead.

"¿Luci, podría invitarte a almorzar?" *Luci, can I invite you to lunch?*

Hours seemed to pass as Izzy stared at her phone, waiting for the screen to notify her of Luci's reply. Deciding it better to distract herself, she set her phone down and tried to get back to the email she was writing. Before she could get another sentence typed out, the phone lit up with a new text.

Sí. Tenemos que hablar.

Before she was able to get to the cafeteria, however, Luciana appeared in her doorway. Izzy's stomach did a backflip and her palms instantly began to sweat. She didn't hate confrontation, but she hated being put on the spot and confronted about something she had done wrong. She physiologically, without intention, prepared her defense.

"Hey, Luci," she said warmly but with hesitation.

"Hola," Luci said in return.

"De acuerdo . . . tenemos que hablar." *I agree: we have to talk.*

Before Izzy could continue with anything she had scripted in her head, Luci closed her office door and sat down heavily into one of the chairs across the desk from Izzy.

"Fíjate," Luci began, "mientras viajabas, fui con el grupo a una fiesta en la casa de Alejandra." *While you were traveling, I went with a group to a party at Alejandra's house. Big surprise that Alejandra would wait for Izzy to be away to throw a party*, Izzy was thinking, but the next thing Luci said stopped her short. "Y me besó Felipe." She stopped, without any further explanation, as if the news that Felipe kissed her would be a bomb and Izzy would explode.

"¿Él te besó? ¿Tu no besaste a él?"

She clarified, that in fact, he had kissed her and not the other way around.

"Sí," she responded, waiting.

Thank GOD! This is your way out! See? He doesn't think y'all are a thing and now you can get out of this! You never even have to say anything about that Blake guy in New York! Was that his name? Whatever, doesn't matter. Her adrenaline flooded away, and she felt as if she might be floating on air.

"Entiendo" Izzy began slowly. This must have been what Ximena alluded to when she said Luci was just as bad as Izzy. At the time, things were feeling patched up and getting back to normal after their weekend together, so Izzy hadn't pressed Ximena for explanation. But it had left her wondering what Luci had done to make Ximena say that. Now she had a pretty good idea. Even if Luci had done it for vengeance, she had done the same thing Izzy did. She went after the man her friend had wanted. Even if they weren't really on speaking terms, it wasn't right.

"Pues, escúchame, Luci. Me caes muy bien, y estoy muy triste que nuestra amistad ha sufrido por este chavo." *I like you a lot, and I'm sad our friendship suffered over this guy.*

Luci's face didn't seem to register agreement or relief. Her look was skeptical. Maybe she was expecting Izzy to fly off the handle, or maybe she had been expecting a huge argument, but she didn't appear to feel the same way about it.

Izzy continued anyway. "Y la verdad es que, no estoy enamorada de Felipe. Y a mi me parece que él será mas feliz contigo." *I'm not in love with him. And it seems to me that he'd be happier with you.*

It was the truth, and Izzy could say it without putting on an act or pretending she wasn't hurt.

Luciana smiled, but didn't seem to buy it quite yet. The girls looked at each other for a minute before she spoke again.

"¿No estás enojada?" Luci asked, making sure Izzy wasn't angry.

"¡No! No, la verdad es que estoy feliz de que él tenga un interés en ti." She answered truthfully that she was actually happy he had interest in her. *So I don't have to feel guilty about cheating on him or ruining our friendship!*

"¿Qué?" *What?* Luci asked forcefully. "¿Cómo puedes decir que no estás enojada? Si él no te gusta, por que valió la pena a lastimarme?" *How can you say you aren't angry? If you don't like him, why was he worth hurting me?*

Izzy tried to get her vocabulary straight to make sure things came out right. Luci had a point, but there was more to it than that.

"Tal vez tu piensas que lo hice todo sin pensar, o con intenciones malas. Y sí, en el principio, no me importaba nada." *You might think I did this without thinking or with bad intentions. And yes, the first moment, I wasn't thinking about anything.* "Pero, el me gustó mucho también, y cuando él me seleccionó, me sentí muy feliz. Pero después de algun tiempo con él, fue claro que no ibamos a quedarnos juntos por todo de la vida." *But, I liked him a lot too, and when he chose me I was really happy. But after spending time with him, it's clear we aren't going to be together for life.*

"Okay," Luciana said and gave a slight smile but didn't seem certain. "¿Y ahora qué?" *And now what?*

"Pues," Izzy took a deep breath and plunged over the edge, "creo que yo tengo que romper con él, y que tienes que comenzar a salir con Felipe de nuevo. Y, espero que podamos ser amigas como antes." *I think I should break up with him, and that you should go out with Felipe again. And, I hope we can be friends like before.*

Luci stared at her. Izzy looked right back at her, confident about what she had just said and believing with all her heart that was the best solution. And the friends thing, well, even if Luci never did agree to that, Izzy could know she had done what was right. Even though it was hard.

Luci got up and hesitated, as if she might want to hug Izzy, but then she decided against it and turned to leave the office. As she opened the door, she turned around to look at Izzy and said, "Gracias por llamarme. Y gracias por entenderme." *Thank you for calling me. And thank you for understanding.*

Damn. Izzy thought. *Couldn't have been any better than that. Even if the friendship isn't restored, she got me back, so now we are both in the drama, and I'm not the only bad guy. Who needs a drink?*

~

"Mom?" she asked into her computer screen that night at home. "Can you hear me?"

"Wait—hang on!" She could hear and see her mom in the Skype window, but she wasn't sure it was going through on the other end.

"Hon, I can't hear her. It's all choppy and the picture keeps freezing." She heard her mom say this to her father and watched his face get closer to the screen, mouth hanging open, to investigate.

"I can see you both; you can't see me?" She was trying not to get frustrated.

"OH!" her mom exclaimed. "I see you now."

Why does she always talk so loud? Izzy smiled in spite of her frustration.

"Okay, so," her mom started, as if settling in for a long conversation, "how was your weekend?"

"It was . . . " She hesitated, looking for the right words. *Enlightening? Frustrating? Trying?* "It was good," she said meekly.

"Well, what did you do?" her mom pressed.

"My friend and I went up to a little beach town called Sayulita and camped and hung out," Izzy reported.

"Who'd you go with?" her mom asked.

"People you don't know," she said rather curtly.

"Okay, well, sorry. I'm just asking how things are going," she said, sounding a bit hurt and leaning back in her chair away from the computer screen, clearly saying she was offended by the tone.

"I'm sorry, Mom." Izzy suddenly felt exhausted. "It's just that the weekend was a little exhausting."

She wasn't ready to go through this with her mom, but she also wasn't ready to sit alone with this feeling anymore. The experience with Luciana and Felipe had opened a wound and exposed a truth to such degree that she still felt like she was bleeding from it. She needed someone to help patch it up. Her mom was tough to talk with sometimes, and things had been strained before her move from Texas as she had plowed deeper into bad relationships, boys, and booze. Mom had judged while Izzy pushed harder to be her own person, claiming inwardly that she didn't need Mom's approval anymore. It couldn't have been further from the truth.

"Oh really? Why?" her mom asked with tempered excitement that perhaps Izzy was going to open up and share something.

"It's just . . . " She didn't know how to start or what to say. Desperately trying to find words that wouldn't paint such a terrible picture of herself, she took a deep breath and tried to frame this better.

"It's just that my friend was pretty harsh," she finally said. "About how I've been conducting myself lately."

"Hmmm," her mom responded, sounding as if she, too, was trying to reserve what she truly wanted to say. Izzy wanted to be annoyed, but she was ready to get it off her chest, and her mom was in the right place at the right time. She'd been trying not to let people control her mood and emotions; she wouldn't let her mom do it today.

"Don't just say 'hmm,' Mom. I know you want to say something. But don't, okay?" She paused, waiting to see if her mom would defy her request. When she didn't say anything, Izzy kept going, somewhat satisfied that maybe Mom would be quiet for a minute and let her talk.

"I mean, I never told Felipe I loved him or anything, so why shouldn't I just have fun while I'm traveling? We weren't exclusive or anything. But Ximena had this big intervention, and she made it sound like I didn't care about anyone and just hurt people's feelings without caring. And it's not like I didn't care about Luciana's feelings during the whole thing with Felipe, but I just didn't know how to tell her. I was going to, though, eventually. But then when I was gone, and she kissed him and then told me, I was like, 'Okay that's fine, you can have him.' So how could Ximena have thought I was still the only one in the wrong and have this entire weekend intervention with me, when she knew what Luci had done anyway? Did she have the same big talk with her? Probably not!"

She took a breath and paused to see what her mom might react to first. Izzy was actually a little surprised how it all came out now that she had said it out loud.

"So you broke up with Felipe?" her mom asked.

"Not yet, but I know I should now," she said, sounding a bit defeated. "And I told Luci I was going to."

"Well, babe, it's not bad to date and have fun. You don't have to always be in a relationship. But if he seems to feel more for you than you do for him, maybe it would be best to end it."

Her mother waited, as if testing the silence to see if she'd gone too far and pissed Izzy off.

Izzy sighed heavily, grateful that she hadn't answered in a judging way for once. "Well, yeah, I mean—I'm worried I was doing to others what Ethan did to me. And I'm worried everyone hates me now."

That was at the core of what was bothering her, she realized. She wasn't only regretful about her behavior, but also that now people might not like her or trust her, and that she had hurt them. "And I feel like a bitch." The tears started again and fell down each cheek as she relived the hurt, anger, and rejection she had experienced the night in the Atlanta hotel room during Ethan's call.

"Well, you're not a bitch," her mom said softly. "And I'm sure they don't hate you. They may be jealous of you, but they can't really hate you."

"Luciana does, I'm sure. I haven't been able to make any real friends here." She sniffled, and more tears burned her eyes at the thought that she was so lonely without any friends.

"Oh, Izzy, you've made some great friends, it sounds like! Maybe just not in Mexico, but all those people you travel with seem to be becoming nice friends." She tried to sound upbeat but sympathetic.

"Why aren't you taking this chance to say, 'I told you so'?" she asked her mom, asking for the additional jab.

"Why would I say that? I didn't tell you anything about Felipe or the lifestyle you're living." She sounded a little confused. Izzy tried to detect the underlying smugness she always seemed to hear, but she couldn't find it. Maybe it was because she didn't want to? Or was her mom not being smug?

"You told me in Houston I needed to slow down, and I haven't done it at all, and now look." Izzy cast her eyes down in shame. She braced for the truth that her mom would lay on her head about her poor choices and poor habits, and how it was her turn to reap the consequences. But it didn't come.

"Baby, I love you very much and am very proud of you," she said tenderly. "I could never do what you're doing—living in another country. The farthest I went was from Indiana to Arizona, and that was scary for me until I met your dad. What you're doing is wonderful, and you're just learning and growing. I *hope* you're learning, at least."

Izzy looked up at the computer screen and felt an overwhelming sensation. Her mom wasn't judging her and making her feel bad. She wasn't saying, "I told you so" or reprimanding her about anything. She was holding her in grace and actually praising her. What?

"Why are you saying nice things?" Izzy asked, not quite believing what she was hearing.

"What do you mean? Why are you so surprised? You're my daughter, and I love you!"

"You're not going to tell me what an awful person I am, or tell me I should have known better, like you have done my whole life?" she said a little forcefully. *Why am I still trying to pick a fight? Why am I trying to get her to say something about that?*

"Of course not! You're not an awful person." Now her mom sounded hurt. "Why would you think I would ever think you're awful? You might make mistakes, but that doesn't make you awful, Izzy. It makes you human, and I love you even with mistakes."

Izzy's tears got bigger and the burning in her throat intensified. *She is proud of me? She really thinks I'm doing a good job?* She hadn't realized how much she needed to hear that. And now, something inside was set free, and it streamed out of her through her eyes.

"Thank you, Mom," she said practically sobbing. "I guess I just needed to hear you say it. I needed my mom to tell me I'm okay."

"Oh, don't cry! You're gonna make me cry!" she said, wiping her eyes. Izzy laughed, and then her mom laughed too.

"I just need a hug!" Izzy said, as if she was a child again.

"I wish I was there to hug you!" her mom said back.

As the tears subsided and she sucked in all that salty humid Mexico air, her chest and head filled with a new weightlessness. A peace came over her that she was, in fact, okay. She was a good person and had maybe made some mistakes, but all was forgivable. And, most importantly, she wasn't a disappointment to her mom. For the first time since Izzy could remember, her mom wasn't showing her where she had fallen short of expectations. She wasn't saying Izzy could do better. She was loving Izzy right where she was. It was all she needed.

Chapter 21

Felipe didn't take the conversation well, but he also couldn't deny that he had cheated on Izzy with Luci. This had given Izzy the chance to tell him the truth, too, about New York. Though it was the right thing, it still felt hard, and Izzy often missed his company and having someone to try new things with. Even though she felt good about it overall, it was still a little rough seeing the two of them—Felipe and Luci—sitting together in the cafeteria at lunch.

The interesting silver lining Izzy hadn't even considered was that everyone seemed to know the entire story, and now Izzy didn't seem so terrible. She had bowed out gracefully and admitted defeat in some versions of the story, but either way it freed Izzy from the uncomfortable tension. Plus, now that Felipe and Luci sat together all the time, Izzy was free to eat with Ximena and Gabe, or Valeria and Alejandra, and even once or twice with Gretchen.

Without Felipe there to distract her between business trips, Izzy was back to walking her beach alone and journaling during her days off. She began to cherish the sunset from her own balcony with a bottle of wine to herself, knowing she wouldn't have that view forever. Only a week ago she had revisited the plaza by the church where the old man had painted her drawings with coffee beans, and had sat watching him from afar as he interacted with tourists and locals alike. In case she never made it back to this town, she wanted to be sure she remembered it well.

As the heat was escaping the day and her stomach reminded her of the dinner hour, she closed the journal where she had been writing about the sights and sounds of the beach. She crossed her legs and squinted in the reflection of the late afternoon sun. Then, she did something she hadn't done much before. Folding her hands and closing her eyes, she prayed.

God? Um, I know we don't really know each other, but if you could maybe, if you're there . . . I mean . . . if you're not too busy . . . could you maybe help me? I really am ready to start another life and leave Mexico. I sort of created a mess. Well . . . maybe you know that . . . Um, but, if you don't mind maybe helping me figure out how to get out of it? That would be great. Thanks. Amen.

"Buenas tardes, gracias por llamar la oficina de ventas. Soy Isabella. ¿Cómo puedo servirle?" She answered with her formal greeting in Spanish these days, without needing her script.

"Izzy? It's Jenny!" Izzy loved hearing from her. "Listen, I have a question. You used to be at the CVB in Houston, right?"

"Yeah, that's how I made the jump to sales. I regret it every day," she said, laughing, causing Jenny to laugh along with her.

"How are things going there in Mexico?"

Izzy could tell Jenny was trying to get to the point quickly. "Well, honestly, they've been better than when I last saw you, but I'm not sure how much longer I'll want to be here." She sensed that might be the question Jenny really had.

"Oh yeah? Why is that? Ready to come home or tired of the travel agents?" It was Jenny's turn to laugh, which made Izzy join in.

"Maybe a little of both," Izzy said with a smile.

"Listen," Jenny said, "here's why I called." She took a breath and paused, building anticipation slightly. Izzy's stomach tightened a bit, and she wondered what Jenny was about to say.

Apparently Jenny's old director, Bob, had moved on to become the director at a new project in Snowmass in Colorado. "It's a brand-new build," Jenny explained. "Should open early next year, but they're already selling it from the CVB standpoint, and they need a contact for the new hotel itself. Bob is too tied up in marketing plans to help sell the projected space." She took another breath, and Izzy waited for what she now understood was coming. "Before Mexico, you did group sales, right?"

"Yes, I did the corporate group meetings at the Houston resort before coming here. That's how I met Gretchen."

"Okay, great; that's what they're looking for! I mean, I realize that's a huge change from a beach in Mexico to a mountain town in Colorado, but hey, could be really fun, and after what I've seen you do in Puerto Vallarta, I know you would be awesome for this!" It wasn't Jenny's full-fledged sales pitch, but she was testing the waters to see how Izzy would respond. Izzy sensed that, so she answered with the most enthusiasm possible.

"Wow! Really?" she exclaimed. "That would be quite the change, wouldn't it?"

"Yeah, huge change. Would you be up for it?" Jenny asked.

"I think it would be worth checking out," Izzy answered slowly.

"Let me send your name to Bob and have him connect with you. Then he can fly you up there to check it out and talk with him. And just keep your mind open, all right?"

"That sounds good—worth the conversation at least," Izzy agreed.

They talked more about Jenny's experience with Bob and what he might be like to work for. Jenny had already mentioned to Bob she had someone in mind, so she talked through details about the flight, rental cars, and where she'd stay in Aspen based on what Bob had told her. Izzy had been thinking about moving to California, and about which of the connections she now had across the US might lead to the next opportunity. Phoenix, San Diego, Portland, and Austin had been in her head, but not Colorado.

Still, she had spent plenty of winters skiing with friends, so maybe it would be fun to live there full time and change her lifestyle completely. *Could I handle snow?* she wondered. *Never hurts to at least see what they're offering.*

Her mind wandered. Lately, after ending things with Felipe and making attempts to repair things with Alejandra, Luciana, and the girls, she had taken to reflecting on the beach as she had months back when she first got there. She had never been a religious person, but she had certainly become a more spiritual person and couldn't ignore serendipities. The job had led her to her friend, and now maybe her friend was leading her somewhere else.

As the sun set across the bay behind the mountains and the tourist pirate ship left its dock for the evening booze cruise outside Izzy's home, she tucked her knees up to her chin, resting her head on them and hugging her legs. *Am I supposed to go to Colorado next? Is a mountain town the right fit for me?* She was excited to find out.

As the plane door opened in Aspen, the cold, dry air hit her face. Closing her eyes, she took in a deep breath and coughed. The gorgeous mountain air made her throat instantly dry. Laughing at herself joyfully, she gathered her carry-on and made her way to the stairs to exit the plane. It was a short walk into the terminal, which was really a small building with windows, looking nothing like any airport she'd ever seen. Before long, her bags were brought in from the plane's belly, and she was off to the rental car counter. They had set her up with a Buick Enclave so she could take time to explore both Snowmass and Aspen since they were close to each other but separated by a highway and a mountain. She was impressed with herself and her luxury ride. Winding through the mountain roads, navigating her way past the valley floor that bore golf courses below the ski runs, she climbed the steady incline up to the village.

As she drove, she looked out the window in awe. Pockets of green seemed like signs of life waking from the winter hibernation among the piles of snow that must have been there for months. From her window she could see, as crystal clear as a painting, the beautiful Rocky Mountains rising above her. Covered in snow, standing stark white against the bright blue never-ending sky, they took her breath away. Years past on a ski trip with her family, she had stood at the top of one of those incredible creations and wondered, *How did He do it?* She was a small child again as she stared, mouth open, out into the distance. Something about the mountains always made her feel small but inspired. The ocean was deep and contemplative, but the mountains were soaring and seemed to call out greatness. After a minute, she realized these were the same mountains that stretched all the way to Puerto Vallarta.

Arriving at the resort site for her interview, she found the small temporary construction trailer, made her way through the cold to the door, and knocked—as butterflies crept up with uncertainty. She heard heavy footsteps make their way to the door, and they rocked the trailer slightly. The door was flung open, and there in the doorway was a plump, friendly man with gray hair and beard reminiscent of Kenny Rogers. She couldn't help but smile and let her guard down.

"Isabel?" he asked, saying her name incorrectly.

"That's me!" she said, deciding it was a bit early to call him out.

"Welcome! Come on in!" he said, stepping back and gesturing her in with a broad smile. "It isn't much for us dudes around here, but we could clean ourselves up for you if you decide to come."

With only Bob and the general manager in the trailer with the contractor, there wasn't much of a "team" to meet. They were all in jeans and boots with sweaters, drinking coffee from Styrofoam cups among cords running everywhere and makeshift desks holding up their laptops and printers. Blueprints were spread across several large tables.

They spent the afternoon telling her the grand stories of what this project would be. It was confidential, even to the locals, as this was the start of a huge development for the village of Snowmass, the "next greatest thing" to compete with Aspen and other ski towns. They talked about the building plans and the vision for the entire area. They talked about the challenges of selling this place, and they talked about what had attracted Bob to this project after being in Aspen for so long. It all sounded wonderful.

Tomorrow she would tour the village and meet with a few people who had places to rent. As she climbed back into the rental car and made her way toward the condo where she'd be staying for the night, she wondered what sort of place she might live in here and what her lifestyle might be like. *Well, guess you'll find out tomorrow when you meet with the folks Bob set you up with*, she told herself.

Her condo was brand-new with granite everywhere, hardwood floors, stainless steel appliances, and adorable pendant lights hanging over the island and the barstools. It was fully furnished and appointed with the amenities she had come to expect in a luxury hotel room, yet with the privacy and unique feel of borrowing someone's condo. Bob and the general manager had left a bottle of wine for her with a note welcoming her to the winter wonderland. *Jenny must have given him some insight*, she thought, smiling to herself. Pouring herself a glass, she made her way to the bedroom with her suitcase to unpack a few things and settle in.

The giant tub caught her attention. After her long flight and this crazy cold weather, it seemed like a perfect plan for her night. As the tub filled with water as hot as she could make it, she perused the in-room dining menu to see if she could have some food sent up as well. To her delight, this condo complex functioned like a hotel, and she was able to get herself dinner. Scheduling the delivery for an hour later, she carried her wine back to the bathroom where she dimmed the lights and lowered herself into the hot water.

This is the life. A nice place with a glass of wine and a quiet night. If only I could have this in my own familiar place, not in a new hotel room every other week.

She sighed heavily. The weight of what she had been truly feeling, what had been building the last few months, finally settled into her consciousness. She wanted to settle. She was ready to find a "home" with her own bathtub and her own collection of good wine, with food she wanted in the fridge. *When is the last time I actually cooked anything? Even at home in*

Mexico, I eat at the cafeteria more than I eat at home. Why do I feel so tired and worn out? Maybe it's the altitude. Maybe it's the stress. Maybe it's the nudge someone is giving me that it's time to make another change. Is that you, God? Are you trying to show me what I need to do next?

She closed her eyes and let herself doze. The red wine and the warm water were enough to melt away all the thoughts she had running through her head, all the doubt about herself and her past, and all the uncertainty about her future. They washed away like rain.

A shiver woke her from her relaxed state as her water was cooling off and slowly draining from the tub. *How long have I been in here? It must be close to time for my dinner to come. Better get dried off and dressed for that.*

She slipped on sweatpants and a long-sleeve shirt, and dug out her fuzzy warm socks she had bought at an airport one cold trip home. They had come in handy more than she could have imagined. Wrapping her hair up and clipping it into place, she heard the knock on the door. *Good timing!*

The man who delivered her food removed all the plates from his serving tray and placed them on the counter for her, along with the water, the ketchup, the silverware, and the napkin. Signing her name to the receipt, she gazed back around the room, this beautiful luxurious room, and thought about the hotel currently vying for her attention and her experience. *Look how far you've come, Isabella.* She had a slight grin as she jotted down the tip for this nice man and handed the receipt back to him.

"Thank you," he said kindly. "Have a beautiful evening, ma'am."

"Thank you," she paused, "and I absolutely will. I hope you do as well."

She closed the door behind him and sighed. She was alone, and she was happy. Not a fiber in her being was anxious or unsettled, wishing she had someone to go hang out with, have come over, or call on the phone.

She finished eating and poured another glass of wine. Moving to the couch by the window, she watched the snow change colors from white to pink to blue in the fading sunlight. She couldn't help but let her mind wander to all this beauty she was surrounded by. Something about the mountains drew her attention to God—at least the idea of what she thought God might be. She didn't really know Him, but the beauty and the serenity of this place seemed to be created just for her to know Him. Like a calling card, she thought.

Chirp! Chirp! Chirp!

My phone! She heard it from the bedroom and walked quickly to retrieve it before the incoming call clicked over to voice mail. *Probably Mom calling to see how I like Colorado.* Flipping open the pink phone, her heart skipped a beat. It was a Houston number. Something about the timing was unsettling.

"Hello?" she answered, trying to sound cheerful.

"Hi . . . hi . . . Izzy?" the voice on the other end asked uncertainly.

"Hi, Ethan," she said back. Not rudely, but not warmly. How did he even know she was in the US? Facebook? Mutual friends? "What's up? Is everything okay?"

"How are you? *Where* are you?" he asked.

"I'm traveling around," she said, hesitating.

"Yeah, I figured," he said with a slight laugh, knowing she was being secretive on purpose. "Look, Iz, I'm not outside your door or anything. I just have been thinking about you a lot lately. Is that okay to say?"

Her stomach turned. Not butterflies or excitement, but dread and nervousness. *What's wrong with me? Isn't this the call I desperately wanted to come?* But that had been months ago, she realized.

"I'm sorry to hear that," she said, a bit more coldly now.

"Um, okay," he said, sounding hurt. "Well, for what it's worth, I'm sorry about how things went down with us."

He paused, waiting maybe for Izzy to respond. When she didn't, he went on.

"Listen, I'm sure you're mad, and I hope you don't hate me, but what I was really thinking is that maybe we could, you know, be friends and just talk sometimes. Maybe see where things could lead to?"

She looked into her glass of wine. "Ethan, while I do appreciate your call, I really don't want to be friends." As the words rolled off her tongue, the knot in her stomach loosened, and the uncomfortable tension she was feeling faded away. "I'm not mad, but honestly, I've moved on. I'm not really interested in rekindling anything."

A weight she didn't realize she had been carrying was lifted off her shoulders. She found her voice and was using it. She truly, in her bones, did not have any longing or desire to hear him continue apologizing. And, surprisingly, she had no animosity toward him. All the crying, all the wishing he would see the error of his ways, all the times she imagined him showing up and getting down on his knees apologizing and asking to have another chance: all those were gone. She hadn't thought about him in so long, and the call only reminded her of that further. She was confident and independent, and she hadn't looked backward.

"Oh." He sounded taken aback, as if he hadn't expected such honesty. "Well . . . ," he trailed off. *Poor guy; help him get out of this with his pride.*

"But hey, thanks for calling," she said quickly. "I hope you're doing well, and of course I wish you the best. You're a nice guy, Ethan, and you'll find someone great."

"Thanks, Izzy," he said tentatively, as if he didn't want the call to end. "Well, I guess take care then. And hey, if you make it through Houston on your travels, maybe we can grab a beer."

"Sounds good," she lied politely. "Take care, Ethan!"

She hung up, closed the phone, and set it on the coffee table. Looking at it for a moment, she took a deep breath. *I won't see you in Houston, Ethan, and that's absolutely perfect with me. I have a new chapter to start in Colorado.*

Chapter 22

"I see," Gretchen said, looking up from the letter of resignation Izzy had just presented her with. "Well, I can understand and wish you all the best. Please be sure to complete all your files, and we'll review them together before you go so I can be sure we don't have anything slip through the cracks."

Izzy had gotten a bit more used to Gretchen's lack of warmth, and in this situation, was actually grateful for it. *No need to dramatize it all. It's just time to part ways. Let's not make this into a breakup.*

For the last few weeks Izzy had been taking meticulous notes and creating detailed files in preparation. Now she could officially start the transition and send her agents' requests to Gretchen directly. Back in her office, Izzy was working on some special requests for an incoming guest when Alejandra appeared in her doorway.

"So, um, I just heard," she said, referring to the resignation letter.

"Oh? Yeah, I miss home and I'm actually excited to go back to corporate meetings instead of selling to travel agents," Izzy said, smiling.

"Well, it has been nice to work with you, and I wish you the best," Alejandra said.

"Aw, thank you!" Izzy said genuinely.

Despite her self-centered approach to every conversation, Alejandra was a nice person. Izzy had been able to let her own ego go and let Alejandra take over without feeling so irritated. It wasn't a competition, after all, and Izzy had realized what she had been irritated about was that *she* wanted to talk about *herself*! When she had finally realized it, her grandma's saying had popped into her head: *Sounds like the pot calling the kettle black.*

"Are you in town this weekend?" she asked Alejandra. "I'm going to have a little going-away party and would love you to come if you can."

"Really?" She seemed surprised to receive the invitation. "Okay, sure; that would be nice."

Izzy and Ximena had been planning the party before she submitted her official resignation. Two weeks wasn't a lot of time after spending a year in this place. They had talked about which club to meet at, and which restaurant to have dinner one last time, but ultimately Izzy had decided she'd like to have everyone over to her apartment. She had only done that once before on New Year's Eve, but it had been a blast. She couldn't think of a better way to say goodbye to everything she had enjoyed.

Instead of going to the cafeteria for lunch every day, Izzy took some time over the last couple of weeks to walk around the resort. The place she had first seen as concrete and piles of dirt had transformed into paradise. The baby palm trees had grown some, the fountains danced underneath the afternoon sun, and the bright pink bougainvillea had bloomed alongside the tropical birds of paradise planted in the gardens. Better than the natural beauty created in this place were all the people relaxing in lounge chairs, walking the once-remote beaches, and enjoying the delicious menus she had helped create. The days of the cramped shared office space were long gone but not forgotten to Izzy. She didn't want to leave any aspect of this to a clouded memory.

~

When the party finally came, Izzy hadn't been surprised about who showed and who didn't. What she was surprised about was how she felt about it. She hadn't expected Gretchen to come, or Ricio, given how far away he lived, and even when Alejandra didn't show up, she knew they had already made their peace, so she wasn't hurt. This night was just about having fun one last time in the space she had called her own, with the people she had called friends, overlooking the beach she had borrowed all those afternoons and evenings.

"¿Un baile más?" Matías had insisted.

"¡Okay!" Izzy had agreed. She even seemed to have improved since La Posada, despite her inconsistent practice.

Valeria toasted Izzy several times throughout the night as she consumed more and more tequila and talked about someday crossing paths when she became a full-fledged sales manager like Izzy. Gabe had brought some of his friends Izzy didn't know, which normally would have irritated her since it was her place, but she let it slide, knowing this was the last time she'd probably see him. Ximena even took time to sit with Izzy and tell stories and laugh rather than spending the entire night making out with Gabe. They remembered ridiculous nights together and watching the sun come up over the malecón.

"¿No me olvides, okay?" she said more than once. *Don't forget me, okay?* "Ahora tengo el Facebook y podemos estar en contacto. Quiero ver las montañas de Colorado!"

Izzy had every intention of staying in touch with Ximena. She had never met anyone like her and had never been confronted by anyone like her, either. She genuinely admired her for that and had such a deep and sincere appreciation for her friend. She could only hope to find more friends as honest and caring as Ximena was—caring enough to hold up a mirror and speak truth, even if it meant being misunderstood.

I want to be that for my friends, Izzy thought.

When the door opened and the couple entered the room, many heads turned, and some stopped to watch Felipe and Luci. They walked through the door, then stopped inside as tension seeped in. He hadn't been to this place for months, and neither had Luci, but Izzy was happy to see them in the doorway.

Setting her beer down, she caught Ximena's eye, winked at her, and walked over to greet them. Giving each a kiss on the cheek and saying she was happy to see them, Izzy instantly defused the awkwardness for everyone. They didn't stay long, but they had made the effort to visit Izzy one last time. Though not verbalized, Izzy could still see something in Felipe's eyes. Maybe it was sadness their relationship hadn't worked out, maybe it was still a wish there could be something in the future, or maybe it was simply a silent "thank you" for the experience. Izzy didn't think too much about it. She was focused on her last moments with Luci. Luci was the friend who had made the transition from being with Ethan to being on her own more fun. Luci had been there for her when she needed her, and she wanted to make sure Luci knew that.

"Luci," Izzy said, grabbing her hand. "Quiero decir que no hubiera disfrutado de esta experiencia sin ti. Y, desde el fondo de mi corazón—gracias, amiguita." *I want to say that I never could have enjoyed this experience without you. And from the bottom of my heart—thank you, my friend.*

Luci smiled, let go of Izzy's hand, and wrapped her arms around Izzy's shoulders.

"Teníamos nuestras difficultades, pero te quiero mucho. Estoy tan feliz con Felipe, y te voy a extrañar mucho. Gracias por tu amistad." *We had our difficulties, but I love you very much. I'm so happy with Felipe, and I'm going to miss you a lot. Thank you for your friendship.*

Both had tears in their eyes as they hugged. Izzy knew she would not see Luci again and would not stay in touch. She was sad for how things had played out, yet it seemed to have been the only possibility. It had to happen that way. Before the girls let go, Ximena joined them, wrapping her arms around both of them together, spilling beer down Izzy's back as it sloshed out of her bottle. She kissed each of their faces, and both Izzy and Luci kissed Ximena's face in return. In that moment, she was grateful to finally be out of "el mareo," which she had been struggling in for so many months. The love fest was too much for Felipe, who had disappeared, but as the girls let each other go, he appeared with new beers for each of them.

"¡Salúd!" they all cried as they clinked the bottles in the air.

With bags packed and piled at the door, fridge empty and kitchen cleaned, Izzy sat in the plastic chair looking out toward the ocean one last time. She took care to look intentionally at every detail—every speck on the mountainside across the bay, every flower, and every wave. She listened for every bird, every wave crash, and every joyful shout, and she breathed in the salt and sand and Mexican air. The knock on the door came too soon. Her taxi had arrived, and the driver was here to help carry her bags downstairs.

Bumping along the marina streets for the last time, she recounted the incredible memories she had made over the past year: the loneliness, the stress, the heartbreak, and the friendships. The adventures and the tequila. Everything swirled in her mind as she fought back tears. Her life had been forever changed, and it was everything she could have asked for. As she looked out the taxicab window at the familiar condos, homes, and marina locals she had seen day after day, one specific memory from several months ago came flooding back clearly.

It had still been winter in most of the US and Canada, but the annual whale migrations had begun. "Whoa! Look over there!" A lady cried out with joy, and Izzy smiled because she felt the exact same way inside. "They're so close!" The local tour operators that put together tours and experiences for visitors had offered Izzy a chance to experience their most popular activity—snorkeling at Las Marietas. Small rock islands inhabited mostly by marine life and birds, like the blue-footed boobies, these islands were an ecosystem of their own, according to the tour guide.

What's a blue-footed booby? she wondered. *Some sort of rodent? Maybe I should ask . . .* She started to raise her hand and then thought better. *Shouldn't you know this? You live here and sell this place! Let one of the tourists ask.*

Someone finally did, and the tour guide answered, "The blue-footed booby is a marine bird native to the tropical and subtropical climates of the Pacific. They are found on islands like Las Marietas as well as the Galápagos Islands."

But now Izzy was curious about the whales. Were they all the same? This time, nobody asked her question. They stared out at the ocean waiting for the next whale to breach the surface. She grew impatient.

"Ma'am?" Izzy asked, somewhat tentatively. "Are all these the same breed of whale?"

"Great question!" the guide said a bit too loudly. "The whales we see here are humpback whales. The Bay of Banderas here is the second destination these whales migrate to from Canada to breed, the other being Hawaii. So interestingly enough, you can say about half of all Pacific humpback whales are Mexican!"

Strangely, Izzy learned, the whales didn't eat anything in the bay, so other wildlife remained protected despite the huge whale presence. In breeding season, the males jumped from the water, slapping it with their pectoral fins on the surface dramatically. Or they leaped and breached the surface, to the gasps of onlookers and the delight of the female whales. The males were quite aggressive in their competition for females, and all the displays of jumps were their attempts to become leader of the pack and, therefore, assert dominance over the females.

Boys could be so much like whales, Izzy thought.

To reach Love Beach, the hidden beach where they would snorkel, required a brief swim underwater. After some time snorkeling, kayaking, and enjoying lunch on the boat, the second guide, who had been fairly quiet, led those who were willing to attempt that underwater swim. The water was still cold, so they were in short wet suits, which made the journey a little more tolerable. But this deeper water offshore didn't seem to warm up like El Anclote and Punta de Mita, and Izzy swam faster, attempting to warm up. As the group approached the edge of the rocks, the instructor herded them in, giving them details about which direction to swim and where. It seemed they'd be in underwater caves or something, which was a little intimidating, but she'd gone this far. She couldn't chicken out now.

The guide took a dramatic deep breath, then disappeared under the surface. A few brave souls at the front of the pack they'd formed followed suit quickly. Showoffs. Izzy wasn't first, but she sure as hell wasn't going to be last. Swimming through a few people who had paused to tread water and watch, she took a deep breath and disappeared under the surface.

It felt even colder under there, and for a quick second she could have sworn she detected a large shadowy figure swimming out of the darkness. Through the snorkeling mask she could see light a little way ahead of her. Following the guide's instruction to swim toward the light, she did, and she surfaced just feet from where she had been but now in a whole new world.

The rocks formed an entire cave, with the top ripped open so the sun could pour through. A secret little hideaway. The water was calm and lapped gently onto the beach, which was stifled slightly by the acoustics of the rock surrounding the area. She was mesmerized.

This place was something special, and she was here alone. Alone again in a romantic place, an incredible discovery place, seeing and doing things she'd never done before. And she was sharing the moment with perfect strangers. They all had folks with them they knew, mostly friends or family, and were creating memories together. But she was on the outskirts by herself.

Each time she'd found herself alone, the longing for companionship seemed to dim. And now, standing on this isolated, serene beach, hidden from the world, Izzy was alone with the universe. Nobody else to interpret the moment for her or have influence over how she would remember this.

It was all her. Something about that realization made her feel free, and her mind wandered to all sorts of things, just as it had as a child. *You think explorers found this place because they got shipwrecked? Maybe there's buried treasure in here somewhere!*

Just then the guide began gathering everyone up to head back through the opening to the boat. The trip back offered a few more whale sightings, but mostly it was Izzy's chance to sit peacefully alone on her corner of the boat. She had fun, and she didn't even have to convince herself or encourage herself as she would have before. It was starting to feel more and more natural. Being herself felt truly amazing.

About the Author

Danielle Ledezma was raised in San Antonio, TX, and attended the University of Texas at Austin. She majored in Spanish and public relations, which led her to a career in international hospitality. Danielle enjoys yoga and fitness, red and rosé wines, and live music of many kinds—from jazz to Carrie Underwood. She currently lives in Texas with her husband, Pedro, and their two fur babies, Cali and Cole.